harem scrolls

endorsements

Harem Scrolls is a fascinating history of King David's life through the eyes of his favorite concubine. With the archaeological find of female-authored scrolls in the City of David's ruins, Joan Campbell weaves together a biblically based tale of what might have been.
—**Mesu Andrews**, best-selling and award-winning author

Author Joan Campbell raises an intriguing "What if?" What if someone had recorded the stories of King David's wives? What might his wives have said about their life with the king? I invite you to read *Harem Scrolls* and find out. Campbell's skillfully woven tale tells the story of King David as his wives and concubines may have viewed him. Consequently, we are treated to a unique female perspective on David the man, the husband, and Israel's greatest king, a leader who experienced devastating lows to go with the exhilarating highs, and who was deemed a man after God's heart.
—**John Maust**, retired president, Media Associates Int'l

If you enjoy reading biblical history/fiction, you will find both in Joan Campbell's compelling stories of King David's wives and concubines. Joan stays true to the historical timeline and brings to life the many characters introduced through one concubine's desire to tell their story. You will recognize several names from Scripture and be introduced to the real-life drama of love, war, hatred, and the faithfulness of Adonai.

—Donna K. Stearns, biblical fiction author, and blogger

Joan Campbell has taken the scant Biblical information on King David's wives, done extensive research on the women, customs, traditions and lifestyle of the times, and has woven it into an attention capturing work of historical fiction. Her characters—both historical and fictional—come to life on the page, portraying a fascinating glimpse into the harem of Israel's greatest king. Jealousies, rivalries, heartaches, love stories, moments of both emotional and military battles lock together into an enthralling and captivating tale. *Harem Scrolls* is most definitely worth reading ... more than once.

—Bryan Andrews, author of *Reuben* and *Connect*

Harem Scrolls chronicles stories laden with open and concealed love, doubts and suspicion, gossip and open rebuke, even treachery and betrayal. But there is also abundant friendship and bonding relationships to brighten the dark side of some characters.

Because no human existence is all evil or all good, Campbell skillfully combines the two forms of characterization to achieve plausibility in storytelling. Perceptive readers will encounter timeless themes that unearth the struggles humanity has grappled with for centuries. In *Harem Scrolls*, real-life characters, suspenseful plots, and lively descriptions are the driving force behind every scene so carefully crafted by Joan Campbell.

—Lawrence Darmani, author, publisher, CEO of Step Publishers, Accra, Ghana

harem scrolls

joan campbell

ELK LAKE PUBLISHING INC.®

PUBLISHING THE POSITIVE
Plymouth, Massachusetts

A Christian Company
ElkLakePublishingInc.com

copyright notice

harem scrolls

INTERNATIONAL VERSION ®.Copyright©1973, 1978, 1984, 2011 by Biblica, Inc.™. Used by permission of Zondervan

Cover and Interior Design: Kelly Artieri, Deb Haggerty
Illustrations: Ashlyn Campbell
Editor(s): Carol McClain, Cristel Phelps, Deb Haggerty

PUBLISHED BY: Elk Lake Publishing, Inc., 35 Dogwood Drive, Plymouth, MA 02360, 2025

Library Cataloging Data
Names: Campbell Joan
Harem Scrolls / Joan Campbell
504 p. 23cm × 15cm (9in × 6 in.)
ISBN-13: 9798891344464 (paperback) | 9798891344471 (trade paperback) | 9798891344488 (e-book)
Key Words: Christian historical fiction harem girl King David; Biblical fiction Old Testament inspirational David; Bible stories David wives scribe faith prophet; Biblical fiction women harem defiance fear love; Biblical Christian fiction King David wives God; Faith-based fiction Old Testament Holy Land woman; Fictional retelling King David woman prophet love
Library of Congress Control Number: 2025046914 Fiction

dedication

For Kayleigh:

> still I bloom.
> roses tumbling from my wounds.
> a wild offering of hope.

(taken from "I will not give up"—Liezel Graham)

acknowledgments

Thank you to everybody who supported and encouraged me throughout the process of writing and publishing *Harem Scrolls*.

Roy, you continue to be my best friend and champion. Thanks for sneakily reading a few chapters of the manuscript when I sent you the file as a back-up, and for telling me the characters and story gripped you.

Nicole, as always you were the first reader of an early draft, and you were as excited about this book as you've been about my others. That means a lot coming from an avid booklover who reads Jane Austen, CS Lewis, and other renowned writers.

Ashlyn, thank you for transforming my boring spreadsheet into a beautiful graphic to depict the House of David. What a talented designer you've become.

Denise, my number two fan, thank you for still encouraging my writing after all these years of friendship. I so appreciated you reading an early draft and giving me valuable insights, especially on the title of 'queen' in royal Hebrew harems. This is why one needs friends with theology degrees!

Tanya, thank you for indulging long discussions on the book over our many breakfasts, and for your "out of the box" thinking that sparked some wonderful additions to the story. Every time you read about Nathan's falcon, know that it's there because of you (and hopefully to entice bird-loving Ashlyn to read the book).

My many MAI colleagues and friends, your love and passion for the ministry of the written word continues to inspire me. You remind me that we write for the glory of God and the extension of his kingdom.

Tim Beals, thank you for taking time to consider my query to your agency, and for giving me thoughtful advice on publication. Your kindness and consideration meant so much to me.

The Elk Lake Publishing team—Deb, Cristel, and Carol—thank you for believing in this story and for helping me refine and share it with readers.

Thank you to everyone who sacrificially took the time to read an Advance Reader Copy and write an endorsement of *Harem Scrolls*. You beautifully model encouraging and building each other up (1 Thes. 5:11). I am grateful.

Many other friends continue to speak into my writing journey. If you've ever told me one of my books or blogs have spoken to you, know that even the smallest word of encouragement touches me deeply, and gives me the confidence and drive to continue writing.

Finally, I want to acknowledge the One who is patiently teaching me to sit at his feet, believe in his love, and listen to his voice. Jesus, thank you for loving me just as I am and for showing me the power and beauty of storytelling. May this book honor you.

prologue

ANCIENT SCROLLS MAY BE WORK OF A WOMAN

Several ancient scrolls discovered in East Jerusalem may be the work of a female scribe. So says Jerusalem University's Professor Naomi Blum, director of the excavation that discovered the four scrolls, and the burned fragments of a fifth, in the area known as the City of David.

From their location in the original Bronze and Iron Age settlement, Blum believes the scrolls date back to the Iron Age. "This makes it one of the most significant archaeological discoveries of our time," Blum said. "But even more incredibly, our preliminary analysis indicates that the scrolls were written by an ancient woman, about the lives of ancient women. Nothing like this has ever been found in Israel or anywhere else in the world."

However, Blum's conjecture that the scrolls are the work of a female scribe has come under attack. Adam Leib, the director of the National Museum of Israel has called Blum's claim "premature." "The scrolls have yet to be accurately dated, and damage to the lid of the clay pot in which they were stored means they were exposed to the elements," said Leib. "This has obscured some of the text. It's too early to speculate who penned them, but it's highly unlikely to have been a woman."

The Jerusalem Times

tabytha

extract from scroll א (hs alef)

On the day of my birth, my father named me Tawaassi. On the day of my betrothal to the Hebrew king, my grandfather changed my name to Tabytha. That day is carved into my memory like letters on stone. I remember how my mother scolded me for the tear in my dress and the blood on my knees. I tried to tell her that Atamu had shoved me to the ground as we ran home along the valley path. My brother's anger always flared up when my stones hit the mark and his didn't, but Mother wouldn't listen that day. Her hands were harsher than usual as she scrubbed the dirt from my face and the blood from my knees, and when the brush snagged in my unruly curls, she muttered curses to every god she could think of. Finally, she shrugged and told me to put on my best robe, the one I wore to festivals.

I'll never forget her words when I objected that we weren't honoring a god that day. *Today you meet your husband, and if the stories are true, he's more fearsome than any god.*

I still remember Atamu, full of questions, trailing behind us as my mother led me to the fort. I had never set foot inside this stronghold. It was no place for women. My grandfather, Ornan—the high ruler of Jebus—held court here with the other Jebusite leaders and warriors. Although I hardly knew my grandfather, my heart still swelled with pride when I heard the respect in people's voices as they talked about their Araunah, the *lord* of mighty Jebus.

When we reached the fort, my mother stopped and looked down at me. There may have been a flicker of tenderness on her face, but it vanished as soon as she pushed me towards the open gate with one last instruction to keep my mouth shut.

I remember clamping my hand over my mouth, suddenly ashamed that my grandfather and all our elders would see my missing teeth. The front ones were only half-grown in.

"This is the Araunah's granddaughter," she said to the men milling at the gate. "Take her to him."

Then she turned and left me there.

One man looked puzzled and said something to his companions. Then he shrugged and pointed towards a stone archway. I realized he expected me to go alone.

Don't cry.

I took a few hesitant steps forward and then a few more, drawing comfort from the thought that this was my grandfather's fort. Through the archway lay a small space that led to another doorway. It was the only one I could see, so I reluctantly approached it.

As I entered the room, the smell of the men struck me. Sometimes, my father, returning from battle, held me to his chest, and I breathed in this same smell—of dust and heat and bravery. My sun-lashed eyes could hardly make out anything in the darkened room, but from the far end of the chamber, I thought I heard Ornan's voice. I shuffled towards it until I found myself blocked by a towering wall

4

of armed men. Even from the back, I could tell they were not my people, not Jebusites. Fear gripped me as I realized these were the infamous Hebrews who had taken Jebus with such stealth and cunning, cutting down the best of our fighters.

The *very* best.

I tried to swallow down the lump in my throat that always preceded the tears. I mustn't think of my father. It was bad enough our conquerors might see my missing teeth—they mustn't see me crying like a child too.

One of the Hebrews turned and saw me. He said something to his companions in a tongue that sounded almost the same as my own but with other notes, like fast-flowing water. As several more warriors turned to look at me, heat rose to my face.

The first man beckoned me forward, and men moved aside, clearing my path. Yet I stood rooted to the spot, not wishing to walk between them. I wanted to turn and run back. To my mother. To the hills that were my freedom. Even to Atamu. But one man clucked impatiently and grabbed me by the shoulder, pressing me forward to where Ornan sat in a circle of men.

When my grandfather saw me, he smiled a defeated smile without any warmth. My father's smile had been so different. It had filled me with a sense of belonging.

Don't cry.

"Here she is, my lord." Ornan held out his arm towards me as if pointing to a fine donkey. "My granddaughter, Tawaassi. Her marriage to you shall unite our houses in peace." To me, he barked, "Bow before your new lord and master, girl."

I did not know which of the seated men now looking at me was to be my husband, but at my grandfather's stern expression, I quickly dropped to my knees and bowed my head to the cold, stone floor, thinking that if I could stay in this position, the men would not see my teeth.

"That's unnecessary." I felt a new hand on my shoulder, not rough like the one that had pushed me forward. "Sit up, Tawaassi, so I can see your face."

He spoke gently, the way I talked to the lambs when they were separated from their mothers, and slowly, so I could make out the words in the fast-river tongue.

I lifted my head and looked at the man resting next to me on one knee. If this was their king, he was much younger than Ornan, for by now, my eyes had adjusted enough to see that his close-cut beard held no grey. The intensity of his dark eyes drew me in, recalling my mother's words. *More fearsome than any god.* Afraid, I looked down, but the man lifted my chin until I again met his gaze.

"She's lithe and lovely as a gazelle." He smiled, and the sense of danger was gone like the sun breaking through clouds. "Shalom, Tawaassi. I am David."

And because his smile lit his eyes like my father's always had, I forgot about my missing teeth and my mother telling me to keep my mouth shut and that he was our enemy, and I smiled back.

part 1

Ten years since King David conquered Jebus,
to rule the twelve tribes of Israel
from within its mighty walls.

chapter 1

Tabytha had known this day would come. Still, on the morning she stood in the courtyard and saw the four Hebrew soldiers descending the street toward her house, she had to fight the urge to run. She knew why they were here.

"Mother!"

Her mother glanced up sharply from where she sat grinding the barley. As she looked at her daughter's face, she knew too. She rose unsteadily and came to stand beside her. Together, they watched the men approach. Tabytha slipped her suddenly cold hand into her mother's warm one, and her mother squeezed it hard as if she could transfer all her stubborn strength to her daughter.

"You are old enough now, Tawaassi." Her mother had been the only one to refuse Ornan's decree that she was to have a Hebrew name. "Nearly ten years have passed. You are no longer a child."

It had been her mother's idea to hide Tabytha's monthly bleeding and to bind her breasts, so her grandfather might forget she was growing into a woman. Might forget to send her to the enemy king.

"Go put the last things into your chest."

The wooden box stood ready. Tabytha just needed to lay her brush and robes on top, along with her sandals and sleeping mat. But she stood frozen, holding on to her mother's hand, feeling her insides turn to water.

The soldiers stood at the entrance of the courtyard now.

"Are you the one promised to the king?" the front one asked without preamble, and when she nodded, he said, "We are here to take you to the palace."

"Can I have a moment to say goodbye?"

He nodded impatiently. "Don't take long. We have more important duties than fetching Jebusite *concubines*."

Pilegesh. The Hebrew word was unfamiliar to her, but the way he said it and the way he looked at her filled her with a sense of shame.

"I'll go find the little ones," her mother said, and Tabytha felt bereft as her mother's hand slipped out of her own and she stood alone with the soldiers.

She fled into the house to roll up her sleeping mat, aware of a wild pounding in her chest and the familiar tightness in her throat that threatened a flood of unshed tears. *Don't cry.* She folded up her robes, trying to draw out the moment as long as she could, and was almost relieved to hear the children's voices. Her two nieces burst into the room and flung themselves onto her. "You're going to the palace to be a queen." Tuhi's young eyes shone with excitement, and despite the fear and grief lodged in her chest, Tabytha smiled.

Her brother appeared from the other room of the house, sleep-creased and grumbling. "What in the storm god's name is going on here, Tab?"

Tabytha silently thrust her chin towards the courtyard and saw Atamu's expression of comprehension as he followed her gaze.

"Hebrews!" He spat out the word like a foul-tasting piece of decayed cheese.

Iuni was suddenly there, too, bustling to pull her children off Tabytha. "Give your aunt room to breathe. She'll never be a queen if you crush her to death."

The children giggled but let go of her and didn't object when their mother sank down and took their place at Tabytha's side.

"It's going to be fine, Tab," Iuni whispered, putting her stocky arms around Tabytha's neck, much as her daughters had done earlier. "You are going to live in the finest of palaces, wear rich gowns, and have servants do your every bidding."

"I don't want any of that." Only now did a few tears escape. "I want to be here, laughing with you as we make bread, playing with the children, going together to ..."

"Hush, my love. We all face this when we leave our mother's house to become a wife. Think of the honor bestowed on you. The city's women swoon when King David passes by, and you get to be his wife."

Concubine. Tabytha glanced at the soldier who had spoken the word.

"There's no honor in being the wife of an enemy." Atamu had moved close enough to hear their conversation.

"He's not our enemy." Their mother spoke softly, casting a worried look at the soldiers. "He's our ally and strong protector. Our king."

"How quick you are to forget your husband's death, Mother," Atamu said.

"Stop, please." Tabytha raised her hands. Theirs was an old, worn argument. She couldn't dwell on her father's death at the hands of her husband's men. Not today. She closed the chest lid with a final thud and swiped away the errant tears.

She rose. "I am ready."

As two of the men stepped forward for her chest, her mother pulled Tabytha into her arms one last time.

"Be strong, Tawaassi, and may our gods protect you."

Tabytha, no longer trusting her voice or her childhood gods, just nodded.

King David's palace stood on the summit of the city, parts of it within the walls of the old Jebusite fortress. Tabytha still recalled the stir in the city when King Hiram of Tyre sent cedar logs for the palace's construction. Not long afterward, the carpenters and masons arrived with their tools. She and Atamu had sometimes snuck to a narrow slit in the old fortress wall and pressed their eye to it. She had hoped to catch sight of the king inspecting the building, but all she ever saw were men—Atamu said they were slaves from the Hebrew king's many conquests— dragging logs around or chipping at stones or passing them along a line to each other. Occasionally, a foreman strutted about issuing instructions.

Now, the soldiers led her through the old fort's gatehouse—the very place her mother had left her on the day of her betrothal. The guards posted there hardly stirred as she passed them. She followed through the archway she still remembered from that one childhood visit, but from there on, everything looked different. The doorway to the room where Ornan had given her away to his enemy was gone. The archway now opened into a quad with broad steps, about ten in all. Above the steps rose an imposing building—King David's palace.

She followed the men up the steps, stopping when she reached the top to take in the sight of her new home. The king's palace was beautifully proportioned. The broad steps had led to a courtyard enclosed by pillars, topped with intricately carved stones. Covered porticos framed the two side wings of the building. On the far side of the large courtyard rose the central part of the palace, its light sandstone edifice exuding warmth but also an inescapable air of strength. Much like the king himself, Tabytha thought, remembering the warmth of his smile but also her mother's words. *More fearsome than any god.*

One of her escorts turned impatiently, and Tabytha quickly fell in behind them again. She let her fingers glide over the cold stone of a pillar and looked at the grand wooden doors directly opposite her.

"This way," one of her escorts said gruffly, pointing to the palace wing on the right side. "That entrance is only for the king and those on the king's business."

Not for a woman. Not for a *concubine*.

She trailed after the soldiers along the covered portico, glancing at the activity in the palace courtyard. A group of older men sat cross-legged on the ground in heated conversation. A large woman haggled with a tradesman over the price of olives and grapes. A young boy bearing a scroll ran across the courtyard towards the steps she had just climbed. Two priests in tasseled robes stepped out of the king's entrance, heads bowed solemnly. And stationed around the courtyard were the king's fighting men, swords strapped to their sides, eyes watchful.

Nobody seemed to notice her. Nobody marked this—the most significant moment of Tabytha's life. For them, it was just another day at the palace.

"Well, well," a voice drawled from behind her. "What have we here?"

Tabytha turned to see two young men walking towards her. The taller one had a strikingly handsome face and thick black hair that reached beyond his shoulders. He flashed her a confident smile. His companion stood a head shorter but broader around the shoulders. He had a ruddy complexion and studied her with a roving gaze.

"An attractive young woman about to enter the Women's Quarters," the shorter one spoke again. "Could our father have found himself another Bathsheba?"

"Forgive my brother." The tall one gave a slight bow. "Being the oldest son of a king makes one rather arrogant. I am Absalom, the third son, and therefore only a third as arrogant as Amnon." Again, the flash of that perfect smile. "And you are?"

She hesitated. She had no desire to tell them her name, but it appeared they were her husband's sons—Hebrew princes—and she was only a Jebusite woman.

"I am Tabytha."

"Tabytha." The older prince rolled out her name languidly. "Do I detect a Hebrew name on a Jebusite tongue? How intriguing. Have you come to serve one of the king's wives?"

"I *am* one of the king's wives." She hadn't intended to sound so haughty, but Amnon's disdainful tone had bristled her into it.

Amnon laughed. "A wife! Surely, we would have been invited to a royal wedding, Brother? Do tell. When did this illustrious event occur that we—the king's favorite sons— missed it?"

She felt her face reddening. The soldiers bearing her chest had stopped and were watching the encounter. One of them might even have snickered. "I have been betrothed to the king these last ten years."

"Ten years, you say?" Amnon frowned and made a show of counting on his fingers. "That would take us back to the very year we conquered Jebus, wouldn't it, Absalom?" The princes, only two or three years older than she, spoke as if they themselves had breached her city's mighty walls. "I suppose that makes you one of the spoils of war."

"I am not a *spoil of war*." She heard the tremble in her voice and hoped fervently that they didn't. She drew a deep breath and straightened her back. "I am the granddaughter of the Lord of Jebus, and my marriage to your father unites our two houses."

"Our two houses?" Amnon appeared to be enjoying this. "You mean your little hovel and our grand palace?" He swept his arm around to take in the majestic building. "Yes, I can see why my father would want *that*."

For the second time that day, her throat clenched closed. This time, it was not tears she forced into submission but rather an outburst of curses. Atamu had taught her a string of those, suitable for every occasion involving a Hebrew. The eldest prince baited her. She knew she should turn away. Isn't it what her mother had taught her to do with all the boys who had mocked her over the years?

"Brother, I fear you are upsetting Abba's latest, lovely mate." The other prince's grin showed that he, too, enjoyed the mockery. "She must be the youngest of the Jebusite concubines Abba acquired when he took Jebus."

There was that word again—*concubine*—and another word that jarred her to the core—*acquired*. "Well, our father has waited long for you. Let's not keep him waiting a moment longer." Absalom pointed to the tall cedar door that hid the Women's Quarters. "Welcome to the house of David, Tabytha."

chapter 2

tabytha

extract from scroll א (hs alef)

On the day of my betrothal, I stood behind my grandfather as the men carried on talking. I can't remember all they spoke of, only that I stole glances at the Hebrew king as often as possible. He was as much a warrior as my father had been. I could see it in his watchfulness, strong shoulders, and the blade scar on his right arm. He spoke more than the other Hebrew men seated in the circle. When those men looked at him, I could see the respect and pride in their eyes. He was their Araunah, the way Ornan was ours. But strangely, Ornan, too, meekly deferred to him and calling him lord. I didn't like that one bit.

No one spoke to me again, and if the Hebrew king looked at me—his new wife—I didn't notice. Finally, the talking stopped. Ornan bowed his head low to the ground before the foreign king. I had never seen my grandfather bow to anyone before. The king inclined his head in dismissal, and as Ornan and our elders rose, uncertainty and fear gripped me. Would my grandfather leave me here alone with my husband? What should I do now?

Suddenly, I remembered a wedding festival I had been to where the bride had sat at her husband's bare, washed feet. Perhaps this is what I had to do too.

I slipped past my grandfather to where the Hebrew king still sat in conversation with his men. I glanced at his sandaled feet. I would have to take them off. I dropped to my knees behind my new husband, reaching for the first sandal. My hand barely grazed the strap when the king spun around, and, quick as a lightning strike, his large hand crushed down on my own small one. I let out a startled cry.

"It's you." The frightening fire in his eyes died instantly. "Forgive me, little one."

Ornan grabbed me by the arm, wrenching me to my feet. "What are you doing, girl?"

"What the brides do ..."

"Don't be a fool," my grandfather said as men's laughter rolled around the room. Tears pooled in my eyes at the shame and the sharp pain in my shoulder. "Go home. The king will send for you in time."

I didn't understand. Was the Hebrew king not pleased with me? Hadn't he called me lovely? He had smiled at me. And Ornan had said our houses were now united.

I allowed myself one last glance at the Hebrew king, his solemn gaze still on me. At least he didn't laugh like the rest of the men. Then I darted between the soldiers and out the door. My sandals slapped up dust as I ran from the fort, the pooling tears finally streaming down my face. When I reached our house, I threw myself into my mother's arms as I did when Atamu pinched me or stole one of my figs.

"I don't think the Hebrew king wants me," I managed to say between shuddering sobs. "He said I was lovely, but then I smiled, and he must have seen my missing teeth. He didn't look at me once after that, and Ornan said I must come home instead of going with him. But if I'm his wife now, shouldn't I go to the fortress and clean it and cook for him, like you did for father?"

"Don't be a fool, girl." My mother's brusque words echoed my grandfather's. She pushed me away and scowled. "You're too young to be a wife. You will go to him when you're older."

"How much older?"

"When you bleed. Then you are ready to bear him children."

Children? The thought shocked me. I had heard the women with swollen stomachs screaming long into the night when a child came. Sometimes, they even died. I didn't want to die.

"Come, child." My mother's tone softened. "You can forget about the Hebrew king for now. Nothing will change for years still."

But my mother was wrong.

chapteR 3

Tabytha breathed a sigh of relief when the tall cedar door closed behind her, leaving the mocking princes and impatient soldiers outside. The royal guards at the door had told her to send servants for the chest. Apparently, they couldn't enter the Women's Quarters to bring it in.

The quarters were quiet and blessedly cool. From deep inside the palace, she thought she heard the tinkling of water—a peaceful sound. The air carried the sweet, fresh smell of cedar wood. She noticed that the roof beams and walls were made of the timber. It felt like stepping into a warm, welcoming cocoon.

She took a few deep, steadying breaths, trying to shake off the shame of the princes' words and the soldiers' laughter. What had Iuni said? *It is like this when we leave our mother's house to become a wife.* Other women shared her plight, and as they had adjusted, so would she.

Tabytha considered which way to go. The passage on the right led to a solid door, but she knew that most of the Women's Quarters must lie to the left, so she slowly set off that way.

She passed several curtained-off rooms and began to wonder where everybody could be when two young boys came barreling down the passage, shrieking with laughter, an older girl close on their heels. "There's nowhere to run now. I've got you," the girl called out triumphantly.

"Quick, Sol. Aunt Michal will open her door for me," the taller boy called. They both darted around Tabytha, not even slowing to glance at her.

The girl, however, stopped and cast Tabytha a curious look. "Shalom. I haven't seen you before. Are you replacing Hannah in the kitchen?"

"I'm Tabytha, King David's ..." she hesitated, recalling the prince's mocking tone when she called herself a wife. "Concubine."

"Ah!" The girl's face lit up as if she had found a long-lost friend. Tabytha estimated the girl's age to be a year or two younger than her own. She had a pretty, open face and eyes that shimmered with laughter. Tresses of her thick hair had loosened from the elaborate style in which it had been pinned, giving the girl a sense of indifferent elegance. "Abigail said you would be here any day now. Welcome. I'm Tamar."

For the first time that day, Tabytha felt the knot of tension inside her loosening a little. If the palace women received her this warmly, perhaps she could grow to be happy here over time.

"We got away! We got away!" Two young voices chorused from the direction Tabytha had come.

"I'll get you next time," the girl called down the passage then turned to Tabytha. "The chase was doomed to fail. Michal would have opened the door for Mica. Although she might have left Solomon outside for me to devour."

Her mischievous smile reminded Tabytha of her niece Tuhi, and she found herself grinning, too.

"Are they both King David's?"

"Solomon, yes. He's one of Bathsheba's. Mica belongs to the cripple, Mephibosheth." She saw the lack of comprehension on Tabytha's face. "Mephibosheth? The grandson of the previous king? Abba fulfilled his promise to Jonathan to look after his offspring. That's why he brought him and his family to the palace."

So many names. How would she ever learn all of them? But one thing struck her. "You said *your father* brought them? Are you King David's daughter?"

The girl laughed and nodded. "You can tell by the robes." She twirled around in the long, full-sleeved gown, made of soft, flowing fabric, the color of a pomegranate flower, with dark blue embroidery around the neck, wrists, and base.

"It's beautiful," Tabytha said, even though the word didn't do the garment justice. She ran self-conscious hands down her own simple, undyed robe.

"All the princesses have gowns like this. It's our mothers' doing." Again, that glint of mischief. "They even turn dressing their daughters into a contest. One at which my own mother excels."

"Who's your mother?"

"Maacah."

"How many wives does the king have?"

"Eight, but Eglah died last year giving birth. The baby died too." A shadow chased over the girl's lovely face. "That leaves seven wives ... and nine concubines. Ten with you," she added quickly.

"That's a big household." Much bigger than she had realized. Tabytha thought of her own small home that had consisted of her mother, brother, and herself until her brother wed and Iuni joined them.

"My mother says that living here makes her feel like fermented wine bursting from a wineskin. But that's usually only when she and Abital are at odds with each other." Tamar shook her head ruefully. "Those two."

"How many children live here?"

"Oh." Tamar shook her head as if the question was too big for her. "I've lost count with the concubine's children. Many of the wives' children born in Hebron have married and live in their own homes now. I'm one of the few remaining ones.

"But come." She grabbed Tabytha's hand to lead her down the passage. "The others will want to meet you. I heard Abigail telling Gilia and Suta to prepare a place for you in their room. They're the youngest concubines and don't have children yet, either. Although," her face broke into the quick grin Tabytha was starting to associate with her, "Suta is getting a little heavier around the waist if you ask me."

At the sound of footsteps behind them, Tabytha turned to see that the smaller boy had returned.

He looked crestfallen as he threw his arm around Tamar and tucked himself into her side.

The princess tousled his hair. "You're not scared of the bear anymore?" She gave a playful growl.

"It's a silly game." He scowled. "I'm too old for it. I only played because Mica wanted to."

"Yes. Five is far too old for such games." Tamar winked at Tabytha over the boy's head. "Where is your trouble-double?"

"With his Aunt Michal."

"Wouldn't she let you in?"

"She did, but I don't think she likes me, so I left again. She's only nice to Mica. Why is she mean to me, Tamar, if we're part of the same family?"

"That's just Michal, Sol. She hardly likes anybody."

This idea seemed to satisfy him, and he turned a solemn gaze to Tabytha. "I'm Solomon, Bathsheba's son. Who are you?"

"I'm Tabytha, the king's ... concubine." Saying the word to a child didn't feel so bad.

"Why does Abba need another concubine? Doesn't he have enough?"

"Sol." Tamar berated him gently. "Our father betrothed Tabytha at the same time as the other Jebusite concubines. She wasn't old enough to come to the palace."

"Your name doesn't sound like the other concubines' names. It sounds more like one of ours."

"Sorry," Tamar said, pulling her half-brother into a playful neck choke. "This one is always full of strange thoughts and questions."

"No, the question is very clever. You're right, Solomon," Tabytha said. "My grandfather gave me a Hebrew name on the day he promised me to the king. Your father. Tabytha—gazelle—is what your father called me when he first saw me. He said I was lithe as a gazelle." *And lovely*. Would he believe her so still?

The boy looked her up and down. "You don't look at all like a gazelle."

"Of course she doesn't," Tamar said. "It's poetic, and you know how much Abba likes poetry. He saw she was tall for her age and had fine, long limbs, and they reminded him of the legs of the gazelle. That's why he said it."

The boy nodded sagely. "I remember Abba telling me about this. It's called a fig of speech."

"Fine. Now run along and find Shimea to play with." A note of impatience had crept into Tamar's voice.

Tabytha thought the boy rather interesting and engaging.

Tamar disentangled herself from Solomon's arm. "I'm taking Tabytha to meet the women."

The boy was not easily dissuaded, however. He fixed Tabytha with a solemn gaze. "What was your first name? Did you like that name more than being called after a gazelle?"

No one had ever asked her which name she preferred.

"My first name was Tawaassi."

The boy studied her expectantly. He seemed about to say something, but Tamar gave him a little push forward.

"Leave Tabytha in peace for a while. Go find someone else to interrogate."

"What does that mean ... interrogate?"

"It's what you do with your incessant questioning."

"What does incessant mean?"

Tabytha couldn't help laughing at Tamar's sigh of infuriation and was rewarded with a hint of a smile from Solomon.

"I'm serious, Sol. Run along, or I'll tell your mother to get the reed out."

"She won't. She says a royal heir needs to know as much as possible to rule well. She says I mustn't be afraid to ask questions."

Still, the lingering threat must have left its mark on his young mind because the boy took off down the passage, leaving Tabytha and Tamar behind.

The princess shook her head. "He's far too clever, that one, but Bathsheba is a fool to put such thoughts in his head. Amnon is the heir, with a string of princes after him. Bathsheba may be Abba's favorite wife, but she can't change that her beloved Solomon is nowhere close to inheriting the throne."

They had passed a few more curtained-off rooms and now reached a split in the passage. From the left, Tabytha could hear voices. Tamar took this direction.

The passage opened into a large courtyard, at least double the size of her mother's house. Tabytha stopped to take in the remarkable sight. The same elegant pillars she'd seen at the front of the palace framed the quadrangle. Three covered steps spanned its perimeter, providing shaded seating for several women reclining on brightly dyed cushions. Laughter pierced their animated conversation. On the far side of the courtyard, girls sat braiding each other's hair. Younger children played in the center. Tabytha caught a glimpse of Solomon and another boy dueling with wooden swords around a pillar.

"This is the heart of our quarters, the Women's Courtyard. No men allowed." Tamar winked. "Except Abba, of course."

chapter 4

tabytha

extract from scroll א (hs alef)

My mother was wrong when she said nothing would change on the day my grandfather promised me to the Hebrew king.

In Jebus, the Araunah's words carried weight, but in our house, his instructions were more than that. Since my father's death, my grandfather was the head of our home, and his word was law. Ornan ruled from a distance, however. A messenger would come telling us all to be at the new moon celebration. Another would come saying Atamu needed to tend our grandfather's goats. Then came that fateful afternoon when a messenger told me to present myself at the fort to meet my husband.

But that same night, Ornan himself came. I could see my mother's nervousness as she washed his feet at the door and bade him sit on the cushion that had been my father's. He waved aside my mother's offer of wine, instead, allowed me to pour him water. I thought he was there to scold me for disappointing the Hebrew king, and my heart pounded wildly as he began to talk. However, he addressed my mother.

"You realize what this means, don't you? The girl is no longer yours. She is the Hebrew king's, and they are a strange people with their belief in one god. She will have to learn their ways, or she will displease him. That would bring shame on our family."

He looked at me sternly from under his bushy white eyebrows.

"She will need a Hebrew name and upbringing. The other Jebusite elders had older daughters to give him to seal this covenant of peace. They are already Jebusite through and through, but the girl is different. She is young and can still learn to be a Hebrew."

"What if she doesn't care to be?"

My mother's brash question and how she held my grandfather's gaze as she asked it shocked me.

"Her wishes—or yours—are irrelevant." Ornan's voice had grown softer, and I felt more frightened than if he had shouted. "She will no longer be Tawaassi. From this day on, her name is Tabytha. And she will no longer attend the festivals of our gods."

My heart sank at this shocking declaration. Only at the festivals did I wear my beautiful robe, eat the special food prepared for our deities, and dance with my friends.

"You will also no longer tell her the stories of our gods," he continued. "I will find her a Hebrew to teach her about their one god."

"You would anger our gods to please a mere man?" My mother's voice rose in anger. "The gods' displeasure will be great, and there will be consequences. They may demand her very life ... or mine or yours, for insulting them so."

"Their anger will be on my head," Ornan said, and again, I glimpsed the heaviness I had seen in him that afternoon. "And El may forgive us if the girl worships only him and not his consort or the other gods."

But it was all the others, woven through my mother's stories, that I loved the most.

"Let El hear your words, Araunah," my mother declared solemnly, "that this decision may be on your head and not the girl's. I will not forgive you if the child is cursed because of this pronouncement."

I had never heard my mother—or anyone for that matter—speak to the Araunah like this before. It was shameful for a woman to address a man this directly, especially when that man was the lord of Jebus. Her words made me realize how worried she was. Would I be cursed from this day on? Wasn't it bad enough that I had to marry our conqueror? Would our gods be angry with me now too?

My grandfather turned to me. "You realize, Tabytha," the new name sounded strange on his lips, "how important this marriage is for us? The fate of our entire family rests on your shoulders. Our future is in your hands. The king's displeasure with you will lead to his displeasure with us, and this King David grows more powerful by the day. He can take our land, our animals, our very lives if he finds fault with you."

As he spoke, I imagined Ornan, my mother, Atamu, and my cousins all sitting on top of each other, on my shoulders. They were too heavy, far too heavy, for my thin body to bear.

"So, you are to learn your lessons well," Ornan said. "You will learn their history and understand their devotion to their one god. You must speak like they do, think like they do, act like they do. Then you will not displease their king. Perhaps, in fact, you will please him, and we will live under his favor."

In the silence that followed, my grandfather again pinned me with his severe gaze. It felt as if he waited for a reply.

"I will learn well, Araunah. I will not let you down." My trembling voice betrayed me. I had wanted him to know I was strong enough to carry them all.

But my grandfather could not find a Hebrew willing to teach a young Jebusite girl. It took two whole years before Ahio came to teach me to be a Hebrew. He was a man you would hardly have noticed in a crowd. His unkempt hair and beard gave him an air of neglect. Although he couldn't have been older than my mother, his shoulders stooped, as if he wanted to make himself smaller—unseen.

I met him in the courtyard that first day.

"Shalom, child." His deep voice was at odds with his timid, disheveled appearance. A whiff of beer emanated from his breath. "Is this the house of Tabytha, the one betrothed to King David?"

I nodded. "I am Tabytha."

He seemed taken aback. "You are younger than I realized. I am Ahio, sent to teach you the history of our people and the ways of ..." He took a steadying breath. "Of Adonai."

My mother had come to stand behind me, her protective hands on my shoulders. I didn't look up at her, but imagining the stony gaze she gave the man wasn't difficult.

"Peace to this house," he greeted her with a tentative smile.

"The peace fled this house on the day your king set his sights on Jebus," my mother said sharply.

The man didn't reply. He shuffled his feet nervously and cast me a long, almost pleading glance. For a moment, I thought he might turn and leave, but then he straightened his shoulders and looked at my mother again.

"I have been appointed to teach your daughter. I will come twice a week as instructed. Where is the best place for us to sit?"

"Stay here in the courtyard."

If my teacher realized the insult of not being invited into the house, he did not indicate it.

"She's a bright one," my mother continued. "Hopefully, you won't need to come more than a few weeks."

"We are a people with a long history, and Adonai has high demands of his chosen people." A boldness seemed to have crept into him as he spoke. "This will not be a matter of weeks or even months. It will require time."

"Tawaassi has chores. Do not keep her from them."

"I'm sure Tabytha will manage both her chores and lessons."

Something in the way he said it, and the small conspiratorial smile he gave me, made me want to do my best for him. How could I let this sad-looking man down?

So began a surprisingly rich part of my life.

Ahio came every week after that. Sometimes, he smelled of sour beer and looked at me with bleary eyes. Occasionally, he didn't come at all, and Atamu would tease me that even my drunk, no-good tutor couldn't bear to be with me. But Ahio always returned, a little broken but as determined as before. "I have failed at so many things. I will not fail at this," he told me once.

Atamu heard from his friend, who heard from his uncle, that Ahio was the only priest willing to teach a Jebusite girl. This was why Ornan had taken so long to find me a tutor. The same uncle said Ahio was an outcast and the other priests didn't speak to him at all. Perhaps this knowledge softened my mother slightly towards Ahio, for she finally invited him inside. The enemy's castaway priest would be tolerated if not wholly trusted. Ahio's deep voice wove together the stories of his people, starting with the story of how his god—Adonai, he called him—had created everything and placed the first man and woman in a beautiful garden, where a serpent had tempted them to eat the forbidden fruit. When I told him this sounded just like our head god, the creator El, Ahio vehemently denied that they were the same.

"Adonai is not just the *head* god. He is the *only* God." It was one of the few times Ahio raised his voice at me.

There were many more stories. Of floods and a noisy, smelly boat filled with animals. Of brothers who sold one of their own into slavery—Ahio gave me a rare smile when I told him my brother might have done the same to me. Of how that slave became the second most important man in Egypt and saved everyone, including his mean brothers who had come begging him for grain. Of an Egyptian princess finding a Hebrew baby floating in a basket on a river. Of frogs in the Pharaoh's bed and Adonai's shining messengers killing babies in every home but passing over the houses of the Hebrews because of the blood on their doorposts. Of how Adonai opened a path through the sea so his people could escape but then closed it again to drown the Egyptians. Of the holy mountain where Adonai gave the Hebrews two stone tablets engraved by Adonai's own finger. Ahio taught me to recite those sacred engravings despite my grumblings that the words were too difficult for one as young as me.

harem scrolls

I loved Ahio's stories almost as much as I loved my mother's stories of our own gods, for, despite Ornan's warnings, she had not stopped telling me them. Those two worlds—Ahio's and my mother's—entwined vividly in my dreams. El and Asertu both walked in the garden as the first man and woman hid, the juice of the forbidden fruit still staining their mouths. In my dream, it was Telipinu, our storm god, who blew the sea apart for the Hebrews to escape from the Egyptians. And it was the protector Inara, Telipinu's sister, who stood by the houses to keep Adonai's heavenly warriors away.

As time passed, I slowly pieced together parts of Ahio's life. He told me he came from the tribe of Levi, the ones chosen to look after their sacred relics. When I asked which items were in his care, he shook his head and told me he had been relieved of his duties.

"Because you drink too much beer?" I asked. "Or did you drop and break something?"

He sat long and stared into the distance as if he had not heard my impertinent question.

"Ahio?"

"Something happened," he finally said.

My childish curiosity knew no bounds, but he would not tell me why he no longer served as keeper of the relics, why he drank too much, or why the other priests didn't speak to him anymore.

I also learned something else about Ahio—his fear of Adonai. Whenever he spoke his god's name, he wiped his brow or swallowed nervously.

"Why are you so afraid of Adonai?" I asked towards the end of one lesson.

"He is a fearful God, Tabytha. Have you not listened to my stories of how powerful he is? Shouldn't we fear the one who can strike down an entire nation's firstborns?"

"But those were your enemy's firstborn."

"He strikes us down, too, sometimes." Surprisingly, his eyes pooled with tears.

"Like when?"

Ahio rose abruptly. "Our lesson is finished."

"But you said you would read me the song Miriam sang." I had been particularly excited to learn that he had brought a scroll with him that contained words composed by a woman.

"Next time, Tabytha."

I snatched the scroll off the low table at which I still sat and unfurled it.

"Careful with that, child."

I studied the small symbols that filled the scroll. Together, these symbols made words, and the words were the thoughts of a woman just like me. How I longed to decipher them, to have access to her mind.

And then I had a thought.

"Ahio!" I grabbed his hands in excitement. "Why don't you teach me to read?"

chapter 5

After five days in the Women's Quarters, Tabytha longed for solitude. She would have escaped into the valley if she had still been at home. She would have walked the paths she had known since childhood, waved a greeting to the herdsmen of her kin, and sat at the river's edge to dangle her feet in the calm flow of the water. She would have looked up at the vast sky guarding the valley of her birth and breathed deeply of the air as the afternoon shed its heat. She would have ...

"May I join you?" Abigail's words snapped her out of her reverie. She, too, lifted her gaze to the small piece of sky visible from the Women's Courtyard. "It's a lovely blue at this time of day, isn't it?"

"It looks even better from the valley."

Abigail gave her a searching look. "Did you spend much time there?"

"Almost every afternoon, around this time of day."

"I remember that kind of freedom," Abigail said wistfully. "Before David became king at Hebron. We were in wild, remote places much of the time. Those night skies in the wilderness were something to behold."

Everything about Abigail was slight and fine—her face, hands, and even the soft way she spoke. Yet Tabytha suspected Abigail's gentleness masked strength. The older woman wielded unrivalled authority in the Women's Quarters.

"It must be difficult to come into such a large household," Abigail said. "Do you miss your freedom?"

"Yes." Tabytha swallowed away the lump in her throat

"I'm sure David will let you visit your family soon." Abigail spoke of the king with warm familiarity. "Then you can walk the valley again."

Tabytha thought it unlikely. She had yet to see the king, who had been away inspecting a distant fortification. That afternoon, word had come he would return to the city by sunset. Excitement had coursed through the Women's Quarters. Children were being scrubbed clean. Hair was being braided. The women were dressing and perfuming themselves. Hence Tabytha had found herself blessedly alone in the courtyard.

"David will be here tonight." From Abigail's smile, Tabytha deduced it was not only the younger women anticipating his return. "We haven't had time to make new robes for you, but perhaps Suta can lend you one of hers."

"She said I could wear one, but I thought this would do."

Of the two concubines Tabytha shared a room with, Suta was the one starting to feel like a friend. Whereas Gilia constantly found fault, Suta seemed particularly content with her life. Being with her felt a little like being with Iuni.

Abigail ran a hand over Tabytha's robe. "The workmanship is fine, and David is not one to judge on appearances," she said gently. "But you may feel self-conscious in a robe plainer than everyone else's."

Tabytha shrugged. She hadn't taken long to realize there were women here who were far more beautiful than she. Haggith, for instance, with her dark, mysterious eyes. Or Bathsheba, with her flawless skin, long hair, and shapely body. In contrast, Tabytha's tall, lean build might be mistaken for a boy's even when she didn't bind her breasts. Worst of all, over the years, she had taken to cutting her unruly hair so it only just reached her shoulders. She hadn't given this a thought until the day she arrived at the palace, and—when she removed her headscarf—the women and girls had let out a collective sigh of dismay. "How are we going to braid *that*," one of the girls had asked, her hand over her mouth in concern.

"At least my teeth have grown in," Tabytha said. "The last time the king saw me, most were missing."

"I'm sure he'll be particularly glad of that." Abigail smiled.

Suta held up a string of beads. "This one suits me better. What do you think, Tabytha?"

Tabytha had returned to her room, one of those she had passed on that first day in the palace. The room was dark. Unlike the wives' rooms, it did not open onto the courtyard or the side of the palace overlooking the city. Instead, its two small, high windows opened onto the passage near the women's entrance. Still, the room's furnishings were better than at home. A woven rug covered the floor, and Tabytha had her own low bed with a blanket softer than any she had had before. Shelves lined the wall for her gowns and other belongings. One corner contained a scattering of cushions around a low table. Here, Gilia and Suta had spread out their jewelry in search of the perfect items to wear that night.

"It's lovely," Tabytha said.

Gilia cast her a critical look. "You're not wearing *that,* are you?"

"It's the best robe I have."

"But not one to wear for a king."

"I don't think it matters much."

"Oh, it matters," Gilia said, rolling her eyes. "A lot. Let me explain something to you, Tabytha. As it stands, you are at the bottom of the household hierarchy."

Tabytha had found the last few days an overwhelming whirl of faces and names, of questions and stories. Wives and concubines, sons, and daughters—she sought to put them all in their rightful place. One thing she was starting to understand was the king's household had a very particular pecking order, and it appeared the women all intrinsically understood where they ranked.

"Why am I at the bottom?"

"To begin with, you're a concubine, and concubines are always lower than actual wives."

"And you're the last to arrive," Suta added. "Seniority outranks new."

"Except if you're beautiful or the king's favorite." Gilia's disdainful appraisal of Tabytha communicated her doubt that the latest concubine would fulfil either of those qualities.

"Or if you're a wife and have given the king sons," Suta said. "Concubines' sons don't count. And the heir's mother will always have the highest rank of all. She is not only the wife of a king but will be the mother of one too. She is the *Gebirah,* the queen."

Tabytha remembered her nieces' excitement that she was to become a queen. How wrong they had been.

"So Ahinoam is the most highly ranked wife? As Amnon's mother?" Tabytha thought of the arrogant prince she had seen when she arrived at the palace.

Suta nodded. "Ahinoam was also the king's first wife, so she has the highest rank."

"I thought Michal was his first wife. Isn't she the queen?"

Her companions both laughed. "Michal? She's hardly a wife, and definitely not the queen," Gilia said. "Come to think of it, you're not the lowest-ranking member of the household. She is."

"Why? What happened to her?"

"Well, to begin with, she *hates* the king. You know her father was his predecessor and tried to kill King David most of his life." Gilia became louder and more expressive when telling such conspiratorial tales. "So, her family and his are sworn enemies."

Tabytha thought of Tamar saying her father had brought the cripple, Mephibosheth, into the palace. Wasn't he the former king's grandson? Would David have done that if he considered their family enemies?

"And then there was the time Michal saw the king dancing in little more than his loincloth before a whole crowd of people." Gilia laughed. "She told him it was undignified, and rightly so. Since then, he has shunned her."

"He didn't shun her," Suta said. "Michal stopped coming to family gatherings. I think the king still has feelings for her. She was his first love, after all. Puduhepa told me he even sent for her once, but she refused to go to him."

"What does Pudu know?" Gilia scowled.

"She was the king's first concubine in Hebron. Abigail told her. You know how close Ahinoam, Abigail, and Pudu are."

"And how would Abigail know? She thinks the sun shines only on her beloved David. She can't bear to think he would treat a wife that way."

"Where does Abigail rank in the family?" Tabytha asked.

"Not as high as she thinks," Gilia said. "Honestly, she acts as if she runs the whole palace."

"You're too hard on her," Suta said. "She's not proud and controlling like some of the others. The king often confides in her and relies on her to arrange things."

Gilia shrugged as if Abigail mattered little to her. She returned to the necklaces, picking up a beautiful one made of blue stones.

"I think I'm going to wear this one."

"Do you want to choose something for yourself, Tabytha?" Suta held up a string of pearls.

"Nothing will match that awful gown." Gilia snickered.

"That should make you happy. If I caught the king's attention, I might soon outrank you," Tabytha said.

Suta howled with laughter. "Young Tabytha is not as tame as you think, Gilia. You'd better watch out." She turned a thoughtful gaze on Tabytha. "What we need to do is find something unique about you and make you shine in that. Abigail is the organizer, and Bathsheba is beautiful. Maacah, the noble, better-than-everyone-else one. Haggith dances and sings. Abital prays half the day and looks down on us pagans for the rest of the day. Puduhepa tends her figs and makes the best fig tarts you've ever tasted. I'm the cheerful one, and Gilia is the one who knows everyone's business better than they know it themselves. Ask yourself,

Tabytha, what are you good at? What can you do better than anyone else? What could make the king notice and remember you?"

Tabytha shook her head. She was just an ordinary Jebusite, the granddaughter of the Araunah. She could throw a stone as well as any boy, but in the palace of a warrior king, she wouldn't exactly need that skill. She wasn't particularly beautiful or graceful or talented at cooking or sewing. She had nothing to offer King David and his household.

Except ...

"There is one thing I can do that most others can't." The words slipped out before she could give them much thought.

"What?" Gilia's tone suggested she doubted Tabytha could do anything particularly worthwhile.

"I know how to read and write."

chapter 6

tabytha

extract from scroll א (hs alef)

Ahio resisted the idea of teaching me to read. His reasons were many. He was only required to teach me the history of his people, not how to read it. Writing was the domain of priests, scribes, and a few of the Levites. He didn't know a single Hebrew woman who could read or write, much less a Jebusite girl. The female mind could not grasp the complexities of forming the intricate Hebrew alef-bet.

But my mother said I had the most stubborn streak of anyone she knew. Over the next two years, I whittled away Ahio's resolve until he reluctantly agreed to bring me a clay tablet with the twenty-two Hebrew letters on it.

That I spent more time studying than helping my mother angered her. More than once, she shouted at Ahio that his teaching took me away from my chores. Once or twice, she even threatened to smash that clay tablet to pieces, and I couldn't help thinking of Moses at Mount Sinai and the stone tablets Adonai himself had engraved.

Atamu mocked me for learning the script of our invaders. I knew Mother's threats to destroy the tablet were idle, but

I feared what my brother might do to my precious tablet, so I took to hiding it in the roof reeds or burying it behind our house.

I also scratched the picture letters into the soil where I hid my treasured tablet. Over and over, I composed them—markings that meant ox heads and swords and doors and camels and hooks and serpents. I tried to puzzle out how to combine them into words. The first word I wrote was the ox-head and the house and the ox-head again. Alef Bet Alef. Abba—head of the house.

When I showed Ahio, a small smile crept onto his usually somber face.

"Your mother was right, Tabytha. You are a clever one." There might have been a hint of pride in my teacher's voice.

After that, he brought me scrolls of religious writings, and slowly—painstakingly—we read them together. Ahio explained the placement of the letters and how they changed the meaning of the phrases. It amazed me the Hebrew's faith was woven into every mark and symbol, and in these holy writings, I understood the lessons about Adonai better than I ever had before.

One day, he arrived a little early, eagerness in his bearing. "I have a surprise for you." He laid a small scroll between us and watched as I unrolled it the way he had taught me.

Unlike the long prophecies and histories we had read together, this was a short piece. I looked up at him in surprise.

"Another one of Miriam's songs?"

"Read it." His eyes—clearer than usual that day—sparkled with pleasure.

I couldn't make out the first word, so I pointed to it.

"Mizmôwr," Ahio said. "It's a poem set to music."

"A mizmôwr of ..."

A name.

I looked up at him. *Could it be?* "... of David."

Ahio nodded proudly.

"The king wrote this?"

"He writes many such prayer poems. The Levites assigned to singing use them often."

Something swelled inside me. My husband was not simply a warrior, not only a man of the sword. He had a tender side. He crafted songs. And he had written the one I held in my hands *right now*. I had only seen him once, but I held a little piece of his heart in my hands.

I continued reading, surprised to see that the first word was Adonai's actual name. YHWH—the name Ahio declared too holy to speak—that whenever the scribes wrote it, they purified themselves first.

I wondered if the king had purified himself, too. I didn't say the name but replaced it with Adonai, the way Ahio had taught me. "Adonai is my ..." I puzzled over the letters of the next word. "Sheep?"

"Shepherd. Adonai is my shepherd."

"Nothing I want," I slowly pushed on. "He makes. Me rest. In ... meadows."

No, this wasn't how I wanted to hear my husband's words for the first time. I held it out to Ahio. "Read it to me. Please."

Ahio always insisted I struggle with the words myself, but he seemed to understand my longing to hear them the way they had been written. He took the scroll from my hand. I closed my eyes and let his deep voice draw me into my husband's words.

"Adonai is my shepherd. I shall not want. He makes me lie down in green pastures. He leads me beside the still waters."

I thought of the river winding through our valley and how the sound of that water always quieted me. He had felt that way, too.

"He restores my soul. He leads me in the paths of righteousness for the sake of his name. Yea, though I walk through the valley of the shadow of death, I will fear no evil, for you are with me. Your rod and your staff, they comfort me."

In my mind, I saw the king walking along my valley path behind a powerfully built man. His god, Adonai, carried a rod and staff and led the way.

"You prepare a table before me in the presence of my enemies. With oil, you anoint my head. My cup runs over."

A table laden with the finest foods appeared in my imagination, and the Araunah and all of us Jebusites were bowing before the king as oil dripped from his hair and beard.

"Surely goodness and mercy shall follow me all the days of my life, and I will dwell in the house of Adonai forever."

A long silence followed as Ahio and I let the poem's words wrap around us. I had never heard such beautiful words.

"Read it again, Ahio."

So, he did.

When he finished, I said, "Why doesn't the king fear Adonai like you do? He speaks of him as if he is his friend."

"He fears Adonai in his own way. He was there when—" Ahio stopped abruptly.

"When what?"

My teacher shook his head. "You must understand, Tabytha, King David is the anointed one. Adonai is our ultimate king, but King David represents him here on earth and, as such, lives under his favor as no other man does."

Although Ahio wouldn't let me keep that scroll, I memorized the king's poem. I said it every time I walked the valley path. When I imagined the king walking there with Adonai, I walked with them, too.

chapter 7

As Tabytha descended the steps of the Women's Courtyard with Gilia and Suta, she marveled at its transformation. Low tables stood where the children typically played, and most of the king's wives and concubines were already reclined on cushions around them. Wafts of perfume mingled with the smell of yeasty bread and herbed lamb. Tabytha was sharply reminded of the festivals of her childhood before Ornan's decree forbade her from attending them. Oil lamps cast warm light onto the faces of the women, looking lovelier than ever in their fine gowns and jewelry. The freshly scrubbed children sat in orderly lines on the far steps under the watchful eye of Tamar and some of the older girls. Although everyone was more subdued than usual, Tabytha sensed the undercurrent of excitement.

"We're late," Gilia muttered. "Now we'll have to sit at Pudu's table."

"You were the one taking so long to get ready," Suta said. "Anyway, it's not like we were going to be invited to sit with the king tonight."

As they made their way to the table, they could hear Puduhepa's laughter. She had been part of David's family for almost as long as Abigail and Ahinoam and radiated a confident sense of belonging lacking in most of the other concubines. This evening, particularly beautiful fabrics swathed her broad body, and her eyes sparkled as she regaled her dinner companions with a loud story.

"I'm going to pinch her if the story's about the king telling her to make fig cakes so that one of his warriors could win over the parents of the woman he loved," Gilia said.

"... and one bite of my fig cakes, and they agreed, of course. Ah, you three ..." Pudu broke off her story as the women reached her table. "There is plenty of room for you to join us. Come, Tabytha, sit next to me. I am telling the others about when King David asked me to make fig cakes for one of his men, Ira, who had his eye on this beautiful girl from Hebron ..."

"We've heard the story before, Pudu. Many times." Gilia looked around. "Now, where is the servant with the wine?"

Pudu lifted her hand and called across to a servant with a wineskin. The girl hurried over and poured the red liquid into Gilia's goblet, Suta's, and Tabytha's. Tabytha seldom drank wine at home and cautiously lifted the goblet to her nose, breathing in the fruity, yeasty smell.

"You'll manage the drink, my dear," Pudu said. "King David always has our wine watered down. He doesn't like drunkenness among his men." She winked. "Or his women, for that matter, although Gilia gives inebriation a good try."

Tabytha took a tentative sip. The wine tasted sweet and warmed her throat when she swallowed. She took a fuller sip.

Pudu watched, nodding like a proud mother. "I knew you'd like the wine."

"When does the king arrive?" Tabytha put down the goblet. She wanted a clear head to meet the king tonight.

"Should be here soon. He got back to the palace about an hour ago." Pudu pointed to a door in the courtyard wall. "He'll come through the door joining our quarters to his."

"Does he bring his guards?"

"Two will be stationed on the other side of the door."

Servants brought platters of bread and an olive spread. Tabytha ate of it, sipping her wine and listening to the women's banter, but her gaze kept drifting over to the door. She hadn't seen the king for almost ten years. Would he remember how she had embarrassed herself that day? Or her gap-filled smile and how she had tried to untie his sandal? She still recalled her grandfather's harsh words, the men's mocking laughter, and the Hebrew king's solemn gaze on her.

After what felt like an intolerably long time, the door opened. Tabytha's breath caught in her throat as King David stepped into the Women's Courtyard. *Her husband*. He was not dressed as a warrior this time but wore a fine, dark brown cloak. She caught the glint of a blade beneath the cloth as he made his way down the steps. Ten years had not weakened him, although she noticed his beard and hair were now speckled with grey. If anything, she thought the king had an even greater aura of strength and authority. The way the conversation in the courtyard hushed as he entered added to the impression. The moment broke as a small boy ran across the courtyard and threw himself into the king's side. "Abba!"

King David laughed, lifting Solomon into the air and spinning him around as the boy squealed with delight. The other young children were close behind their brother, clambering around the king for a turn to be lifted high, even as their mothers called for them to leave their father alone.

"You'd think those women would have better control of their unruly young. And the king is far too indulgent," Gilia said. "Sometimes he doesn't act like a king at all."

Tabytha smiled as the king bent down to a little girl the stronger boys had pushed out of the way. Gilia was wrong. Protecting the weak was precisely what a king should do.

Finally, the younger children made way for the older ones. These approached the king with more gravity, with tiny bows and solemn words. Tamar, however, tucked her arm around her father and laid her head on his shoulder before saying something that made him smile.

Now, the king made his way to the table where his wives sat. Only Michal was absent. Tabytha had yet to see her. The women rose, and each came forward to greet their husband. Tabytha watched closely, trying to understand the protocol, but couldn't discern a pattern. Some wives bowed more deeply than others.

Maacah hardly inclined her head.

"Typically arrogant, just because her father is the king of Geshur," Gilia whispered, watching the greetings with as much interest as Tabytha did.

Abital, on the other hand, bowed so low her forehead almost touched the ground.

"She treats him like he's Adonai on earth." Gilia's tone was scathing.

Haggith's bow was dancer elegant, Ahinoam's confident and familiar. Abigail bowed briefly before exchanging words with the king. Bathsheba lowered her head but lifted her eyes coquettishly while touching the king's shoulder.

To that, Gilia merely let out a derisive snort.

"So, what should I do?" Tabytha asked her companions nervously. "They all greeted him differently."

"It doesn't matter, my dear." Pudu patted her arm. "He's not one to stand on ceremony."

Tabytha did not know what that meant and continued to watch closely as the next table, the first of the king's concubines, rose to greet him. Finally, the women at her table rose, and Tabytha fell in behind Suta as they made their way to the king.

Her hands sweated as she watched her companions greet him. Gilia, cool and formal; Pudu exuberant; and Suta, shy. Tabytha still hadn't entirely decided what to do when she found herself face-to-face with King David. But even before she could kneel, he spoke and held out his hand. "You are finally here, Tabytha. Welcome."

Tentatively, she slipped her own hand into his. It felt warm and comforting. She had almost forgotten that deep, gentle voice. It stilled something in her.

"My lord and king." She bowed as low as she could without letting go of his hand.

"Are you settling in well to my home?"

"I am, my lord. Everyone has been very kind." She dared to look up at him then, into those dark, dangerous eyes. Yet as he met her gaze, the king smiled, and it felt like a ray of warm sunshine fell onto her. She suddenly understood why Abital bowed as if the king was Adonai's envoy on earth, why Suta became shy and giggly, and why Bathsheba reached out to touch him. All those urges raced through Tabytha at once, leaving her flustered, warmth rising to her cheeks.

"I look forward to hearing how your grandfather and family are doing," he said as if he didn't notice her discomfort. "I recently bought Ornan's threshing floor."

"I know, my lord. When the plague ravished the land."

"Yes." His expression darkened, and she wished she hadn't mentioned the plague. Rumor had it the king had disobeyed Adonai, and the plague that killed thousands had fallen on his nation as a punishment.

"I hope you enjoy this evening." As he dropped her hand, she felt slightly bereft. "They have prepared my favorite meal."

"I will, my lord." She stood a little longer, not wanting the moment to end. "I hear you sometimes play the lyre. Will you do so tonight, my king?"

"Do you like music?"

"I do. Especially your songs."

He lifted a quizzical brow. "You have heard my songs?"

"I had a Hebrew tutor. He sometimes brought scrolls of your poems." *For me to read*. Perhaps he, too, would disapprove she had been taught what Hebrew priests considered a man's domain.

"Which did you like the most?"

She didn't even have to think. "Adonai is my shepherd; I shall not want ..."

"He makes me lie down in pastures green. He leads me beside the still waters," the king continued, his gaze on her face. "Then that is the one I will sing tonight."

Somehow, she made it back to her table on her suddenly shaky legs. She hardly tasted her food or heard the conversation around her but kept looking over to where the king sat next to Bathsheba and Ahinoam, opposite Abigail. Their comfortable conversation. Their easy laughter. She felt a pang of jealousy like a sharp shard in her throat. Why couldn't she have been born a Hebrew? Why couldn't she have been chosen instead of being the Araunah's granddaughter, the peace offering he hadn't even sent for until now?

"She's got it bad, doesn't she?"

Gilia's voice broke through her thoughts, and Tabytha drew her gaze away from the main table to find her table companions looking at her, a few with knowing smirks.

"He had that effect on most of us, my dear." Pudu looked over at the king with a glint of mischief in her eye. "Still does, in fact."

"Not on me," Gilia said. "I don't forget that I'm a Jebusite of high birth, and he the lowly throne-snatcher who stormed my city."

The words, so like those of Atamu, doused Tabytha's heady feeling.

But only until the king picked up his lyre and began to play. As his fingers danced across the strings, Tabytha felt the longing in the notes—the hope but also the joy. She knew the words of his poem by heart, yet when his deep voice wove through the melody, they came to life as never before. When she read the words with Ahio, they transported her to a river and a valley and a table laden with rich foods. Only now—on his lips—did she hear the king's deep devotion and love for Adonai. She had previously imagined the three of them walking the valley floor, but now she knew this was a love song for only two. The king sang it for her tonight, but she suddenly understood his first love had never been Michal, Abigail, or even Bathsheba. David's heart belonged to only one—Adonai. Strangely, this insight stilled the jealousy she had felt towards his wives.

When he finished the song, the king looked over at her and nodded, and she touched her heart and bowed her head, willing him to know she had never heard anything more beautiful.

That night, Tabytha fell asleep, the words of the king's song still echoing through her mind. She slept more soundly than she had since arriving at the palace.

A voice calling her name awoke her.

Daylight had already crept into the room. She must have overslept. Suta and Gilia were not there.

Surprisingly, the boy, Mica, stood on the other side of the curtain.

He earnestly peered into the room, then said, "Aunt Michal told me to make sure you were alone. She says you must come see her now."

"Right now?" Tabytha shook her sleep-heavy head in confusion.

He nodded emphatically. "Aunt Michal hates to wait."

chapter 8

tabytha

extract from scroll א (hs alef)

One other event stands out starkly from my childhood. It happened three or four years after my betrothal to the Hebrew king. My brother and I were scampering down the valley path with his friends when I saw a flutter of movement on a small ledge above us.

I called the others to stop, and we backtracked to higher ground for a better view.

A large bird with a long tail, curved beak, and yellow-rimmed eyes perched on the rock. The bird was the color of ash after a fire had burned out. One wing hung lower than the other.

Atamu immediately picked up a stone. "It can't fly. Watch me knock it off the ledge before any of you can!"

The other boys scurried to pick up stones as my brother threw the first one. In the last two years, Atamu had grown almost as tall as a man and strong, too, so the stone flew far and fast. It hit the rock close to the bird. He fluttered his whole wing wildly to escape, even as the other hung limply by its side.

"No!" I screamed, pushing Atamu as hard as I could. Yet even as my brother sprawled on the ground, other stones flew through the air. One of them found its mark, to the delight of the boy who had pitched it into the air, and I watched the bird tumble off the ledge.

"No! No! No!" I screamed again, pummeling my tiny fists into their much larger bodies, anywhere to keep them from throwing their stones.

"Stop that *now*."

We had not seen the man approaching from behind us, but at his stern command, we all froze and spun around. Tall, with a full, black beard and eyes the color of dark basalt, the man wore a rather fine cloak over his homespun tunic.

"The king's seer," one boy whispered, and his fear compelled us all to start running. I dared to look back one last time and saw that the man had left the path and now climbed to the ledge where the injured bird had been perched until the stone had struck it. I stopped running and took a few tentative steps back, trying to get a clearer view of the seer.

By then, the boys were far down the path. I could hear my brother calling to me. His voice rankled me, rekindling my anger that he would try to hurt the beautiful creature. As afraid as I was of the seer, I ignored my brother and slowly walked back up the path.

I watched the man take off his robe and bend down. When he straightened again, I saw he carried the bird in his cloak. He picked his way carefully back over the rocks. I knew I should run, but something kept me standing there, even though I felt a tremble pass through me. Perhaps it was the desire to see if the bird lived. Perhaps it was something else—a draw to this strange man who men said could see the future. When the seer reached the path, he nodded, silently acknowledging my presence.

It gave me the courage to take a step towards him. "Will the bird be fine?"

"He lives. I will do what I can." His voice had lost its sternness. "Come closer, child, and see him. He's a beauty."

I stepped closer and peered into the folds of his robe. The bird fought the constraint of the robe. It looked up at me with eyes that held a wild fierceness. Somewhat like the seer's eyes.

"I've seen these falcons in the Judean desert," my companion said. "They breed on the cliffs in summer and hunt small birds. In winter, they fly south."

"Will you catch birds for it?" I asked. "Until it can hunt on its own?"

"Birds could prove difficult. It might have to live off other meat with me." The seer's attention shifted from the bird to me. "You were brave, child, protecting him from those big boys." He looked at me then, long, and intensely.

I wanted to look away, but the same compulsion that had kept me standing on the path drew me into that gaze.

He finally looked away. "You are no ordinary girl, I see."

I didn't know what to say. I felt ordinary enough. Except that I was the Araunah's granddaughter and betrothed to a king, so maybe his words were true.

"What is your name, child?"

"Taw ... I mean Tabytha."

"Tabytha? A Hebrew name."

"The king gave it to me."

He nodded as if this did not surprise him. "I have heard," he said after a little while, "that men use such birds of prey in the eastern lands to hunt."

"Truly?" I tried to imagine it. The birds could go where hunters couldn't. It was clever.

"Perhaps I will try myself if I can get this one's wing to heal."

"I don't think it will work. If his wing gets better, he'll fly away. I would. Wouldn't you?"

"Yes." The seer looked at me with the same intensity as before. "Yes, indeed. We all long for freedom. No one wants to be a captive."

His gaze shifted to something behind me, and I turned to see Atamu and two of his friends hesitantly making their way up the path, rocks in hand.

"Your friends have returned to rescue you." His lips twitched with amusement. "You should tell them nothing good comes of throwing stones at falcons or prophets."

"My brother." I shrugged. "He doesn't really care for me, but he knows my mother would kill him if ..."

"... if you fell into the hands of the prophet Nathan?"

I grinned.

"Go before one of those rocks strikes me too," he said. "And Tabytha?"

I turned back to him.

"You are no ordinary girl. Adonai sees your heart. Remember that his hand is on you. Remember especially when you have a broken wing. Shalom, child."

They were the strangest of words. My chest tingled as he spoke them. Those words branded onto my heart with searing intensity, both frightening and comforting me. Years later, I could still remember them. Above all, I could recall the feeling that a divine hand had reached down and touched my heart.

It would be a long time before I saw the prophet or the falcon again.

chapter 9

The boy waited outside while Tabytha dressed. He escorted her to Michal's room at the end of the passage, even though she told him she would go alone.

He pounded on the door.

No curtain for the king's wife.

"Aunt Michal. I brought her like you told me to."

Tabytha blinked in surprise when a finely dressed woman who seemed too old to be Michal opened the door. The woman scowled at Mica and said primly, "Your aunt says not to make such a commotion."

"But she promised me dates for fetching the concubine."

The woman held out a bowl of fruit. The boy snatched a handful of dates, stuffing one into his mouth before whirling around and running down the passage.

"Such vile manners." The woman turned her attention to Tabytha, her stern gaze lingering on Tabytha's short hair. "Come in. The queen doesn't like to be kept waiting."

Tabytha couldn't have been more surprised by Michal's quarters. She had expected the exiled wife's room to be small and dark, but this room was spacious and light, with tapestries on the walls, carpets on the floors, and fine ornaments scattered on chests and tables. Her gaze snagged on several small statues. Were those Asherah, the fertility goddess? Surely not in Israel's palace?

One small, latticed window looked out over the central palace square, but most of the light came from the other side, which opened onto an enclosed courtyard filled with flowering pots. Michal bent over one of these pots, trimming a branch. She straightened and turned, frowning as Tabytha stepped into the courtyard.

"You're the Jebusite concubine who can supposedly write?"

"I'm Tabytha, yes."

"Fine. But can you write?"

Michal might have been beautiful in her day. Possibly, she still was with her high cheekbones and slanting eyes. But Iuni had always said that true beauty lies inside you, in the way you speak to others and the kindness you show them. If so, Michal wasn't at all attractive.

"I can write, yes. Who told you?" She'd only shared it with Gilia and Suta the day before.

Michal's smile held no warmth. "Just because everybody thinks I'm as good as dead doesn't mean I don't know what's happening. Here's some sage advice to serve you well in this madhouse palace, Talita. Don't tell Gilia anything you don't want the world to know. By now, David's lowest serving boy probably knows you write."

"Tabytha."

"Mmmm?"

"My name is Tabytha." She was surprised to find herself matching the woman's abrupt tone. "And what is it to you if I write?"

"You are to write my story." Michal stared down at her hands as if only now aware of the soil on them. "Hannah, my dove? Could you bring some water?"

The woman who had opened the door appeared almost instantly with a bowl of water and held it while Michal washed her hands. The servant carefully put the bowl down, took a towel from around her neck, and gently dried them.

"What would I do without you, dear Hannah?" Michal looked up at Tabytha. "Hannah is my sister-in-law. My faithful companion all these years."

"You're the king's sister?" Tabytha asked, turning to Hannah. Surely, she would have heard if King David's sister lived in the Women's Quarters? And why would she be serving Michal?

Michal snorted derisively. "Not David's sister. Paltiel's sister."

"Paltiel?"

"My first husband. David took me from Paltiel when he and Abner were scheming to get my brother's throne."

"But weren't you King David's first wife? The wife of his youth?" That's what Gilia had told her.

"Hardly a marriage," Michal said. "He went on the run for so long I forgot what he looked like. David and I were both young. Naïve. He was ..." For an instant, something wistful crept over her face. She looked at Hannah almost guiltily before she continued. "Well, you know how it is when you are young and impressionable. I fell in love with most of my father's young warriors."

"And Paltiel?"

"I was furious when my father told me he was giving me to another man. But his decision proved wise. At that time, David lived the life of an outlaw. Paltiel was the husband David could never be. He loved me, truly loved me as David never has. David cared only for my father's throne. That, and his precious *Adonai*."

The contempt in Michal's voice shocked Tabytha. Ahio had always spoken of Adonai with awe and a good dose of fear. The king wrote of him with deep affection and closeness. Abigail spoke his name with reverence. Even Tabytha's own people, the Jebusites, seemed afraid of the powerful Adonai. He was not a god to anger, surely not a god to hold in contempt.

Michal laughed. "Don't tell me you're as taken with Adonai as David, Abigail, and the rest of these fools. Adonai destroyed my family. Didn't he destroy yours too when he gave David your city?"

Tabytha thought of her father. Her father could still be alive if the Hebrews hadn't claimed Jebus for themselves, if Adonai hadn't given them this land and told them to drive everyone else out of it.

"Anyway, let's get back to why I called you here." Michal gracefully lowered herself onto the cushions on the floor and patted the one next to her own—an invitation for Tabytha to sit. When Tabytha was seated, she spoke again. "You are to record my story."

"Why?" Tabytha ran her fingertips over the silky cushion, marveling at its softness.

"Because nobody else will. David has scribes and historians writing down the smallest thing he does. I am the daughter of a king, yet nobody spares me a thought. I am forgotten here in this god-forsaken corner of David's palace. Who mourns for me or my husband, driven apart all these long years? Only Hannah remembers with me." She reached for Hannah, who had bent down to tuck a cushion behind her mistress's back.

As the women gripped hands, Tabytha considered them united in their loyalty to Paltiel and their disdain for King David. As much as she wanted to hear Michal's story, she realized she liked the king, *really* liked him, and didn't want that poisoned by these two women.

"No." She began to push herself up. "Find yourself another scribe."

"No?" Hannah's voice quivered with suppressed anger. "You dare deny Queen Michal this simple request?"

Tabytha noticed Hannah's use of the high title. Obviously, she didn't share Gilia and Suta's view on the women's rankings in the king's court.

Michal lay a restraining hand on her lady's arm and studied Tabytha. "Stay a while longer, Tabytha. I fear I have gone about this the wrong way," she said softly. "I was so amazed to hear we had a woman among us able to write that I could hardly restrain my excitement. Your gift should be put to good use, wouldn't you agree?"

Tabytha shrugged, sinking back into the cushion. She had never thought of her ability to read and write as a gift she had to share with others.

"I believe you and I are not that different," Michal said. "We've never had a voice. Our wishes have never counted. Our fathers and brothers, the men who should have protected us, have been the very ones to trade us away as if we were nothing more than well-bred mares, all so they could gain more power. We have been acquired and discarded at the whim of kings. Our lives have turned on the hinge of history, on who fell and who lived on the battlefield."

Michal's impassioned speech stirred uncomfortably in Tabytha. She thought of her grandfather giving her to the Hebrew king when she was but a child, and of her father's battlefield death that brought about her betrothal.

"I was young once too. I trusted too easily, held nothing back in love, and dreamt of what my life would become."

Michal shook her head. "But none of it proved true. Whenever I found a breath of happiness, it was snatched away by *men* who claimed to care for me."

Michal and Tabytha looked at each other in the long silence that followed. Something in the woman's gaze and words touched on Tabytha's deepest fears and longings. Had Michal felt these same feelings before her?

"Can you understand why I say you have a gift, Tabytha? If you give me a voice, you grant me power. On a scroll, my words will carry the weight they never have in this world of men. I will live beyond my time. I will exist beyond these walls and all that imprisons me. So, I ask you again, will you write my story?"

"But you hate him," Tabytha said. "You hate the man I am trying to learn to love."

Michal looked down, and Tabytha's gaze followed to her small finger and the slim ring she twirled around, almost unawares.

"Perhaps," she said. "But one day, you will understand. Often, love and hate are opposite sides of the same coin. I could never have hated David if I didn't love him first."

chapter 10

michal
extract from scroll ב (hs beit)

I am Michal, youngest daughter of King Saul.

I first saw David in Gibeah at my father's palace.

At that time, when my father had one of his rages, I often hid out with Rizpah, my father's concubine. Hers was the room furthest from the main hall and my father's sleeping quarters. My mother's room was next to his, so if I went there, I could hear all too clearly the ranting death threats and shattering of whatever object he had hurled at an offender.

And besides, my mother would never take me—a fourteen-year-old—in her arms the way Rizpah did, rocking me from side to side, whispering this would pass as it had always passed before.

"What makes him so angry, Rizpah?" From a young age, I had known that she understood—and loved—him better than my mother did. "Is it an evil spirit, like the servants say?"

"I don't know, Mici." Her face creased with concern. "He sometimes tells me he cannot feel Adonai inside him the way he used to. The emptiness terrifies him."

"But I can't feel Adonai either. Can you?"

She shook her head. "Your father is not an ordinary man, my love." The pride in her voice lit my own. "Adonai chose him to be king and gave him his spirit to rule."

"Then why did Adonai leave him? It's all because of that Samuel, isn't it?" How I hated that old prophet for ruining my father's life. If Samuel hadn't been so late coming to the battle, my father would not have offered the sacrifices that made Adonai so angry. Samuel and Adonai were to blame for making my father the way he was. He hadn't always been this way. I could still vaguely remember when his eyes lit up as he looked at me, when he called me his pretty princess and let me clamber onto his lap to twirl his beard around my fingers.

"You see." Rizpah sat up straight. "It's already passed."

I listened intently, expecting another crash at any moment. Instead, I heard snatches of music.

"Can you hear that, Rizpah? It sounds like a lyre."

She looked puzzled. "I can't hear anything. And there aren't any lyre players at your father's court."

"I'm sure of it." I rose and tugged at her arm. "Come. Let's go see."

"We're women. We can't march into the king's hall."

"I know a place near the back, behind a pillar. Merab and I often stood there when we were younger."

"You go." She smiled. "A concubine could get punished for spying on her lord, the king."

"Could I get punished?" *What if my father turned his terrible anger on me?*

"Step lightly, my dove. That way, he won't hear you." She kissed my forehead and gave me a little pat on the back. "And report back on everything you see. You're my spying ears and eyes now."

I found the darkened steps, feeling my way carefully down them over the rough stones. An oil lamp flickered at the bottom, casting strange shadows on the roof and walls. I could now hear the music coming from the hall to my right. Pure, soft, and soothing, the notes sounded more beautiful than anything I had ever heard—strings vibrating with life and emotion. It drew me forward despite the flutter of fear.

I crept into the back of the hall, towards the pillars. Disappointment stabbed through me as I saw Merab. My sister's arm hugged a pillar, her face peering intently around it towards the throne where I knew my father sat. She hadn't seen me yet, and for a moment, I considered going back to Rizpah before her sharp tongue—so like my mother's—could lash out at me.

But the music pulsed all around me. It stole right into me and echoed into my heart. It made me think of rushing water or a night sky. Of wonder. I had to see the one who could create such enchantment.

Merab heard me and turned. Her usually sullen face was lit with the same wonder I felt.

Wordlessly, she beckoned me forward, and I pressed against her to peer around the pillar. My father sat on his throne, elbow leaning on the armrest, his head resting on his fist. His eyes were closed. I thought him asleep for a moment, but then I saw his other hand tapping to the music's rhythm. My brothers stood near him, Jonathan to his right, Abinadab to his left, and a host of men around them. I followed their rapt gazes to the lyre player, the only man—besides my father—seated in the hall.

He was younger than I had expected; perhaps his age lay somewhere between mine and Merab's. Thick curls framed a contoured face, browned by the sun. His eyes drew me.

Darkly beautiful and long lashed, they gazed upwards as his fingers danced across the strings, and I saw in them a love and desire unlike any I had ever encountered before. At that moment, I wanted nothing more than for those eyes to be turned on me.

"Who is he?" I whispered.

"A Judite."

"Where's he from?"

"Bethlehem. They say he's a shepherd." My sister's words were tinged with a hint of contempt. However, the news of his humble position did nothing to diminish my impression of the lyre player. As I continued to gaze at him, I knew he was no ordinary shepherd. Everything about him spoke of a quiet confidence, of strength. He looked more like a prince than a shepherd.

The song ended, and a strange hush fell over the hall as if nobody wanted to breathe or move for fear of breaking the spell. My father stirred, opened his eyes, and looked at the lyre player for a long time.

"Come here, boy. You have a remarkable gift. One rather wasted on sheep, don't you think?"

The men laughed uneasily—the uncertain laughter that filled the hall of a king whose reactions could never be gauged. The lyre player rose to his feet, lay his instrument down, and walked to my father's throne, where he dropped to his knee.

"For a while, my dark thoughts fled from me." My father signaled for the musician to rise. "How do you explain that, young shepherd?"

"It is often so with music, my lord." His voice was not as deep as my father's, but it was warmer—a voice inviting trust. "But I believe only Adonai can truly soothe a troubled heart."

I heard my sister's sharp intake of breath, and the men around the throne stirred nervously. Talking to my father about Adonai often ended badly.

"Adonai? That's a lofty thought for a lowly herder." My father gave a snort of laughter, echoed by a few of his men. "But let us keep such talk for the prophets and priests. Play me another song."

"My lord." The lyre player bowed again and returned to his instrument.

I sank to the ground behind the pillar, watching him as he plucked the first notes of the new song.

"What are you doing?" Merab hissed. "You can't stay here."

"Says who?"

"We're not children anymore. We got our glance of the shepherd. Now it's time to leave."

"You go then. I'm staying."

"Fool!" She turned to leave. "Don't come crying to me when Father finds you here."

I stayed there, pressed against the pillar, and watched the lyre player. Everything else around me faded. I did not glance again at my father or his men. I no longer feared the king's fury. I didn't feel the cold of the stone floor creeping through my robe. I saw the shepherd briefly close his eyes at the end of each song as if in prayer. The strength in those tanned arms. The smile that played on the corners of his mouth as the music coursed through his body. His long, graceful fingers as they worked the strings.

I didn't notice someone standing behind me until I heard his low voice.

"Spying on the king, princess?"

I jumped but stifled my squeal when I saw Jonathan looking down at me with a wicked grin.

"Jonathan!"

My eldest brother was almost as tall as my father. His face held laughter. If I had often wished Rizpah was my mother, I had just as often wished Jonathan to be my father. He was an adult when I was born, so I ran to Jonathan as a child in need of comfort. He would pick me up and spin me around and around. His smile held the paternal love and pride I wished to see on my father's face.

"He's a remarkable musician, isn't he?" Jonathan's gaze followed my own. "His music lifts you above the darkness and dreariness of our world."

"He's remarkable."

My brother studied my face carefully, and I felt my cheeks redden.

"Guard your heart, dear Michal. You know well enough it's not yours to give away."

I rose, angry he could read me so well. "If I did, it wouldn't be to a shepherd."

"The daughter of a king through and through." Jonathan gazed back at the lyre player.

"What is his name, this lyre-player?" I asked.

Jonathan looked at me again, and in the long pause that followed, I knew he had seen right through my haughty tone.

"His name is David. Son of Jesse."

Over the next few days, I heard the sound of the lyre coming from the hall at different times of the day, sometimes when my father awoke, sometimes late at night. Whenever a rage threatened, David would play, and the storm within my father would abate. A little of the king's old joviality returned, and the atmosphere in the palace lightened.

Men walked easier. Women were not afraid to laugh. Even Mother and Merab grew a little more patient with me.

But I hardly noticed the changes. David consumed my thoughts. I had managed to watch him a few more times from behind the pillar, yet, over time, I wanted more than just to see him. I wanted him to see me. A king's wives and daughters were not like other women. We did not roam around freely. Mostly, we lived out of sight, behind palace walls. But I saw one chance, and that was Jonathan, for my father permitted me to visit my brother's house next to the palace. From the whispers of servants, I gauged David spent much time there. Rumor had it my brother, one of the greatest warriors in all of Israel, taught David how to wield a sword.

Exactly a week from the day I first saw David, I dressed in my prettiest gown—one passed down from Merab— slipped a matching veil over my hair and marched to the palace gates. I had learned that if you held your head up high and walked with enough confidence, people seldom questioned your right to do something.

Only the guard at the gate asked me where I went and why I didn't have a companion, but when I told him I was visiting Jonathan, he opened the gate.

My heart pounded with anticipation as I reached my brother's door. He lived alone except for the few servants who attended him. Jonathan had resisted all my father's attempts to choose a wife for him. I'd asked him about this once, and his brow had furrowed.

"I know I am the heir to the throne, and I will need to produce an heir of my own, but the thought of leaving a woman I love to go into battle terrifies me."

Jonathan? Terrified? He was the bravest man I knew. "Nothing terrifies you," I'd objected.

"Breaking someone's heart does."

Today, I was grateful I would not have to make my way past a wife and children, for women's small talk and gossip would hinder my goal. I only wanted to be near David and have his dark eyes take me in.

I pushed the door open and stood a moment in the dim interior. I could hear Jonathan's voice coming from the courtyard. "Watch you don't overstep and expose your side."

"You can take the shepherd from the field, but can you take the field from the shepherd?" Ish-Bosheth's sardonic voice drawled.

Drat. I had hoped to be alone with Jonathan and David. Now, I had another brother to contend with. Still, I walked the length of the room and came to stand in the doorway to the courtyard, watching David and Jonathan circling each other, dulled practice swords in hand. David caught sight of me, and Jonathan took the moment of distraction to thrust the blunt tip of the blade at David's chest.

"You are dead, my friend." He laughed before turning to the door to see what had given him the advantage. His smile wavered momentarily as he saw me.

"Ah, we have a visitor. Little wonder you lost your focus." He came to me and threw an arm around my shoulder, drawing me out into the courtyard. "This is my youngest and, it appears, boldest sister, Michal."

David stepped forward, dipping his head in respect. "Your brother speaks highly of you, Princess." Then he looked up at me. Not fleetingly as some men did. Not lustfully or appraisingly or indifferently. He looked at me intensely, searching for something in my face and eyes. Knowingly, as if a part of him already suspected one day I would be his.

And I wondered if something stirred to life within him at that moment the way it did in me.

chapter 11

"Where have you been?" Gilia asked sharply as Tabytha slipped into the room. "No one ever knows where to find you." Her eyes narrowed. "I hear Michal has taken you into her confidence. Beware of that one, dear Tabytha. She's the serpent in the palace garden."

"I was playing with some of the young ones."

Michal had made clear that Tabytha could not tell the others of the parchment and ink Hannah had bought from the old scribe near the Traders Gate. She didn't want anyone to know of the project secretly occupying them these last weeks. Still, Tabytha suspected in time, Gilia would discover what they were doing.

"It wouldn't surprise me if the king knows you are consorting with his banished wife. That would explain why he hasn't sent for you. Then again ..." Gilia's lip curled the way it always did before she said something particularly cruel. "Maybe he mistakes you for a boy."

Tabytha touched her hair self-consciously but didn't reply. The king had never seen her short hair. She always wore a headscarf when he came to the Women's Quarters for a meal. Yet Gilia's remark knotted unrest in her belly, for it was true the king had not chosen to spend time alone with her. Usually one of his wives, often Bathsheba, accompanied him back to his own quarters. Sometimes, Tabytha felt relieved her husband hadn't called on her, but lately, she worried he didn't find her attractive enough.

"That's not true," Suta said. "He gave us all time to settle in before he sent for us. Besides, how long has it been since *you* spent time with the king, Gilia?"

Gilia shrugged as if she didn't know and didn't care.

"At least five months by my calculations."

"My, my. Haven't you grown smug since his royal seed began to grow in you?" Gilia glanced disdainfully at Suta's belly, now showing her to be with child.

When she first arrived, Tabytha had believed Gilia and Suta to be friends, but something had shifted between them in the last weeks. Suta seemed more sensitive and Gilia more scornful than before.

"Is it true the king and his army leave next week to go to war?" Tabytha asked, changing the subject in her role of peacemaker.

"The army always goes to war in the spring," Suta said wistfully. "But I wish, like in past years, the king wouldn't go with them."

"You fear for his life?"

"No. He is a mighty warrior and won't be easily defeated. Besides, his men will guard him with their lives. But with the babe coming ..." Suta lay her hand on the bulge of her stomach. "I'd rather he stayed here."

"Better he goes than pacing around the palace, restless as a young lion. That's never ended well," Gilia said.

"True." Suta shook her head as if to shake off her pensive mood. "We've still got the Sabbath meal with him tonight."

"At least the day Sabbath starts is not as boring as every other day in this palace," Gilia said.

Tabytha didn't find the days boring. Life at the palace had begun to take on a comfortable rhythm for her. The Women's Quarters offered a certain amount of freedom. Tabytha spent her mornings with the younger concubines, grinding wheat and barley while tending to the youngest children and discussing the palace happenings. Initially, that the king's own women would do these menial tasks surprised Tabytha, yet she didn't mind. She found comfort in the familiar routines and the chatter of women's home life. Once the flour had been combined with olive oil and flattened into breads, they entrusted them to a few of the servants to bake. Then, they usually made their way to the Women's Courtyard and turned to their needlework.

The weekly Shabbat market provided the women with a steady supply of beautiful fabrics. Each was at a different stage of making or embroidering a garment for herself or a child. Often, Abigail, Ahinoam, and Pudu would join them in their needlework. Haggith sometimes came too, although Tabytha seldom saw her sewing. Instead, the wispy woman would sit quietly and lift her face to the sun. Then, suddenly, she would rise and make her way to the courtyard's center, lift her arms to the sky, and twirl around to music only she could hear.

The children loved this moment. The girls would grab each other's hands and spin around. The boys would clap or drum out a beat with their wooden swords. A quiet joy would well up in Tabytha, especially if Tamar grabbed her hands and pulled her down from the steps to dance.

In the afternoons, most of the women rested or—if the king was joining them—prepared themselves and their children for the evening meal. Usually, Tabytha went to Michal's quarters to record her story.

"The Sabbath is my favorite day, too." Suta's words broke through Tabytha's thoughts. "We're going to the Shabbat market. Come with us this time, Tab."

The palace women loved the market. It was the one time they were free to mingle with outsiders. Select traders arrived in the palace courtyard with food, fabrics, and other items to tempt the nobility. The king's wives and concubines would wear their headscarves and leave their quarters to mingle with the royal servants and the king's guard. Often, the king's older children—those who no longer lived in the Women's Quarters—would be there too, talking to their mothers, sisters, and younger brothers.

Tabytha had never ventured out to the market. Instead, she savored the peace and quiet of the empty quarters or visited Michal without the need for furtiveness.

But today, Suta insisted. "It's time you found fabric. You can't keep wearing your common, undyed robes that make you look like a servant. Besides, I'm tired of you wearing my gowns in the evening. I'll help you choose something. Last week, Elik said he would probably have new fabric."

"Fine." It was probably time for her to make robes of her own instead of only helping with children's clothing. "I'll come."

Suta jumped up, beaming. "Quick, Gilia. Before our reticent Tabytha changes her mind." She grabbed a headscarf off the chest and pushed it into Tabytha's hands. "You'll love the market. Come. We must get there before Maacah chooses all the best fabric. As if her daughter Tamar needs any more robes."

Her friend's enthusiasm was contagious, and by the time Tabytha stepped into the busy palace courtyard, she felt a little like she had as a child when her mother took her and Atamu to the market and bought each of them two dates from the trader with the deeply lined face. She couldn't remember the man's name, only that her brother mockingly called him 'the Prune.'

Now Suta wove her way through the crowd, pulling Tabytha beside her. The traders—wares lined up on the ground or on low tables—called to Suta.

"My lady, let me show you the latest beads ..."

"... the best blanket to swaddle your child."

"... you will be irresistible to your lord the king if you wear this."

Tabytha almost stopped to sniff the perfumed oil this last man held out to them, but Suta shook her head.

"We can come back for it. First, the fabric. Elik is always the busiest." As she led Tabytha down the courtyard steps, she groaned. "They got here before us."

A huddle of women stood around a fabric-laden cart. Maacah draped a fine green cloth over Tamar's shoulders, exclaiming at her daughter's loveliness.

"It's a particularly flattering shade for her, my lady," a tall man with sun-darkened skin said.

"We will need something for her collar and hem, Elik," Maacah said.

Tamar spotted them as they reached the bottom step, and her face lit up. "Elik, this is Tabytha, the latest woman of our household. We must find something wonderful for her to wear."

The tall man looked at her, taking in her plain robes. "It will be an honor to serve you, my lady." His words lacked conviction,

"Not until you are finished with us." Maacah glared at the newcomers.

"But, Ima, I have plenty of gowns." Tamar pulled the fabric off her shoulders and walked towards Tabytha, draping the cloth around her neck. "This would be perfect for you, Tab."

"We had it first." Maacah stalked over and grabbed the fabric away.

"This is what I miss the most about the Women's Quarters," a voice drawled from the steps behind them.

Even without turning, Tabytha recognized that arrogant tone—the king's eldest son. Every part of her wished she could run back up the stairs and hide away in the safety of the palace so she wouldn't have to face him again.

"Nothing quite as interesting as women bickering, wouldn't you say, Jonadab?"

Finally, Tabytha cast a quick backward glance at Prince Amnon and his companion. The prince didn't look at her—he appeared to be studying Tamar. The man with him, Jonadab, was taller and older than Amnon. His unusually light brown eyes held a glint of astuteness as he watched the prince.

"I wouldn't know my prince. I am only the nephew of the king and not his son, so I did not enjoy the privilege of growing up in the royal palace." Jonadab took the last step and strode over to Maacah and Tamar. He bowed. "My lady. Princess."

"Cousin." Tamar inclined her head, her manner guarded.

"Where are my royal manners?" Prince Amnon strode over to Maacah and her daughter, giving a slight bow. "Lady Maacah." He turned towards Tamar. "You're looking as lovely as always, my sister. And I absolutely agree with your mother this fabric will be wasted on anyone else. Especially *her*."

At the dismissive flick of his head—he didn't even look at Tabytha—she felt the same rage she had at their first encounter. "I'm going back," she whispered to Suta.

Suta grabbed her arm. "But you haven't even seen the fabric."

"Next time." She pulled free of her friend's grasp, hitched her robes, and ran up the steps. As her vision swam with tears, she didn't see the man standing at the top of the steps and careened right into him. His arm steadied her.

"Careful, my gazelle."

She looked up into the king's face and felt a moment of panic. Tears had swollen her eyes, and, in her mad dash up the stairs, her headscarf had fallen askew, exposing her hair. Why, oh why, would he be here now to see her like this?

"My king!" She grabbed the scarf and pulled it over her hair as she dropped into a bow. "I didn't know you came to the Shabbat market."

"Not often." He drew her up and looked at her closely. At his nearness and the intensity of that look, Tabytha felt a keen ache in the pit of her stomach. She stood like a frozen doe as he lifted his hand and wiped away a tear. "Something has upset you, Tabytha."

"Nothing, my lord."

He looked in the direction from which she had come. "Ah," he said with the smallest of smiles. "I believe the cloth trader is the cause of most of our family disputes. Come, let's go choose a fabric for you. You will need something special to wear soon." Again, his gaze lingered on her face, and she felt the ache even more keenly.

He tucked her arm through his own, and they descended the steps together. This time, Maacah and the other women made way for them. Deference replaced Amnon's rudeness and instead of a disapproving glance, Elik bowed low and exclaimed what an honor it was to serve the king himself.

"Your very finest fabric for my wife, please," the king said. Tabytha felt the warmth and belonging the word wife spread through her.

"The finest, your Majesty?"

At the king's curt nod, the man lifted the pile of fabrics and pulled out a cloth bag from the very bottom of his cart. He unfolded the bag and deftly drew out the fabric to a collective sigh from the women who stood there.

Tabytha had never seen such a fine weave, or cloth the color of a late summer sky. Rich and regal, this fabric was far too good for her.

Elik seemed to agree with her assessment. "This is fabric for royalty, my lord, for a king's robe. The azure dye is made from mollusk shells in the same time-consuming process as the royal purple dye. Very rare and precious."

Tabytha caught a whiff of the sea on the fabric.

"In that case, I think it will do," the king said. He turned to her. "Do you like the cloth, my love?"

My love. Her heart pounded at those words.

"Of course, my lord, but this is fabric for a royal robe."

"Exactly." The king looked around, and his gaze snagged on Amnon and Maacah, standing together. "You are a member of the royal household now, Tabytha, which all would do well to remember." He turned his attention back to Elik. "Ensure that the fabric is brought to the royal seamstress immediately."

"Yes, my king." The trader bowed low again.

"Tamar?"

"Yes, Abba?" Tamar stepped forward, laughter in her eyes.

"Take Tabytha to the seamstress this afternoon. Tell her I say the robe is to be complete two days before I leave for war."

He turned back to Tabytha and drew his face close to hers so only she could hear his next words. "And it would please me greatly if you wear it for me that night, Tabytha."

chapter 12

michal

extract from scroll ב (hs beit)

Something about David drew us all. My father made him his armor-bearer. Jonathan became not only his sword master but his closest friend. I was infatuated—thinking and dreaming about him and sneaking visits to Jonathan's house whenever I knew he visited my brother. Jealousy flared up in me whenever I saw Merab smile at him or a serving girl giggle as he passed by.

Sometimes, I sensed David might be drawn to me too. I would catch him looking at me, and when we met at Jonathan's, he would smile and hold my gaze attentively when I spoke. But he always remembered his place. I was the king's daughter, and he was a mere shepherd in my father's service. I could never be his.

The spring in which the Philistines gathered at Sokoh everything changed. My father, brothers, and warriors in the king's service left for war. David left too. Too young and inexperienced to fight, he returned to the hills of Bethlehem and to his father's fields. I wept into my pillow every night.

The palace lay still and abandoned. No men's voices or lyre music wafted from the hall, and Jonathan's quick laughter was not there to break the heaviness that settled on those left behind. Word came the Philistines were mighty, and their champion stood three heads taller than any of our men, with a spear shaft as thick as a weaver's rod. Every morning, they said, this champion taunted and challenged our men until fear crept into their hearts at the sight of him.

Four weeks passed. We heard Father had promised Merab's hand in marriage to the warrior who defeated the giant. My sister and I spent days contemplating which of my father's warriors it might be. I said Calah. She said Ebal. Another two weeks passed before we heard rumors the Philistines had scattered. Their champion lay dead, and my father's army pursued them. Philistines bodies piled high, food for ravens on the road to Gath and Ekron.

Merab and I had one burning question—who had defeated the champion? Which worthy warrior would become Merab's husband and son-in-law to the king? No one knew his name, although stories about him abounded. They said he was young and hadn't worn any armor. Apparently, he wasn't even a real soldier, for he had gone to battle without a sword, wearing nothing more than his tunic. Some said the giant had tripped on a rock, others that the sight of the unarmed youngster enraged him so much he had a fit and fell to the ground. Whatever had happened, the unknown Israelite had somehow wrestled the giant's sword from his hand and killed him with it.

Finally, we heard the news that the army returned. Every place they passed, women celebrated the king with song and dance. Rizpah had longed for my father's return, worrying constantly about his safety, so she begged me to go with her to meet the victorious army. "With all the men gone, who will stop us from leaving the palace, Mici?" She gave me a scarf to pull over my hair and face so no one would recognize me.

And what joy we felt as we saw the dust of the approaching army. When they were still a long way off, we began to sway to the timbrels, and the voices around us rose to chant about my father's victory. "Saul has slain his thousands." If only it had stopped there, but their voices proclaimed another's victory even louder. "And David his tens of thousands."

I remember the look that passed between Rizpah and me as we stood in that jubilant crowd, the refrain filling the air around us. "Saul has slain his thousands and David his tens of thousands. Saul has slain his thousands and David his tens of thousands."

Only now do I know Rizpah's shock was different than mine. Looking back, I realize she understood what those words would do to the man she loved. That victory chant would be the seed that fell into my father's jealous heart on that scorching summer afternoon, to grow into a tree whose deep roots would split the foundations of his family and kingdom. Rizpah saw it even then, but I did not. Only one thought burned through me. The man who had slain the champion, the man to marry my sister, was the man I loved. David. On hearing the news, Merab couldn't hide her elation. She would wed not a greying warrior but the young, handsome man all of Israel now hailed as the greatest savior since Samson. And knowing I loved him only added to her pleasure.

I returned from the victory procession, threw myself on my sleeping pallet, and wept, refusing to eat or even to be comforted by Rizpah. Only when Jonathan sought me out the next day did I finally sit up.

My brother sat next to me and drew me close. "This is about David, isn't it? That Father promised him Merab?"

"Will you speak to Father? Tell him I am the one who loves David. If he promised him a daughter, it doesn't have to be Merab, does it?"

"You know how it goes, Mici," my brother said. "The eldest daughter marries first. Like Leah marrying before Rachel."

"And look how that turned out. Doesn't Father want me to be happy?" Even as I said these words, I knew their futility. The king only did what was best for *him*.

"It may not happen, you know. David claims he is not worthy to be the king's son-in-law."

"Really?" The thought my haughty sister wouldn't get him lifted my mood considerably.

"Which means he would refuse your hand too," Jonathan said with a glint of amusement in his eye.

"Maybe not." I pushed myself to my feet. "Do you know where David is?" I had only seen him briefly the day before as he marched into the palace grounds, wearing what looked like Jonathan's robe and sword.

"With Father. Playing the lyre." Jonathan laid a restraining hand on my arm as I grabbed my best cloak. "Stay, Mici. The king broods today."

I paused at that. My father's moods had lightened since David came to his court, but how well I remembered those dark days. When those unpredictable rages came on Father, he became someone else, someone frightening.

"But David's playing soothes him, doesn't it?"

"It used to, but now ... well, I'm not so sure." Jonathan frowned as if thinking about our father and David together worried him. "I'd better go."

I waited until I knew my brother would be down the stairs, and then I slipped out of my room to the king's hall and the pillar from which I had first seen David. As on that first day, my father sat on his throne. His eyes were closed, and his lips moved. Jonathan had reached his side and bent over to him, listening attentively. My gaze found David. His fingers danced across the strings. His eyes were closed, too, and his voice harmonized with the music. He had told me before that when he sang, he did so for Adonai, not for Father. I studied him. He had changed these last months. A little taller and broader in the chest, a new strength and confidence now radiated from him.

A movement caught my eye. My father had risen from the throne, snatching a spear from the hand of the guard to his right. Momentarily, Jonathan and the others around the throne looked on with confusion. My father glared at David with such intense hatred I suddenly understood what he intended.

"David!" I screamed.

David startled, jerking backward at the same instant my father threw the spear. Its deadly tip grazed David's cheek before thudding into the wall behind him. David dropped his lyre, his fingers reaching for his cheek. He looked dazedly at the blood on his hand before turning to the king. Father shook with rage, and for a moment, I thought he would reach for the spear again and thrust it into David, but Jonathan had reached them.

"Go!" he shouted at David as he threw restraining arms around the king.

"Let go of me, you son of a whore!" my father bellowed. But my brother held him until David leaped up and ran from the hall.

I ran, too, unable to catch my breath, a strange weakness in my limbs. Somehow, I made it to Rizpah, collapsing at her feet.

"My dove, what is it? You are as pale as sun-dried bones."

"Fa-Fa ... Father threw a spear at D-David."

That was the first time my father tried to kill David. Other times would follow, although he hatched more subtle plots to rid himself of the man he now considered the greatest threat to his kingship. Several times, he gave David command over a thousand men and sent him into the fiercest battles with the Philistines. Always David returned victorious.

Then, my father found the perfect weapon. Learning of my love for David, he decided to use *me* as a snare. Although David had resisted marrying my sister and initially resisted marrying me, my father insisted he would have him for his son-in-law. At a small price. A rather deadly price.

I—Michal—could be bought for a hundred Philistine foreskins.

chapter 14

"David chose well, Tabytha," Abigail said. "You look wonderful in that gown."

In two days' time, the king's army left for battle. The women and children gathered in the Women's Courtyard, awaiting his arrival to the farewell gathering. Tabytha wore the robe the king had chosen for her and sensed the women's envious glances. The seamstress had offset the deep blue fabric with silver trimming on the neckline and sleeves. Unlike the gowns Tabytha typically wore, this one had been cut to fit her perfectly, accentuating her curves while still flowing softly around her.

"It's lovely, isn't it?" Tabytha nervously adjusted the matching headscarf, edges embroidered with delicate silver patterns.

At the king's command, she and Suta sat at the main table tonight with Abigail, Ahinoam, and Bathsheba. The two older women had been warm and welcoming, but Bathsheba said little. She hardly looked at the two concubines, instead she watched the children play on the steps and glanced occasionally towards the king's door.

Tabytha felt the usual flutter of anticipation as that door opened, and the king stepped through. The children flocked around him, and as always, he took his time greeting them. Tabytha usually enjoyed watching him with his children, but today, impatience gnawed at her. When the king finally approached them, Tabytha felt his gaze on her. Self-conscious, she pulled the headscarf around her and looked down. The others rose to greet the king, and Tabytha hastily followed them.

"My lord, my love." Bathsheba reached him first. "I can't believe this is our last night together."

"Let us hope we quell this Edomite rebellion swiftly." A note of formality marked the king's voice. "Abigail. Ahinoam." He greeted his older wives before turning to Suta with a smile. "How are you and the child, Suta?"

"I am well, my lord, as is the child. This last week, I felt him moving."

"Him?" The king laughed. "You believe I need another son?"

"Of course." Suta smiled. "A king can never have too many sons."

Finally, he turned towards Tabytha, extending his arms and shaking his head slightly. "I am speechless. The cloth I bought was beautiful, but I could not have imagined anyone looking as lovely as you do tonight, my gazelle."

"My lord." Tabytha bowed, heart pounding. "It is the most beautiful of gifts."

For Tabytha, every moment of that evening filled her with joy. The breeze carried whiffs of the spring flowers she had picked on the hills as a child. Bright stars and a sliver of moon jeweled the dark sky. The bread tasted better, the fruits sweeter, and the meat more tender. All because she sat opposite the king. He spoke about the surrounding nations and their leaders and the upcoming battles they would face. Abigail asked him probing questions, and he answered each as if he were talking to a trusted advisor rather than a wife. He enquired after their days and seemed interested in the small things that occupied them.

Throughout the evening, women and children came to wish him well in the coming campaign, and, close up, Tabytha saw his tenderness as never before. He spoke soothing words to his wives and concubines and had a personal word of blessing for each of the children. He had also brought out his lyre and sang a new song to them. One line echoed into her heart. *Whoever dwells in the shelter of the Most High will rest in the shadow of the Almighty. I will say of the Lord, "He is my refuge and my fortress, my God, in whom I trust."* Tabytha again felt the longing for Adonai the king's previous songs had stirred up in her.

Towards the end of the evening, as Ahinoam, Abigail, and David reminisced about their early days together running from Saul, the king turned his gaze on Tabytha.

"How does Michal fare, Tabytha?"

She stiffened at the unexpected question.

"Few in the palace see her, yet I am told she has befriended you."

"Yes, my lord. I attend to her occasionally."

"How is it that she rejects the rest of her family but embraces you?" His tone was curious rather than accusatory.

"I don't know my lord." She flushed at the lie.

Suta sensed her discomfort. "How are Amnon and Absalom doing in their role as advisors, my king?" she asked.

"They have much to learn." His thoughtful gaze remained on Tabytha.

"I am sure Solomon could advise you."

They all laughed at Bathsheba's comment, and to Tabytha's relief, the conversation moved to a long one about the king's children.

At length, the king said, "My army prepares tomorrow. It will be a long day if we are to march out the day following it, so I will retire now."

Bathsheba stirred, and briefly, the king's gaze found his favored wife, but then he turned to Tabytha.

"Do you care to join me, Tabytha?"

"Yes, my lord." She lowered her gaze shyly, feeling self-conscious as he rose and extended his arm to her. All the women of the court watched her. Excitement and fear mingled as the king led her to the door through which he had come earlier. It opened when he rapped on it.

Two armed guards stood on either side of a passage lit by flaming torches. They bowed, averting their gaze from her. One of them closed the door, shutting out the familiar sounds of children shouting and women laughing. The sudden quiet felt strange, unsettling.

"My lord," one of the guards said. "Joab requests an audience with you."

The king sighed. "What now? I made it clear I did not want to be disturbed."

"A messenger from the Beersheba garrison arrived earlier with news of the Edomites. Joab wishes to give you an immediate account, my lord."

"Fine. Send word I will see him outside my chambers shortly." As the guard hurried off, David called after him, "Benaiah, tell him to keep it short. We have all of tomorrow to discuss these matters."

They continued down the passage. "My apologies, Tabytha. Joab is head of my army and not easily dissuaded."

Tabytha had heard of the man who—according to the women—ruled second only to the king. He had taken Jebus for David. Perhaps her own father had even died by his blade. Brilliant and dangerous, loyal, and ruthless, all agreed that Joab was not a man to have as an enemy.

Unlike the newer Women's Quarters, built on more level ground, this part of the palace had been the old Jebusite fortress. Built into the highest hill of Jebus, its passages wound around in a confusing maze. Tabytha and the king—trailed by the remaining guard—descended a flight of steps, turned into an adjoining passage, and then ascended a further flight. Off the passages, she glimpsed rooms of varying sizes. Some were empty. Others contained individuals—a scribe poring over a scroll, two men in discussion. They passed a large room where several soldiers ate a meal in near-silence.

She found herself trailing her fingers over the cold stone wall and wondering if her father had ever walked here. Perhaps his fingers had touched this precise spot. Perhaps he had ... *No. she mustn't think of her father. Not now.*

She forced cheer into her voice. "I don't think I'd ever find you again if I needed to, my lord."

The king laughed. "Fortunately, I know where to find *you*. And here we are."

They stood at the end of a passage. Ahead of them lay a chamber closed off by a brown curtain. The king began to pull it aside when they heard someone approach.

"My king."

Despite his short stature, the man striding towards them had an air of supreme command and strength. "Joab. I suspected you were lying in ambush. Surely, Benaiah hadn't found you yet?"

"True. I awaited you." Unlike the guards, Joab did not divert his gaze from Tabytha. He inclined his head towards her. "My lady. It's good to see you again. I remember well the day your grandfather promised you to David."

"Wait here, Joab." The king held the curtain aside and bade Tabytha enter.

She stepped into the chamber and looked around in surprise. She had expected luxury, but the room was simple. Flickering torches lit up a bed raised slightly off the ground, several chests, and a large table strewn with parchment, ink, and reeds. Shelves lining the wall contained more parchment rolls. A lyre hung on a hook above the bed, and a spear—thick as a weaver's rod—stood in one corner.

The only truly remarkable feature of the room was the view. Several open shutters looked out over the city. The king pointed to another curtained-off entrance on the same wall as the windows.

"There are cushions on the terrace if you want to wait for me there. I find the view of the city rather lovely."

He left, dropping the curtain closed behind him.

"Could this not wait till tomorrow, Joab?" The heavy curtain muffled his voice. "I clearly said tonight was for my family."

"I see now why you didn't want to be interrupted." Joab laughed. "She has all the long-legged grace of the gazelle she is named for. But no, this couldn't wait, David."

"Walk with me then."

Their voices grew softer, and Tabytha turned her attention back to the room. She followed the king's suggestion and stepped out onto the terrace. Below her lay Jebus, now the king's city. She could make out some of its walls, lit up by the moving torches of guards on patrol. Countless windows shed the soft glow of oil lamps within. A cool breeze blowing up from the valley carried the sound of distant voices. She tried to find her mother's house, but it lay too far down, in the shadows of a wall.

How remarkable the king could look out from here on his subjects.

After a while, she glanced at the cushions but felt too restless to sit. She went back inside and, without giving it much thought, found herself at the king's table.

She bent over an unrolled parchment to see the words the king had penned on it. Another song. Ahio had said songs were for the ear, not the eye. They needed to be read aloud. So, she began.

"Blessed is the one who does not walk in step with the wicked or stand in the way that sinners take or sit in the company of mockers, but whose delight is in the law of the LORD, and who meditates on his law day and night. That person is like a tree planted by streams of water, which yields its fruit in season and whose leaf does not wither—whatever they do prospers."

"It is true then."

She spun around at the sound of the king's voice. He stood a few paces from her, incredulity on his face.

"I'd heard rumors that you could read, but I didn't believe it true."

"Forgive me, my lord." She dropped her gaze to the ground, not wanting to see the moment his amazement turned to anger.

"For what, Tabytha?"

She shook her head, unsure herself. For reading his private thoughts. Perhaps for merely reading—doing what only men were supposed to do.

"I'm not angry." He stepped towards her and took her cold, clenched hands in his own warm ones. "Look at me, my gazelle."

She obeyed, looking deeply into those dark, expressive eyes. Instead of anger, she saw tenderness and something else—longing. Tabytha tentatively stepped closer to him. He let go of her hands and put his arms around her, drawing her against him. She felt his solid strength and a warm desire pulsed through her.

"My love," he whispered before his lips closed on hers.

chapter 14

michal

extract from scroll Ტ (hs beit)

I didn't think of the bride price or of my father's intent to kill my husband on that first night with David. I was the most blessed of women and nothing could make my happiness more complete. We were finally free to vent the slow-burning passion that had built in us both over the last months. Now I see we made love with the intensity of those who know their love is fated to fail, but then I believed it to be the truest meeting of lovers—body and heart.

David and I were happy.

But Adonai ruined everything. Over and over, he gave David battle victories, and my father's hatred grew with every triumph. Eventually, he told Jonathan and his attendants to kill David on sight and again tried to pin him to the wall with his spear. David always evaded him, and his God always protected him.

Then, my father sent men to our house. So little did he care for me, his youngest daughter, that he told violent men to watch my house and slay my husband in our bed. I saw the men lurking in the shadows. From the day I married

David, I had looked for them, knowing one day they would come at my father's command.

So ended our brief life together. Our last conversation is seared into my memory like a brand on flesh.

"If you don't run now, you'll be dead tomorrow."

"I can't leave you, my love. Surely your father …"

"David, how many times does he have to try to kill you before you believe he means you harm?"

"He is my king and father-in-law. I owe him my allegiance."

"He is your sworn enemy. You owe him nothing."

"Don't I owe *you* my allegiance, Michal?"

"We'll be together again, my love."

I lowered him from the window, and he fled into the night. I placed one of my idols in our bed, even adding goat's hair to its head. The ruse bought David the time he needed to escape.

I, then, had to face my father's fury.

The men brought him *me* instead of David. They thrust me to the floor before his throne and told him of my deception. Never have I looked into eyes so cold, so deadly. *This was my end*. Desperate to save myself, I told him David had threatened to kill me if I didn't help him escape. Perhaps my father believed me. He let me live. Jonathan came to me afterward and held me while I cried.

In the following weeks, word came David had fled to the prophet Samuel at Ramah. My father sent the same men who had burst into my house to bring back David, but they returned ashamed. They had fallen to the ground and prophesied of David's greatness. This happened three times until my father decided to go himself. Although he denied it afterward, men recounted even King Saul was slain with the Spirit, stripped off his garments, and prophesied of a kingdom not his own.

How I hoped to hear from my husband. Surely, he would send word, or better still, send for me? But he didn't. Jonathan said David didn't want to put me in harm's way. The life of a fugitive was no life at all, especially for the daughter of a king. But jealousy burned through me when I heard that David had sought out Jonathan, and the two of them had made a covenant—as if my brother meant more to him than I did.

Time passed, and life in my father's court continued. Whenever he heard rumors of David's whereabouts, he would send men to hunt him. They always failed. He raged when he heard of Jonathan's covenant with David. If his own family turned against him, no one was above suspicion. Fear stalked our palace passages, and innocent blood soaked its ground. My father ordered eighty-five priests to be killed under the tamarisk tree below my window. Their crime? They had given David bread. I see those splayed bodies still in my dreams.

Jonathan reluctantly told me David had taken two wives. Only then did I have an inkling of my father's rage, for it boiled through my blood too. David had replaced me, not with one but with two women. If time eroded my hope, that betrayal eroded my love.

I was almost glad when my father gave me to Paltiel— glad to escape the king's madness and glad to be with a man who wasn't David. Paltiel was everything David would never be. Women didn't look at him. Men didn't praise him. He didn't overshadow but rather doted on me. Paltiel didn't set my heart on fire as David had, but I was no longer that young, passionate woman. Passion is fickle. Paltiel was steady, and my father didn't hate him. With him, I would learn to forget David. I would begin to live again.

chapter 15

The sweltering summer months stretched on. The palace women sought shelter from the heat inside and the restless children with them. Little ones cried, older children bickered, and women's tempers frayed like unfinished fabric. Relief flooded Tabytha when the sun lost its ferocity, and a breath of cool air announced the approach of evening. They made their way to the Women's Courtyard to shake off the day's lethargy. But evenings lacked luster without the king's presence and his joyful songs to sway and dance to. Even the music inside Haggith must have grown quiet, for she no longer twirled around, hands held to the sky.

Tabytha longed for the king with a deep ache. She sometimes thought it might have been better if he hadn't chosen her that last night. Perhaps the longing would be less if she hadn't lain in his arms, hadn't breathed in the scent of him, hadn't felt her softness melt into his strength. But then she wouldn't have had the tiny treasures she turned over and over in her mind like a gem catching light. The way he had laughed in delight when he saw the shortness of her hair. The way he had whispered 'you're beautiful' when her blue robe dropped to the floor. The way he spoke her name as if it was the only name that had ever been on his lips.

No, she wouldn't wish their one night together away.

She had secretly hoped she carried his child and had felt bereft when her bleeding came. Now and then, she found herself looking at Suta's large belly with a pang of jealousy. How wonderful to have the king's child sleeping below one's breast. Yet her envy dissipated when she saw the sheen of perspiration that constantly coated Suta's body and heard her restless thrashing in the night. No one struggled more with that summer's heat than Suta did. No, there would be time enough to bear the king a child once this oppressive summer passed.

Two things lightened the oppressive season—gifts from the king. Abigail had been the bearer of both. A week after the king left, Abigail sought out Tabytha, an enigmatic smile on her face.

"Come," she said. "David wanted me to take you somewhere."

"Where?"

"Come. Bring a headscarf."

Intrigued, Tabytha followed Abigail to the entrance of the Women's Quarters, where Ahinoam waited for them. The two women shared a smile as Abigail knocked on the door. A guard opened it and nodded at them.

"Are the men who are to accompany us ready?"

"They are, my lady."

Two armed men had fallen in behind them as they crossed the palace courtyard that early morning. They descended the palace steps to the gate, which another guard waved them through. For the first time since her arrival at the palace, Tabytha found herself on the streets of her old city. Everything about the city felt familiar, yet also tantalizingly new. The way the sun warmed the limestone walls, the press of people and the hum of voices, the braying of donkeys, and the smell of bread. Tabytha reveled in the sense of being ordinary, just another woman of a living, thriving community.

She wiped away a tear, not wanting Abigail or Ahinoam to see her emotion. "I can't believe how much I've missed this."

"Freedom." Abigail gripped her hand and squeezed it, her gaze full of understanding. "That's what we lose as David's women."

It hadn't taken long for Tabytha to realize where they were going. Joy had welled up in her as she quickened her step. By the time she saw her mother's house, she had broken into a run.

Her mother knelt precisely where Tabytha had left her, preparing food in the courtyard as if mere moments had passed instead of months. She looked up as Tabytha appeared and rose—more unsteadily than before. Tears pooled in her eyes as she took her daughter in her arms. "Tawaassi, Tawaassi. My precious girl."

Joy marked their reunion. Atamu had appeared, scowling at the guards, and Iuni and the girls crowded around her, asking questions without giving her pause to answer. Tabytha couldn't believe how much her nieces had grown. Initially, Iuni and the girls had been shy around the king's wives, but Ahinoam had brought Pudu's fig cakes, and soon, they were eating, talking, and laughing together as if they had been born of the same people. Even Atamu had smiled at something Abigail said as he stuffed yet another fig cake into his mouth. Tabytha hadn't wanted the morning to end.

As they walked back up the hill towards the palace, Abigail again squeezed her hand. "David said he wronged you by keeping you from your family for so long. He says you may visit your mother's house once a month if you take one of his men with you."

At Abigail's words, Tabytha recalled lying in the king's arms and telling him about her family. She had even spoken of her father's death on the day Jebus fell. He had looked away then and said, "You were too young to lose him, my gazelle."

She understood then, that in granting her access to her family, the king attempted to atone for what she had lost.

The king's other gift had been even more surprising, coming near the end of the summer months. Abigail had again appeared one morning and told her to follow. This time, they walked further into the Women's Quarters, past the courtyard, and down a short flight of steps Tabytha had never been down that led to a cedar door. Abigail pushed it open and beckoned Tabytha inside.

Although smaller than the room she shared with Gilia and Suta, light bathed this room with warmth. Tabytha stepped towards the window, which looked down on some roofs and—raising her gaze—to the hills outside the city.

"It's a lovely room." The furnishings were similar to those of her own room but included a small table pushed against one of the walls. On the table lay ink, reeds, and parchment. "Whose room is this, Abigail?"

"Eglah's, David's seventh wife. She died last year giving birth."

"Tamar told me."

"Before he left, David told me this room is to be yours if you want it. He instructed me to get a table, bench, and writing supplies." She shrugged apologetically. "It took longer than I expected."

"He wants *me* to have it? But I am the least of his women. What of the others?"

"You are obviously not the least in his eyes." Abigail watched her intently.

"But what of the others?" Tabytha repeated. "They will resent this."

"They might, but they will accept it as David's will. You will be the only concubine besides Pudu to have your own quarters. They will assume you have found favor with him."

"Have I? Found favor, I mean?"

Abigail looked around the room again, her eyes lingering on the table. "I would say you have. But there's more to it than that. David seldom does anything without a good reason." She reached under the collar of her gown and drew out a chain with a key on it. "He told me to have a lock put on the door, another first in the Women's Quarters." She pulled the chain over her head and dropped it into Tabytha's hand.

"Under the table is a large clay pot," Abigail said. "The scribes store their scrolls in them. David says you can keep Michal's scroll in there, so her story is preserved for posterity."

"He knows about Michal?" Tabytha couldn't hide her dismay. "Nobody but her lady Hannah knew."

"David is no fool. He knows Michal well enough to realize she wanted something from you that nobody else could give her."

"Is he angry with me?"

"No, Tabytha. If he were, would he give you the pot and key to keep the scroll safe?"

"I deceived him."

"It looks to me like he's forgiven you. Go and fetch your belongings. And Tabytha?"

Tabytha turned back to her.

"Don't let Michal's hatred of David affect how you see him. He's a good king and an even better man. Despite what she thinks, claiming her back was his right. She belonged to him long before she did to another man."

"I know."

"David is a complex man with contradicting emotions and motivations," Abigail said. "You can ask each of his wives and concubines, and they will have a different impression of him. He is an enigma, as powerful men often are."

"Even to you? I thought you knew him the best. And loved him the most."

Fleetingly, sadness shadowed Abigail's face. "Years ago, I would have agreed. David has a way, doesn't he, of making you feel special. But something changed. Maybe when Bathsheba arrived. Seeing him with her." She shrugged. "Still, I am glad to be his wife, and I do love him."

A thought pushed into Tabytha's mind then.

"Abigail. What if you tell me your story, too? I can write it down and store it in the pot, and if anyone reads it, they will see another side of the king, not only Michal's."

"Michal wouldn't like it." Abigail laughed. "Perhaps I'll do it for that. I'll think about it, girl. Go now and fetch your things."

chapter 16

ABIGAIL

EXTRACT FROM SCROLL א (hs GIMEL)

I heard of David long before I saw him marching down that ravine, intent on destruction. Word had spread of his defeat of the Philistine champion and his successful campaigns for Saul. Some even said the prophet Samuel had privately anointed him in Bethlehem to be Saul's successor. My father didn't believe it. He had been at Mizpah when Samuel drew lots for Israel's first king, and it pointed to the tall, regal-looking Saul. And when that same King Saul came to Carmel to set up a monument in his own honor, my father, and his friend Nabal—both wealthy men in Carmel—brought wine, figs, raisin cakes, and bread for him and his troops. Adonai had clearly chosen King Saul, my father said. Who was this sling-wielding shepherd in comparison to Israel's mighty king?

My mother was a wise and godly woman, and not as enamored with Saul as my father. When she looked at the king's monument, she saw not greatness but pride. "God does not share his glory with men," she often said, although never to my father. She never spoke out against her husband, even on the day he gave me to Nabal. Not a murmur of protest passed her lips when her young daughter became the wife of a middle-aged man known for his foul temper.

As she had, I learned to survive an unhappy marriage with a difficult man. His selfish demands. His anger. His drunkenness. Over time, I realized that despite my youth, I had a skill for managing the household and servants. Nabal saw and resented this. But above all, he was a lazy man, and my competence allowed him to do even less. We forged a tentative, unspoken understanding. I would manage his household, but on occasion—usually when there were visitors—he would oppose and belittle me to ensure everyone knew him to be the man of the house.

One day, everything changed.

The shearing season arrived, the busiest time of all. For days, I oversaw the preparation of meals for the shearers. I awoke well before dawn and worked with the servants throughout the day. We dried figs, roasted grain, pressed olives, made raisin cakes, and hundreds of loaves of bread. We slaughtered goats and sheep, skinned and cut them, and built fires to roast the meat. By the time Nabal's servant, Heber, sought me out, tiredness consumed me.

"Mistress?"

"What is it, Heber?"

"I'm afraid Master Nabal may have insulted David."

I stared blankly at him, my exhausted mind struggling to recall a servant named David. Nabal always shouted at and insulted his men. Why would Heber bring this particular incident to my attention?

"We know what he's like. Let this David go home and lick his wounds. Tomorrow, all will be forgotten."

Heber shook his head. "You misunderstand. The master didn't insult one of our men but David, the fugitive warrior."

David, the Anointed? A wave of fear drove into me, instantly dispelling my exhaustion. I'd heard David hid in the Desert of Paran with his men. Rebels and discontents, Nabal had called them. He had a good mind to let King Saul know where they were, so he could come to deal with them. But our shepherds told a different story. David's men had been good to them, they said. They had never stolen from them and, in fact, had kept them and their flocks safe from harm.

"What happened, Heber?"

"Ten young men arrived this morning and greeted Master Nabal in David's name, with a blessing for health and long life for him and this household."

This morning? My heart sank. Why only tell me now?

"They said they had protected our men and flocks in the desert and asked for our master's favor since they came at a festive time. They asked to be given whatever could be found for them."

"What did Nabal say?" I asked, even though I could imagine exactly what he had said.

Heber swallowed nervously. "I should have told you this sooner, shouldn't I? But Master Nabal has been in a foul mood since then, keeping us all busy with his demands."

His brow furrowed in thought. "Something like, 'Who is this David? Many servants run from their masters, so why should I take my bread and water and the meat I've prepared for my men and give it to the likes of you?'"

My heart pounded with fear. The words were rude enough. Add to that Nabal's enraged expression, thundering voice, and waving fists, and David's men had seen the very worst of my husband.

"I can't stop worrying what David's reaction might be," Heber said. "He is a man of the sword, after all. Did you hear how he saved the town of Keilah from the Philistines?"

I had heard. David and his men were strong and fearless. More than rebels and discontents, he now had real soldiers—even some Philistine mercenaries—loyal to him. Moreover, they were a large force, six hundred men by our shepherds' estimation.

"Think it over, Mistress Abigail, and see what you can do, because I think disaster is hanging over our master and this household. But you know how it is with him. No one can talk to him."

Yes, I knew Nabal's bull-like stubbornness. And I didn't need to think. If I acted quickly, I could still save us.

"Fetch eight donkeys. Saddle one of them for me to ride. Now!"

"Chava!" I called.

Heber's portly wife appeared almost instantly, flour on her hands and brow.

"What is it, Abi?"

"I need supplies for David and his men. There's no time to waste. Pack all the bread we made today and the roasted grain, figs, and raisin cakes onto the donkeys. Also, the two large wineskins put aside for tonight, along with the five dressed sheep. I must leave within the hour, do you understand? And not a word to Nabal."

She didn't question me but bustled back to the kitchen, where I heard her strident voice issuing instructions. Only then did I look down at my robe and hands, covered with the stains of a hard day's work. I hurried back to my quarters. Young Jacoba, sweeping the floor rushes, looked up in surprise.

"Mistress Abigail, I thought you would still be preparing food for tonight."

"Bring me water to wash my face and hands and the brush for my hair. I'm going to meet the king."

Her eyes widened. "King Saul?"

I shook my head. "There's no time to explain. Hurry, please."

I took off my robe and waited impatiently for her to return. It felt like an eternity before she returned with the water. She brushed my hair, as I washed my hands and face.

"Shall I pin it for you, Mistress?"

"Just a quick plait. I'll cover it with a scarf."

Her nimble fingers worked quickly. When she was finished, I dressed in one of my finer robes.

She stepped back to admire me. "You look beautiful. Is the king coming here?" Excitement lit up her face.

"I'm afraid so. Pray I find favor with him."

Back in the courtyard, Chava and Heber oversaw the donkeys' final loading. A youngster held the lead donkey while two other boys kept the additional animals in line.

Chava shook her head at me, and I could tell Heber had told her everything. "Nabal won't like that we gave away his meat and bread for the night. I've sent Oren to fetch more wineskins. If we keep their cups full, perhaps they won't notice they're eating dried meat."

"You're a wise woman." I allowed myself a small smile.

Heber had come to stand with us. "Can I help you mount, Mistress Abigail?"

I allowed him to steady me as I lifted myself onto the donkey's back. How I had come to care for these two faithful servants and all the others who worked on Nabal's estate. I had to stop David from coming here in anger, not for Nabal's sake but for theirs. *Please help me, Lord*, I prayed as I set off.

chapter 17

Suta's birth pangs started in the early hours of the morning. Tabytha spent the day walking the passages with her friend as she labored in pain. By the evening, the exhausted Suta seemed no closer to giving birth. Abigail finally sent Tabytha away that night. Despite her anxiety for Suta and the baby, she slept soundly in her own room until the light awoke her. She threw on a robe and ran to her old room, already hearing Suta's cries as she rounded the corner. Gilia stood outside the room, eyes closed, and hands pressed to her ears, and Tamar stood with her, weeping silently.

"Gilia, is the child not yet born?"

"No. The midwife is here. She says the babe lies the wrong way."

"Like with Eglah." Tamar wept. "We will lose them both."

Tabytha took Tamar into her arms and stroked the girl's hair. "Perhaps Adonai will spare them," she whispered.

"Well, well. The Jebusite concubine has faith in the Hebrew god," Gilia mocked.

Tabytha bit away her sharp retort. She had only intended to comfort the girl, although she *did* find herself hoping that

Adonai would care for a Jebusite concubine and her child, especially because that child was King David's. These last weeks, recording Abigail's story had churned up memories of Ahio's lessons. Abigail's faith appeared as strong as the tutor priest's, but somehow—untinged by his fear—sweeter to Tabytha.

"If only Abba were here to pray for them," Tamar said.

Gilia scowled. "It didn't do much good with Bathsheba's first child, or with Eglah's for that matter."

"Gilia, you've stood vigil long enough," Tabytha said. Why don't you go break your fast? I will call you if anything changes."

A while later, Pudu stepped from the room, her brow furrowed. "The child's head appears but then disappears again. The midwife says the shoulders are too wide."

"A big baby, then?"

Pudu shrugged. "Or Suta is too small."

"Have you seen this before?" Tabytha asked. Pudu had helped at many of the women's birthings.

The concubine shook her head. "The midwife says she knows what she must do, though. She has Suta on her hands and knees instead of on the birthing stool and told her to push only when the child is in the right place. If that doesn't work, she may need to snap the babe's shoulder."

"No!" Tamar cried.

"Better a live, broken babe than a dead, whole one."

It had taken another five hours for the child to emerge. Although the midwife hadn't snapped any bones, the girl, whom Suta called Bashemath because she had come so close to being the death of them both, was not entirely unbroken.

Her skin had been grey when she finally escaped the cage of the womb. Instead of the lusty cry of a newborn, Bash greeted the world with a weary whimper. In the following weeks, she did not suckle well or grow strong. Her body remained limp as a lifeless doll, and she cried often. There was a wrongness about the king's newest child that caused others to lower their voices and look away quickly, and that caused Suta to withdraw into a world only big enough for her and her newborn. If the first barrier to entering that world was Suta's deep melancholy, the second was Gilia, who took on the role of fierce, and only, protector.

Without the talk and laughter of her closest friend in the palace, the days were long and lonely for Tabytha. She greeted the rains that broke the unbearable heat of that long summer with relief.

The rains also marked the return of the king and his army.

Tabytha stood at the window of her room. She could hear the stir at the Fountain Gate—distant voices cheering and calling—and her heart leaped with anticipation. The voices swelled as the army drew nearer, kindling longing and joy to life in her. Now that King David was here everything would be better. He would draw Suta back to her old self. He would hold little Bash and beg Adonai to heal her. He would come to the Women's Courtyard, and children would run into his arms. He would strum his lyre and sing to lift all their hearts to heaven. He would look at Tabytha with longing and take her into the safety of his arms. Yes, everything would go back to how it had been before.

The next night, when the king came to greet his wives and children, had indeed held the promise of all that had been good before. Tabytha had chosen her gown carefully, not the beautiful blue one the king had chosen for her but a light green one she had made during the summer from fabric Tamar helped her choose. She wore one of Tamar's necklaces and left her hair—which had grown during the summer—loose, with two small side plaits as a crown to frame her face.

Tabytha smiled when she saw Suta coming down the steps of the Women's Courtyard, wearing one of her fine robes, her hair neatly pinned back. Suta had swaddled Bashemath and, trailed by Gilia, carried the whimpering infant to the table where Pudu, Tabytha, and several other concubines sat.

The conversation stilled at her approach.

Suta stared at them defiantly, face pale and eyes shadowed. "I've come to present Bashemath to her father."

"Of course, my dear," Pudu said. "He'll be delighted to see her."

There was a long, uncomfortable silence as they contemplated her words.

"Sit, Suta." Tabytha moved over to make space for her friend. "It's good to see you about again. Do you want me to hold Bash for a while so that you can eat something?"

"I'll hold her." Gilia took the child from Suta, who relinquished her reluctantly.

Suta picked at her food, all the while watching Bashemath. The new mother's face did not reflect the group's keenness and joy when the king finally appeared. She gripped Tabytha's hand and whispered, "I failed him. He'll see the child and know I am cursed."

Tabytha dragged her gaze away from the king and the children running across the courtyard.

"No, Suta. He'll be glad he didn't lose you, like Eglah. And Bash is his daughter. He will not think her a curse."

Still, even Tabytha felt anxious as they eventually crossed to the main table to greet the king. He watched her as they approached the table, and desire fluttered inside her at the warmth she saw in his dark eyes.

"My king, I'm so glad you're home." She dipped her head before looking up at him and smiling.

"As am I. Abigail tells me you are well settled in your new room."

"I am, thank you, my lord. And for the visits to my mother. It's been good to see my family again."

He nodded. "Family is one of the greatest treasures Adonai gives us."

At this, he turned his attention to Suta and the swaddled child. "I hear I have a new daughter." His voice and smile held a note of restraint, hinting that he had been told all was not well with the child. He held out his arms, and hesitantly, Suta placed Bashemath in them.

Fortunately, the baby had stilled. Her eyes were closed, and her mouth pinched in her usual pained expression. The king gazed at her for a long time before looking up at Suta, whose cheeks were stained with tears.

"Could you pray, my king, that your god will make her well?" Suta asked. "The way you prayed so fervently for Bathsheba's first son?"

"That child died," the king said.

"Yes, but you cared enough to pray. Because he was a boy and Bathsheba's."

Briefly, anger chased across his face. "You think me unconcerned about my daughters? Or my concubines, for that matter?"

"No, my lord." The tears again flowed down Suta's face. "I only ask that you pray for her."

The king held out the baby for Suta to take. "I will, as I do for all my children."

A taut silence hung between them when they returned to their table.

Gilia finally spoke. "He didn't even ask her name. Did you notice? That's how little he cares about her."

"Of course, he knows her name," Tabytha said. "Someone would have told him." Probably the same person who had told him the child was not right.

Suta rose without a word and, gripping the now wailing child, fled back to her closed-off world, Gilia on her heels.

Suta's child cast a long shadow over the night. The king seemed more distant, the conversations more muted. He did not play his lyre. Haggith didn't dance.

At the end of the evening, Tabytha's heart jolted with disappointment when she saw Bathsheba rise to follow the king across to the door that led to his quarters.

chapter 18

abigail

extract from scroll ⅃ (hs gimel)

My sure-footed mount followed the pack of donkeys on the narrow trail into the Judean mountains. The three boys leading the donkeys whistled, laughed, and called to each other, unaware of the danger Nabal had put them in. Their jovial voices did not dispel my fear. If anything, they multiplied my terror. Their lives rested on me and my words to the man destined to be our king. *Give me the right words, Lord, and give David a heart to hear.*

The air cooled as I rode into the first shaded ravine. Usually, I would have slowed to admire the mountains rising on either side of me, but today, my thoughts churned on my coming confrontation. I thought of all the men I had ever known—my father, brothers, and Nabal. None of them had ever listened to a woman. We were always silenced with a severe stare, a harsh word, or a clenched fist. What chance did I have to change the mind of this powerful man and the warriors he commanded?

Then I saw them—a flood of men pouring into the dry wadi. They raised their swords and voices as they crested the hill, and the words chilled me to my core. "Vengeance for David! Vengeance for David!"

My young servants stopped the pack of donkeys and looked back at me, finally an inkling of fear in their eyes. I held up both my hands and nodded, hoping it communicated control and calm. I slipped off my donkey and clung to the saddle, afraid my legs would betray me as I waited for the men to reach us.

The approaching men had seen us. Their voices stilled as they strode towards us. I knew instantly which of them was David, for he walked slightly ahead of his men with the confidence of a born leader. The men closest to him glanced at the pack donkeys and then looked towards David the way my servants had looked towards me. But David's intense gaze, having taken in the donkeys and my servants, was on me.

I let go of the saddle and stepped towards him. When he was three paces away from me, I dropped to my knees and put my head to the ground, the posture of a servant before her king. "Pardon your servant, my lord, and let me speak to you. Hear what your servant has to say."

I waited.

Finally, he said, "You come from Nabal?" He spoke my husband's name with cold fury.

I lifted my head. "Yes, my lord."

The men around him stirred. One grabbed my young servant roughly by the arm and put his knife to his throat. "You just made an oath to kill every man of Nabal's, David. Well, here's the first."

"Wait. Let go of him." David looked from him to me. "Let's hear what she has to say first."

The man instantly lowered his knife and took his hands off my servant. It was good to know David had firm control of his men. Now, to convince him not to follow through on his vengeance oath.

"From your fine clothing, I take it you are Nabal's wife?" David asked, his gaze still filled with simmering anger.

I nodded.

"Rise. It will be easier to hear you." He held out his hand, and I took it, allowing him to draw me up while looking into those dark, menacing eyes.

As soon as he released my hand, I said, "Please pay no attention, my lord, to that wicked man, Nabal. His name means fool, and folly goes with him." A few of his men chortled at this, but David's expression didn't change. "As for me, I did not see your men this morning. Now, my lord, as surely as the Lord your God lives and as you live, since God has kept you from bloodshed and vengeance, may every one of your enemies intent on harming you be like Nabal."

I saw David's expression soften, not I suspected, at the curse I spoke over his enemies, but at my mention of God. My heart pounded at the words that had come unbidden to my lips, for that was the moment I knew Adonai would indeed punish Nabal for scorning his anointed one.

I pulled my thoughts back to the reason I was here. I pointed to the donkeys. "Let this gift be given to the men who follow you."

His men murmured appreciatively. They pressed around the donkeys, opened saddle bags, and exclaimed at what was inside.

David studied me intently, and heat rose to my cheeks. He wasn't much older than I was, but he had already faced so much. My life hadn't been easy, but his was one of danger at every turn. To be the king's enemy, to hide in caves and the barren wilderness, to keep moving, never sure if you were walking into a trap—how could a man not grow bitter, angry, and disillusioned? Yet I saw integrity and faith under that struggle-hardened strength. I yearned to bless him then, to tell him to keep his hope and faith alive.

"Please forgive your servant's presumption." I stepped closer to him and lowered my voice so only he would hear the words. "The Lord your God will certainly make a lasting dynasty for you because you fight his battles. Even though someone is pursuing you to take your life, God holds you securely in his hand, while your enemies will be hurled away like a stone in a sling." I saw a flicker of a smile as we both remembered how David had defeated the Philistine champion. I dared to grasp his hand then. "When the Lord has fulfilled all his promises to you and appointed you king over Israel, you will not have the burden of needless bloodshed on your conscience. And when the Lord brings you success, remember me, your servant."

We stood like that for a moment until, self-consciously, I dropped his hand. What had overcome me to speak to him like that? To hold his hand, for goodness sake? He had not yet called off the attack on Nabal's estate. We were still in danger, still completely under his power. And, lest I forget, he was a man and unlikely to be swayed by a woman.

But then David smiled, and my fears melted away.

"Praise be to the Lord, the God of Israel, who has sent you today to meet me."

My spirit leaped with joy at his words.

"What is your name?"

"Abigail."

"Bless you for your good judgment and for keeping me from bloodshed and vengeance today, Abigail. The Lord kept me from harming you. If you had not come quickly to meet me, every male belonging to Nabal would have died by daybreak. Go home in peace. I have heard your words and granted your request."

He wasn't like all the other men I knew. He believed I was sent by God and had granted my request. He even blessed me instead of cursing my name, as my father and Nabal had done so often.

And as I made my way home that night with my three herders, I couldn't help but think how easy it would be to love a man like David.

chapter 19

ABIGAIL

extract from scroll ג (hs gimel)

It was dark when I got back to the estate with my three young servants and the donkeys, saddle packs empty. Loud shouting and laughter came from inside the house.

Heber and Chava waited outside the entrance, an oil lamp in hand. They came running as they saw me. Chava embraced me tightly.

"I was so worried, Abi. I thought perhaps they had taken you captive. I kept saying to Heber I should have gone instead of you."

Heber grabbed my shoulder in a fatherly way. "Mistress. Praise Adonai, you are back. He gave you the favor we prayed for?"

"He did. We are saved." A deep tiredness washed over me at that moment. "What about Nabal? Did he ask where I was?"

"Only once, Abi. He wanted to know where all the fresh meat was."

"What did you tell him?"

"That you were still preparing it. Then, I filled his cup. I thought it would help him forget he was eating dried meat."

I laughed. "It sounds like you did a good job of helping him forget. It would be useless to speak to him now if he is drunk. I will tell him in the morning."

"Perhaps he doesn't need to know," Chava said anxiously. "What will he do to you in one of his foul moods?"

I shrugged. Nabal did not often lay a hand on me, but undoubtedly, this would make him angry enough to do so. "It matters little. Adonai averted David's justified anger today. I'm sure he can avert Nabal's unjustified anger tomorrow."

I slept soundly that night and woke well before my husband. I knew what I would say by the time he appeared, squinting into the light and shouting for someone to bring him water for his parched mouth.

"Where were you last night?" He glared at me as he sat down at the table. "And what was that old, fetid meat I had to serve my guests?"

"I went out to the wilderness with several donkeys laden with food for David and his men," I said as if reporting a minor household incident. "Including the fresh meat. I thought it a small price to pay for our lives."

"You *what*?"

"I heard of his request to you yesterday. I know he is a man of the sword and would not take your offense lightly, so I took immediate action to keep him from coming to kill you. We owe him much for keeping our herds and shepherds safe."

Nabal slammed his fist down so hard the cup of water I had placed before him jumped, spilling water on the table.

"Owe him? I owe the traitor nothing." He rose, trembling in rage. "You are a worthless whore of a woman! A despicable wife." Spittle flew into my face.

He grabbed me by the arm.

"Nabal. You're hurting me."

"Hurting?" He laughed then, a cruel sound. "This is nothing, Abigail. When I'm finished with you, you will never walk beside a donkey again to give outlaws my food."

"Master!" Chava had appeared. "Let her go."

Nabal glanced at her but didn't loosen his grip on me. "It wouldn't surprise me if you and your worthless dolt of husband helped her deceive me. Once I've dealt with her, you'll be next."

"You're a fool, Nabal," I said quietly. "That outlaw will be king one day. I came across him and his men in the wadi, armed and ready to slay you and every man on this estate."

Nabal's face reddened with rage. "*King*! Saul is king. David will never be anything more than ..." His words wavered. I saw the surprise in his eyes and then a flash of fear. His hand fell from my arm. "Abi ... Abi? What is hap ...?"

And Nabal fell to the ground like a heavy sack of legumes.

"Nabal?" I knelt next to him and looked into his eyes, which were filled with wild terror.

Chava called for Heber before kneeling next to me.

"Master? What happened? Can you speak?"

But Nabal could do nothing but stare at us and mumble incoherently. He would never raise a fist or a voice against any of us again.

Ten days later, Nabal was dead.

We buried him behind the homestead, where the sycamore fig trees grew.

Numbness shrouded me as two young men lowered my husband into the ground. Sand thudded onto the wrapped body as Heber filled the grave. I had not loved Nabal, but I had grown accustomed to life here with all who served him, now standing beside me and staring silently into the grave of their harsh master.

I hoped that their lives would be better under their new master, but I had my doubts. I looked across the grave to Nabal's brother, Buz. He was tall and imposing. Although he didn't seem to raise his voice as often as Nabal had, there was something cold and calculating in the gaze he gave me now. As the next in line, the kinsman-redeemer, he had the right to claim me as his wife, even though he already had a wife. Our first son would be deemed Nabal's and would inherit the estate. My father had been in discussion with him since last night, arranging it all.

"Come, Abi," Chava said gently. "It's over. Let's find you something to eat. You haven't eaten anything since yesterday."

I let her lead me away and even ate the food she brought me.

I waited a day and another while my father and Buz decided my fate. Buz stalled. He wanted the estate—his greedy gaze told me that much—but he didn't want to be burdened with a wife whose first son would steal his new property away from him.

The waiting and uncertainty exhausted me, and I found myself falling into fitful sleep during the days.

"Mistress?"

I awoke to Jacoba shaking my arm. It took a moment to remember where I was.

"Heber sent me to fetch you."

Perhaps Buz had finally decided. Perhaps I was to learn my fate today. It wouldn't surprise me if he agreed to take me to get his hands on the property but never lay with me so it would always stay his. Strangely, I was almost past caring.

I followed Jacoba out into the courtyard, where Heber and Chava stood with four young men, strong and browned by the sun. Knives glistened on their hips. *David's men*, I realized with a jolt.

One of the four stepped forward.

"David sent us with a message for you. He heard of your husband's death." The man didn't express any pity. If anything, his words showed a sense of vindication.

"It is kind of your master to send his sympathies."

The man smiled at that. "He's not sending sympathies. He's sending for *you*."

I shook my head in confusion.

"David asks if you will become his wife," the man said plainly.

Chava gasped, and Heber stared at the man in disbelief. Perhaps they thought of my father, at that exact moment, arranging to give me to Nabal's forbidding brother, who didn't want me.

I thought only of the strong, young leader who had met me in a wadi, listened to me, changed his course of action because of my words, and blessed me instead of cursing me. I thought of the faith I had seen in him, the kindness and admiration in his eyes as he looked at me, and my sure belief that he was the anointed one of Adonai.

So, I sank to my knees and said, "I am your servant and am ready to serve you and wash the feet of my lord's servants."

Then I rose and told Heber to fetch my donkey. Right away. For I was going to become the wife of the man destined to be king.

Chapter 20

Tabytha blew on the ink of the last word, king, and then wiped the tip of the reed. She carefully placed it with her other reeds before putting the stopper on the ink jar. She looked up at Abigail, who stared out of the window, still lost in her memories.

"It's a fine story, Abigail. I'm not sure I would have had your courage to face a band of mercenaries like that."

"I sometimes marvel at it myself." She smiled. "I was young. Only a few years older than you are now. But Adonai's hand was on that meeting."

"You are fortunate indeed to be one of his people."

Abigail looked at her thoughtfully. "You said you had a Hebrew tutor from a young age?"

"Yes. A priest. Ahio."

"Ahio? I wonder ..." She furrowed her brow. "Never mind. Did this Ahio tell you about the Canaanite woman who hid the spies in Jericho?"

"Was that the city the Israelites marched around until the walls fell down?"

"Indeed. There was a woman in that city called Rahab, a prostitute who hid the Israelite spies. Adonai saw her faith and rewarded her faithfulness to his people by keeping her and her family safe. Her house in the wall was the only one that didn't crumble to the ground." Abigail smiled. "David told me about her. She was his father's grandmother."

"Truly? She was his forebearer?"

"But more than that. Adonai *saw* her even though she wasn't an Israelite. He protected her and gave her the legacy of a royal line."

Tears sprung up in Tabytha's eyes. "Do you think he sees me too?"

"I am sure of it, Tabytha." Abigail gripped her hand and squeezed it. "You are now as much one of his people as I am."

She wanted to believe it—how she wanted to—but so many doubts assailed her. Her mother's voice proudly telling her the stories of their gods. Her brother's voice telling her never to forget she was a Jebusite. Ahio's voice telling her Adonai's instructions to the conquering Israelites to destroy everyone who roamed the land and to smash every one of their gods to pieces. The king's voice singing of Adonai as his shepherd and her own girlish dreams that they walked together beside the still waters in the valley below the city. Then, the dawning realization his love for Adonai was far bigger than his love for her could ever be.

"You doubt it?" Abigail's voice was gentle.

"No. Well, perhaps." How could she explain everything that shouted she was not one of Adonai's own? Not chosen. Not loved. Finally, she said, "Ahio made me fear Adonai. He spoke of his wrath and his judgment. Never of his love, the way you do."

Abigail rose and stretched. "It's a mystery that he is both judge and redeemer. To be feared and to be loved. The most difficult of all is to accept he could know and love us. Me *and* you, Tabytha. But I believe he does."

"The king believes it too," Tabytha said. "I hear it in the words he writes about Adonai."

"Yes." They shared a smile as they thought of David's faith-filled words. Then Abigail said, "It's been a long morning. Shall we continue recording my story the day after Shabbat?"

Tabytha nodded. They only met once or twice a week, and the work was slow, but it had become one of her favorite times. Meeting with Michal made her anxious, mainly because Michal insisted no one was to know about it, but the time with Abigail felt different. They had become friends, and now that she hardly saw Suta, she valued Abigail's companionship.

"I'm glad for this time." Abigail's words echoed her own thoughts. "I'm not doing it for the same reason as Michal, but I'm still grateful others will be able to read about my life with David. Thank you, Tabytha."

My life with David. A pang of jealousy pierced Tabytha. Yes, Abigail had spent years with the king before there were too many wives and concubines to share him with. Even now, Abigail sat at his table. He confided in her and asked her to arrange things, unlike Tabytha, who sat at the table furthest from him and had spent only a single night in his arms.

"I wish I knew him as you do."

Perhaps that was what her time with Abigail, and even Michal, was giving her—insight into her own husband, who was little more than an alluring stranger to her.

Abigail considered her intently. "It's not easy for you to be thrust into his court at a time when David is busy and distracted. To compete for his attention against Bathsheba. We all do, I suppose, but most of us spent time with him. We bore him children. We grew to know him."

Tabytha shrugged, suddenly ashamed. She was not as desirable as Bathsheba, and everybody, including Abigail, could see it.

"It matters little. My life here is good. I have everything I need and even the ability to record history." She waved to the parchment and reeds. "Rahab's legacy was to be the mother of royalty. Maybe my legacy is these writings. Perhaps our children's children will read them one day." She smiled at the thought. "Do you think that could happen, Abigail?"

"If you store them in those clay pots, it might," Abigail said with a laugh.

The next night, the king chose Tabytha over Bathsheba. Even as she followed him through the door, shame washed over her at the thought he was doing so only at the urging of Abigail. Yet their lovemaking was as tender as before, not as slow and gentle but more urgent and passionate.

When it was over, he rested on his side, looking at her as she lay in the crook of his arm.

"I've missed you, my gazelle." He twirled his fingers into the curls of her hair. "You are as beautiful and passionate as I remember."

"I've missed you too, my lord."

"My lord is a little formal for lovers. When are you going to start calling me David?"

"I can start now." She smiled coyly. "David."

"Better." He kissed her again, deeply, and desire stirred within her.

He pulled away, smiling. "I'm not as young as you are, my love. I need rest."

He lay back, and she stretched out against him, marveling at the feel of his warm body against her own. In the long silence that followed, she thought he had fallen asleep until his voice broke through her lazy thoughts.

"How far are you with Michal's account?"

She didn't want to think of Michal. Not now.

Reluctantly, she said, "Her father has given her to Paltiel as a wife."

"It was not a valid marriage. She was mine."

She said nothing. The king raised himself onto his elbow again. "I'm sorry, Tabytha. Michal has a way of digging under my flesh like a thorn." He stroked a finger down her forehead and nose, lingering on her lips. "I have broken my own rule never to speak of one wife while lying in the arms of another. Do you forgive me?"

"I don't," she said playfully.

He grinned. "How can I make it up to you?"

"Will you answer a question? Truthfully?" She grew more serious. "Did you choose me tonight because of something Abigail said?"

"And you force me to break my rule a second time." He sighed and lay back, looking at the ceiling. "Abigail reminded me—rightly—that I have been neglecting you and some of the others and you have the right to get to know me as a husband." He turned to look at her just as she turned away. "Your face shows me everything, my gazelle. If you think I didn't want you in my arms tonight, you're wrong."

She swallowed away her tears.

"Tabytha. Look at me."

She turned back and looked into his dark eyes, as beautiful and intense as the first time she'd gazed into them as a child, kneeling at Ornan's feet.

"I am sorry I have hurt you, my love. First, by keeping you from your family and, now, by neglect. I will try to be a better husband to you. To all of you. Being king demands much of me. That doesn't excuse it, but ..."

"No." She lifted her hand to his cheek. "You have given me much. The parchment and the reeds and the ink pots. My room with a view of the hills I used to roam. Time with my mother. Friendship with Abigail and Suta. Your songs and your love of Adonai. I am grateful to be here in your royal court. And even more grateful to be here, in your arms."

He cocked his head to the side. "You are the first of my Jebusite women to show a genuine interest in my songs about Adonai. Why is that?"

She shook her head. "I don't know about the others, but I was a child when I heard of the Hebrew God, the one true God. When I look at all the miraculous things Adonai has done for his chosen people, how can I not believe he is all you say he is?" As she spoke the words, she knew they were true. She truly *did* believe in King David's powerful God.

The answer seemed to please him. "Adonai himself has given you this wisdom and insight, Tabytha. May he bless you and your offspring for your faith."

That blessing lingered with her. Tabytha carried it back to her own quarters like a warm, protective cloak. Every day that followed, she wrapped those words around her when the inner voices tried to tell her she was not loved and not chosen by Ahio's fearful God. Adonai's anointed king had told her his God had given her wisdom and insight. He had spoken a powerful blessing over her. Surely, Adonai would see her now?

chapter 21

abigail

extract from scroll ג (hs gimel)

As I hurriedly packed my belongings, Jacoba begged to come with me. When I relented, she told her sister, who also worked on the estate. By the time I finished, Jacoba, her sister, and three other women stood ready to go with me.

David's men merely shrugged at this. "We have a shortage of women," one said, looking at Jacoba in a way that made her blush.

We left before the news could reach my father or Buz. I doubted either would follow us into the wilderness to face the armed men. I suspected Buz would be somewhat relieved if I disappeared for good, although he might curse me for taking four of the pack donkeys.

The men led us away from the estate towards the hills that marked the edge of the wilderness, then through the wadi where I had bowed before David and over the mountain I had seen him and his men stream down. As the sun set and the cold crept in, they halted and made a fire, passing around bread and water. The women and I huddled together, whispering about what lay ahead, listening to the men's easy talk and laughter. Eventually, we rolled out our sleeping mats near the fire. Despite the hard ground and the biting cold of the night, I slept soundly for the first time in two weeks, with a sure sense that Adonai's hand had brought me here.

We set off early the following day. I would come to know and even love that wilderness, for it would be my home for many months before we moved to Gath and Ziklag. But on that first morning, riding into the heart of it, the vastness and barrenness of that land unsettled me. We followed the narrow contour paths the shepherds and flocks walked, and I began to notice more life in this land than the stark hills hinted at. Grasses and small tufts of green bushes sprouted between the rocks—this was why Nabal's men brought the sheep here for winter grazing. Occasionally, I would spot a mountain goat, sure-footed, on the crags above us. As the sun rose higher, a large bird of prey circled lazily above us until it was a mere speck in the sky.

Despite the heat, the men pushed on, keen to reach their camp. We dropped into a ravine, stopping briefly at a stream to quench our own and the donkeys' thirst and splash water on our faces and arms. From there, we walked along the wide riverbed. The plaintiff bleating of goats was the first sign that we neared David's camp. Soon after, a voice called out from above. I looked up to see a smiling sentry waving from a large, flat rock. Other men appeared too, running—as sure-footed as the wild goats—along the steep slopes in the same direction we were going.

Word of our arrival had reached the camp by the time we arrived, for a large contingent of men awaited us, all with the same strong, sun-darkened look as our companions. I saw women and children, too, more than Jacoba's admirer had indicated. The warmth of our welcome—cheers, laughter, and a few good-hearted jibes about David's new woman—struck me.

I looked for him in the crowd but couldn't see him. However, as I slid from my donkey, a hand suddenly appeared to steady me.

David stood next to me, laughter in his dark eyes. "You said yes."

I dismounted and started to kneel, but his strong grip held me up. "No need for that today, Abigail," he said softly. "The wilderness is not a place for formality."

Still, I bowed my head. "My lord. I am honored by your proposal."

"And I'm honored you accepted it." He swept his hand towards my female companions, who looked at him in wide-eyed appreciation. "Welcome all of you to the fugitive life. It's not an easy one, and if any of you wants to return to Carmel, my men will take you back." His eyes lingered on me. "That includes you, Abigail."

"There's nothing for me there, my lord. From this day forward, my life is bound to yours." I wanted to say more about how I believed Adonai's hand had directed me here, but I sensed in his gaze he felt it, too.

"And mine to yours. I will do all in my power to make it a good life for you. Come, let me show you our modest dwellings. The men will bring your possessions."

He led me and my female companions up a narrow path that seemed to climb out of the ravine.

"The men with families tend to live in tents up there," he said, pointing to the top of the ravine. "It's easier for them to take our herds out to graze. My younger men prefer to stay in the ravine, simply sleeping on the riverbed." He shook his head ruefully. "They were almost caught in a flash flood a few weeks ago, so most have moved to higher ground."

"You have a large group, my lord."

"Almost six hundred men, not to mention the growing number of wives and children. This way." We branched off from the main path, soon reaching the wide entrance of a cave. "I stay here with a few of my men."

The cave was blessedly cool, and the smell of smoke lingered. Inside the entrance, we stepped over a circle of blackened rocks enclosing kindling, ready for the next fire.

David followed my gaze. "Those of us who stay in the caves tend to eat our evening meals together around the fire. It gets cold here at night."

He led us past sleeping mats, rolled and stacked against the stone walls.

"How many men stay here?"

"About twenty of my most trusted warriors. Several smaller caverns branch off from this one. I had my men move out of one in preparation for your arrival. You and your women will be able to stay there."

He stopped at a rock ledge, where several clay oil lamps and flint stood.

"It's dark in the back caverns. Let's take lamps."

He lit three lamps, passing two to Jacoba and me before leading us on. The air here smelled musty and was even cooler than at the entrance.

We reached a cavern closed off by palm branches.

"There are palm trees here?" I hadn't seen any.

"No." He pushed them aside. "These came from our previous camp. Ahinoam insisted we bring them. She has not quite mastered the nomadic life of a single bag of possessions."

I thought of my own large pack of belongings and felt a sense of understanding for this Ahinoam, whoever she might be.

"She thought you would want privacy from the men."

I had to duck down to enter the cavern, but once inside, the light of our lamps showed a high roof above our heads. Jacoba's sister screamed as a winged creature flew narrowly past her face towards the exit.

David laughed. "Our loyal bats. We've chased them away, but they keep returning."

Someone had made a rough mattress of grasses, wool, and goat skins along the far wall of the spacious cavern. Besides a large bowl and jug for washing, the cavern was bare. *The nomad's life.*

"I'll ask Ahinoam to find more bedding material for your women."

"Thank you."

"Rest a while. The men will bring your things into the main cave shortly. And the women will bring water for washing."

I nodded my appreciation, suddenly aware of my tiredness.

"We'll go up later when it's cooler, and I'll present you to my men and their wives. The women are particularly keen to meet my Abigail."

My Abigail. Warmth flooded my body at the simple words and the intensity in his eyes as he said my name.

"I look forward to it. And will Ahinoam be there too? I must thank her for all she has done to prepare for my arrival."

"Yes, of course." He looked at me closely and seemed to come to some understanding. "You don't know, do you?"

"Know what?"

"Ahinoam is my wife."

Wife? For a moment, everything tilted around me. *David had a wife?*

"I didn't know."

He must have seen my disappointment, for he reached out and took my hand. "I assumed you knew. I'm sorry, Abigail. If this changes things for you, I will take you back myself tomorrow."

"No, I ..." I believed Adonai directed me here, didn't I? "I need a bit of time to think about it."

"Of course." He turned to leave but then looked back at me. "I am also married to King Saul's daughter, Michal."

I nodded. I had heard that, but also that King Saul had given her to another man. Michal wasn't here to vie for his affections. Ahinoam was.

"How does Ahinoam feel about me coming?"

He glanced to the side. "Much the same as you do, I suspect. But she accepts it." We stood in silence for a while. "One day, I will be king and will marry not for love but for alliances. You will not be my last wife."

The strong, practical part of me understood this. But another part longed to be the special possession of a man such as David.

"What do you gain by marrying me?" I could not hide the hurt in my voice.

"A wise, godly, and beautiful wife." He smiled languidly. "Tell me your answer by the morning. We are planning a wedding celebration tomorrow night."

He ducked through the entrance, and I remained standing in the cold cave, my thoughts in turmoil, my companions tittering excitedly behind me.

chapter 22

tabytha

extract from scroll ג (hs alef)

I look back over the years and see that my second year at the palace was the happiest of all—before everything tore apart. When David still came to the Women's Quarters for meals and joy infused the words he wrote and sang. When laughter still echoed in our corridors.

David had stayed behind that spring when his army left for the border skirmishes with the Philistines, dedicating himself to the administration of his kingdom. As he had promised, he showed attentiveness to me. Some of my favorite memories are of us sitting together, poring over the words of his latest prayer poem. As when I first heard the Shepherd Song, I marveled at the beauty of his words. Truly, a poet's heart beat in his warrior's body. The praise songs he created for Adonai moved me to write my own songs. I felt shy the first time I showed him one, but his eyes glistened with tears as he listened to me reading the words. I can still hear his voice saying, "Beautiful, my gazelle. Beautiful."

As I penned my songs, I grew to understand David better—how his words shaped his faith almost as much as his faith shaped the words he wrote. It started to happen to me, too. Through writing, I gained insight into Adonai. As I poured my doubts and fears onto the scroll, my faith budded and I sensed Adonai's closeness, almost as David and Abigail described it. At those times, I believed the God of Israel saw me, a Jebusite concubine, the way he had once seen Rahab, the Canaanite prostitute.

There are other precious memories. I recall us sitting on his terrace, looking out over the city's roofs as the sun set. We were talking about our brothers. I remember how he laughed as he said, "You had only one mocking brother—I had six." And I still see the glint of amusement in his eyes as he went on to tell me about his brothers' expressions on the day the fearsome old prophet anointed him.

He told of the day with a storyteller's flair and humor.

How Samuel had come from Ramah to Bethlehem, on the instructions of Adonai, summoning David's father Jesse to bring all his sons to a sacrifice. How Jesse called his sons together, and they consecrated themselves and— with a sense of pomp and honor—went to meet the grand old leader of their people. But how they all conveniently forgot to tell David.

How Samuel saw the strong, tall Eliab and thought, *surely the Lord's anointed stands before me.*

Adonai whispered, "This is not the one."

Next came stately Abinadab, and again Samuel thought, *surely this is the Lord's anointed,* but Adonai whispered, *this is not the one.*

How Jesse had stood by anxiously watching as his third and fourth and fifth and sixth son came before the old prophet. But how Samuel shook his head with each one.

And how finally Samuel turned to Jesse and said—David acted this out until my sides ached from laughter— "Are these all the sons you have?"

How they sent his brother Ozem, the worst of his tormentors, to fetch David from the field and how Ozem muttered angrily at having to tend David's sheep.

David had grown more serious as he talked of the moment Samuel saw him. The old man's eyes had locked on his own and a sense of knowing settled on the prophet's face at that moment. How the prophet had told him to kneel and had taken a horn of fragrant oil and poured it over his head before kissing him on the cheeks with the words, "The Lord has anointed you ruler of his inheritance." How, when he rose, his father and brothers' faces reflected a mix of shock, jealousy, and anger.

And then, David spoke of the warmth that had suffused his heart. Adonai became more real to him on that day than ever before, he told me.

I remember, too, the day I asked him about the spear that stood in the corner of his chambers, thick as a weaver's rod. Again, David the storyteller emerged to recount how he had slain the Philistine champion when he was but a few years past his boyhood. I didn't tell him Michal had spoken of the incident. I knew by then how brooding he became when I mentioned her name. So, I let him tell me how his father had sent him with provisions for his brothers in King Saul's army who camped in the Valley of Elah. How his heart jolted in his chest the first time he saw the vast Philistine army and how anger boiled inside him when Goliath, the largest man he had ever seen, stepped out and shouted his defiance of Adonai's army.

How Eliab had mockingly told him to return to tending his few sheep in the wilderness and leave the fighting to the real men, but how he paid his brother no heed and told the king he did not fear facing this giant. How the king, thinking he sent a young man to his death, insisted he wear his armor. But, realizing he couldn't move well in it, David stripped it off. How he took his staff, sling, and five smooth pebbles from the cold stream running through the valley, and how deep the silence had been as he stepped out to meet the Philistine.

Then, how the silence broke with Goliath's bellow of rage that a mere boy would come at him with a stick as if he were a dog to be beaten down. And how a strange peace had settled on him as the Philistine's curses and threats echoed through that valley.

"The words came to me unbidden, my gazelle. From deep inside." His eyes held a faraway look. "You come against me with sword and spear and javelin, but I come against you in the name of the Lord Almighty, the God of the armies of Israel, whom you have defied. This day, the Lord will deliver you into my hands, and all will know that it is not by sword or spear that the Lord saves. The battle is the Lord's, and he will give all of you into our hands."

Then, how true that first pebble had flown from his sling to strike the Philistine between the eyes and how the ground shuddered as the giant fell before his feet.

I had to urge him to tell me the rest. He thought a woman should not hear of such horrors. Finally, he relented and told me how he had used the Philistine's own sword to hack off the giant's head and present the bloody offering to the king.

I never looked at that spear the same way again.

By the end of my second year at the palace, I knew I loved David the way Abigail spoke of loving him. Deeply. Fiercely. Wholeheartedly. I whispered it to him in the dark of the night when I knew he slept. He was not a man to burden with such depth of emotion. He never whispered the words back to me. But sometimes, when he looked at me with tenderness, amusement, or curiosity, I could almost believe he loved me too.

When my monthly bleeding stopped, and I secretly knew I carried King David's child, my joy was complete.

chapter 23

Tabytha and Tamar sat on the steps of the Women's Courtyard enjoying the sweet figs Tamar had bought at the Shabbat market.

"I saw Sharai at the market, Tabytha, and he smiled at me. You have never seen a smile like that."

Tabytha laughed at Tamar's flushed face. "Did he speak to you?"

The princess shook her head. "It wouldn't be proper. But my mother told me that Abba said Sharai and his father came yesterday to discuss marriage."

"Truly? What did your father say?"

"I'm not sure, but I expect he'll send for me today and ask me what I think." Tamar clasped her hands together like a young child receiving a gift. "And then I'll tell him I think it's a wonderful match."

Tabytha smiled. David was an unusual father, especially where his daughters were concerned. It wouldn't surprise her if he asked Tamar's thoughts on the matter. The young man in question was the son of one of David's most celebrated warriors.Sharai had proven himself almost as courageous and skilled as his father in this last campaign against the Philistines. He had returned with something of a reputation and, apparently, plenty of confidence, for few men his age would be bold enough to approach the king and suggest becoming his son-in-law.

"You don't think Abba's already turned him down, do you?" Tamar suddenly looked crestfallen.

"No. I'm sure he will consider it as carefully as he does all the important decisions he makes. He'll do what is right for you, Tamar. You know that, don't you?"

"I know."

"Even if that's deciding Sharai's not a good match for you."

"But he *is* a good match."

"Because he has a nice smile?"

"No." Tamar grinned at Tabytha's teasing. "Because he's as strong and heroic as Abba himself."

Tabytha lifted her face, enjoying the sun's touch after a week of rain. The air held a note of warmth, hinting at the nearness of spring. Tabytha still remembered the stifling heat of her first summer at the palace. Last year's summer hadn't been as bad, but she fretted about being with child through the coming summer months.

She pressed on the side of her stomach and smiled at the slight flutter of movement.

"Is the baby moving?"

"Feel here." She directed Tamar's hand to the place and watched the delight on the girl's face as she felt the movement.

"A whole new life, hidden inside you."

"Incredible, isn't it?"

"Are you afraid?" Tamar looked at her somberly, and Tabytha wondered if she thought of Bashemath. The child was a year and a half old and did little more than whimper, lift her head, and occasionally roll over. She should have been toddling around them in the courtyard by now, chortling happily and saying, Ima. How different Suta would be then.

"A little."

"I want a child. But seeing what happened to Eglah and then to Suta ..." The girl swallowed. "It makes me afraid to marry."

"But think about his smile."

The girl laughed. Her eyes creased with the mischievous joy Tabytha loved so much.

Maacah arrived just then. She seldom came to the courtyard during the day when all the other women were there.

"Ima!" Tamar jumped up. "Is there word from Abba?"

"Yes. He sent a message for you."

"Did he give Sharai his permission?"

"Sharai? No." Maacah scowled. "It had nothing to do with that."

"Oh. I thought ..."

"Your father recently came from Amnon's house. He's been ill."

"Amnon?"

"He's asked for you to come and make his favorite dish, that herb bread we used to make in Hebron."

"But why me?"

"How must I know, Tamar?" Her mother sighed. "You'd better go soon. Your father says Amnon looks feverish."

"How is herb bread going to help a fever?" Tabytha asked.

Maacah cast her a derisive glance. "Why don't you go question the king's wishes now that you're as favored as Bathsheba herself?"

"Someone should go with her," Tabytha said. She thought back to the day at the Shabbat market when David bought the blue fabric for her dress. Of Prince Amnon's arrogance and how he had looked at Tamar with a kind of … possessiveness.

"He's her brother. Why would she need a companion?"

"If Abba wills it, I'll go," Tamar said. "And then, perhaps I can speak to him tonight about Sharai. Do you think he'll say yes, Ima?"

Her mother smiled indulgently. "You might be able to convince him."

"Come with me to the kitchen, Tabytha." Tamar rose. "I'll see if there's ground flour for the bread."

Tabytha trailed behind Tamar, still thinking of Amnon. "Perhaps I should come with you to help make the bread."

"You can't simply go." Tamar laughed. "You'll have to ask Abba first, which will delay everything."

They'd reached the kitchen by then, and Tabytha watched as Tamar playfully wrangled a jug of flour and olive oil from one of the servants.

Once the woman had relinquished the supplies, Tamar grabbed Tabytha's hand. "Walk me to the gate, and I can tell you more about Sharai."

"What more is there to tell?" Tabytha laughed but let Tamar lead her out of the Women's Quarters and across the bustling palace courtyard to the gate. There, a palace guard stepped forward to accompany the princess, but another man, leaning against a pillar, straightened and intercepted them. *Jonadab, Amnon's cousin and friend.* Tabytha still recalled his sly look on her first visit to the Shabbat market.

"Princess." Jonadab bowed. "Prince Amnon sent me to accompany you."

Tamar seemed unsure but then nodded. "No need to come with us," she said to the guard. "My cousin will ensure my safety."

Tabytha watched them go, unease stirring inside her.

Just then, something caught her gaze. A bird streaked down, like a rock falling from the sky. She watched in amazement as it dropped towards a lone figure on the city wall. The man stood silhouetted, his arm held up to the sky. The bird slowed, landing on the man's arm as if it were a tree branch.

The guard who had offered to accompany the princess watched the bird too. He shook his head and looked at Tabytha. "Unnatural, if you ask me."

"Who is he?"

"The king's prophet. But how he came by the bird, I wouldn't know."

But Tabytha knew. And the words that the king's seer had spoken to her all those years ago returned to her with the same strange heart-stirring as when he had first spoken them. *You are no ordinary girl. Adonai sees your heart. Remember that his hand is on you. Remember, especially when you have a broken wing.*

chapter 24

ABIGAIL

extract from scroll א (hs gimel)

On our first evening in the camp, David led us up the ravine path to a large plateau dotted with tents. Groups of warriors sat around fires, drinking, eating, and laughing. A few women roasted bread on a separate fire while the handful of children with them poked sticks into the flames. We made our way to one of the men's fires, close to a pen of lambs and young goats.

The men rose at our approach. I felt their gaze on me.

"May I present the new women of the camp." David didn't call me his wife. After all, I hadn't given him my answer yet.

A short man with a powerful build and gaze as sharp as an eagle searching for prey inclined his head in my direction.

"Welcome to the house of David, my lady. I am Joab, and these are some of the men under my command."

"Joab, Abishai, and Asahel," David pointed to the two men standing on either side of Joab, "are my sister's sons. Few are as skilled with a sword as they are."

"Except perhaps David himself." Joab smiled mockingly.

"Perhaps. Best we don't find out. I hope always to have your blades on my side of a battle."

"Our blades are wholly yours, my king," Joab said, bowing his head.

"I'm not king yet."

"Only because you cut off a piece of Saul's robe rather than his head when Adonai gave him into your hands."

"I will not lay my hand on the Lord's anointed, Joab." A hard note in David's voice made me think this was an old area of contention. "Come, let me introduce you to the others."

We made our way around the fires, finally reaching the one where the women sat. A young woman with a round, pleasant face rose and made her way toward us.

David murmured, "My wife, Ahinoam."

Ahinoam smiled and gripped my hand. "I'm glad you are here, Abigail. David speaks highly of you."

I couldn't help but respond to her kindness. "Thank you, Ahinoam. And for preparing the cavern for me and my women. I hope we'll be friends."

"So do I." She looked shyly at David, and I thought I saw a shadow of sadness in her eyes. It vanished almost immediately. "I'll be glad to have women in the cave. It has been the domain of men far too long."

David gave her an approving nod. He turned to me then and said, "So you see, I'm not the only one that wants you to stay. I hope you are persuaded?"

"I am." As I looked at the woman prepared to be kind to her husband's next wife, I knew I could do the same. "It will be my honor to stay and be your wife, my lord."

The next day rushed by in a whirl of preparations. Ahinoam, Jacoba, and my other companions led me to the women's pool in the river to wash. Back at the cave, they rubbed scented olive oil over my skin and helped me dress in my finest gown, the same one I had worn when I wed Nabal. I couldn't help but remember my younger self, naïve and fearful of being wed to a man known for his bad temper. Today, however, I felt a flush of anticipation at becoming the wife of the strong, attractive man destined to be king.

Jacoba plaited my hair and wove leaves through it. I let the women darken my eyelids and rouge my cheeks, and then we waited nervously at the cave entrance.

Near evening, we heard the distant sound of men's voices, of laughter, and tambourines.

"They come." Jacoba clambered to her feet.

"Here. Let's take oil lamps with us." Ahinoam went over and lit them as my ladies flapped around me, straightening my hair and the rumpled fabric of my gown, putting on my sandals, and dabbing perfume on my neck.

My hands sweated by the time David and his men arrived. My heart leaped as I saw him. For the first time, he was not dressed in a warrior's rough, knee-length robe. He had washed his hair and trimmed his beard, , and wore a long cloak of fine fabric. He had never looked more like a king.

"My lady." He bowed playfully, laughter in his eyes. "I couldn't imagine a more beautiful bride."

I smiled and lowered my head, murmuring, "My lord."

"I wish I had the same costly gifts to give you as Abraham's servant gave to Rebecca. One day, you will be my queen and have all your heart desires. But for now, please accept this, my wedding gift to you." He held out a silver bracelet inlaid with three red stones. "Three stones to remind us that Adonai is part of our union."

"It's beautiful." The bracelet lacked the value of the *mattan*—the wedding gifts—Nabal had bestowed on my family, yet as I slipped it on, I knew it would remain my favorite throughout my life.

"Come." He took my arm and led me from the cave. "Now to celebrate."

Joab and his brothers went ahead of us, and the rest of the men fell behind the women. It was a joyful procession of music, singing, and laughter. My nervousness dissipated as I clung to the arm of my soon-to-be husband. I let myself enjoy it. I couldn't remember the last time I celebrated. My years with Nabal had crushed the joy out of me.

The plateau teemed with people, and a loud cheer spread through the crowd as we arrived. *David, David, David*, the voices chanted, a display of loyalty for the man they had followed into the wilderness. We pushed through the crowd of well-wishers towards a slightly raised, covered platform, where a single, solemn man stood.

"I have asked my priest, Abiathar, to bless our union," David said into my ear.

"He doesn't seem very pleased about it."

"Since Saul killed all his relatives, he bears the entire weight of the priesthood on his young shoulders. At times, he is torn between the rigid demands of the Torah and my wishes."

"Does he think Adonai is against our marriage?" The thought startled me. Hadn't I sensed Adonai leading me here?

"He has nothing against you, but he likes to remind me of Moses' words that a king should not take many wives lest his heart turn away from God. We disagree on how many wives are too many."

I laughed at his slightly self-satisfied smirk.

"Besides, I told him you were a particularly godly woman and far more likely to turn my heart *towards* Adonai."

As we stepped onto the platform, I glanced at the young priest. He had a long, thin face and dark, sorrowful eyes. Yet the smile he gave me felt real, a momentary glimpse of who he had been once before a mad king slaughtered his entire family.

The crowd grew silent, straining forward to hear the words of blessing. The priest cleared his throat nervously.

"David Ben-Jesse, you acquire this woman, Abigail of Carmel, to be your wife. Speak out your covenant now before these witnesses."

David turned and took both my hands in his own.

"Abigail, when I first saw you in the valley, I knew you were a woman of God. You bless me by becoming my wife. For as long as I live, I will protect you, provide for you, and honor you before Adonai. I will care for the children born to you. Never will you or they be cut off from my house. May Adonai and all these bear witness between us."

Tears sprang up in my eyes at the surprising words and the conviction I saw in David's eyes as he spoke them. Nabal had made no promises. He had bought me from my father like one buys a lamb or a donkey.

"My lady," the priest said, "you wish to be this man's wife?"

"I do."

David smiled at me, and the priest put his hands on our heads and spoke his blessing.

"David, may this wife bring you love, honor, wisdom, and joy. My lady, may Adonai bless you with the love of Rachel and the womb of Leah. Blessed are you, O Adonai, who makes the bridegroom to rejoice with the bride."

A cheer arose around us as he lifted his hands from our heads. The lone, almost haunting, sound of a ram's horn carried over it, and the juxtaposition felt right, declaring the moment to be both joyful and solemn.

I was the wife of David, the anointed of Adonai.

chapter 25

Abigail rose and stretched. "I'm glad we're doing this, Tabytha. It's good to remember those early days with David."

Tabytha blew on the ink of the last words and looked at the older woman. "When I met him as a child, I was afraid of him. I wish I could have seen him through your eyes even then."

"He is much the same man now as then. Older, yes, but still strong and kind."

"And handsome," Tabytha said. They both laughed.

"Next week, same time?"

"Yes." Tabytha rose as Abigail opened the door. "Abigail? Did you see Tamar last night or this morning? I couldn't find her."

"I didn't." Abigail furrowed her brow. "Could she be ill?"

"She wasn't in her room last night. I'll ask Maacah. She'll know where she is." Tabytha couldn't shake her sense of unease.

"I'll come with you."

They walked together to Maacah's room. Tabytha had never been there, although she'd heard from the other concubines that it was particularly fine. It didn't surprise her. Maacah enjoyed reminding everyone of her dual status as both wife and daughter of a king.

Abigail knocked on the door.

"Who's there?" Maacah asked belligerently.

"Abigail."

After a while, Maacah opened the door. She scowled when she saw Tabytha.

"I've been looking for Tamar since yesterday," Tabytha said without preamble.

"Absalom sent word last night. She's staying with him for a few days."

Maacah began to close the door, but Tabytha pushed her hand against it.

"Why?"

"How must I know? She's young and capricious."

"But she planned to ask David about Sharai last night. She wouldn't have missed that chance."

"I can't know another's mind, least of all Tamar's of late. All she thinks and talks about is that boy."

As Maacah pushed the door closed in their faces, Abigail regarded Tabytha. "So, we know where she is, Tabytha. But you still look worried."

"It's not like her to go without telling us, is it?"

Abigail shrugged. "Maacah's right. Children grow up and yearn for their own lives. Tamar may be spreading her wings as much as a king's daughter can. I'm sure she'll be back in a day or two with plenty of tales to tell of her adventure."

But Tamar did not return the next day or the day after that. On the third day, Tabytha sent a message to David asking if she could visit Tamar. As soon as his reply came, she packed a few of Tamar's gowns, found a guard to accompany her, and let him lead her to Prince Absalom's house.

It was a fine residence for a prince of his age, standing out from the homes around it by its size—double-storied— and grand entrance pillars, as well as the fact that two men stood guard on either side of them.

One of these went to call the prince.

Absalom emerged, dressed in a fine purple robe. Had he been wearing it in his home or just put it on to impress her? Either way, he was Maacah's son through and through. As he approached, her gaze snagged on his thick, long hair. If only Adonai had blessed *her* with such hair instead of an unruly mass of curls.

"Tabytha, isn't it?"

She drew her gaze away from that hair and inclined her head. "Greetings, Prince Absalom."

The perfect smile he flashed her highlighted his good looks. Yet, the smile lacked the sweetness and warmth of Tamar's.

"I see you bear my father's child. My congratulations."

She flushed uncomfortably under his gaze and said hastily, "I've come to see Tamar. I hear she is staying with you. I brought her some gowns."

"My sister isn't well." He stepped closer, and she caught a whiff of aloe and spice. He took the gowns off her arm. "I'll give them to her."

"What's wrong with her? Is it what ailed Amnon?"

Something darkened in the prince's expression. "I couldn't say."

"Can I see her? I won't stay long."

"She sleeps."

"Has someone been tending to her?"

"My wife."

"Could I just ..."

"I'll tell her you came."

And with that, he turned around and strode off.

She thought of following him, but a glance at the faces of the prince's guards told her she wouldn't succeed.

Tabytha had no alternative but to return to the palace, her mind churning with worry for her friend.

Through the course of Tabytha's life, many had underestimated her determination and persistence. If she could wear down a Levitical priest into teaching her letters, she could surely wear down a young prince into allowing her to see his sister.

Tabytha returned the next day, this time with Pudu's fig cakes.

Again, Absalom barred her entrance, snatching the fig cakes from her hands and promising that Tamar—again sleeping—would receive them.

The day after that, Tabytha returned, this time with the unfinished gown Tamar had been working on. When the prince tried to take it from her, she spun away from him.

"I insist on giving it to her myself, Prince Absalom."

His perfect smile wavered.

"In that case, she will not finish the gown. Now stop bothering me, or I will send a message to my father to take his unruly concubine in hand."

"At the same time, you can explain to him why you are hiding Tamar away from everyone."

She saw a flash of panic in his expression. "I'm not hiding her. She's unwell."

"Even more reason for her to return to the palace where her mother can care for her."

"*Our* mother?" The smile returned, this time filled with genuine humor. "You've met Maacah, have you? A particularly fine dresser, but maternal care is not one of her greatest strengths."

Tabytha acknowledged the truth with a wry smile. "Please, my prince. I won't stay long. I'm worried about her and seeing her would put my heart at ease."

He considered this and finally relented, signaling for her to follow him. He led her to a room, closed by a curtain, and told her to stay outside while he spoke to Tamar. She thought she heard crying through the curtain and then his voice, soft but pleading.

"Come, my sister. Father's concubine is here to see you. Dry your tears. And remember, say nothing of the matter."

Tabytha stepped through the curtain. "What matter?"

The sight of Tamar startled her. The princess sat huddled against the wall, her knees pulled up, her usually beautiful hair unwashed and disheveled. Her eyes were swollen and dark-ringed. All the usual lightness and joy had seeped out of them, replaced with the kind of sorrow Tabytha had only ever seen on the face of the grieving.

"Tamar!" Tabytha ran across the room and dropped to her knees, pulling the princess into her arms and feeling the sobs shudder through her friend's body. "What's wrong, my love? What happened?"

Absalom sighed. "Didn't I tell you to stay outside? She's not in a state to see anyone."

"Leave us alone."

The prince flinched at Tabytha's sharp command. She held his gaze, briefly fearing he might retaliate violently for being addressed as a servant rather than a prince. Yet anger kept her from asking for his pardon. Absalom had denied her request to see Tamar when the girl needed her the most.

She was almost surprised when the prince pulled aside the curtain and left.

Tabytha turned back to Tamar and held her as she wept, stroking her hair and whispering that all would be well. Even then Tabytha feared the words would never again be true for the king's daughter.

When the princess finally quieted, Tabytha drew back a little, placing her hands on Tamar's cheeks and lifting her face so that they were eye to eye. "Please tell me, Tamar. What happened at Amnon's house?"

The look in the girl's eyes at the mention of the name confirmed Tabytha's worst suspicions.

"Come back to the palace. Your family is there, and we will take care of you. Your father will make this right."

A spark of hope kindled in the girl's eyes for the first time that day.

"Do you think so? But Amnon ... after he ..." Tamar closed her eyes and clenched her fists on the fabric of her gown. "He doesn't want me anymore. His servants dragged me out and bolted the door."

A hot rage burned through Tabytha at the thought of Tamar begging the brother who forced himself on her to keep her.

"Your father loves you, Tamar. He is king. He will know what to do."

"But how can I face Abba or Abigail and Ahinoam?" At the mention of Amnon's mother, fresh tears sprang into Tamar's eyes, and she shook her head violently. "I can't. I can't. I am ruined."

"The shame is not yours! It is Amnon's."

Of all she had seen and heard that day, the look in Tamar's eyes at that moment pierced Tabytha the most. Everything that delighted her about Tamar—that sweet, lively, hope-filled girl—was gone, replaced by something worn and world-weary.

"Don't you know?" the princess said. "The shame is always ours."

chapter 26

abigail

extract from scroll ג (hs gimel)

I still remember the night David decided we should leave the wilderness. We were at the fire by the mouth of the cave—David and Ahinoam, Joab and his brother Abishai, and Abiathar, the priest.

"It's those godforsaken Ziphites that betrayed us again, David," Joab said. "We need to deal with them once and for all."

"My fight is not with them." David stared into the flames.

The night before, David's scouts had brought word that Saul and three thousand men camped a mere stone's throw away from us near the hill of Hakilah. Ahinoam had pleaded with David to flee, but that wasn't David's way. Instead, he took a few of his men to the hill above the king's camp in the darkest part of the night. Then he and Abishai snuck right down to where Saul slept.

"Who exactly do you fight?" Joab said. "If, as we all know, it's Saul, you should have let my brother thrust his spear through him instead of merely stealing his water jug.

We could be crowning you king now instead of hiding like animals in a cave."

David said nothing.

"Perhaps you believe Saul this time when he says he will not harm you, that you are like a son to him. Perhaps we can all go and have a merry feast with him tonight."

Abishai lay a restraining hand on his brother's arm. The men stirred uncomfortably. Ahinoam looked away. Only the crackle of the fire broke the silence.

"Enough." For a moment, I thought David reprimanded Joab, but he was looking at me and Ahinoam. "We've been on the run for far too long. We will settle where Saul cannot reach us."

"And where exactly does Saul's long arm not extend, cousin?" Joab asked.

"Philistia," David said. "In the morning, we will leave for Gath."

It took a few days to reach the Elah Valley. David stopped to show us the precise spot where he had brought down Goliath. I followed his gaze to the distant hill city that had been the Philistine giant's home. Gath.

"Will they welcome the killer of their champion?" I asked him softly.

"King Achish is no fool. I am his enemy's enemy, and my men are known for their fighting skills. He will not turn down the offer of our blades."

I wondered if he felt as confident as he sounded.

"And let's not forget the last time King Achish saw David, our celebrated leader was a rather harmless madman," Joab said.

David gave a wry smile. "I can't keep that act up again. If anyone asks, Joab, my madness has been miraculously cured."

Of course, we had been seen from that distant hill. By midday, a large force of Philistines approached us, armed with round shields and impressive spears and swords. David had told me the Philistines were renowned for their iron weapons. Several of the men stood head and shoulders taller than their companions. These were the feared Anakim, the race of giants that had terrified Moses's spies and kept our forebearers from taking the land.

Surprisingly, their leader was a man even shorter than Joab, with a much finer build. He carried no shield and wore only a short blade at his side.

David called his men to a halt and stepped forward to meet him.

"David, I suspected it to be you." The Philistine spoke with a soft voice and a soothing lilt. He assessed our group with an astute gaze. "Your company has grown considerably."

David bowed his head. "Greetings, Prince Iyasala. We come in peace."

"Passing by or on your way to Gath?" the Philistine prince asked.

"I seek an audience with your brother, the king. I wish an alliance with your people against our mutual enemy, Saul."

"I've heard of your troubles with the Hebrew king but also that you spared his life on occasion." The Philistine prince cocked his head to the side thoughtfully. "He is your father-in-law, isn't he?"

David nodded. "But he has sworn to kill me. My men and I come to offer our blades to Gath."

Iyasala considered this for a moment. "In that case, you will not object if Gath takes your blades. Please tell your men to disarm."

"My men will not take kindly—"

"Your men will not enter Gath carrying weapons." He spoke as gently as a mother might to a disappointed child.

David exhaled slowly, then nodded to Joab, who spread the command among the men. Reluctantly, they surrendered their weapons to the Philistines.

"May I say your mind appears better than the last time we met, David?" Iyasala said. "My brother still berates me for allowing a madman into his presence. If I take you to him, I trust you will not start drooling into your beard again?"

"I have not had another such attack," David said tersely.

"I'm sure." Iyasala smiled. "And now, while we gather your men's blades, perhaps you will introduce me to your wives." His gaze found mine. "I heard of the loveliness of the Carmelite widow. For once, the reports were not exaggerated."

"You're as well informed as always." I detected a note of tension in David's voice. Surprisingly, this mild man appeared to make him nervous. "This is my wife Ahinoam." He held out his arm to her before pointing to me. "And Abigail of Carmel."

We both stepped forward and bowed to the Philistine prince, who nodded in acknowledgment.

"Well, let us be on our way. We wouldn't want to delay your happy reunion with my brother. He'll be delighted your mind has returned to you."

Enclosed by Philistine troops, we marched towards Gath. I had never seen such a city. Its high walls spoke of power, its size of prosperity. The city sprawled over the coastal plain, but the summit where the imposing palace of King Achish stood drew my gaze.

Iyasala stopped and addressed David. "Your men will stay here, guarded by mine. You may accompany me to an audience with my brother." His gaze snagged on me. "And your Carmelite wife will come too. Achish has always been partial to beautiful women."

"I insist on coming." Joab stepped forward. "Let's leave the woman behind as we discuss men's business."

Iyasala studied Joab impassively. "I recall you—the outspoken, impetuous one. Joel, was it?"

"Joab," he said stiffly.

"You are to David what I am to my brother, so I will allow you to attend your leader. The Carmelite comes too." He turned and strode away. Three men—his personal bodyguard, I assumed—followed closely behind him, one of them a giant.

David, Joab, and I peeled away from our company.

"We're completely at their mercy," Joab whispered to David. "They have us surrounded, *and* they have our weapons."

"What did you expect? We have come to plead for our lives."

"Our sworn enemies." Joab watched the giant with the broad back ahead of us. "And we're walking right into their lair. Perhaps you are a madman after all."

"When will you stop questioning my every decision?"

Joab said nothing.

Prince Iyasala led us through a massive gate in the thick walls. Everything about this city appeared large. The young soldiers at the gate bowed to the prince, but most looked at us with impassive faces. We passed a large temple, many impressive dwellings, and a building that rang with the clang and hammering of metalwork. We made our way through a busy market, where I admired tables of beautifully decorated pottery and exotic fabrics.

The path climbed steeply upwards to an inner wall protecting the summit fort. More guards stood watch here. The prince led us across a courtyard, where several soldiers dueled with dulled blades. Most stopped and watched us, this time with greater hostility than the guards at the gate to the city. These men, at least, appeared to recognize David.

Inside the buttressed fortress, we were taken directly to the king's quarters. I felt uncomfortable in this foreign, male domain, but David—glancing at me—took my hand and squeezed it briefly. Some of my courage returned.

King Achish, standing by a large window that commanded a sweeping view of the city and the Elah valley, turned as we entered. A large, barrel-chested man with a thick beard, his bearing was that of a powerful king.

"Well, well. As you thought, brother. The infamous David in the flesh." Loud and jovial, I wondered if the king was a little drunk despite the early hour.

David knelt on one knee. "It is a pleasure to see you again, King Achish."

Joab stepped forward, too, and sank into a bow, but Achish paid him no heed. He was watching me.

"You come with a gift for me, David?"

Prince Iyasala, standing beside me, said dryly, "Not for you, I'm afraid. This is David's wife, the Carmelite we had reports about."

Achish bellowed with laughter. "You tease me, brother. Bringing this pearl of great beauty into my presence, only to tell me I cannot have her."

"David has come to pledge himself and his men to you." Iyasala's smile belied his calculating words. "It would pay him to remember that should he fail in his duties, say if he has another bout of madness or still secretly serves his old master Saul, you—as his vassal lord—will have first rights to *all* his treasures."

I understood then why Prince Iyasala had brought me to the fort and why he made David so nervous.

"In that case, let us hope madness prevails." The Philistine king picked up a stone goblet, held it high in salute, and took a long swig.

chapter 27

Tabytha found Abigail in the Women's Courtyard, laughing with Ahinoam and Pudu. "Abigail? Can I speak to you?" She had cried all the way home. "Alone."

The woman took one look at her and quickly rose to her feet. The others cast her worried glances.

Tabytha couldn't meet Ahinoam's gaze. How would she react when she learned what her son had done?

"Let's go to my quarters." Once they were in Abigail's room, she said, "Is it the babe? Are you bleeding?"

"No. The babe is fine."

"Thank Adonai." Relief washed over Abigail's face. "What then, Tabytha? Is it your mother?"

"It's Tamar. I saw her."

"Tamar," Abigail said, confused. "Is she ill?"

Tabytha shook her head. Suddenly, she understood why Tamar had hidden away all these days. How could she possibly put into words what had happened, this most terrible thing?

"Amnon, he ... Amnon took her against her will."

"He took her from Absalom's house?" Abigail's brow furrowed in confusion.

"He forced himself on her. When David sent her to cook for him."

"Forced himself? You mean ...?" Understanding finally dawned on Abigail's face. She took a step back from Tabytha. "No. No, he wouldn't do that. Not to his own sister. Not to any woman."

"He did, Abigail. I saw her. She's completely ..." Tabytha couldn't even think of a word to describe Tamar. "She's like a pot shattered into a hundred pieces. Broken." Actual pain stabbed through Tabytha as she realized the truth in the words. "Amnon has completely broken her."

"No."

"We must tell David."

"No." Abigail gripped her arm so tightly it hurt. "This is a misunderstanding. Surely, we women can resolve this between us."

"How? We can't undo this. No one can undo this."

"Give me time to think. This is a shocking accusation. We'll find a way to ..."

"To what? Hide it like Absalom wants her to do? No. David must hear of this. He'll know what to do with Amnon."

"With Amnon?" Abigail shook her head decisively. "He's David's firstborn. Crown prince. Nothing can be done to Amnon."

"But he ..."

"If this rumor spreads, it could ruin him."

"Ruin *him*?" Anger flared up in Tabytha. "He did this to Tamar, yet you're worried about *him*?"

"We don't know what happened between them, Tabytha. Neither of us was there."

"You think Tamar is lying? Why would she lie about this? Her life, her dreams, her future ... all gone. No. She wouldn't lie."

"But I know Amnon. He was always such a good boy."

"He's not your and Ahinoam's little boy anymore. He's a man." *An arrogant man who believes he is entitled to take anything he wants.* "You know Tamar. She wouldn't lie about this."

Abigail sat down on her bench and put her head in her hands. When she finally looked up, there were tears in her eyes.

"This will tear David's house apart, Tabytha."

Till then, Tabytha had only thought about Tamar, but Abigail's words rang with an ominous truth. She sat down next to her and took hold of her hand. They sat in silence, Tabytha thinking, Abigail weeping softly for all that had been—and all that would still be—lost.

They went together to see the king. Tabytha felt glad not to go alone. A guard led them to a small room in the old part of the palace, where David held counsel with Joab and several of his palace administrators.

David rose when they arrived, his expression grave. "A few moments, please, men. We will finish this later."

"My lady," the men murmured, bowing towards Abigail as they left.

Only Joab remained standing at David's side. "It's unusual to interrupt important administrative discussions for trifling women's matters, my king."

"This is no trifling matter." Abigail walked over to David and gripped his arm. "Send him away, David."

"If it's truly important, he'll want me to hear it too," Joab said.

"Leave us, Joab," David said, not taking his gaze off Abigail's face.

"As you wish, my king." Joab inclined his head, glaring at Tabytha as he passed her.

"I'm sorry, David," Abigail whispered.

David looked from her to Tabytha. "Have you lost the babe, Tabytha?"

Tabytha shook her head.

"We wouldn't interrupt you for that," Abigail said.

"It's what I feared," he said. "But what's worse than losing a child? Just tell me."

Abigail looked away as she said, "Amnon lay with Tamar when she went to bake for him."

David said nothing. Only the smallest clenching of his jaw betrayed his emotion. "Forced or willingly?"

"Forced," Tabytha said. "She begged him not to, and afterward, she begged him not to throw her out, but he did anyway."

He turned away from them and walked to the small window overlooking the valley. He put his hands against the stone wall and lowered his head.

They stood in silence for a long time. Finally, he turned around, his expression as cold as flint.

"Where is she?"

"With Absalom," Tabytha said. "I went to see her. She is ... broken."

Grief flickered in David's eyes.

Tabytha remembered the first time she had seen Tamar flinging her arms around her father's neck. The way he had smiled at her. He loved her deeply, no doubt about it. He would do the right thing.

"What are we to do?" Abigail asked. "We need to tell Maacah. And Ahinoam."

"Yes, but ..." He shook his head. "They will ..." He looked up at them almost pleadingly. "What will it do to them? To our family?"

"Tear us apart," Abigail said softly.

"Out of your own household, I am going to bring calamity upon you," David said. "Those were the words Adonai spoke through Nathan after I sinned with Bathsheba. After I ..." He closed his eyes. "Killed a friend. The prophet's words are coming true."

"This is not your fault, my king." Tabytha stepped towards him, taking his large hand into both her own. "Amnon must pay the price."

"How can I make him pay for a lesser sin than my own?"

"This isn't the same as you and Bathsheba, David," Abigail said softly.

"Her husband perished on the battlefield. At my command. What sin can compare with that?"

Shock jarred through Tabytha. Could David truly have done something like that? Still, this wasn't about what David had done but about what Amnon had done.

"Amnon must surely be punished, my lord?" Tabytha said. "This terrible act against Tamar demands a price."

David looked from Tabytha to Abigail, his gaze finally resting on his wife. "No one will have Tamar now. No amount of tears will change that. But must we ruin Amnon's future, too?"

chapter 28

ABIGAIL

EXTRACT FROM SCROLL ג (hs GIMEL)

Those months in Gath were strange, unsettled ones. We lived in the fortress palace of King Achish, along with about forty of David's men and their families. The rest of our company stayed in the Philistine barracks at the lower gate or camped outside the city walls with our flocks.

As David's wives, Ahinoam and I were given special privileges. We ate with King Achish's wives and concubines and often accompanied them to the market. The Philistine women were civil but not warm towards us, and Ahinoam and I found ourselves drawn together more often. Our friendship deepened.

I did not like this inactive life. I yearned for the wilderness days of fetching water, milking goats, baking bread, laughing with the men around the fire, and speaking to David about the words and ways of Adonai. But Ahinoam and I hardly saw him, for the Philistine king kept him busy and close to him at all times.

I did not fully understand the motives of King Achish, but one new moon celebration, I had the opportunity to observe his interaction with David. Once a month, a large feast was prepared for the entire king's household. The women ate at their own tables, but on this night, King Achish, loud and cheery, declared that his two senior wives and the two wives of David should sit at the royal table.

"Let us see all these beauties side by side!" he bellowed.

Four men were shifted to other tables, and we dutifully took their place. Ahinoam and I hardly spoke, but King Achish's wives drank freely, spoke seductively, and laughed loudly. Prince Iyasala, seated on the king's right, said nothing but, I suspected, observed all. Sitting on the king's left, David smiled and interacted courteously with the king and his wives, but I sensed his discomfort was as great as mine, particularly when the younger of the king's wives directed her flirtations to him.

The king had noticed this, too, but from his reaction, he hardly seemed to care. "Salum knows a good man when she sees one, don't you, my dear?" He laughed.

"You are the best of all men, my love," his wife purred.

"But you rate David a close second?"

The woman lowered her chin and smiled coquettishly at David. "A very close second."

David looked away.

Ahinoam gripped my hand and whispered, "This is disgraceful. How can the king allow this?"

"He encourages it. He's drunk."

The king had noticed our whispering. "Your wives have something to say. Perhaps your beautiful Carmelite finds me the best of men too?"

I looked down at my plate and said nothing.

"Don't be shy, lovely pearl," the king said. "I am David's liege lord and therefore your lord too. I demand you answer me."

I locked eyes with him. "I only have one lord, King Achish, and that is Adonai, the one true God. I answer only to him. He has made me the wife of David, his anointed one. I would not dishonor Adonai or my husband by speaking to you as your wife speaks to David."

A discomforting silence descended. I glanced at David, but he did not meet my gaze. *What had I done?* To shame a man was dangerous. To shame a king could prove fatal. David and his entire company might pay the price for my words.

King Achish's face darkened like a sky before a storm.

Only Prince Iyasala looked at me. Was there amusement in that perceptive look? "Well, this is entertaining." He broke the taut silence. "A woman of noble bearing who speaks her mind even to a powerful king. You have a treasure here, David, no doubt."

King Achish's wives tittered nervously. The king released a long, pent-up breath and turned to a servant, demanding more wine. David finally looked up at me. I read no anger in his eyes.

Perhaps the initial danger had passed, but my words had ruined the jaunty banter at the table. King Achish said little after that, casting occasional brooding looks at his wives. They, too, were subdued. David asked questions about the trade in the city and the capacity of the iron forge. Iyasala's answers were short and uninformative, those of a man wary of giving information to an enemy.

Much earlier than usual, the Philistine king rose and declared the feast over. Ahinoam and I escaped back to our quarters.

On our way past Salum's room, we heard low, angry words and a plaintive woman's voice. A while later, a cry of pain hinted that Achish's anger had found its target—his flirtatious wife, Salum.

I lay on my bedroll, restlessly replaying the night's events in my mind, when David slipped into the room.

"Abi?" he whispered, putting down the clay oil lamp he carried.

"David!" I clambered to my feet and into the safety of his arms. "I'm sorry."

He held me tightly, silently stroking my hair. I rested my head against his chest, breathing in his warmth, allowing the sense of his strength to quiet my unease.

"I was foolish tonight. Forgive me," I said.

"There is nothing to forgive, my love. Achish forced you to answer. You merely spoke the truth."

"But he could have ..." I shook my head, not wanting to think or speak of what might have been. What might still be if the king's anger rekindled.

"There is much he could have done, but Adonai honored your courage and integrity tonight. He kept us all safe." David continued, "You put me to shame tonight. Not in the way you think," he said as I stiffened. "No. You reminded me I should speak the truth courageously. To put my trust in Adonai instead of trusting my own wiles and ways of finding favor with the king."

"Sometimes I wish we were back in the wilderness. At times, Gath feels more dangerous than the desert."

"We are among dangerous men," David acknowledged. "Many of them still hate me for killing their champion. But they won't move against us if we are under Achish's protection."

"He's a drunk, David. And erratic. There's no knowing what he might do."

"No. He's nothing like King Saul with his violent rages. Achish drinks too much, but it makes him talk more and laugh louder. He is growing to trust me. Yesterday, he even talked about making me his bodyguard. That's not something you say to a man you fear might stab you in the back."

"What of Iyasala?"

David looked towards the small window. A few lights shone in the city below.

"What do you think of him?" It always warmed me when he asked what I thought. Nabal had never valued my opinions. "You're an observant woman, Abi. What do you make of Achish's brother?"

I closed my eyes and imagined that mild-mannered, soft-spoken man.

"He's clever." I opened my eyes again. "And sees everything. He also has a lot of influence over the king."

"Yes. He may be more dangerous than Achish. We must not make an enemy of him."

"But tonight, he protected me." I thought back to that moment with a rush of gratitude. "He protected *us*."

David nodded again thoughtfully. "I do wonder what he had to gain."

chapter 29

The first woman Abigail and Tabytha told about Tamar was Ahinoam. She stared blankly at the two of them as if she hadn't heard or understood their words.

Abigail reached for her hand and gently said, "Ahinoam, did you hear what I said? Tamar claims that ..."

"I heard you." Ahinoam gripped her chest. "It's not true. It's a lie."

Tabytha was about to speak, but Abigail shook her head, so she bit down her defense of Tamar. Ahinoam needed time to accept this. Tabytha rose and slipped from the room, looking back at the two women, heads bowed together, whispering to each other.

She waited outside the room for Abigail. They'd agreed to tell Maacah together, too. That might be even more difficult than telling Ahinoam.

Abigail finally appeared, her face streaked with tears. They walked in solemn silence to Maacah's room.

"I wish it didn't fall on us to tell Maacah," Abigail said as they neared the room.

"David should do it. She's his wife and Tamar, their child. He could comfort her in a way we can't."

"No. These are women's matters."

They stood outside Maacah's door by then, both unwilling to do what had to be done. Abigail's hand shook slightly as she lifted it to knock.

Maacah opened the door sooner than either of them wished she would. "You two again. What now?"

"Can we come in? We have news of Tamar," Tabytha said when Abigail didn't immediately answer.

Maacah's eyes widened. "Is she ill?"

"Please, Maacah." Abigail finally spoke. "Sit down, and we'll tell you."

"She's dead!" Maacah's voice rose hysterically at the last word.

"She's not dead." Abigail took Maacah by the arm and led her back into the room. Tabytha followed.

Maacah's room was as beautiful as Tabytha had heard, filled with fine furnishings and expensive-looking objects. But the silky orange fabric draped over the window darkened the room, and the cloying smell of perfume felt oppressive. Tabytha had the overwhelming urge to run from the stifling room, to escape David's palace and this terrible news of which she had become the reluctant bearer. She wanted to run into the valley of her childhood, back to vast skies, wild spaces, and carefree innocence. Into the strong arms of her mother. Away. Away. Away.

A keening sound drew her back to the present. Maacah lay crumpled on the floor, Abigail kneeling beside her.

"David says he'll provide for her every need," Abigail said. "She'll be able to stay with Absalom for the rest of her life."

Maacah's wail filled the room and pounded painfully into Tabytha. It resonated with her own unbearable grief for her friend.

"Hush, Maacah. All the palace will hear," Abigail said.

"No," Tabytha said. "Don't silence her, Abigail. This is the only response to what has happened to Tamar. We should all lament. All tear our clothes to shreds and weep for that beautiful young girl lost to the world. We should not take this quietly and hush it up to protect the one who did this to her. No! We should ... we *will* wail out our grief for all Jerusalem to hear."

And Tabytha went down on her knees, threw her arms around the grieving mother, and finally gave voice to all the pain and anger inside her.

Before nightfall, everyone in the palace knew of Tamar and Amnon, and the following day, Jerusalem was astir with the shameful news.

Just as Abigail had predicted, the house of David tore along the inevitable fault lines of such a complex family.

Ahinoam vehemently defended her son. Tamar had slept with another man, she claimed, but on fearing the discovery of her lost purity, she and her mother devised the evil story against Amnon. After all, everyone knew that Maacah held a grudge against Ahinoam and would do anything to ruin her son.

Not many believed this version of events, but those who did spread Ahinoam's claims with relish. Gilia, loudest of all, always enjoyed a story that cast people in the worst possible light. Under Gilia's influence and too absorbed in caring for Bashemath to hold an opposing view to her outspoken friend, Suta claimed to believe it, too.

Ahinoam's loyal friends, Abigail and Pudu, had raised Amnon as one of their own. Although they did not believe Ahinoam's claims against Tamar, between themselves they speculated if Tamar had encouraged her brother's attention. "Isn't it true," Pudu said, "that Maacah always dressed the girl in the richest, loveliest gowns? No wonder she drew her brother's gaze. He is a man, after all."

Abital, who had always looked down on Maacah because she was not a Hebrew, claimed that what had befallen Tamar reflected Adonai's judgment on David's union with a woman of impure blood. "Maacah's children were cursed by God—Tamar and Absalom alike." To the few wives Abital deigned to speak, she was fond of saying, "Watch and wait. Adonai is not yet done judging Maacah's offspring."

Besides Pudu, Gilia, and Suta, most of the concubines sided with Maacah and Tamar, but their interest soon faded. Only Tabytha had been particularly close to the princess. The others had their own concerns. Tamar's situation occupied almost all their discussion for a week or two, and then they went back to talking about other matters.

Haggith was the only wife who wept on hearing the news. She sought out Tabytha and asked after Tamar and if there was anything they could do for the girl. Bathsheba, too, had surprised Tabytha. The aloof wife had pressed a small item into Tabytha's hand as she passed her in a passage. "A gift for Tamar from Solomon." Tabytha's eyes filled with tears when she saw the boy's rough carving of a horse's head.

The evenings grew somber and quiet in the palace. They no longer gathered as a group in the Women's Courtyard. Only the small children still played there, with one or two of the younger mothers keeping watch. David did not come for meals anymore. He did not visit Tamar. He rebuffed all Maacah's attempts to speak to him. Many weeks passed before he sent for Ahinoam.

Above all, he refused to speak out against Amnon, his son and heir.

Tabytha could not easily forgive him for that. *Perhaps this is what happened to Michal. Perhaps even true love could erode with the passing of time and the growing of disappointment.*

chapter 30

ABIGAIL

extract from scroll ג (hs gimel)

The night I spoke so plainly to King Achish changed everything but not—as I had feared—for the worse. Instead, that night set in motion the events that took us away from the Philistine city. Perhaps that night Achish wearied of our presence in his citadel or possibly Iyasala saw a way to be rid of us. Following that night, David, more trusting of Adonai's protective hand than ever before, grew bolder in his interaction with the king.

The very next day, David asked for an audience with Achish. Later, he told me that the words he had spoken to Achish had simply come to him as if Adonai had put them in his mouth.

"What did you say?" I asked.

"If I have found favor in your eyes, let a place be assigned to me in one of the country towns, that I may live there," David replied as if the words were still imprinted on his lips by Adonai. "Why should your servant live in the royal city with you?"

I marveled at David's directness and brashness but even more at Achish's response. The king had apparently looked at his brother, Iyasala, and then nodded as if the two of them had reached some unspoken agreement.

"I will give you Ziklag," the king said without hesitation. "It's a small town, half a day's walk from Gath. You can build it up and protect our lands from Judah's raids. In fact," Achish added, "it will make a strategic base for you to raid into Saul's territory."

David said he had felt the prince's gaze on him, gauging his reaction to the statement.

He had tried to hide his aversion to the suggestion that he attack his own countrymen. Instead, he bowed low and thanked Achish for his generosity, all the while praising Adonai in his heart.

David wasted no time putting out the word to his men. Three days later, our company—men, women, children, and animals—began the journey eastwards. I remember Ahinoam and I singing a few lines of Miriam's song, so glad were we to leave the oppressive Philistine city. "Who among the gods is like you, Lord? Who is like you—majestic in holiness, awesome in glory, working wonders? You stretch out your right hand, and the earth swallows your enemies. In your unfailing love, you will lead the people you have redeemed. In your strength, you will guide them to your holy dwelling."

More and more voices joined in, and as we sang, our journey transformed from a move to a country town into a declaration of faith and hope. We felt it. We all felt Adonai's mighty hand at work.

Ziklag lay at the base of the Judean hills, a cluster of stone buildings occupied mainly by Philistine farmers and a small posting of Achish's warriors. The Philistines met our arrival warily. They appeared glad for the added protection of six hundred armed men, but we read mistrust in their eyes.

David worked hard to put their doubts to rest. Not a Philistine was to be harmed, not a home to be invaded, not a woman to be slept with, he warned his men on threat of death. Only good reports should reach Achish's ears. In our times alone, David confided his suspicions that one or two of the warriors were Iyasala's spies.

Our men set about hewing rock from the hills and building homes. We women helped where we could, usually tending and watering the flocks to allow the men time to build. How good to be away from Gath. Within a few months, David, Ahinoam, and I lived in our own two-roomed house with a small courtyard. Jacoba's sister, the only one of my women not yet wed to one of David's warriors, stayed with us while Jacoba's husband built the house they would all move into.

I delighted in managing a home again and fell back into it with ease. I traded one of our Philistine neighbors a goat kid for barley and wheat seed and set about planting my crops. David laughed at this, saying he hoped we wouldn't be here long enough to see multiple yields.

My heart, however, yearned to settle down, have a child, and live in peace in this remote, beautiful place where I could convince myself we were safe from Saul's hatred, Iyasala's schemes, and Achish's power.

For a while, my dream felt within reach.

Ahinoam's monthly bleeding stopped, and I rejoiced with her even when jealousy whispered to my heart, "Why couldn't it be me?" The men began to go out for long periods, always returning with sheep, cattle, donkeys, camels, and clothes. David was generous to the Philistines among us. They gratefully accepted his gifts, never asking where they came from. But on his regular visits to Gath, Achish—another recipient of David's generosity—was less circumspect. "Where did you go raiding this time?" he would ask, and David would answer, "The Negev of Judah," or "The Negev of Jerahmeel," or "The Negev of the Kenites."

He always told the king he raided in the east, against our own brethren and homeland, but I knew he didn't go east. I knew where his loyalties lay and once overheard him telling his men to take plunder to the elders of Judah. He directed them to take a circuitous route and ensure not to be followed by any of Iyasala's spies.

We only talked about it once.

I lay in his arms as he traced his finger down my forehead, my nose, my lips. These were the moments, the perfect moments, when I feared losing him. "You must stop, my love," I said.

He drew away, a bemused smile on his face. "I thought you liked it."

"I like *that*." I laughed. Then I grew serious again. "You must stop the raids, David. Soon Iyasala will discover you're not going to the Negev."

"He won't."

"But undoubtedly a report will reach him."

"Trust me, it won't." He sat up abruptly and I berated myself for ruining the intimate moment. He swung his legs off the sleeping pallet and stood up.

"How can it not David?"

He turned back to me. The expression on his face was one I had seen only once before, in that valley near Carmel, on the first day we met. Cold. Ruthless. Frightening. Then I understood—there was no-one left to send a report.

"Even the women?" I whispered.

"One day, I will be king of this land. Every enemy I kill now is one I don't have to kill then," David said before stalking from my bed.

I tried to see it his way. *The plunder of an enemy,* I thought when I looked at the sheep and cattle, the donkeys, and camels. But when I washed a patched garment, I thought *mother* and when I wiped dried blood off a pair of small sandals, I thought *child.*

INTERLUDE

TABYTHA
EXTRACT FROM SCROLL ג (HS ALEF)

All these years later, I try to untangle my feelings for David. As a child, I feared him. As his young wife, I adored him. But something eroded in me over time. After Tamar, I could no longer see him with Abigail's blind, shining devotion, but neither did I want to see him through Michal's eyes—as ruthless, selfish, and uncaring.

Even now, after all that's happened to me, after all that he did, I will not think of him that way.

I remember Abigail once describing David as a complex man. Perhaps this explains my contrasting emotions. He was the man who stirred passion in me, who I shared every part of myself with—thoughts, writings and dreams. He was the one who awoke in me a love of words and poetry. He was the father of my son.

But he was also the one who discarded those who loved him as easily as a worn-out garment. At first, I thought he didn't care enough. With the insight of years, I think the truth is that he cared too much. Perhaps for such a man, it is easier never to look one you love in the eye again rather than to look and see their pain.

Sometimes, that thought comforts me. Sometimes, I am angry, that even with all his power and courage, he was not stronger in the ways that mattered, in the ways that might have saved Tamar and Suta and me. In the ways of the heart.

But even after Tamar, I remember good times with him, tender times that still fill me with a pang of longing.

Once, just before Beninu's birth, he sent for me and helped me lower my heavy body onto the terrace cushions.

"Listen to these lines from my song, Tabytha. I wrote them after I felt our child move."

We had reclined in the same place a few weeks earlier, and he had laid both his hands on my belly as the baby kicked. We had laughed together, marveling at this hidden masterpiece growing inside me. Finally, he had closed his eyes and prayed for our child, that he would be born healthy and strong and that Adonai's favor would rest on him.

That second time, he strummed his lyre and began to sing. These are the words of that song. Still, they move me to tears:

"For you created my inmost being; you knit me together in my mother's womb. I praise you because I am fearfully and wonderfully made; your works are wonderful; I know that full well. My frame was not hidden from you when I was made in the secret place, when I was woven together in the depths of the earth. Your eyes saw my unformed body; all the days ordained for me were written in your book before one of them came to be."

If I close my eyes, I can still see him with that lyre, face to the sky, his resonant voice singing words of praise inspired by our unborn child.

But I always have to open my eyes again, and the reality of where I am—and who put me here—comes rushing over me like a startling splash of winter rain.

pArt 2

15 years since King David conquered Jebus,
to rule the twelve tribes of Israel
from within its mighty walls

chapter 31

"Mine!"

Beninu stood with bunched fists and a trembling lip as Shobab mockingly held his wooden toy out of reach.

Tabytha looked up from the small table at which she sat with Miriam, Haggith's daughter. At Haggith's request, she was teaching the girl to read and write. Two years older than Solomon, the princess had her half-brother's keen intelligence and confidence, and quickly mastered every lesson.

"Shobab's always been mean to the little ones." Miriam sounded older than her twelve years. "Don't worry, Sol's there. He'll make it right."

As the girl predicted, Tabytha watched Solomon snatch the toy away from his brother and pass it back to Beninu. It was, in fact, a toy he himself had made for the young boy.

Miriam let out a self-satisfied huff. "See? Sol loves being the judge of everyone."

"I'm glad of it today."

Beninu toddled over to the table where they sat and pushed himself into his mother's side. "Sab naughty," he grumbled, glancing back at the prince, who appeared to be receiving a stern lecture from Solomon. Tabytha pressed her face into his dark curls and breathed in his sweet, warm smell.

"You're strange." Miriam watched her closely. "What smells nice about a boy?"

Tabytha laughed. "Let's carry on. Read the next line."

The girl slowly but meticulously formed the words, and Tabytha felt a rush of pleasure. She wondered if Ahio had liked instructing her as much as she did Miriam. She suspected he had. Ahio had the gentle patience of a natural teacher. Where was he now? Perhaps David could ...

"Tabytha?" Miriam looked at her impatiently.

"What?"

"You didn't hear a word I said, did you?"

"No. Sorry."

Miriam sighed. Tabytha liked the girl, but sometimes, it was difficult to believe she was Haggith's child. She had none of her mother's mild, soft-spoken ways. "I'm named after a great prophetess," she had told Tabytha more than once. "Prophets must always speak their minds."

"I asked how old you were when you learned to read," Miriam said.

"A little younger than you. Why?"

"Sol was younger too. If my mother had let you teach me when you first arrived, I'd be as good as him now."

"It's not a contest." Although with Miriam, most things were. "It also took me a long time to convince Ahio to teach me."

"And I'm tired of reading Abba's songs."

"Really?" Tabytha felt a little affronted at this.

"I want to start reading Moses's writing," the girl continued. "He was our greatest prophet, and I want to read as many prophecies as possible. Don't you find prophecies amazing?"

Tabytha shrugged. She didn't care to know the future. In her experience, things grew more difficult with the passing of time. Prophecies unsettled—whereas poetry soothed—one's soul.

"Sol says he's read everything Moses wrote." The girl glared at Solomon, now lining up all the children to play a game he had invented. Beninu had wandered back, too, standing at a distance from the older ones. "But he says the priest won't give the scrolls to a girl to read. Sol says they're too sacred for a girl to touch. That I'll *defile* them. Can you believe it?"

Tabytha laughed. She *could* believe a priest saying that. Ahio had been an unusual one to treat her with such respect.

"It's not funny." Miriam glowered at her.

"I know, but what can we do? That's how things are. The best thing is for you to learn to read and write. Then, one day, you can write your thoughts and maybe change someone else's."

"But women won't be able to read my thoughts, and men probably won't think they're worth reading."

"So, you think I'm wasting my time recording the stories of the women?"

She was now recording Michal, Abigail, and Ahinoam's stories. After Tamar, Ahinoam asked Tabytha if she would write down hers too. Tabytha had said yes, not because she wanted to hear it but because she thought it might be good for Ahinoam to talk. At times, though, recording all the glowing things Ahinoam said about Amnon felt like a betrayal of Tamar.

"No, it's a good thing," Miriam said. "Ima says those who record history shape it too."

Haggith had said that? Perhaps, under Haggith's dreamy exterior, stood a bedrock of strength.

"So, you'll ask Abba?"

"Ask him what?"

"For the scrolls."

"What scrolls?"

"Tabytha!" Miriam pounded her fists on the table. "Moses's scrolls."

"Ah. I suppose. When I see him." She flushed a little, too ashamed to admit it had been close to three months since David sent for her. It wasn't only her, though. Since Tamar, David had cut himself off from most of his wives and concubines. Only Abigail and Bathsheba still saw him regularly. "I'll ask Abigail. She sees him more than I do."

She considered telling Miriam to ask David for the scrolls herself, but the children also hardly ever saw him. Only on feast days did he still come to bless his family. Beninu was growing up without his father. He would scarcely know him. This thought made Tabytha even sadder than the loneliness she experienced herself.

"Are you crying?" Miriam asked

"No." She quickly wiped away the offending tear. "Carry on reading."

Miriam did as she was told, but Tabytha struggled to pay attention. She watched her little boy tagging behind the other children. How could one love another as fiercely as she loved him? From the moment the midwife had laid him, soft and so surprisingly warm, on her chest, she had felt it. She thought back to her first glimpse of him. His dark, wet hair. His earnest eyes squinting up at her. His pinched mouth and the small mewling sounds that had replaced his first lusty cries.

As the midwife handed him to her, she had asked what name the king bestowed on the child. "Beninu," Tabytha said, not admitting that David had told her to choose a name. Already, the king appeared distant from the child. Beninu might be her first son, but he was one of many for David. Beninu. *Our son.* Had she chosen the name to remind herself or David that the boy was jointly theirs?

As Miriam's voice faltered over her father's words, Tabytha wondered if David had chosen the names of his older sons or his beloved Bathsheba's sons.

"What does this say?" Miriam's voice broke through Tabytha's thoughts.

She leaned over the scroll. "Cherubim."

"Those are the ones that have swords and guard the entrance to the Garden of Eden," Miriam expounded. "Abital told me about them. Do you know that there's a prophecy that one of Adam's offspring will crush that serpent Satan for good?" The girl stamped her foot to illustrate the point, grinding a small, imaginary foe into the ground with her heel. "And Abital says that he will be of Abba's line. Did you know that?"

Tabytha shook her head.

"No, you wouldn't. You're a Jebusite."

She heard Abital's condescending tone in the words. It was to be expected, Tabytha thought, that David's most religious wife would talk to the girl who believed herself destined to be a prophetess. She did hope Haggith didn't allow Miriam to spend too much time with the haughty woman.

"Keep reading, Miriam. I must go bathe Beninu."

The princess bent over the scroll again, her finger finding the place where she had stopped. "He made …

darkness his ... co ... vering," she continued, and Tabytha's mind returned to those first moments with her son.

Only the midwife had been there to witness his arrival into the world.

"Could you let Abigail know my child is born?" Tabytha had asked her.

"In the morning," the stoic woman had replied. "She won't thank me for waking her if there's no need."

There is a need, Tabytha wanted to say, longing for someone who cared to mark the moment with her, to look on her child with the delight she felt.

She knew now what she had only begun to realize then—that Beninu, *our son*, had only ever been hers.

chapter 32

ahinoam

extract from scroll ᴛ (hs dalet)

Abigail caught Amnon as he slid from my womb. She was the one who slapped him on the buttocks to elicit his first angry intake of air. She cleaned and swaddled him and lay him in my arms, and her tears of joy and wonder mirrored my own as he latched onto my breast. As he grew older, he would lift his arms to her as much as he did to me. Until the age of five, he called us both Ima, only stopping when Abigail's little Daniel told him—with pudgy clenched fists—that she was only *his* Ima.

Amnon was David's firstborn. And David, Abigail, and I loved him fiercely.

Perhaps this is surprising to Hebrews who know the story of Leah and Rachel—sisters who were jealous of each other and fought for their husband, Jacob's, affection. It was never like that with Abigail and me. Of course, I was sad when David told me he had sent for her, but I was not surprised.

He first spoke of her on the day he and his men returned from their mission to destroy Nabal. Instead of stories of vengeance and blood, I heard of a woman who had bowed at his feet, brought him donkeys laden with supplies, and spoken of Adonai's plans for him. I could see the admiration in his eyes as he spoke of her, and envy stirred in me, but she had a husband of her own, so I soon forgot about the woman from Carmel.

Then came word that her husband was dead. David acted immediately and only told me once his messengers had left that he had sent for her. I cried. *Wasn't I enough for him? Why hadn't he told me? What did she have to offer him that I couldn't?*

I didn't understand why David wanted her. He had married me because my father opposed Saul and—more importantly—was wealthy. My father gave us livestock when we wed and readily supplied us all we needed. What would this Abigail bring to David? Her wealth had belonged to her husband, and surely his heir would not be our benefactor.

But the first time I saw her, walking by David's side towards the fire where we were baking bread, I knew she had the bearing of royalty. She looked *right,* walking by his side in a way I never would. Him, handsome and strong. Her, fine-boned and attractive. They had an elegant compatibility that drew everyone's gaze. I wanted to detest her at that moment. But not only did she look like a king's consort, she had the grace of one too. Her soft-spoken words were insightful and over time, I fell under her spell as much as David had.

David, too, had a role to play in our friendship. Unlike Jacob, who had clearly favored Rachel, David took care to give both of us his time and affection. I remember those early days with fondness. Later, when Maacah joined us, things changed, for she tried to dominate David. And with every woman he added after that, our share of him lessened. So even though not easy, our wilderness time was good, perhaps even the best time we had.

Still, in the early days, I secretly hoped wilderness living would defeat Abigail. Life in a cave among rough men, always aware that the deadly king of Israel pursued us, brought strain. Yet under that fine, delicate exterior, Abigail had a down-to-earth toughness that surprised me.

I once saw a flower blooming in the wilderness. Its yellow and orange bell-shaped petals were the most beautiful thing I'd ever seen. Something about that flower reminds me of Abigail. She, too, thrived in the starkness of that Judean wilderness, her loveliness even more evident because of the harsh surroundings.

I saw the same strength in her when she faced down the king of Gath that night we sat at his table, and his wife flirted with David. But let me tell you when Abigail's quick wit and strength saved me and Amnon from certain death.

After we had left Gath and settled in Ziklag, the Philistine king often called David to fight for him. On one such day, David and his men left to fight with Achish against Israel. David wasn't happy about it, but he kept saying that Adonai would make a way for them not to bloody their swords with their brothers' blood. They'd only been gone about three or four days when we saw the dust cloud rising in the south.

I still remember the wave of dread that washed through me, particularly for the baby growing inside me. Fear coursed through the camp as that cloud grew closer. No men remained in the camp, only a few old Philistines. How would we women defend ourselves and our children? Knowing that the approaching party came from the land of our people's great enemies—the Amalekites—only added to our terror.

But Abigail stepped into the middle of the turmoil of crying children and whimpering women, calling out, "Shalom. We are under Adonai's protection. Stop crying and listen to my instructions." Surprisingly, everyone quietened. She told the women to bring all the food and wine they had in their tents. We were to set a feast for the invaders, she said. They might not treat us as enemies if we treated them as guests. When everyone had left to do as she said, Abigail pulled me aside.

"Go with Hannah and put on one of her largest, oldest robes to hide your babe. Stay near the back, out of sight. Do not tell them you are David's wife."

Hannah was a large woman, and her clothes were plainer than ours.

By the time the large group of Amalekites arrived, some on camels and others on foot, everyone stood with an offering of food in their hands, quietly praying to Adonai.

I wanted to run, but fear rooted me to the spot as those first ungainly camels paced towards us, bearing turbaned men wearing ferocity on their faces and swords on their sides. Their slaves ran forward and forced the camels to their knees, allowing the men to slide from their backs. My own knees wanted to give way, but I watched as Abigail walked forward to the first camel rider and sank down, bowing her head to the ground.

"Men of Amalek." Her voice remained steady. "Welcome to our camp. We have prepared food, wine, and water for you."

The man, long scar slashing his cheek, towered over her. For a moment, I thought he would smash his fist down on her. "Adonai, Adonai, Adonai," I whispered.

But instead, he laughed. Then he bellowed back at his men, "Hear that, men? They have prepared food for us. The food we would have taken by force will now be handed to us on platters by these Hebrew lovelies. Come! Eat and drink from their hands, men. Then we will slay them all."

The men jostled around the women, who offered them bread, olives, figs, and grapes while pouring cups brimming with wine. Abigail tended to the cheek-scarred leader. I marveled at her calmness as she spoke to and even laughed with him. And I watched as some of the hostility seeped out of him. *Abigail's plan was working.*

But my blood ran cold as the scarred leader emptied another cup of wine and shouted, "Where are the wives of the whore-son David? Do you know how many of our women he has slain? Let me start by killing one of his."

Hannah gripped my hand in the silence that followed.

Abigail spoke.

How could she stay so calm?

"I am Abigail, David's wife, my lord. But I feel I will better serve you alive than dead."

"You?" The man narrowed his eyes. "Pity. I was starting to like you. But he has another wife, no?"

"He does, but she has gone to her family in the Negev. But I have heard the Amalekites are shrewd men, and I see it in you, too, my lord. It grows late, and every moment you linger, our men's return draws nearer."

At this, the man let out another bellow of laughter. "We know full well they fight with the Philistines, woman!" He reached out and jerked Abigail towards him by her hair. His voice dropped dangerously low. "You're a clever one, aren't you, Wife-of-David? Giving us food and wine and talking so smoothly."

"My lord." Still, Abigail sounded calm. "The men have indeed gone to see if they are needed in the fight, but they may well return if the Philistines do not trust David to fight against his own people. Many among them don't trust him."

Uncertainty flickered in the leader's eyes. He looked in the direction of Gath. "Rightly so." The man shoved Abigail away. "I wouldn't trust him with his own grandmother."

"It would be good if you are well on the way when he returns, my lord," Abigail said. "I have seen his temper, and he and his men fight like wild animals. I will direct the women to load your camels with the goods in our tents and houses. We have clothes and jewels and even excellent swords and shields. And if you want to take the livestock, too, the boys will round up the sheep and goats for you. Then you can be on your way well before nightfall."

The man considered this. "Fine," he said. "Tell them to bring everything of value to the camels. My slaves will pack the goods, and my men will go through the houses and tents to ensure they're not hiding anything. If they find something, someone will die."

For the next two hours, the camp buzzed with activity, with Abigail and the leader directing the packing. Abigail's calm had infused to the women and children, and they worked quietly and steadily, bringing all their possessions and livestock to the Amalekites. As I watched Jacoba bring my wedding robe to the camels, I let out a small cry of dismay.

"She's giving them *everything*," I whispered to Hannah.

"Hush," she said sternly. "They would have taken it all anyway but slain us as they did. All Abigail is doing is saving our lives."

As if to prove Hannah's words correct, we heard shouting from one of the Philistine houses, followed by a bone-chilling scream and loud wailing. We learned later that one of the old Philistine men had tried to stop them from taking his ring, and they had plunged a sword through his chest.

The calm, cooperative spell broke at that moment. The Amalekites began shouting, shoving the women and children to go faster. Children cried. Mothers tried to push past the raiders to reach them.

Abigail called for calm, but it was too late. One of the raiders threw a lit torch into a house, and the men laughed as two of our women rushed forward to stomp it out. More torches were thrown, and the flames grew and spread.

The leader called for the camels and livestock to be moved away from the fire, and then told his men to round up the women and children.

"But my lord." Abigail pleaded with him over the hiss of the flames. "We will slow you down. Let us stay so you can get away quickly."

The man sneered at her. "You are right, Wife-of-David. I am a shrewd man, and I know the value of a slave. A few hundred slaves, in this case. But you ..." He grasped her by the chin, and the sneer became a lusty leer. "You I might keep for myself.

chapter 33

"I saw him at the Shabbat market, Tabytha, and he smiled at me."

Miriam's words unsettled something in Tabytha. A vague, indistinct memory fluttered at the edge of her mind. Had she heard those words before?

"Jonadab has a nice smile."

"Jonadab?" Tabytha shook her head, trying to shake off the strange feeling. "Prince Amnon's friend?"

"Our cousin. My Uncle Shimeah's son."

Tabytha recalled the young man who had been with Amnon when David bought her the blue fabric. He had those strange, light eyes that seemed to take everything in. Wasn't he the same man who had taken Tamar to Amnon? On *that* day.

"Be careful of him, Miriam."

"Why?"

Tabytha shook her head. "Never mind. Did he speak to you?"

"Not then. But Adonijah was there and told me that Absalom had just gone to see Abba to ask him and all his sons to a feast at Baal Hazor."

Haggith's oldest son, Adonijah, had more of his mother's fine-boned elegance and soft-spoken manner than Miriam did. Tabytha liked him the most of all the older, Hebron-born princes.

"Then I said, why couldn't he invite the king's daughters too, and they laughed as if I'd said the most ridiculous thing. And then do you know what Jonadab said?"

"What?"

"He said I must stop letting the king's Jebusite concubine fill my head with foolishness. That I would never find a husband if I insisted on acting like a man and learning to read."

Tabytha laughed.

"You always laugh at things that are not funny!"

"But it is. Think about it. I read and write, and I married a king. Don't believe all the ridiculous things men say."

The girl scowled at this. "You're not really married to Abba. Abital says ..."

"Yes, yes. Abital has a lot to say, but the point is your father values my writing and reading. He's not narrow-minded like so many other men.

"Is your father also going to Absalom's feast?" Tabytha tried to direct Miriam's thoughts to something other than her cousin's cutting words.

The princess shrugged. "I didn't see them again after that. But ..." And here the girl's countenance finally lifted. "Ima bought some beautiful fabric and says she'll make me a new dress." A girl, through and through. Tabytha hid a small smile. With fine dresses and an even finer mind, David was sure to find Miriam a husband when the time was right.

Tabytha found Ahinoam in high spirits when they met together that afternoon to record her story. Ahinoam had just seen Abigail, who had heard from David that Absalom planned to hold a feast for all his brothers. "All the older ones, at least," she clarified. "Isn't that wonderful?"

Tabytha nodded, not saying she had already heard the news from Miriam. A vague sense of discomfort stirred inside her. "Is David going too?" she asked.

"He doesn't want to burden Absalom by going with his whole retinue, but he's given his blessing for Amnon and the others to go."

His blessing. Just as he gave Tamar when Amnon called for her.

"The time is ripe for Amnon and Absalom to reconcile," Ahinoam said. "They need to let the past be the past. To forgive and move forward."

Tabytha clenched her jaw, biting back a quick retort. How could the past be the past when Amnon's selfish, evil act had poisoned Tamar's present and future? How could everyone, including David, forgive him so readily?

She was surprised Absalom had invited Amnon to his feast. On the few times Tabytha had seen him when visiting Tamar, she had sensed a simmering anger towards his older brother. He hid it well with his smooth words and charming smile. Yet now and then—usually when he looked at Tamar—the façade shifted to reveal pain ... and something darker. She would not have expected Absalom to forget and forgive. Surely, he didn't plan ...?

Ahinoam's cheery voice broke through her dark musings. "Tabytha?"

"Mmm?"

"I said that if our sons reconcile, perhaps David will return for meals in the Women's Courtyard. Then Maacah and I can sit at the same table again. Wouldn't that be wonderful?"

"Yes." Tabytha thought back to those family meals. The beautifully dressed women. The children's excitement. David playing his lyre and singing joyfully over them all. Yes, she shared Ahinoam's longing for unity to return. The House of David had been divided for long enough. Perhaps a new, happier season was about to begin.

chapter 34

ahinoam

extract from scroll ⊤ (hs dalet)

Terror coursed through me as the Amalekites drove us southwards. They set a brutal pace. Once or twice, I saw a young slave fall, too weak to continue. Their masters didn't bother to slow down or pour water into their parched mouths. What would happen if the youngest or oldest among us could not go on? Would we, too, be left behind to die? By the end of the second day, I could hardly breathe, and pain jabbed through my side. Hannah spurred me on. Abigail cast me the occasional backward glance from where she marched at the front of our group. *We are under Adonai's protection.* I recalled Abigail's words.

"Please, Adonai," I whispered, "protect David's unborn babe."

I almost cried with relief when the scarred leader called his men to a halt for the day. We had spent most of the afternoon crossing a long valley—the Besor Valley, Hannah told me. As a boy, her father had grazed his master's flocks here. She prattled on, but I hardly heard her anymore. I sank onto the hard ground and curled into a ball. *I will never rise again. This is where I die.*

I awoke to Abigail leaning over me with a water skin. "Drink." She lifted my head and held the water skin to my lips. When she produced a fig cake for me to eat, I shook my head. She insisted. "You must keep up your strength. For the babe."

I took a small bite, doubting I could even keep it down. All I wanted to do was lie down again. "I won't make it through another day, Abi."

"You may not have to." She glanced back at the hills we had skirted that afternoon, and I followed her gaze. "I saw movement there earlier."

"David?" My heart pounded at the thought.

She nodded.

"What's he waiting for?"

"Look." She gazed across the vast stretch of land where the Amalekites had settled for the evening. "Soon, they won't know which side of their swords to hold."

Saddlebags littered the ground, and the men sat among the food and wineskins they had taken from us, drinking and laughing wildly at the success of their raid. I looked away when I saw that quite a few of them had our youngest, prettiest women with them.

"I hope he doesn't wait too long."

He didn't.

David and his men emerged like silent shadows as the sun dipped towards the horizon. A few of the Amalekites were slain before anyone even raised the alarm. But Abigail had underestimated our enemy. Even half-drunk, the Amalekites fought with ferocity. I sat frozen, watching the bloodshed until Abigail pulled me to my feet.

"We can't get caught in this. I've told everyone to move. We will head away from the battle that way," she pointed, "and then try to make it to the hills if we have a chance.

"But what of our girls with the Amalekites?"

"David will make sure they're safe. Come."

I would not have thought it possible to take another step that day, but fear—and Abigail—drove me on.

"Just a few more steps. Look, we're almost at the hills. You can rest there." She pushed, cajoled, and encouraged until, when darkness enveloped us, we were in the relative safety of the hills. More and more of our women and children joined us there. Behind us, we could still hear the distant sounds of the battle—the ring of swords and strangled death screams.

Abigail made a place for me to lie, her outer robe a pillow for my head.

"Rest now. I'll be right here. I'll wake you if we have to move."

I slept fitfully, dreaming of leering men with swords. Of children falling, lying limp and unresponsive, even as I screamed my throat raw for them to rise before the enemy trod on them. Of David bleeding to death in my arms.

I awoke in the dark, a startled cry on my lips.

Abigail sat near me, and she quickly drew me into her arms. "It's fine, Ahinoam. Everything's fine."

"David?" In my mind, I could still see his blood on my hands.

"Still fighting. But he sent one of his men to check on us. He wants us to get away as soon as there's light. Two hundred of his men are camped on the valley's far side. We are to join them there."

"That's a third of his men. How many Amalekites are there?"

"More than a thousand."

"They're so outnumbered."

"Just the way David likes it." I could almost hear the smile in Abigail's reply. "He says that's when Adonai fights the best."

At dawn, all the women and children who had made it to the hills set off across the valley, accompanied by a handful of David's men. It was a solemn procession. I thought of those who had not made it to the hills, of the young women who had been among the Amalekites. We tried to list the missing and came to twenty-three. I thought, too, of David and his men—so outnumbered—and of Abigail's faith that Adonai fought for them. But every time I looked down at my hands, I remembered the dream of my husband's blood.

Still, shouts of joy echoed across the valley when we reached the two hundred men. Women and children ran into the arms of husbands and fathers and wept as they told their tales. The men told us how Prince Iyasala had advised his brother to send them away from fighting against Israel, fearing David's men would turn on them in the heat of the battle. David had put on a good act of indignation at this insult but had been secretly pleased he wouldn't face Saul and Jonathan on the battlefield.

Only Joab had been disappointed. "Another chance missed to kill your enemy," he'd said, to which David replied that Adonai didn't need his help to deal with Saul.

They told how they had returned to find Ziklag smoldering and silent, and how they had wept until their tears ran dry. One man admitted they had turned on David in their grief, even threatening to stone him, but David had stayed calm, even though his own wives were among those taken. He had called for the priest Abiathar to bring the ephod and had enquired of Adonai if they should pursue the Amalekites. Adonai had said they should go, for they would overtake the raiders and succeed in the rescue.

Even though nightfall encroached, they had set off straight away and followed the trail through the night with their torches. In the daylight, David had pushed them harder than ever. They lost the trail on the rocky ground but found an Egyptian slave whom the Amalekites had discarded when he grew too weak to continue. The men pointed to the dark-skinned man sitting to the side, beaming broadly, clearly proud of his role in guiding David to the Amalekites.

"Why did David leave you all behind?" Abigail asked. "The raiders number well over a thousand."

The men looked away, and one of them finally said, reluctantly, "We couldn't go on anymore. The pace ..."

I nodded, remembering how I had curled up on the ground, thinking I would never rise again. "Shouldn't you help him now that you have recovered your strength?" I ventured to ask.

A few of the men, whose wives and children were among the missing, wanted to go immediately, but the man David had left in command forbade it. David had told them to stay with the supplies, and stay they would.

I slept more soundly that night, secure in the knowledge that the men encircled us. Yet fear of what the morning would bring, still lingered in my mind. What had happened to our army? To David? Would my child lose his father before he was even born?

But by the end of the following morning, we saw them coming across the valley. Men and cattle, camels, and donkeys. Abigail reached David before I did, throwing herself into his arms. He spun her around, laughing wildly. David lived! I still had a husband. My child still had a father.

Our greeting was more subdued. He held me tightly, then drew away and looked at me. "The babe?" he asked.

"I felt him kick this morning."

"Praise Adonai." His voice shook, full of unshed tears. "I was so afraid."

"Did you recover all our women?" Abigail asked. "There were—"

"Twenty-three. We've got them all. Not one of our group was lost."

Our joy was marred by some troublemakers who didn't want to share the plunder with those who had stayed behind with the supplies, but David held firm. Adonai had given them the victory, and everyone would share in it. That night, we danced and sang under the stars, celebrating Adonai's goodness to David.

chapter 35

Tabytha took a long sip of the wine and looked at the darkening sky. The small, high clouds above caught the gold and orange of the last light. She let out a long, contented sigh.

"Happy?" David laughed.

"Look at that. How can you be anything but happy with such artistry?"

He looked up, too, and nodded. "The heavens declare the glory of God. The skies proclaim the work of his hands. Day after day, they pour forth speech. Night after night, they display knowledge."

"David! That's beautiful. You should write it down."

"I already have." He looked at her intently. "You have a poet's eye and ear, my gazelle. It's why I enjoy spending time with you."

Then why had he taken so long to send for her? No, she shook off the thought. It was enough to be here now, on his terrace, under a perfect spring sky. She leaned back against him, and he encircled her with his arms.

"How is our son?"

"Growing fast. He follows the older children around, and mostly, they let him. He learns a lot by watching them, I think."

"Brothers are the best teachers, if not always the kindest. I wouldn't be the man I am if it weren't for them."

"They're kinder to him than yours were to you. And there's always Solomon to watch over him."

"Does he?" He cocked his head to the side. "I know he's clever. It's good to hear he's also kind. Bathsheba says the same, but one can't always trust a mother's glowing description of her child."

"Well, Beninu is surely the cleverest, strongest, bravest two-year-old you've ever come across."

He laughed. "I trust *you* completely, of course. And with a clever mother and a brave, strong father, why wouldn't he be?"

"That you are, my king."

She twisted around and kissed him, and he kissed her back. But then he pulled away and lifted his head.

"What is it, David?"

"Someone at the Fountain Gate."

She listened, too, and heard the stir of voices and the pounding of hooves coming towards the palace.

"Leave your attendants to deal with it." She smiled coyly. "You have more pressing matters here."

But David had already risen. "Messengers seldom come with such haste at night."

He pulled on his cloak and sandals.

"Shall I stay and wait for you?"

"Better for you to return to the Women's Quarters."

"But, David—"

She doubted he even heard her objection as he hurried through his room and into the palace passage. Tabytha's heart thudded with disappointment at the thought of returning to the Women's Quarters. She had been overjoyed when David sent for her and didn't want the evening to be cut short.

In a flash of bravado, she decided to follow David to the throne room. If she stayed in the shadows, he wouldn't see her. Then, as soon as he had dealt with the messenger, she could return to his room and be waiting for him there.

Tabytha put on her headscarf and slipped into the well-lit passage. She passed several startled soldiers and administrators, but she lifted her head and strode on confidently, acting as if David had sent for her—which he had, after all.

She had never been to the throne room. Women were not often permitted entry to this, the heart of the palace. She hesitated at a fork in the passage, unsure which way led to the king. From the right, she heard voices and followed them, a shadow of doubt forming in her mind. Would David be angry with her for following him?

The passage opened into a large room. At least a dozen men stood in small huddles, whispering. David paced along the far wall, where several soldiers stood guard at another door.

Tabytha slunk into the room and pressed herself into a shadowed corner to await the messenger's arrival. She was startled when a shadow moved, and a man materialized from behind one of the pillars closest to her. She glanced in the direction from which she had come, but before she could escape, he spoke.

"Stay. You have a right to hear this."

It was the king's seer.

"Hear what?"

"The fulfillment of the words I spoke to the king on the day you and I first met."

"The day of the bird?"

He nodded.

"What did you say to him?"

It was an impudent question to ask any man, especially one as powerful as him, but it felt important to know. The seer looked towards David, and Tabytha saw tenderness and pain in his expression.

"That for his sins, warfare would come upon him. And that it would come from inside his own house."

Warfare? What could that mean? Did an old enemy revolt against David? Could there be an enemy inside the very walls of the palace?

Just then, the soldiers stirred, and a man ran into the room. Even if his speed didn't warn he was the bearer of bad news, his haunted expression did. He looked around wildly, and when he saw David, he stumbled towards the king and sank to his knees.

"Oh, my king, my king." Emotion choked his voice.

David stood as stoically as when Tabytha and Abigail told him about Tamar. He looked down at the messenger and murmured, "Tell me."

"Your sons, my lord. They are ... dead. Absalom has struck down every one of them."

The words hit Tabytha like a blow. She watched David's face. She saw his shock and unbelief, and the precise moment when her strong lover, the all-powerful king of Israel, crumbled. First his face slumped, and then his body, as if all the life inside him breezed away.

He staggered to his knees, but even these were not strong enough to hold him up. He sank to the ground, a hiss escaping from his lips like the last breath of a dying man.

Tabytha ran towards him even as the men around him stood like stone pillars. She threw herself onto him and held his limp body.

"My love. My love. My love."

Another man bent over them. "It's only a rumor, my lord. Do not believe they have killed all the princes."

David's face lifted to look at the man who spoke. Hope lit his eyes. "It's not true?"

Jonadab had spoken, the man who had taken Tamar to Amnon.

"Absalom would not kill all his brothers, my king." He looked away from David to Tabytha. Was there a fleeting moment of guilt? "Only Amnon will be dead. This has been Absalom's express intention ever since Amnon had his way with Tamar."

"Do you think ...?"

"My lord, the king should not be concerned about the report that all the king's sons are dead," he repeated. "Only Amnon is dead."

"Dead?"

The single word held a lifetime of fatherly love and loss in it, and as much as Tabytha despised the king's eldest son, she longed with all her heart for Amnon to be alive so that David would be spared this grief.

"Perhaps it's a rumor, my love," she said. "Perhaps they all still live. Amnon, too."

Yet even as she said it, she recalled Absalom's simmering anger and hatred. She looked at Jonadab, the one other person who had seen it, and she knew. Absalom had invited Amnon to his feast for one reason—to cut him down for what he had done to Tamar.

Just then, another messenger came running through the door. He, too, looked for David and seemed momentarily confused to see the king down on the ground. He walked over to the king and slowly dropped to his knees beside him.

"My lord, I stand watch on the western wall. I see many people coming at great speed from the direction of Horonaim."

"You see, my lord," Jonadab said. "Your sons have come, just as I said."

Tabytha heard the wailing before she saw the movement at the door. The princes! She watched as the weeping men poured in, Adonijah in the lead. Shephatiah and Ithream were behind him, and Pudu's three sons followed. Absalom and Amnon were missing. The princes' faces and torn robes told a story of shock and pain.

They converged on the king, who had risen—unsteadily—to his feet.

Adonijah fell into his arms, weeping loudly. "Abba! Amnon has been slain."

"I was standing right next to him. They struck him down. Over and over." Shephatiah punctuated the words with short, sharp stabs of his hand.

Tabytha couldn't stop looking at the blood spatters on his robe.

"Absalom gave the command," Adonijah said. "Our brother, Absalom."

"A moment earlier we were raising our cups and laughing." Ithream's eyes glazed over. "Then everything changed. How could this happen?"

"It was inevitable. From the moment Amnon lay a hand on Tamar," Jonadab murmured. "We had not considered Absalom's reaction. How rage would consume him until he could think of nothing but Amnon's death."

Tabytha looked up and met the seer's gaze. He still stood in the shadows. Fleetingly, she wondered what other words he had spoken to the king on the day they first met—the day of the bird.

David had closed his eyes. His fists were bunched on the fabric of his cloak, and as he ripped his hands apart, the sound of tearing, of grief, echoed through the throne room.

chapter 36

abigail

extract from scroll ד (hs gimel)

David grieves like he does everything in his life—wholeheartedly. I first witnessed it on our return to Ziklag after the Amalekites had captured us. We returned to our burned houses and immediately set about cleaning up and rebuilding. On the third day, a young man staggered into the shell of our town. He wore torn clothes, and dust coated his hair. He fell at David's feet, words of homage on his lips.

David would have none of it and told him to rise. "Where have you come from?"

"From the Israelite camp, my lord."

"What happened?" David asked warily. "Tell me."

"The men fled from the battle. Many of them fell and died. And Saul and his son Jonathan are dead."

At the mention of Jonathan, I looked up sharply at David's face. I knew the depth of their friendship.

David's face remained impassive as stone. "How do you know that Saul and Jonathan are dead?"

"I happened to be on Mount Gilboa, and saw Saul, leaning on his spear, with the chariots and their drivers in hot pursuit. When he turned around, he called out to me, and I said, 'What can I do?'

"He asked me, 'Who are you?'"

"I said, 'An Amalekite.'"

"Then he said to me, 'Stand here by me and kill me. I'm in the throes of death, but I'm still alive.'"

The man seemed to revel in his account, but I watched David's face and saw the anger simmering below that cool surface. The messenger appeared oblivious to the danger, enjoying the fact that every pair of eyes watched him.

"And did you?" David murmured. "Did you slay the king?"

The Amalekite nodded confidently. "I stood beside him and killed him because I knew that after he had fallen, he could not survive. And I took the crown on his head and the band on his arm and brought them here to my lord."

With a flourish, the young man drew a small gold circlet and thick armband from the pouch on his side. His hungry smile as he presented them to David, hinted at the anticipation of a grand reward. What man would not honor the one who lay a crown at his feet? What man would not heap treasures on the head of the one who announced him to be king?

Fool. You do not know the man you speak to.

David's face drained of color at the sight of that crown. He seemed to sway for a moment. Behind him, Joab stood transfixed, enthralled by that circlet of power.

"The king is truly dead," David said with disbelief, as if speaking to himself. The messenger nodded eagerly, but something changed in his expression as David took hold of his own cloak and ripped it. "King Saul is dead. And Jonathan. *Jonathan.*" His voice wavered the second time he said the name, and he ripped again at his cloak. And again. And again.

Around him, the air filled with the sound of ripping cloaks as David's men followed his lead. Several women began to wail. I did not raise my voice with them, although I would weep quietly with David that evening as he spoke of his friendship with Jonathan, the covenant they had made, and how many times the prince had saved his life.

But at that moment, I only stood and watched as my husband raised his voice, calling us to fast and grieve for the anointed king of Israel and his son. I watched the anticipation of the messenger-crown-bearer turn to bewilderment and then to fear. He edged away from David, as well he should have. I knew David's righteous anger, and his decisiveness. He would not deal lightly with the man whose hand had slain the anointed of Adonai.

Later, we would learn the young man was a liar, not a killer. He claimed to have slain the king but had not actually done it. Saul had indeed begged for someone to end his life, but this appeal had been made to his sword-bearer, not to the young Amalekite. When his sword-bearer refused, Saul had fallen on his own sword.

Would David have spared the young man's life if he had simply told the truth? I believe he would have. My husband is not a cruel man. But he had heard the man confess to striking down Adonai's anointed, and David's first act as king-in-waiting was to avenge his predecessor's death.

The young man died that night.

The weeks after that were unsettled ones. With our permanent dwellings burned to the ground, we lived again in makeshift tents. The rich plunder from the Amalekites gave us some comforts—poles, skins, and fabrics for shelter—and a good supply of food and wine. David mourned deeply. He went for lengthy walks, prayed, wept, and wrote long laments.

The men grew restless, and Joab, confrontational. One night, he spoke his mind as we sat at the fire's last embers. "It's time you went back to Judah. Your own tribe will crown you king. In time, the rest of Israel will swear allegiance to you when they see what a weak king Ish-Bosheth is."

"Leave me, Joab. The time is not yet right."

"What are you waiting for? You've been plying the men of Judah with plunder. They're soft soil, David. They're yours."

"I grieve for my king and best friend, Jonathan. Closer than a brother. Do you know how that feels?"

"Your *king*?" Joab scowled. "The man who spent years trying to murder you, you mean? And here you sit writing pretty poems about him. You're a fool. You love those who hate you and hate those who love you."

He stalked away, leaving just me and David sitting there.

My husband dropped his head into his hands. His shoulders shook with silent sobs.

I moved towards him. "My love. Your loyalty to Saul and love for Jonathan is a strength, not a weakness. Adonai sees your heart."

His weeping stilled. Finally, he looked up at me with red-rimmed eyes.

"Recite it to me again, David. That last part that starts 'daughters of Israel.' I am a daughter of Israel. I want to remember those words."

"Everyone will remember them," David said. "I will make sure of it. Saul and Jonathan will not be forgotten."

And even now, all those years later, I remember his lament. David taught it to us all.

"Daughters of Israel, weep for Saul, who clothed you in scarlet and finery, who adorned your garments with ornaments of gold. How the mighty have fallen in battle. Jonathan lies slain on your heights. I grieve for you, Jonathan, my brother; you were very dear to me. Your love for me was wonderful, more wonderful than that of women. How the mighty have fallen. The weapons of war have perished."

chapter 37

The palace grew silent after Amnon's death. All the tentative life and lightness that had started to grow again was snuffed out. Only a few strayed into the Women's Courtyard to speak in hushed tones. The children grew solemn, and Solomon took it upon himself to hush those who dared to raise their voices or laugh too loudly.

Ahinoam was inconsolable. Her beloved Amnon lay dead in a cold tomb, and even Abigail could not draw her friend back from her all-consuming grief. Tabytha stopped recording her story, for no more words came. Only tears.

Maacah became even more isolated than she had been before. She refused to see the other wives, so Tabytha was surprised when Maacah finally opened the door to her, the fifth day she stood outside pleading for entry.

"You are ridiculous." Maacah threw the door open and turned her back to Tabytha as she stalked back to her bed. "Why can't you leave me alone?"

Tabytha followed her into the warm, stuffy room. The orange curtains were closed, and the dull light filtering through them cast the room into gloom.

Why *had* she come, Tabytha wondered. Maacah had never been kind to her and didn't even try to hide her disdain. Then again, Maacah didn't seem to like anybody except David and her own two children. *This* thought moved Tabytha to keep trying with her. David had cast Maacah off. Tamar was lost to them all. And, if the rumors were true, Absalom had fled to his grandfather, the king of Geshur. Maacah had nobody left.

"Shall I open a curtain and let in the light?" Tabytha strode to the window.

"No! Did I ask you to come and rearrange everything?"

Tabytha left the window and sank down next to the bed where Maacah lay, her hair uncombed and her eyes puffy. The usually proud, beautiful woman looked ragged, as a beggar might look dressed in rich clothes.

"I came to see how you were. Nobody has seen you for over a week."

"My maidservant sees me," Maacah said belligerently.

"She says you hardly touch your food."

"What is this? Are you spying on me?"

"I'm worried about you."

Maacah snorted. "Nobody's worried about me. I'm more of an outcast than Michal."

"Only because you choose to be. Just as she does."

Maacah shook her head. "This is different. I am the mother of the crown prince's murderer."

It was true. Tabytha couldn't refute the statement.

"I'm glad Amnon is dead," Maacah said. "I'm glad he paid for what he did to Tamar. Does that shock you?"

Tabytha shook her head. "I always thought he should pay too."

"So, how can I come and mingle with all the women who thought Amnon the golden prince of the palace? David's beloved heir? How can I pretend to be sad when I'm glad he's dead?"

"This is a small room to live out a life in." Tabytha looked around at the room stuffed with objects. This space pushed the very breath out of her.

"At least I don't have to pretend here."

"Perhaps I can come visit you now and then? So that you see someone."

Maacah shrugged noncommittally. Tabytha considered it a small victory. Perhaps Maacah did long for some company.

"Have you heard from Tamar?" Maacah asked after another long silence.

"I haven't had a chance to visit. I'll go soon."

Tabytha dreaded the thought of going to see the princess. Tamar's world was small and sad, too, and with Absalom gone, it had become smaller.

"And Absalom?" Maacah's voice trembled on the name of her outcast son. "Is there any further news of him?"

"I hear he is with his grandfather."

Maacah nodded. "He'll be safe there. David won't pursue him onto my father's lands for fear of starting a war."

"Why don't we visit Tamar together? Seeing you will lift her spirits." Maacah had only visited Tamar a few times in the last two years.

But Maacah shook her head. "If I can't set foot in the palace for fear of everyone's judgment and hatred, I definitely can't set foot on the streets of the city."

No amount of cajoling would change her mind.

Tabytha went to visit Tamar alone the next day. She found the house as it had been before—well guarded—and wondered why the men had not joined their master in Geshur.

She discovered the answer inside, where Absalom's young, pregnant wife hastily wrapped jugs and cups into cloaks.

"Shalom, Bilhah."

The girl, not glancing up, gave a curt nod.

"Where are you going?"

Bilhah looked up then, her eyes darting furtively over Tabytha's face. "Away. I can't stay here without Absalom."

"Is Tamar going with you?"

"Ask her yourself. All she's done this last week is cry."

Tabytha found Tamar perched by the window of Absalom's room. She sat so still that for a moment, Tabytha imagined her to be a statue. She studied her friend's profile, a silhouette against the bright light streaming into the room. How beautiful Tamar had been, still was, in fact, until you looked into her eyes and saw only a brittle shell.

"Tamar?"

The princess looked up and smiled wanly. Tabytha went over and sat next to her at the window. She could see the edge of the palace.

"I sometimes sit here and imagine what the king might be doing. I've done that a lot this week."

King instead of Abba. She whispered, "How is he?"

"Grieving deeply. I haven't seen him since he heard the news."

"Does he blame me?" Tamar's eyes swam with tears. "This is my fault, isn't it?"

"No, Tamar. He doesn't blame you. And it's not your fault. Amnon and Absalom made their choices. You had nothing to do with either."

"But if it weren't for me, Amnon would still be alive. Absalom would still be here. Bilhah is right. I should never have been born."

"You can't believe that."

"She blames me. She says Absalom wouldn't have had Amnon killed if he hadn't been looking at my downcast face every day. She says I should have put aside my grief by now and gone on living."

Tamar bowed her head, and Tabytha pulled her into an embrace.

"I don't know how." Tamar's shoulders shook as she wept. "I don't know how to go on living. There is no future for me."

When the princess finally drew away, Tabytha asked, "Where is Bilhah going?"

"Absalom sent word for her and his men to join him in Geshur."

"Are you going too?"

"I don't want to leave. I don't want anyone to see my shame, least of all my mother's parents. But I can't stay here by myself." Her eyes were those of a young, frightened child. "Where can I go?"

"Come back to the palace," Tabytha said impulsively. "We're your family. Your home. There are people there who care for you."

Longing replaced the fear in Tamar's gaze. "You think I could?"

"Yes." *But what would David say?* "Let me ask your father," Tabytha cautioned. "I'll let you know what he says."

chapter 38

abigail

extract from scroll ⊤ (hs gimel)

Not only Joab grew restless while David grieved for Jonathan. The men did, too, and with them, their wives, and children. The women asked me and Ahinoam what David intended to do. When would he claim what was rightfully his—the throne? How long would he keep us all in this god-forsaken Philistine village?

Ahinoam, close to giving birth, avoided the women. She evaded David's advances too, which meant he spent more time with me. One night, as I lay in his arms, he asked me what the women were saying about him.

"They grow as restless as their husbands," I admitted.

"What about you, Abi?" He propped himself up on his elbow to look into my face. "Do you grow restless too?"

I shook my head. "I trust you, my love. Adonai will show you when the time is right. You are his anointed, after all."

He smiled. "Your trust in me is a gift." Then, he grew solemn. "I am afraid. I don't feel ready to be a king. I am young and inexperienced."

"You will rule well, David, precisely because you do not feel ready. You will rely on Adonai's strength and wisdom instead of your own."

"I keep thinking of Saul. He started off with Adonai's anointing on him, too, until Adonai took it away from him. I'm just a man. Undoubtedly, I will fail. Will he cast me aside too?"

"You are not Saul, my love. I doubt his heart was ever fully Adonai's. Yours is. I've seen it for myself."

David nodded, but I still saw the doubt in his eyes. "Everyone is but a breath. Jonathan. Saul. Me. Will my heart stay steadfast? Will I stay the course?"

"You will, my love," I whispered.

But now—years later—I have seen the power of temptation, the allure of sin. David foresaw it even then. He knew his own frailty and that he could fail the ones he loved—could even fail the God he yearned to serve with such wholehearted devotion.

Still, something must have shifted in him while we spoke, for the next day, he called for the priest, Abiathar, to bring the ephod. With all the men watching, he asked, "Shall I go up to one of the towns of Judah?" And Adonai said, "Go up." David asked, "Where shall I go?" And the answer came back, "Hebron."

Two days later, we left for the place that would be our home for the next seven years.

How good to be back among our own people. At first, we camped by the Oak of Mamre, where Abraham and Sarah had entertained angels. There, at the very place Adonai had promised Abraham a son, Ahinoam gave birth to Amnon.

His was not the first birth I had attended, but it would be the one that touched me the most. Tears ran down my face as I drew that small, warm body into the world. Seeing that dark, wet hair and red face filled me with hope. This was David's own—the offspring of the man I loved—and I knew then I would love his child fiercely, too.

"Is it a boy?" Ahinoam cried out.

I laughed. "It's a boy!"

David had an heir.

That night, we celebrated. We forgot the years of running, hiding, living among enemies, and endless waiting. A new season had dawned. We all felt it. David would soon be king, and today's birth of a prince ensured his dynasty would continue.

We ate and drank, sang, and danced. I kept glancing at my tall, striking husband in that crowd. No trace of Ziklag's grief showed on his face. Tonight, he beamed with pride.

Within a month, the men of Judah came to Mamre. Old and young, they came to bow before David like Father Abraham had bowed before the angels under that same tree. As Sarah had done, we women prepared bread for our guests and plied them with curds, milk, and meat.

David sat with them around the fire and talked long past the time my eyes drooped with tiredness. They spoke of Saul and his son, Ish-Bosheth, and how choosing David as king would divide Abraham's covenant people.

Joab reminded them Adonai had rejected Saul and his descendants, and Samuel himself had anointed David as the next king of Israel. "Ish-Bosheth is the illegitimate imposter on the throne, not David."

"It will bring war." The elder Jeriel's face was as dark and worn as parchment. The men deferred to him not only for his age, but also for his wisdom, for he spoke with unhurried clarity. "One tribe fighting against eleven. Will we survive?"

Abiathar, our quiet priest, spoke up then. "David is the anointed of Adonai. With God on his side, he brought down a giant. Even though we are only one tribe, we are stronger than they, for God fights with us."

His words brought no comfort to Jeriel. "We should not wish to slay our brothers in other tribes. Even with Adonai's help."

The men left as solemnly as they had arrived, deep in discussion. David watched their departure pensively, but Joab paced and spat on the ground.

"Cowards and fools. Why did we waste our best plunder on them, David? Shall we forever live as outsiders in the land you were born to rule?"

A few days later, as the women and I washed clothes by the river, David appeared. The women scrambled to their feet and bowed their heads. Some of the younger ones blushed, but David didn't appear to notice because his gaze sought me.

"Abigail, would you walk with me?"

I left my wet clothes with Jacoba and followed him. Out of sight, I slipped my hand into the crook of his elbow. "Where are we going, my love?"

He smiled, that languid smile I loved so much. "I want to show you something."

We walked along a narrow path, forcing me to drop behind him. David extended his hand to help me over rocks or across narrow gullies. I liked these Judean mountains with their layers of hills, blue and hazy in the distance. This land also blossomed with life—grasses, flowers, and small shrubs. I bent down to study one when David stopped.

"We're here," he said.

I looked up to see the gaping mouth of a cave set in a stony knoll, bringing to mind our cave in the wilderness. Surely David didn't want us to go back to living in a dark, bat-infested grotto?

"The Cave of the Patriarchs," he said.

So, not a home but a burial place, and a particularly sacred one at that.

"Abraham and Sarah lie here?" I pushed past him for a better look.

"Isaac and Rebecca, too. And Jacob and Leah."

I walked to the entrance then halted, unsure. But David took my hand and led me into the cave. We stopped at a low, flat rock and sat down.

"Where do you think they are?" I whispered, looking around as my eyes adjusted to the dark.

"Abiathar showed me the cave yesterday. He says it extends that way, which is where the bones were placed and covered with stones."

I sat and thought about the hardships and courage of our ancestors then and raised a silent prayer of thanks that Adonai had made them into a nation. Finally, I understood old Jeriel's reluctance to slay the men of the other tribes.

"Abiathar read from the scroll of Moses." David's voice echoed in the reverent silence of the cave. "I will make nations of you, and kings will come from you. I will establish my covenant as an everlasting covenant between me and you and your descendants for the generations to come, to be your God and the God of your descendants after you."

As he recited the words, a cold wave rippled across my flesh. "Kings will come from you," I whispered. "Adonai had *you* in mind when he gave Abraham that promise."

David smiled enigmatically. "Not only me. My son after me. And his son. And his. *Everlasting*, Abi! That's what Adonai promised."

I thought of Amnon, small and helpless, suckling at his mother's breast. Would he grow to be as fine a man as his father? A strong leader? King of Abraham's offspring? Only time would tell.

chapter 39

And time did tell, thought Tabytha, as she recorded Abigail's final words for the day. Amnon had not been a fine man or a strong leader. He would never be king of Israel. Would that role now fall on Abigail's son, Daniel—next in line for his father's throne?

"Will Daniel come back to live in Jerusalem now he is heir to his father's throne? He's still in Hebron, isn't he?"

Abigail shook her head. "Daniel won't rule, though I believe he would make a fine king. He has David's heart for our people."

"Why won't he rule after David?"

"He fell off a mule as a child and damaged his back. It disfigured him and has left a weakness on the right side." She mimed a spear thrust. "He could never lead an army into battle."

"Surely others can do that for him? David doesn't go out with his army anymore."

"But David is respected as a fine warrior. That's why men give him their allegiance. Daniel will never have such respect, and he knows it. He left Jerusalem for that reason. If he makes a bid for the throne, one of David's other sons may well contest it. It would tear David's family—and the country—apart."

Amnon and Absalom have already done that. Thinking of the murdered and exiled prince reminded Tabytha of her promise to Tamar. She had returned from visiting the princess and immediately sent a message asking David for an audience. Four days had passed, and she had not yet heard from him.

How would David react to her suggestion of bringing Tamar back to the palace? Perhaps if she and Abigail went together, he would concede.

"I saw Tamar the other day."

Abigail looked up, her expression troubled. "How is she?"

"Absalom's leaving has affected her. Bilhah is following him to Geshur, but Tamar doesn't want to go. I think she should come back to the palace."

"Impossible." Abigail's brow furrowed. "Can you imagine how Ahinoam would feel having to look at the girl daily?"

"How would she feel?"

"Tamar's the reason Amnon was murdered. You can't expect his mother to sit at the same table as her."

"Amnon brought Absalom's wrath on himself. That wasn't Tamar's doing." Tabytha felt the heat in her face. "And none of us ever sit at the same table anymore. This family is more broken than Daniel could ever make it."

"She can't come back. David will never allow it." And with those parting words, Abigail stalked out of Tabytha's room.

It took two more messages and another five days before David sent for Tabytha. She hadn't seen him since the night of Amnon's death, and the tightness in her neck and shoulders betrayed her anxiety. As she entered the same small room where she and Abigail had told him about Tamar, David turned from the window and looked at her out of dark-hollowed eyes. He seemed smaller somehow, and it took her a moment to realize the cause—his fine, straight warrior's back held a stoop as if he had aged ten years since they sat together on the terrace that fateful night. What had Abigail said? *David grieves like he does everything in his life—wholeheartedly.*

She went down on her knee in a bow. "My king." The action and words felt too stiff and formal, a product of her tension.

"Tabytha. Rise." He held out his hand and helped her to her feet. "How are you? How is our son?" Did his voice quiver a little on that last word?

"I am well, my lord. And Beninu is ... he's busy. As active as any boy his age. Full of life." It seemed David flinched a little at her last words. *You fool!* Telling the king his youngest son was full of life when his eldest lay lifeless in a tomb on the hill.

"Forgive me for those thoughtless words, my lord."

"No. I'm glad of it." He smiled wanly. "It's how it should be. Those are good years. Difficult on the mothers, though."

"No. He's a gift to me. The best gift."

"I'm glad of it, my gazelle." A flicker of tenderness softened his gaze. "You wanted to see me?"

"Yes." She rubbed her hands together, glancing away from his face to the window.

She thought of Tamar looking from her window to the palace. Could the princess see this particular window where her father now stood? She looked back at the king, who watched her silently. Why had she told Tamar she would ask David if she could come back? This was the very worst time for it, too.

"Many come to me with difficult petitions, Tabytha. Most find it best to speak simply and clearly." Fleetingly, he smiled. "I am a reasonable king, after all."

"I know. But this request is not for me. It's for a very dear friend, and I'm so afraid you will say no."

"Then I will try to say yes. What do you need?"

"It's Tamar, my lord." She looked up to gauge the effect of the name on him, but his expression remained unreadable. "With Absalom gone, she has nowhere to live. I wanted to ask if she could return to the palace. To be with her family."

David stood silent and unmoving.

She longed to say more, to tell him how empty and sad his beautiful daughter had become. How desperately she needed to be with those who cared for her. How she yearned for her father's acceptance. But she didn't say any of it. Simply and clearly, David had said, and that's what she had done. Now he had to decide.

"No."

One word. Was that all David had left for his daughter?

"No? But why not? She's your daughter!"

"You know why. My son is dead because of her."

"Your son is dead because he *violated* her."

His expression, which had held tenderness and humor moments before, now turned cold as a stranger's, his voice as hard as flint.

"She can never come back. That is my final word on the matter."

Rage seeped into Tabytha. She felt its heat in her limbs and its pressure in her head. Her vision jumped a little, and her throat tightened. A small warning voice sounded in her head: *this is the king, your husband. Don't say anything you will regret.* But the fury demanded release. It wanted to inflict pain, a tiny retribution for all the injustice inflicted on Tamar. "Do you know what Tamar asked me, David? She asked if you blamed her for Amnon's death. And I said no. Because I thought you were a good father. A man of integrity. A *reasonable* king. I was wrong. You are none of these."

Silence followed the final words of her outburst. She thought she saw pain in David's eyes, the pain she had a moment earlier longed to inflict but now wished she could take back.

Finally, he nodded. "You are right. I often fail those in my charge. Those I care for." Then he turned back to the window.

She stood, awash with shame at her words, unsure whether to stay or go. She wanted to run to him, throw her arms around him, beg for forgiveness.

"My lord?" She took a step towards him. "I am so sor—"

"You are dismissed," he interrupted without looking back at her.

Tabytha fled back to her room, her heart pounding wildly. What had she done? Why had she said those things to the king of Israel? Over every other thought, one fear clawed to the surface. Would she become like Michal? Would the man she loved ever send for her again?

chapter 40

abigail

extract from scroll ת (hs gimel)

As David had predicted, Jeriel and the other Judean elders returned. Again, they sat around the fire, eating our bread, cheese, and meat. Joab sat on David's right, his face aglow with anticipation. I sat in the shadows behind David and ensured my eyes did not droop closed this time. I wanted to remember this moment.

"The elders of Judah have spoken long on the matter, my lord," Jeriel said. "We believe you are Israel's elected king, chosen by Adonai, anointed by our Prophet Samuel. You have proven yourself to be a true son of Judah, loyal to our tribe and people. You protected and even provided for us while you were in exile. No man would make a better king than you."

He paused as if to let the words settle on everyone present, reminding me of the *selahs* that David put in his songs.

"And so, we have come to ask you, David, son of Jesse, of Judah, will you be our king? Will you rule according to the Law of the Kings Moses gave our forefathers, the same law that Prophet Samuel bade your predecessor follow?"

David bowed his head towards Jeriel then looked around the circle of seated men. "It would be my honor to serve as Judah's king. And I will indeed obey Adonai's law as laid down by Moses and Samuel."

Excitement stirred among David's troops at this solemn declaration, but Jeriel held up his hand for silence.

"Thank you, my lord. It would please us if you came to the town to formalize our covenant the day before the next Sabbath. We will, of course, prepare a celebration feast." David's men cheered at this news, and even earnest Jeriel smiled. "There is also a home near the town's summit that may suit you and your wives as a residence. It would be my pleasure to show it to you."

"Thank you, Jeriel," David said. "We will be glad to come."

I was the only woman who went to Hebron on the day David became king although Ahinoam might have come had she not been nursing Amnon. Joy lightened my steps as I followed David and his inner circle of men—Joab, Abishai, Asahel, and Abiathar—to Hebron's gates. Cheering youngsters sat on Hebron's walls, waving palm branches. Many others had spilled out of the town and crowded around the entrance where the elders waited to receive their new king. Some threw their robes on the ground for David to walk on.

Something swelled inside me as I watched him receive their adulation. He walked tall, with the bearing and dignity of a king, yet he took time to smile at the people and even to speak to them.

One moment of that day remains with me still. A young boy, no older than five or six, wielding a stick sword, escaped his mother's grasp and ran towards David. As he reached the large group of men, the boy faltered. He stared open-mouthed at David just as the frantic mother broke free of the crowd. David bent down on one knee and asked the boy his name.

"Caleb," the boy said.

"And are you a good swordsman, Caleb?"

A gap-filled smile appeared on the boy's face. He nodded proudly.

"I'm always in need of good swordsmen. Practice hard, and you can become one of my men when you are older."

A king who took time to speak to an insignificant child—how I admired him at that moment.

Jeriel and the elders invited David and his close men to sit with them outside the gate. I joined the rest of our men, standing in an arc around the seated ones. Our arc met that of Hebron's locals as the cheering died, and Jeriel unrolled a scroll.

He cleared his throat.

"On this day, we, the elders of Judah, elect as our king, David, son of Jesse, of the tribe of Judah." A murmur of approval ran through the crowd, but Jeriel's surprisingly strong voice hushed it. "David, Son of Jesse, we ask of you this day if you will lead us with Adonai's guidance, keeping all his statutes? Will you obey the commands Adonai gave Moses? That a king must not build up a large stable of horses. That a king must not take many wives for himself, lest they turn his heart from the Lord."

At this, David turned his head to the side to look at me, his mouth twitching slightly. I smiled back, glad he knew where I stood in the crowd, and had drawn me into the moment.

Jeriel's reading continued. "That a king must not accumulate large amounts of wealth in silver and gold for himself. That a king must copy for himself this body of instruction on a scroll in the presence of a priest and read it daily as long as he lives. This reading will teach him to fear the Lord his God by obeying his instructions and decrees. It will keep him from pride and acting as if he is above his fellow citizens. And it will prevent him from turning away from the commands in the smallest way. Then he and his descendants will reign for many generations in Israel."

Jeriel looked up from the scroll and met David's gaze. "Do you so promise, Son of Jesse?"

Not a whisper of sound broke the silence. Like everyone in that crowd, I felt the sacredness of that moment. This was not only a promise to Judah. This was a promise to Adonai.

The silence stretched—a long, holy selah—and then David spoke. "I promise I will do everything I can to fulfill this charge. I cannot do it alone, but with Adonai's strength and guidance, I will be Judah's king."

The crowd roared deafeningly. The men around me raised triumphant fists to the sky, chanting, "David, David, David." One even dared grab me by the waist to twirl me around. They had waited long, faithfully serving their fugitive leader. Now, they gained their reward.

Jeriel rose to his feet, clasping a small flask in his hand. When the noise finally died down, he spoke. "Once before David was anointed as Adonai's chosen king. Then, Samuel poured a flask of oil over his head. Today, we anoint him again as a reminder that this man is Adonai's chosen one and rules with his authority. For as long as he lives, we will bow our knee to him in obedience, pledging our allegiance to him."

He gave the flask to Abiathar, and David kneeled before him. As the priest poured the oil over my husband's head, I caught a whiff of its rich scent. Joy filled me as that liquid trickled over his hair, down into his beard, and onto his shoulders. David's eyes were closed, and his mouth moved in a silent prayer. *Adonai,* my heart whispered with my husband's, *help him to be the king you desire.*

What a feast we had that day—the best wines, roasted lamb with herbs, fresh-baked breads with olive spreads, cheeses, figs, and pomegranates. The elders' wives seated me in a place of honor and glanced at me with some of the same adulation with which they'd welcomed David.

For the first time, I realized that being David's wife carried power but also distanced me from people. And I saw the danger, particularly for David, of being surrounded by people's adoration. If everyone treated you as better than them, would you eventually believe it? What could that kind of pride do to a man?

Towards the end of the day, Jeriel and his four adult sons took us to the town's summit to show us the dwelling assigned to the king and his family. It consisted of four houses, enclosed by a low stone wall and gate. As I saw a flicker of sadness on one of the son's faces, I realized that this compound must have been their family's. Some furnishings remained—curtains, benches, and reed mats—but the people had vacated their homes.

David had realized it, too.

"This is a wonderful, spacious home, Jeriel," he said. "But I have only two wives and one son. The space is too large for me. We've grown accustomed to living close together in tents. Let me rather stay in a smaller home close to my men."

"No, my lord. This is an ideal place for you. You will take more wives," the elder looked apologetically at me, "and have more children. Some of your personal guards can stay with you, and you can receive any who wish to petition you. The wall means you can also keep a few goats here."

"Was this your home?"

"Yes." He held up both his hands as David began to protest. "I am no longer Hebron's leader. It will be good to live out the rest of my days nearer my flocks and lands."

"But what of your sons?" David looked at the men standing behind their father, nervously shuffling their feet. "Surely, they don't feel the same way? Should I make enemies of Hebron's young men on the first day I set foot in their town?"

Jeriel smiled. "They will lay down their lives for you, my king. Giving you a building or two is no sacrifice at all."

Two of the four sons nodded at this. One of the two even smiled.

David looked around at the houses again. "It will be a fine home for my family, but I insist on buying this property from you."

"No, my lord." Jeriel shook his head. "It is our great honor to serve you."

"Name your price."

"No, my lord."

David walked to the young men. He addressed the one who appeared to be the eldest, who had neither nodded nor smiled before. "This is your inheritance. What do you think it is worth?"

"One hundred and twenty shekels of silver, my king," the young man said without hesitation.

"Nonsense," Jeriel said. "My lord, please ..."

But this time, David held up his hands. "I agree to the terms of the sale."

All four young men smiled for the first time since we arrived at their home. It made me think David probably should have negotiated with them.

CHAPTER 41

Tabytha didn't speak to anybody about her conversation with the king, although she re-lived it many times over the following days. How she wished she could step back in time and change it. If only she hadn't promised Tamar she would speak to him or had waited a little longer before talking to him. If only she had listened to Abigail, who surely knew David better than any of his wives. If only she hadn't lost her temper.

She sent Miriam away when the girl came looking for her, claiming she felt too sick to give her a lesson. The princess offered to look after Beninu until Tabytha felt better.

After three days in her room without seeing her son, Tabytha returned to the Women's Courtyard in search of him. She heard his throaty chortle before she saw him. Miriam had him in her arms as they chased after some of the young boys. Seeing her son's happiness felt like the first light of dawn breaking through a long, dark night.

Miriam noticed her and stopped running, pointing towards her as she whispered something to Beninu. He waved a chubby little hand in her direction but then flapped his hands towards the children. Miriam shrugged at Tabytha before taking off again after the running princes.

Finally, Miriam put a slightly disgruntled Beninu down and came over to Tabytha.

"Thank you for taking care of him so well. He looks happy."

"Ima helped. Are you better?"

"Yes."

"Can we have a lesson then? Abba sent the scrolls you asked him for."

"Scrolls?"

"Of Moses."

"He did?" Tabytha tried to remember when she had asked him. Their last conversation had taken over every other one she had ever had with David.

"He sent them three days ago. I was coming to tell you, but then, you said you were sick."

Now Tabytha remembered. When they had sat on the terrace, moments before they heard of Amnon's death, she'd told David how well Miriam's lessons were going and that the girl wanted to read Moses's writings.

And he sent them to Miriam the day *after* Tabytha's last conversation with him. A warm rush of gratitude filled her. Did that mean he had forgiven her?

"So?" The girl stood with her hands on her hips.

"Fine. Fetch the first one."

At least it would keep her mind away from her other duty—telling Tamar her father had said no.

As much as Tabytha wished she could lose herself in teaching Miriam and playing with Beninu, more than a week had passed since her conversation with David, and she knew she owed Tamar an explanation. She arrived at Absalom's house before the heat of the day set in. No men stood at the gate. She walked across the courtyard slowly, struck by the silence. When she reached the door, she pushed on it, but it resisted.

She knocked against it. "Bilhah?"

Nothing stirred inside. Again, she tried to open the door, but it did not open.

She stepped away from the door and looked up at the windows of the upper floor.

"Tamar?" she called to the shuttered window at which her friend had last sat, the one with the view of the palace. "Tamar!"

She walked around to a ground-floor window on the side and rattled the shutter.

"Why the din?" An old man ambled around the corner of the house. "No one's here except me."

"Where have they all gone?"

He shrugged and looked at her suspiciously. "Who's asking?"

"I'm Tabytha ... a friend of Princess Tamar." She didn't identify herself as David's concubine. If he had served Absalom and was loyal to the prince, he might be hesitant to tell her anything.

"She left two days after the master's men and wife left."

"Did she go to Geshur?"

"Weren't you listening? I told you she didn't go with them."

"Do you know where she went?"

Again, the non-committal shrug.

"Please, sir. She's my friend." A tear trailed down her cheek. She hastily wiped it away.

Something softened in his expression. "I remember you now. You're the one who bothered the guards so much until the master let you see his sister. Aren't you one of the king's women?"

She nodded—no use in denying it now.

"Well, then, you'd better ask the king where he's hidden her. I heard he bought a house for her to stay in. A guard and an older woman came to fetch her."

The guard she understood but ... "An older woman?"

He looked past her towards the palace.

"The king must have realized how alone she would be without Master Absalom. Perhaps the woman is to be her companion.

"Yes, perhaps."

"I'm a father myself. I wouldn't have wanted to be in the king's position."

"No."

"If you ask me ..." He moved closer and squeezed Tabytha's arm kindly, the way Ornan might have done if he wasn't the Araunah. "He's trying to do right by her."

She nodded. Her throat clenched closed with tears she didn't want to shed in front of a stranger. "When did this happen?"

He thought a moment. "A week ago. Yes. I've been alone a week."

That had been a day or two after Tabytha spoke to David.

chapter 42

ABIGAIL

EXTRACT FROM SCROLL ⊺ (hs GIMEL)

How wonderful to live in our own settlement, not hiding from one king or relying on another's fickle favor. While David spent his time at the town gate meeting with the men of Hebron and traveling to other towns and villages to speak to Judah's elders, Ahinoam and I settled into home life. We stayed in only one of Jeriel's houses. David's inner circle of men and their wives stayed in the others. Together, the women cared for the handful of young children, although Amnon clung only to Ahinoam or me. We drew water together and milked the goats, ground wheat, and baked bread over the fire in the courtyard. We talked and laughed and teased each other. It was a gentle, joyful time.

Sometimes, I slipped away to the market by myself. Since our capture by the Amalekites, Ahinoam felt anxious in crowds, but twice a week, I wound my way down to the small area near the gate where the traders sold their goods. I enjoyed the communal bustle, the merchants' respectful greetings, the smell of spices, and the soft feel of the fabrics traders pressed into my hands. In Gath, we had gone to the large, busy market in the company of King Achish's wives, but here, I had the freedom to wander, look, and speak to whom I chose.

I often sought out the woman who sold herbs and oils. She had an arched back and hands disfigured by time, but her eyes were bright and lined with laughter.

One morning, she grabbed my hand in her gnarled one and looked at me intently. She nodded as if in confirmation and dropped my hand, reaching for a small jar from among her oils.

"My lady." She held the jar out to me. "This will protect the seed you carry."

At my blank stare, she slapped her hand against her side with mirth. "You do not know?"

"Know what?"

"You are with child, my lady."

"Child? But I ... No. It can't be."

"When last did you purify yourself?"

"I ... I don't know." I realized it had been a while since my monthly bleed and the purification ritual that followed it. There had been so much to do since we left Ziklag and set up home in Hebron I had hardly given it any thought.

"How old is the king's heir now?"

"Amnon? About half a year."

"Before he reaches a year," the trader lay her hand on my stomach and triumphantly declared, "he will have a brother."

If that encounter in the market delighted me, another unsettled me, for it caused much unrest in our usually peaceful household. It happened a few days after I learned I was with child.

This time, I didn't speak to the oil trader but to a cloth merchant called Baalis. He was a large man with a loud voice, fond of telling anyone who stopped to look at his wares of his extensive travels and, particularly, of his visits to royal courts. He seemed disappointed that Judah's new king and his wives were not a little more lavish. I believe he would have respected me more if I came with an entourage of finely dressed women, especially if those fine fabrics had been bought from him.

But that day, he was as lively as I had yet seen him, with wide smiles, deep bows, and many *baraks*.

"What are the congratulations for, Baalis?" I thought slightly reproachfully the oil trader must have told the others I was with child.

"Why, my lady, for your husband's alliance with King Talmai. And what a fine, fine king he is. A court to remember. He once invited me to ..."

"Talmai?" I interjected before he broke into another lengthy account of finely dressed foreign royalty.

"The king of Geshur, my lady." His haughty tone implied that my ignorance proved the low status of Judah's royalty.

Of course, I knew of Geshur, our powerful Aramean neighbors to the north. David often expressed his concern to Joab of the threat they posed, so an alliance would put his mind at ease.

"... and the princess is always clothed in the finest of fabrics," Baalis was saying. "She will bring true refinement to your lord's household."

"Princess?" Only then did I realize an alliance with Geshur would probably entail marriage. I had known this when I married David, but still, I felt lightheaded at the thought that another would share his bed—or worse, his heart.

"Princess Maacah. What a beauty she is too."

"How do you know of this alliance?" And why hadn't David told us? Why did I hear it from this stranger on the street?

"I happened to be on the road between Geshur and Hebron, my lady, when King Talmai and his men passed by, discussing the matter. I heard only snatches of the conversation, but I asked the king's recorder, who I know from my many visits to the court and who walked a little behind the others, what the men spoke of. He told me the betrothal has caused quite a disturbance at the Geshur court. Many think the match too lowly for the princess."

"You speak of my husband, trader."

"I mean no offense, my lady." He held up his chunky hands in surrender. "Everyone knows what a mighty warrior your husband is, and King Talmai is wise to befriend him. I tell you only what the man said."

I went home that day with a troubled heart. I understood David's decision was political and nothing else—a way to secure our northern border. Yet it worried me that Adonai's anointed joined himself with a woman who did not worship his Lord. Would she lead David astray as Adonai had warned in his commands for kings? Above all, I wondered why he hadn't discussed it with me, for he had always shared his thoughts and plans before.

I did not tell Ahinoam. I knew she would cry and pout, and David would close up like a desert flower in the cold night air. I would speak to him alone first.

My chance came the next night. David returned to Hebron and sat with his men by the fire. As I brought them food and wine, I listened intently for any mention of Geshur or King Talmai, but the men didn't speak of it. They were weary from the long day of travel and soon left for their own beds.

I stooped to pick up a cup when David spoke. "Sit with me a while, Abi."

I straightened and went over to him, lowering myself to the ground. He drew me against him, and the warmth and strength of that embrace eased the knot of anxiety that had been tightening inside me since I spoke to the trader Baalis.

"Why was Ahinoam not here to help you tonight?" His voice sounded muffled in my hair.

"Amnon's teeth push through his gums. He's been crying most of the day."

"And Ahinoam with him, I'm sure. But what about you?" He pulled away from me to study my face. "You are more solemn than usual this evening."

It still surprised me David noticed such things.

"My heart is unsettled." I looked away from him, towards the dying embers.

"Abigail." At the command in his voice, I looked back at him. His gaze roamed over my face. Finally, he said, "So. You heard about my new alliance. Who told you?"

"A cloth trader. He learned of it on the road between Geshur and Hebron."

"I planned to tell you both tonight."

"Why didn't you tell us before you left?"

"Do I need to explain my decisions to anyone?" David dropped his hand from my shoulder. "I am the king. And your husband."

I had seen this cold side of David before—it had just never been directed at me. Not since that first encounter in the valley, at least.

"It's a wise alliance," I murmured. "It will bring security to our northern border."

"I thought you would understand its significance."

"And this Maacah. When does she come?"

"She asked her father for a week to prepare. I will ride the day after the next Sabbath to fetch her."

We sat in silence as the fire cooled. I wished for him to draw me back against him again, for the warmth—and comfort—of his closeness. But he kept his distance and his thoughts to himself. Did he think of her? A beauty, the trader had said. I wanted to ask David if it was true but feared hearing the admiration in his voice.

"I will clean these now." I reached for a plate, hoping he would grab my hand, as he often did when he had been gone a while, but he only nodded. I thought of pressing into him then, asking if I could be with him that night, but he was already rising to his feet.

"I'll sleep with my men tonight. You can tell Ahinoam in the morning."

He did not return the next day to witness her tears.

chapter 43

Beninu loved the sights and sounds of Jerusalem. Once a month, Tabytha took him out of the palace to make her way to her mother's house. Even with a guard leading them, leaving the stifling Women's Quarters behind felt good. The three years since Amnon's death had been lonely ones for Tabytha. The rift between her and David had not entirely healed, although he still sent for her occasionally. She valued those few short hours with him even though they lacked the easy closeness of before.

Abigail had grown a little cooler towards her since Tabytha's confrontation with the king, although she still came once a week to record her story. Suta had Gilia. Michal had Hannah. Abital was too holy to befriend her, Maacah too proud.

Miriam had learned her letters well and didn't need Tabytha to teach her anymore. The girl had read all of Moses's scrolls and now spent long hours arguing with Solomon about the finer points of the law. Sometimes, Tabytha would listen to them and try to follow their reasoning, but usually, her mind wandered to the latest story she had recorded for Abigail about her life in Hebron or to thoughts of Tamar. She once asked Abigail if she knew where Tamar lived, but Abigail shook her head. Tabytha had been too afraid to mention Tamar's name to David again. She accepted that her one true friend from the Women's Quarters was lost to her now.

The visits to her mother soothed her loneliness, however.

As her mother greeted Beninu, Tabytha embraced her sister-in-law. Tears welled up in Tabytha's eyes at the feel of Iuni's comforting arms. "Hush, dear one," Iuni whispered. "All will be well."

"Aunt Tabytha," Tuhi said. "Can I take Beninu to Rach's house and show him the new lamb?"

"Please, Ima." Beninu's dark, earnest eyes—so like David's—were difficult to resist.

"Fine." Tabytha looked at the guard. "Could you go with them, Isaac?"

He nodded and followed the children, leaving the women alone.

"How is the king?" her mother asked.

"I do not see him often." Tabytha looked away, ashamed. "Abigail tells me he pines for Absalom."

"So, he has forgiven him?" Iuni asked.

"I don't think he ever will. I suppose his grief has eased, though. Now he wishes that Amnon's death hadn't cost him *two* sons."

"And one daughter," Iuni added.

He lost Tamar long before Amnon's death.

"Have you learned where she is yet?" Iuni asked.

"Only David knows, and hers is not a name one mentions in his presence."

She listened as Iuni and her mother spoke of Atamu's latest venture. Apparently, her brother had financed a trader to bring spices from Arabia, but it had been five months, and there was still no sign of the merchant's caravan. Atamu always tried to find an easy way to make money. Most of his exploits ended in failure. More than once, Tabytha had sold a piece of jewelry or fine clothing to ensure her nieces didn't go hungry.

The children returned, Beninu full of wonder at the lamb. They ate the bread Iuni had made that morning and goat's cheese from the palace. Tabytha tried to stretch out the moments, but the guard grew restless, and eventually, they took their leave.

Beninu tucked his small hand into hers as they wound through the streets of Jerusalem. Isaac kept looking back impatiently, but she merely shrugged and pointed to her son. Yet it wasn't Beninu who walked slowly, it was Tabytha. She watched the common women, walking and laughing together, carrying water jugs or children or flagons of beer. She lived in the house of a king, fed, and sheltered and dressed in the finery of royalty, but in all the ways that truly mattered, these women's lives were richer than her own.

"Can I have a lamb, Ima?" Beninu interrupted her musings.

"No, my love."

"But Abba is king and owns the whole land."

"Where would we keep it?"

"In the courtyard."

"It would make too much of a mess."

"The servants would clean up. That's what they do."

"No, my love. They have other work to do. Besides, the palace is too far away from the land. Animals need to graze every day."

"I don't want to be a prince." Beninu pulled his hand from her grasp. "I don't want to live in a palace!" He ran, darting down one of the narrow side alleys.

"Beni. Come back!"

Tabytha took off after her son, with Isaac close on her heels. The dwellings here were small, connected by a maze of narrow passages. Beninu had disappeared.

"Beninu." She stopped, listening for the sound of his running feet. "Beninu!" The name hardly carried over the sounds of daily life in the city, and Tabytha's throat constricted with fear.

"Beninu!" Isaac bellowed. He looked at her, anxiety creasing his brow. "Someone will bump into the lad. He can't go far here."

His words proved to be wrong. They searched and searched, but there was no sign of her son. They knocked on doors and asked if anyone had seen the boy. Several men and older boys offered to help in the search when they realized the missing boy was the king's.

Tabytha couldn't hold back her tears any longer.

"Let me take you back to the palace." Isaac gripped her elbow. "I'll return with guards to look for the boy. Everyone here knows to watch out for him. They'll bring him back if they find him."

She objected, but he was adamant. They were nearing the palace gate when a man strode towards them. Through her tears, it took Tabytha a moment to recognize him—the king's seer.

Isaac took a step back at the commanding hand the seer held up, but Tabytha moved towards him. She dropped to her knees and sobbed.

"Get up." The gentleness in his eyes tempered his stern tone. "Your son is fine."

"Is he here?"

"Almost." He looked in the direction from which she had come, and she followed his gaze. A large bird circled lazily above the buildings, then glided towards them. Below him ran Beninu.

"You see?" The seer's mouth twitched with amusement. "I *did* eventually teach that bird to hunt."

She ran towards the boy and swooped him up in her arms. She should reprimand him for what he had done, but she was too overcome by the warmth of his little body pressed against her, the smell of dust in his hair, and the feel of his hot hands around her neck.

"Ima. I got a little lost, but then I saw that bird ..." He pointed at the falcon now perched on the seer's shoulder. And I went where it flew, and it came back to you."

She wanted to say *well done* and *clever boy,* but all the pent-up fears of the last hour came out then in shuddering sobs.

"Ima. Are you hurt? Sol says only babies cry."

She shook her head. "I was scared because I couldn't find you."

"Well, the bird found me," Beninu said as if birds led lost boys home every day. "I don't want a lamb anymore. I want a big bird."

chapter 44

ABIGAIL

EXTRACT FROM SCROLL ᴛ (HS GIMEL)

It wasn't Maacah's youth or beauty or prideful resistance to work that I held against her. Not even that David initially favored her over me or Ahinoam. What I resented the most was how quickly she was with child.

On hearing the news, jealousy twisted inside me. It had taken me years to conceive, and this was meant to be *my* time to give David a son. Now, years later, I berate myself for my envy. David built not only a nation but a dynasty, and wives and sons were a part of that. My unborn child and I were privileged to be in his household. But in those early days with Maacah, and with the intense emotions of pregnancy, I considered her a rival.

Could things have been different if Ahinoam and I had welcomed Maacah with genuine warmth? Would she and her children have felt more included instead of always standing on the outskirts of our family? Would Amnon have seen a sister when he looked at Tamar instead of an object of desire? Would brotherly love have overcome the hatred that eventually tore our family apart? These thoughts sometimes wake me in the hours before dawn.

Geshur was not the only alliance David made as king of Judah. Other important leaders sought his favor, too, and marriages were the seal and strength of those unions.

Haggith arrived only a few months after Maacah, a mere two weeks before I gave birth to Daniel. Where Maacah had been confident and forward in her claim on David, young and timid Haggith shied away from him. She said almost nothing to us wives, although she was quick to offer help, especially in caring for Amnon. Whereas Maacah had claimed her own room in one of the other houses, Haggith was content to sleep with me, Ahinoam, and Amnon.

I remember the moment, about a week after her arrival, when Haggith first looked at David without fear. The men had been in deep discussion around the fire. Gradually, they departed, leaving David alone. Haggith followed me out to fetch the cups for washing, just as David picked up his lyre and played the first notes of a song. Unlike me, Haggith had never heard him play before. I watched her walk over to him almost as if she was in a dream. *Like a moth to a flame*, I described it to Ahinoam the following day.

Haggith stopped a step away from David, her face filled with wonder. He looked up at her and smiled, and Haggith smiled back. Then she did the loveliest thing I had ever seen. She lifted her hands to the star-cloaked sky, closed her eyes, and danced. David's face mirrored my surprise, but he continued playing all the more joyfully as Haggith danced around him. We both saw that dance for what it was—an outpouring of praise.

He finally stopped playing. The dream broke. Haggith reluctantly came to a halt and dropped her arms to her side.

I felt bereft for a moment, as if a songbird had fallen from the sky in mid-song. Haggith opened her eyes and looked shyly at David, but no trace of her previous fear remained. After that night, she often slipped from our room, and we would hear the music of lyre and laughter wafting from David's quarters. It always made me smile.

As I had been present at Amnon's birth, Haggith stayed close to me at Daniel's. She squeezed my hand when the pain became unbearable and laid a cool cloth on my forehead as I struggled to bring my son into the world. Haggith never left my side during the long day and even longer night. And she wept tears of joy at Daniel's first shrill cry of life.

In the days that followed, when I was still weak from the difficult birth, Haggith hovered near me, quietly sensing my needs before I even expressed them. I would wake to find her sitting with Daniel in her arms, an expression of wonder on her face as his fingers curled around her own.

Unlike with Maacah, I felt no jealousy when Haggith told us she carried David's child.

David married Abital next. She came from the same priestly line as Abiathar and had been young when Saul murdered her father. Although I couldn't tell how David gained politically from the marriage, I think he still bore guilt at what had happened to the priests of Nob. Had Saul not heard of David's visit to the priests, perhaps they would all still be alive.

Abital was a young woman of extremes. As much as she revered David for being Adonai's anointed, she disdained Maacah for being his gentile wife. For a while, she refused to eat at the same table as Maacah. She insisted all the other women and children gather for prayers twice daily and would not even pour a cup of water on the Sabbath. In the months before she conceived, Abital fretted endlessly she had done something to displease Adonai. According to her, it was the marital duty of a wife to bear her husband as many children as possible. I reminded her of Sarah, Rebekah, and Rachel's struggle to bear children, but to no avail. In her world of extremes, the righteous wife would be blessed with children and the unrighteous cursed with barrenness. This left her no way to explain why Maacah had given birth to the beautiful baby Absalom other than to say the curse that should have been Maacah's would carry onto her child.

Eventually, Abital did bear David a son, and even in naming him Shephatiah, she reminded us all, especially Maacah, that the Lord is a God of judgment.

Puduhepa was the next woman David took as his own, although she had no important father or brothers to insist he make her his wife. Still, she was content to be in his household and became like a sister to me and Ahinoam.

Eglah was the last of David's wives. She was small, plump, and, compared to the other wives, rather plain. But like the heifer of her name, she had a gentle gaze and manner that endeared her to everyone. She managed to draw Maacah back to the table and into the fold, softening some of Abital's harshness towards her. Eglah was the peacemaker—the strongest and best of us all.

When I think back on those early Hebron years, I think of jealousy and births, tears and laughter, sleepless nights and first steps. I think of women bickering and three small brothers pressed together at their father's feet, hearing how a single stone felled a giant. I think of Haggith dancing, Abital praying, and Ahinoam smiling down on her sleeping son. I think of a family, far from perfect yet living life together as well as we could.

I hoped then that our family was complete, but David had not forgotten the wife of his youth. Whether because he had once truly loved her or because it would strengthen his claim to the throne of the remainder of Israel, David set his heart to claim her back.

David had not forgotten Michal.

chapter 45

"Listen to this, Tabytha." Miriam held up the scroll and read. "Now then, tell my servant, David, 'This is what the Lord Almighty says: I took you from the pasture, from tending the flock, and appointed you ruler over my people Israel. I have been with you wherever you have gone and cut off all your enemies from before you. Now, I will make your name great, like the names of the greatest men on earth.'" She looked up proudly. "Abba is among the greatest men on earth. That's what Adonai said to the prophet Nathan."

Ever since Tabytha had told her about the seer's bird leading Beninu home, Miriam had been fascinated with every word the man had ever spoken. She had cajoled Solomon into getting all the scrolls that captured the seer's words from the king's recorder. Solomon had complied, mainly Tabytha thought, because he was as curious as his sister to read what the seer had said to their father. The two of them had pored over this particular scroll, the Covenant Scroll, for hours on end.

Tabytha wondered if a scroll existed from the other time Nathan had spoken to the king. She only knew of that time because the seer had spoken of it as he stood with her in the throne room on that terrible night three years earlier, the night the messenger came with news of Amnon's death. The seer had told her on the day they had first met, the day of the bird, that he was returning from prophesying to the king warfare would come from inside his very household.

If such a scroll existed, Solomon and Miriam had not received it.

Miriam continued to read. "'I declare to you that the Lord will build a house for you. When your days are over, and you go to be with your ancestors, I will raise up your offspring to succeed you, one of your own sons, and I will establish his kingdom. He is the one who will build a house for me, and I will establish his throne forever. I will be his father, and he will be my son. I will never take my love away from him, as I took it away from your predecessor. I will set him over my house and my kingdom forever; his throne will be established forever.'"

The girl read well—quick and confident. In fact, Miriam had surpassed Tabytha's abilities, a realization that gave Tabytha a measure of pride.

"Do you know," Miriam said, looking up from the scroll, "that Solomon says *he* is the one in this prophecy? He says he will build a house for Adonai. I told him he's a fool. You don't become king if you're one of the youngest princes. But he says Adonai can do anything he wants, and he saw the prophet Nathan once in the palace courtyard, and the prophet *almost* told him he'd be king."

"Almost?" This piqued Tabytha's interest. She remembered well how intently the seer had looked at her on the day of the bird, and his words were weighty. She hadn't told Miriam of that encounter either. "What did the seer say to Solomon?"

"He's a *prophet*, Tabytha. And he said that Solomon must remember one thing." The girl thought for a moment and then recited, "When offered the world or wisdom, be wise." Miriam shrugged. "It doesn't seem like a prophecy to me."

"No. What made Sol think it was?"

"Because the prophet also said a ruler needs wisdom to rule well. Sol now thinks *he* is that ruler."

"He could have been talking about David or any other king."

"That's what I said too, but Solomon is adamant. He said he saw it in the prophet's eyes."

Tabytha could well believe it. She had seen something in those eyes, too—a strange foresight of what would become of her.

"Here." The girl's attention turned back to the scroll. "See here. The prophet said it again. 'Your house and your kingdom will endure forever before me; your throne will be established forever.'" She looked up to see if Tabytha had grasped the significance of the words. "Solomon says the priest told him that if a prophet repeats something, it's very important. And here it is." She shook the precious scroll in a way that made Tabytha flinch. "He said a few times that Abba's dynasty will last forever."

Forever felt like a long time to Tabytha. She thought of her grandfather, the Araunah. Jebus had probably felt invincible when he ruled the city. Perhaps he had believed his son and grandson would rule after him. Then, a stronger man had taken it away from him. Wasn't that the way of the world of men? But she kept her thoughts to herself and simply enjoyed Miriam's enthusiasm. The clever young princess had brought joy to her life these last few years, and Tabytha was grateful for it.

"I was telling my mother's servant girl about the scroll. She says she thinks Solomon would be a good king, and she wants to be his scribe."

Tabytha laughed. "A king would never let a woman scribe for him."

"She asked me if I could teach her to read and write," Miriam said. "So, I said I would if Ima didn't mind. And Ima said she could have an hour a day to sit with me to learn her letters."

"That's wonderful, Miriam."

"And I already told Solomon that when he is king, he *must* use her as a scribe."

"What did he say to that?"

"That a wise king might consider it if she is faster than the fastest scribe he has. So now I've told her to practice doing her letters very fast."

"As long as they're still legible." Tabytha laughed again. "What is this girl's name?"

"Evie. But from now on, she wants everyone to call her Sophereth."

"Sophereth?" Tabytha tried the unusual word on her tongue. "Doesn't that mean ... scribe?"

"It means," Miriam beamed triumphantly, "a *woman* scribe. And she's told me to talk a lot about her to Solomon so he doesn't forget his promise that if she's faster than all the other scribes, he will let her be in his court. So now, every time Sol and I study a scroll, I tell him how fast Sophereth is at letters."

"Let's first see if Solomon actually has a court."

As Tabytha left the Shabbat market, she saw a strange sight. Joab, the king's commander, walked slowly across the courtyard with an old woman dressed in mourning clothes. Joab didn't strike Tabytha as one to pay attention to the king's petitioners unless they were wealthy or influential. Still, he and the old woman had their heads close together and were talking in a conspiratorial way. Could she be his mother? Tabytha slowed her steps and watched as the king's commander led the woman down the steps toward the palace gate. Despite her mourning clothes, the woman chuckled at something Joab said. The two of them looked rather pleased with themselves.

Tabytha soon forgot the unusual sight, but a day later, the Women's Quarters simmered with the news that Joab had left that morning to bring Absalom back to Jerusalem. Not surprisingly, Gilia was the one who told the women gathered in the courtyard that Joab had schemed with a wise woman from Tekoa to bring this about.

"Yes." Tabytha suddenly recalled Joab and the woman. "I saw him at the Shabbat market, walking with an old, grieving woman."

"Truly? What did she look like?" Zurata, one of the other concubines, asked.

"Well, she walked ..."

"Tabytha knows *nothing* of the woman," Gilia snapped. "Don't ask her. My man in the court told me all about it. Apparently, she wasn't really in mourning. Joab had merely told her to dress that way to gain an audience with the king. And Joab told her everything to say. It was all simply a story to get the king to agree that her one son wouldn't be harmed for killing the other."

"Oh, how terrible." Zurata said. "Did her son kill his brother?"

Gilia sighed loudly. "A lie constructed by Joab. Don't you ever listen, Zu?"

Zurata drew back from Gilia's sharp tongue. Tabytha knew she wouldn't ask any more questions. She was the quietest of them all, usually lost in her simple musings.

"So, when David agreed the woman's son would not be punished ..." Gilia glared at Zurata. "The woman said, 'the king convicts himself for not bringing back his banished son.' And then David perceived the lie and said, 'Did Joab make you say this?' And the woman fell before him, and then Joab fell next to her. And my man says they were both trembling that their deception had been discovered, terrified at what the king would do to them."

Tabytha glanced at the faces around her. Gilia had everyone's full attention with her dramatic retelling of the events. Even Zurata leaned forward again.

"And my man says the throne room grew quiet as a grave as the king rose. Everybody thought he would tell his guards to seize the two for their deception, but instead, he said, 'Go and bring back the young man Absalom.'"

"Has someone told Maacah?" Tabytha was one of the few women still visiting Absalom's mother.

Gilia let out a dismissive huff and then continued with her story. "But, when Ahinoam heard the news, she wept, and sent word to the king to beg him to reconsider. Ahinoam says that ..."

Tabytha rose and slipped away. Every day, she and her son lived in a household divided by the sins of its men. She didn't need to listen to Gilia to know it.

chapter 46

abigail

extract from scroll ⊤ (hs gimel)

I would have been content in Hebron, but I knew David
was destined for more. He knew it too, and one other person
never let him forget it—Joab. With every report from the
north, David and Joab's restlessness grew. When the news
came that Saul's cousin, Abner, had put Ish-Bosheth on his
father's throne to rule over Ephraim, Benjamin, and all of
Israel, they sat late into the night discussing it.

"He's a weakling," Joab said. "Within a year, they'll
come begging for you to be their king."

"Don't be so sure," David replied. "Abner is strong. He
will hold them together. And under his command, their
army will be difficult to defeat."

Joab's scowl showed he didn't like David's words or the
grudging admiration in his voice. Abner threatened Joab.
Not only was he the commander of Israel's army, but men
called Abner the kingmaker. If he had the power to put Ish-
Bosheth on the throne, he could just as easily remove him
and replace him with David. Where would that leave Joab?

He would no longer be David's right-hand man. Abner would usurp him.

A few months after that report, Joab's dislike of Abner turned darker and more dangerous. It started with a report that Ish-Bosheth's army was on the move and heading south.

"Let me take our men and stop them," Joab told David.

"They're outside our borders."

"They're at Gibeon and could easily push into our lands from there—if we don't show our strength."

David finally agreed. "Go. But show restraint, Joab. They're our brothers, after all."

And at first, that's what Joab did. While their armies camped on opposite sides of the Pool of Gibeon, he and Abner met, even sharing some of the bread we women had baked. Their closest men sat around the two leaders, watching each other warily. All agreed later Joab goaded Abner to have a contest—twelve of Ish-Bosheth's men would fight twelve of David's.

The contest was quick and bloody. Every man grabbed his opponent and sank his dagger into his side. Twenty-four fine young warriors died that day because of the rivalry between Joab and Abner. But that's not where it ended. Seeing their men slain, the two armies attacked each other. Even more blood spilled in that place that would forever be known as the Field of Daggers. Finally, Abner came to his senses and called the retreat.

If Joab had shown the restraint David had commanded, his brother Asahel would have lived. But Joab allowed his men to chase Abner's army and did not call Asahel back when he set his sights on Abner. It suited his purposes for Abner to die that day, but that's not what happened. Abner begged Asahel to leave him alone. "Why should I strike you down," he said. "How could I look your brother Joab in the face?" But Asahel did not turn away, and eventually, Abner had no choice but to thrust his spear into him.

At a hill in Gibeon, Joab finally called his men back. They returned to Hebron subdued. Despite losing his brother, Joab declared the battle a victory, but I could see in David's eyes that he disagreed. He grieved not only for his cousin Asahel and the other men who fell on that foul field but for Ish-Bosheth's valiant warriors. They all had paid the ultimate price for the enmity between two power-hungry men and the kings they upheld.

That was the first battle in the war between Israel and Judah. Many more sons of Jacob would die.

Until the day the kingmaker changed his allegiance.

"Ima!" Daniel ran to me, throwing his arm around my leg. "There are men here, and Amnon says they are Abba's *emnies*." He scowled when I laughed at his struggle with the word. "Amnon says we must fetch our swords and fight them."

"Your wooden sword against their sharp blades? Where are these men?"

"Talking with Abba." He pointed.

I looked out the door and saw the three strangers standing with David just inside the gate. From my husband's tense stance, I deduced he did not receive them with his usual warmth. *Who were these men?*

"Abba's not drawing his sword, so he won't want you to draw yours. They are our guests. Let's offer them water instead."

I hurried to fetch a water skin and cups, giving Daniel two to carry. He grumbled at having to take cups instead of a sword but, realizing that as cupbearer, he would get closer to the men than Amnon would, he followed me outside.

David turned as I arrived, and I inclined my head towards him. "My lord, may I offer your guests water after their journey?"

He nodded brusquely, and I poured water to the brim of the first cup and handed it to the oldest of the men. He took it without glancing at me and continued speaking. "I speak for my commander, Abner. He says, 'Whose land is it? Make an agreement with me, and I will help bring all Israel over to you.'"

My hand jerked at the words, and the water spilled to the ground. Had the kingmaker finally decided to throw his weight behind David?

I glanced at my husband to gauge his reaction to the messenger's words. I saw the longing in his eyes, followed by a look of unyielding determination. Before he even spoke the words, I knew what he would demand in return.

"I will make an agreement with your master, but tell him this. Do not enter my presence again unless you bring Michal, daughter of Saul, when you come to see me."

chapter 47

Over time, Maacah's joy that her beloved Absalom had returned to Jerusalem grew into a brooding discontent. Finding it increasingly difficult to be around her, Tabytha visited the isolated woman less frequently. On some days, Maacah did nothing but weep for Tamar and Absalom. On others, she ranted against her husband for the way he treated their son. On the occasional good day, she speculated endlessly on when David would name Absalom his heir.

Today, Maacah's mood had fluctuated wildly between weeping and ecstatic praise for Absalom, who would—according to her—be the most beloved of all Israel's kings.

"My maidservant tells me the people already love him. He receives all who come to him with a kiss and warm words."

"Have you gone to see him yet?" Tabytha knew she hadn't. The woman seldom left her room. "If he greets strangers warmly, imagine how he will welcome his mother."

Maacah looked away. She didn't like being confronted about her reclusive habits. "One day soon, he will visit me here. When David sends for him."

It had been well over a year since Joab brought Absalom back to Jerusalem, and in all that time, David had not sent for his son. Nobody mentioned the prince's name to the king. Even Joab had not pressed David into seeing him. Tabytha chose her words carefully when she spent time with David. She didn't want to repeat the mistake she had made before. But she sensed the prince was never far from his father's thoughts. Sometimes, she wished David had simply left him in Geshur. Things had felt lighter with Absalom far away.

"Do you know," Maacah broke into a rare smile "that Absalom's wife bore him a daughter?"

"I hadn't heard. That's wonderful."

"Three sons and now a daughter. Isn't he the ideal ruler, already blessed with heirs himself?" Maacah's expression grew wistful as she added, "He named the babe Tamar. May she grow up to be as lovely as my poor child."

"Truly?" Tabytha considered how good Absalom had always been to his sister. The name proved he had not forgotten her. Or had he chosen the name to taunt David, who appeared to have forgotten his daughter altogether?

"Do you have news of Tamar?" This question often brought Maacah to tears, but Tabytha hoped that, having mentioned her daughter herself, today would be the exception.

But no. Already, the tears pooled in Maacah's eyes.

"She should be bearing children herself now instead of staying in a dark, cramped house with a lowly serving woman. He ruined her." Maacah never spoke Amnon's name. "He *ruined* her. How glad I am that my son didn't let that vile deed go unpunished, even though it has cost him dearly."

Tabytha had yet to discover where David had hidden Tamar. Now that they were speaking of Tamar, she might as well broach the subject again.

"Have you asked the king where Tamar lives? He would not deny you, her mother, that information. Then we could visit her together. She would want to hear of Absalom's new child, her namesake."

But the overwrought Maacah shook her head. As far as Tabytha could tell, David never saw his wife anymore. Their children's fate had driven a wedge between them. She cast around for a topic that might draw Maacah out of her melancholy state. "Does Absalom still have such fine hair?"

Maacah sat up straighter and wiped the tears away with the back of her hand.

"Oh, the finest in all Israel. You have never seen such beautiful, thick hair. Once a year he cuts it, for it grows too heavy. My maidservant tells me it weighs two hundred shekels by the royal standard. Can you imagine anything finer?"

Tabytha had heard all this before but smiled and nodded in all the right places. She sighed when she finally closed the door behind her. Maacah had not asked her a single question about Beninu. Did she even know Tabytha had a son?

Tabytha worried about Beninu. At seven years old, he should have been running, jumping, laughing, and playing pranks. She remembered the freedom she and Atamu had enjoyed at that age. Her own nieces and the king's other children had appeared carefree and full of childlike joy when they were young. But Beninu watched the world with solemn, mistrustful eyes, and hardly engaged with his brothers and sisters.

Looking back, Tabytha could see how the last years' events had left their mark on the boy. He had been born a mere month or two after Amnon violated Tamar, the act that first opened the rift in David's household. When Beninu was two, Absalom murdered Amnon, and the rift grew into an even deeper chasm. The women were divided and often hostile towards each other, and the children followed the patterns of their mothers.

Deep in mourning his eldest son and aware of the division in his household, David seldom visited the Women's Quarters. He had only seen Beninu three times in the last two years, and such fleeting moments did not make for a relationship.

Tabytha saw the hunger in her son's eyes when she spoke of David, but she could not give Beninu what he needed the most—a father who valued him. Today, she saw how much this grieved her young boy.

They were returning from visiting her mother and brother when Beninu said, "Uncle Atamu told me he wished he had a son instead of two daughters."

Tabytha shrugged. Her brother had said the same thing for years. It had only grown worse since Iuni gave birth to a stillborn son.

"I wish I could be *his* son," Beninu said. "Then we would both be happy."

Tabytha stopped and reached for his arm, forcing him to stop, too. "But you are the son of a king."

"I'm a nobody. If Absalom killed *me*, Abba wouldn't even cry."

"How can you say that? You are his flesh and blood. Of course, he would."

"He wouldn't." Anger flared in Beninu's young eyes. "And it's *your* fault. He doesn't love you because you're a nobody, and that's why he doesn't love me either. I wish I were Uncle Atamu and Aunt Iuni's son instead of yours."

"Beninu, you can't ..."

"I hate you!" He spat the words out the way a cruel man might spit at his lowest slave.

Her son shrugged off her grip, and—although he didn't run away as he had once before—strode away from her, closing the gap between him and the guard. She walked alone, her heart beating wildly with both the pain she saw in her son's eyes and the pain his words had driven into her.

He didn't mean it. He is a hurting child. Yet even as she told herself this, she remembered the loathing in her son's eyes as he said the words.

chapter 48

michal

extract from scroll ב (hs beit)

The morning the soldiers came for me, Paltiel and I had made love. Afterward, I lay in the crook of his arm, my head against his chest, as he smiled down at me. How safe I felt at that moment, safe enough to speak of the one painful truth in our marriage.

"It's been more than ten years, my love, and still, my womb remains closed."

A shadow of pain crept across his face. "Hush. Let us enjoy this moment."

I pushed up onto my elbow, my hair spilling down on his shoulder. "I've longed to give you a son."

"I know." He reached out and wiped a tear from the corner of my eye. "Let's not give up hope. Adonai may yet hear our prayers."

"*Your* prayers." I didn't hide the scorn in my voice. "Adonai has never listened to mine." I knew how distressed Paltiel grew when he sensed my animosity towards Adonai, so I quickly continued. "I've been thinking about it. Perhaps it's time for you to take a second wife."

My husband stiffened as if somebody had woken him with a splash of winter water.

"You need an heir. Your father resents me, and I see what it has done between you and him."

Without a doubt, Laish broached this subject with his son. I saw the simmering resentment every time my father-in-law's gruff gaze met mine. His wife had given him five sons and three daughters.

"It's not his decision." As meek as Paltiel appeared to those around him, he asserted himself when it mattered the most, sometimes obstinately so.

"What if I never bear you a son?"

"I won't love you any less."

"But I want you to have the joy of having a son. Even if it means sharing you with another woman." It pained me to say those words, although I knew them to be true.

Paltiel shook his head. "You are the only woman for me, Michal."

Foolish man, I thought, even as relief washed through me. How I loved him for those words right then.

Paltiel sat up and cocked his head to the side. I heard something, too—the sound of approaching voices. He clambered off the sleeping pallet and pulled a robe around himself to cover his nakedness. I jumped at the sudden pounding on the door.

He strode towards the door and then looked back at me, his brow creased with worry. "Get dressed. I'll see what they want."

As he unlatched the door and slipped out, I caught a glimpse of soldiers. Fear clenched my innards. *King's men*. What could they possibly want with my husband? He showed my brother the same unquestioning loyalty as he had my father.

I pushed myself up and quickly threw on my undergarments and robe. Perhaps they had the wrong man, and if they saw me—the king's sister—they would realize it. Yet my thoughts ran in every direction as I pulled on my sandals. Was Israel under attack that they were summoning men such as Paltiel to fight? Or had somebody said something to Ish-Bosheth to make him doubt my husband's allegiance? Perhaps Paltiel's oldest brother, who always sought ways to ingratiate himself with the king. I strode over to the door. I would tell them that my brother-in-law was a liar and far too fond of the wineskin to be trustworthy.

As I opened the door, my husband turned to look at me. All the color had drained from his face.

"What is it?" I asked him, but he shook his head, like the mute who begged at the corner.

I looked at the front soldier. "If this has something to do with my brother-in-law, know that …"

"Your brother, the king, has sent for you." The man gave me no chance to explain.

"For *me*?"

"David demands you back."

David? … Back?

"But I'm married to Paltiel." The man's expression remained as stoic as before, so I tried to explain again. "I've been Paltiel's wife for more than ten years."

"The king orders it. We are to bring you to Commander Abner, who will arrange to send you to Judah."

At the sound of Abner's name, dread pounded through me. If this was Ish-Bosheth's scheme, I could talk him out of it. My brother had always been little more than a wavering reed. But Abner? Abner was an unmoving rock.

"Please. This can't be." I looked at Paltiel. "Tell them, my love. Tell them I'm yours."

But my husband slumped against the doorframe as if he didn't trust his legs to hold him. I reached for his arm to pull him back inside. We would close the door and push the heavy chest against it. They would have to go away then.

The front soldier reached for the door, holding it open even as I tried to close it. My strength was no match for his.

"Fetch what you need. We leave immediately."

I realized then what Paltiel had grasped from the moment he opened the door. We were powerless to prevent this. Today, we would be torn apart at the whim of the distant king of Judah, and the resolve of an unyielding kingmaker.

The soldier released the door, and Paltiel and I stumbled back inside. My husband closed the door, and the soldier didn't stop him. I understood why—they would simply break the door down if we tried to barricade ourselves inside. I sank to the floor, my body trembling as if winter had taken me into its icy grip.

Paltiel stood for a short while and then slowly moved around the house. I heard him opening chests and rifling through garments. When I finally looked up, I saw that he had laid all my clothes on the sleeping pallet.

"You're going to let them take me? Even help them carry all my clothes to David?"

"What can we...?"

"You're a weakling! Why don't you fight for me, Paltiel?" The words were unreasonable, but my anger needed release. "Take your sword! Show you are a man. Didn't you just tell me you loved me?"

"You want me to fight David? *David?*"

"Yes! He's fighting for me. Why don't you?"

Paltiel sank down next to me. "I'm only a man. He is an anointed king. Adonai's chosen one."

"But you are the one who loves me." Grief raged inside my chest. "Only you love me."

Paltiel drew me closer and cradled me in his arms as I wept. At some point, the soldiers opened the door and came in. When I eventually looked up, the stoic soldier stood at the entrance, with two men behind him holding bundles of my clothes under their arms.

"Let's go," he said.

"I'll come with you," Paltiel said with a sudden urgency. "I'll speak to Abner. Perhaps he will reconsider."

He didn't know my father's cousin like I did, but I merely nodded.

"You know I can't fight David, don't you, Michal?"

"I know."

We set off for the place where Abner awaited us. The two of us walked with soldiers ahead and behind us. They set a fast pace. Paltiel and I, both lost in our own thoughts, didn't speak, yet I sensed he glanced at me often. I set my gaze forward. My tears had been wept, and now only a strange numbness remained.

As we neared Bahurim, another group of men approached, and even from a distance, I could make out Abner's imposing figure in the lead. On meeting, the men in our group moved aside so that Paltiel and I stood directly before Abner.

Abner's gaze briefly brushed over me and then came to rest on Paltiel. His brow furrowed.

"My soldiers were capable of bringing the woman to me. There was no need for you to come too."

"But I wanted to speak to you, Commander. Michal and I have been married all these years. More than ten, sir, and I ..."

"I know precisely when Saul took her from David and gave her to you. It's irrelevant. She was David's wife first."

"Only for a few months, whereas we have built a life together."

"By law, she is his, and you have been committing adultery with another man's wife. A king's wife." He glared at Paltiel. "Be glad King David is willing to pardon your offense."

"Offense? No. It wasn't like that. We ... I mean, King Saul ... gave her to me because David abandoned her."

"Well, that abandonment ends today. He has sent for her." Abner turned away from us and signaled for one of his men. "Bring her to King David and remind him I have accomplished the first thing he asked. Tell him I will meet with the elders of Israel soon, and then I will come to him again."

"Please, sir," Paltiel tried again. "Please can we ..."

"Go back home and find another wife," Abner said sharply. His words reminded me of my own words a few hours ago. A lifetime ago.

A soldier took me by the arm and led me away. Behind me, I heard Paltiel weeping. I still heard him as we crested the first hill and even as we descended into the valley. Only once, much later, did I dare to turn around to see if he still followed us.

But Paltiel was gone.

chapter 49

Beninu had grown increasingly sullen since he told Tabytha that he hated her. He rebuffed every attempt she made to embrace him or engage him in conversation. Even Miriam, who used to have a knack for drawing the boy out and making him smile, admitted to Tabytha that she no longer understood him. Over the months, as her son's melancholy grew, Tabytha found that she, too, began to wake up with a stifling sense of despondency. Sometimes, such a heaviness settled on her she battled to rise from her sleeping pallet in the morning.

Tabytha welcomed the task of recording Abigail's story. For a short while, Tabytha could forget her worries about her son, losing herself in a different time and place. As the story of David's rise to power unfolded, Tabytha gained a better understanding of him. Just as revealing was all she learned about his wives and children. Through Abigail's eyes, Tabytha had the sense they had been content in Hebron, at least as content as one could hope to be as a woman or child in David's household.

Even though the scribing cheered her, something in Tabytha's countenance must have shown her growing anxiety, for Abigail came to stand behind her and laid her hands on Tabytha's shoulders.

"You look tired today, Tabytha."

She shrugged. "No more than usual. I often wake early."

"You're worried about Beninu?"

It didn't surprise her that the older woman knew something was amiss with the boy. Abigail still sought to calm the restless family waters, and in her role as palace peacemaker, tried to know what was happening. Beninu's name must had come up in a conversation.

But what could she say? That her own son hated her? That he wished he wasn't David's?

"He's been … sad. Little interests him lately."

"He doesn't play with the other youngsters?" Abigail came to sit down in front of her. "And Miriam? I recall they had a good bond. He always seemed to like being with her."

Tabytha shook her head, fighting the rising tears. She didn't want Abigail to see the extent of her concern.

Abigail reached for her hands. "I've seen many little boys grow up, and they all give their mothers seasons of worry. This will pass."

Her words were kind, even if Tabytha didn't truly believe them.

"He doesn't like swordplay? Wrestling? Hide and seek? Pebbles and bones?"

With every shake of her head, Tabytha felt she had failed her son.

"Is he good at his letters?"

The tutor that had taught all the princes had recently sent for Beninu. The boy had returned in tears. Apparently, the tutor did not think much of the fact that Tabytha had taught her son the Alef Bet. He had told the boy that a woman could not be trusted to teach sons anything of value. Another confirmation to Beninu his mother was worthless to him. A nobody.

"Didn't Solomon teach him to carve wooden horses?" Abigail persisted.

"His didn't look as good as Sol's, so he stopped. Although ..."

Abigail looked up and nodded encouragingly.

"He did try to carve a falcon by himself. He worked on it for a long time." Her son had seemed almost happy as he did it.

"A falcon? Has he ever seen one?"

"The seer has one."

"You mean Nathan?" Abigail shook her head. "A falcon? I've never seen him with one."

Tabytha considered how often *she* had seen the seer and his falcon. That first time on the day they had rescued the bird, as the seer returned from prophesying to David. She had glimpsed them again on the day Tamar went to bake bread for Amnon. And she'd met the seer in the throne room on the day of Amnon's murder, and the day Beninu was lost in the city. That day, the falcon—or perhaps the seer—had saved the boy.

"Beninu is fascinated with that bird," Tabytha said.

"Well, then, I think we have our answer." Abigail smiled triumphantly. "The key is the bird."

"The bird? But the seer hardly ever comes here, much less brings the bird. You said yourself you haven't even seen it."

"True. And one doesn't tell a prophet when to come or go. They do so at their own volition. But Nathan seems to show himself to you far more than to the other women here."

And always when something significant was about to happen.

"So, if you happen to see the prophet again, ask him if the boy can spend time with him and the bird."

Abigail made it sound easy but as Tabytha thought about the seer's intense gaze, she wondered if she would have the courage.

A few weeks after that conversation, Tabytha had her chance. She sat in the Women's Courtyard stitching a new robe for Beninu. He had already outgrown the two robes she had made him earlier that year. When she called him over, he came reluctantly and held the robe against his shoulders while she kneeled to measure its length. Suddenly, he jerked the robe away.

"Stand still, Beninu."

"Look, Ima!"

The excitement in his voice and the surprising fact that he wanted to share something with her made Tabytha look up at her son.

He leaned back and looked intently into the sky, his face filled with wonder. Tabytha couldn't pull her gaze away from her son's enraptured expression, until Beninu looked down at her and scowled.

"Up *there*!" He pointed, and this time, she followed his gaze. A bird of prey circled high above them.

"It's the prophet's falcon," he said.

"It could be another."

"No. I know that bird. I'm going out to see him."

She suddenly remembered Abigail's advice. "I'll come with you."

Her son hesitated and seemed on the verge of objecting but then shrugged and ran for the steps. Tabytha clambered to her feet, left the half-finished robe lying on the ground, and followed him down the long passage to the entrance of the Women's Quarters. When she arrived at the door, the boy had already swung it open and was well past the startled guards.

"We won't go far," she said, hurrying past them. "Just to the gate."

Tabytha strode across the Palace Courtyard and down the main steps to the gatehouse. She looked up to see if the bird still soared above them but couldn't see it. She had lost sight of Beninu too but doubted the guards would let the prince go out into the city alone.

Finally, she spotted him near the gatehouse. He stood with the seer. She slowed, a prickle of her childhood apprehension returning. The seer didn't even look up at her approach. The falcon perched on his leather-padded arm, and he lowered it so Beninu could take a better look. Her son was so engrossed in studying the bird that it seemed the rest of the world had fallen away from him.

"Where did you get him?" Beninu didn't take his gaze off the bird.

"Along the valley path," the seer said. "He was young still and hurt because some boys had thrown stones at him."

At this, Beninu looked up, his expression troubled.

"But a young girl chased them off before I came along. A very brave girl only a little older than you are now." The seer glanced at Tabytha, a glint of humor in his eyes. "Do you want to know that young girl's name, Beninu?"

Her son nodded, his intense gaze now on the seer.

"Her name was Tabytha."

Beninu swiveled around to look at his mother. "You, Ima?"

Tabytha felt a warm rush of gratitude to the seer for how her son looked at her right then.

"Yes. I couldn't bear to see their cruelty."

"I would've chased them off, too," Beninu said.

"Undoubtedly," the seer said. "You have your mother's courage."

Beninu turned back to the seer. "How did you make the bird better?"

"I kept him still and made a splint for his wing. I caught insects and lizards for him to eat so he would grow strong again."

"Why didn't he fly away when his wing was better?"

"By then, he had grown too dependent on me. He never really learned to hunt well for himself."

"Do you still catch food for him?"

"He eats meat from my table. Sometimes, he manages to catch a bird or two."

Tabytha marveled at her son's insightful questions and felt grateful that the seer answered each one thoughtfully. Not many would afford a child such attention and respect. But hadn't he done the same for her when she was a child? The words he had spoken to her were still carved into her memory. *You are no ordinary girl. Adonai sees your heart. Remember that his hand is on you. Remember especially when you have a broken wing.*

"Can I touch the bird?" her son asked.

"Come from the back of him and scratch him here." The seer pointed to a spot on the falcon's back. "He has a sharp bite and will nip you if you come from the front.

Beninu stepped closer and tentatively reached for the bird. As his fingers stroked the falcon's feathers, he smiled. Joy leaped inside Tabytha when she saw it.

She looked up to find the seer watching her with his usual astuteness.

"Thank you." She knew she didn't have to explain. Recalling her conversation with Abigail, she added, "Could the boy meet you again to see the bird?"

Beninu raised his head, his expression full of hope.

The seer nodded. "Next week, this time." He addressed the boy directly. "I will bring a leather glove and teach you how to hold him."

Then the seer looked up and addressed Tabytha. "The smoke from the south brings change. For all of you."

Only then did she notice the slight tang of smoke in the air. Looking to the south, she saw white puffs rising and wafting towards them.

"What burns?"

"Joab's barley fields have been set alight."

"Who would dare do such a thing?"

The seer looked towards the horizon as if he saw far more than just burning barley. "A bold and desperate man."

chapter 50

michal

extract from scroll ב (hs beit)

I hated Hebron from the moment I walked through its gates. Even as we ascended the hill to David's homestead, people turned to look at me. I heard their whispers—*Saul's daughter, Ish-Bosheth's sister*—and saw their animosity in the quick downturn of their heads, the narrowing of their eyes, and the pursing of their lips. I wasn't one of them. I was of the enemy.

I have never felt so alone as the day Abner tore me from my home and marched me up Hebron's hill like the captive of a conquering king. Every glance and every whisper fueled the fire of my anger. By the time I walked through David's gates, anger beat through my bones like a drum.

"We bring the king's wife," Abner's soldier said to the guard at the top gate.

As the guard hurried off to call David, I glanced around at my surroundings. An open space framed by four low buildings, David's home throbbed with noise and activity. Soldiers sat in circles with children darting between them.

Servants carried water or swept the ground with long rushes. Older men reclined against a wall in conversation. Two women appeared at the entrance of one of the buildings and gazed across the courtyard at me. Were these David's wives?

My eyes caught the movement from the side. *David.* A strange feeling enveloped me as I watched him approach. Even after all the years, that first instinctive attraction remained. As handsome as I remembered, David's confident stride now exuded an easy authority that made him undeniably more attractive. As our eyes met, familiarity jolted through me. I had pined for this precise moment for so long after he left that now my body betrayed me. Warmth rushed to my cheeks like the very first time I saw him at Jonathan's house. Perhaps he noticed, for he smiled.

"My lord." The soldier stepped between us with a curt bow. "Commander Abner says he has done the first thing you asked and brought you your wife. He will come to you once he has met with Israel's elders."

The soldier's words broke that first mesmerizing moment with David. It afforded me time to recall all that had happened that day. Paltiel's grief and Abner's indifference. The selfish schemes of powerful men. By the time David had sent Abner's soldiers to recline with his own, and turned his attention back to me, my anger was once again in control.

"Michal. It's good to see you again." He stood so calmly, so self-assuredly among his men. "Welcome to my home."

"David." I stifled the traitorous memory of the first time I had lain in his arms and whispered that name.

He watched me in silence as if trying to catch a glimpse of the girl I had once been. Perhaps if I'd told him then that little of her remained, it would have saved us years of opposition. But the day had worn me too thin. I merely stood and met his gaze with all the strength and pride I could still muster. *He had treated me, the daughter of a king, like worthless chattel.*

One tiny flame of hope remained—that the young man who had once loved me would consider my wishes and send me back to Paltiel. I would not ask him now, however. David would show no weakness in front of his men. When we were alone, perhaps he would listen to me. Yet even as the hope formed, I wondered if—like me— David had changed beyond recognition. What if too little of his former self remained to appeal to?

David turned to his men. "Join Abner's soldiers while I show Michal her quarters. Perhaps you will learn something of Israel's plans."

"Why don't you come too?" the shortest of the men said. Something in his brashness reminded me of Abner. "I'll send Abigail for the woman."

"I'll join you later, Joab." David's gaze returned to me.

The men inclined their heads before turning away. I swallowed nervously. I hadn't expected to be alone with him so soon. Should I raise my appeal now or wait until I knew this new David better?

"You have nothing with you? No clothes or serving women?"

"They came for me this morning. I had no time to prepare." I suddenly remembered the bundles of clothes. "I think they brought my robes."

David looked towards the soldiers. His gaze, when it settled on me again, seemed troubled. "It shouldn't have been that way. I will ensure you get them back, Michal. And anything else you left behind."

When I said nothing, he said, "Come," and walked towards one of the buildings. I fell in step next to him. Another wave of familiarity washed over me as I caught a whiff of the balsam and olive soap he had always favored.

"You will share the house of my first two wives, Ahinoam and Abigail. Another, Haggith, also lives there."

I wanted to say that *I* had been his first wife, but I held my tongue. After all, I wanted him to forego his claim to me.

He led me to the house where I had seen the women in the doorway. The same two appeared as we reached the door, a gaggle of young children thronging around them.

"This is Ahinoam." David pointed to the plainer of the two women, who gave me an unsmiling nod.

"And Abigail."

Abigail, at least, smiled. "Welcome, Michal." She was slim and graceful. *A threat*.

"And these," David pointed indulgently at the children, "are mostly mine."

"Fortunately, not all mine and Ahinoam's." Abigail chuckled and the way David echoed her laugh increased my mistrust of her.

"Did you bring a bedroll?" Abigail asked.

"She has nothing with her," David said. "Provide her with everything she requires."

"Of course."

"And bring her to the fire later so I can introduce her to the rest of the family. I will go speak with Abner's men now."

I watched his retreating back, suddenly anxious to be left with these strangers. Reluctantly, I turned back to the women. They were watching me. My gaze fell on the children, looking at me with equal wide-eyed wonder—David's offspring. Instant dislike rose in me at that moment.

"Didn't your mothers teach you it's rude to stare?" I snapped. "What am I? The serpent itself that I'm so interesting?"

One of the children, a particularly striking boy, chortled at this. "She's the serpent," he cried in a throaty, child voice. "Sssss. Run!" And the children scattered, shrieking as they went.

Abigail's lips twitched. "If only we'd known it was that easy to get rid of them. Come, Michal."

As they led me into the house to the corner of a room—the one miserable space that would become my own—jealousy stabbed through me. Once David had been mine, and mine alone. But I had stepped into a world where everyone's claim to him was stronger than my own—wives, sons, and daughters.

Far from being the first wife, the one who should have born him an heir, I had become the last. The last and childless one.

CHAPTER 51

Tabytha lay with her arm propped up on a terrace cushion watching David play his lyre. It had been a long time since she had heard him play. The soft music mingled pleasingly with the sounds of the night. Contentment stirred inside her. She watched him in the soft light of the lamps they had brought from his chamber. Although he had aged these last years, she still found him attractive despite his greying hair and deeply lined face. And never more so than now, with his eyes closed, lost in the music.

"I like the tune," she said when his fingers stopped strumming, and he opened his eyes. "But what of the words?"

He laughed. "I almost forgot that you love the words more than the tune." He plucked softly at the strings again. "Look up as I sing it, my gazelle."

She did as he told her to. The moon was a thin crescent. Against the dark sky, the stars were a breathtaking swirl of light. And along with the sight of the vast night sky, David's words lifted her soul high into the heavens.

Lord, our Lord, how majestic is your name in all the earth.

You have set your glory in the heavens.
When I consider your heavens, the work of your
fingers,
The moon and the stars which you have set in place,
What is mankind that you are mindful of them,
Human beings that you care for them?

The words David sang resonated with the truth of what
she saw as she looked at the night sky. Lost in wonder, she
hardly noticed when he stopped playing. When she did
finally let her gaze drop to him, he was watching her with a
tenderness that she hadn't seen for a long time.

"Yes," she whispered. "Yes, David. Your God is majestic
and glorious and great."

"*Our* God," he said.

She nodded at that, for as Adonai had watched over
Rahab, the harlot, she believed he watched over her and
Beninu too. She felt Adonai's eyes on her when she prayed,
when she sat with David, and—on looking back—all the
times she had met the seer. Thinking of their first meeting
with the bird, she realized that even as a child, Adonai had
had his eyes on her.

"What are you smiling about, my gazelle?" David asked.

"A childhood memory. The first time I sensed Adonai
watched over me."

David looked at her expectantly, but she said no more.
Nathan was *his* prophet, after all, not hers. She wasn't sure
what he would make of the fact that the man had spoken to
her as often as he had.

"I hear Joab's fields were alight yesterday." She sought
to change the conversation, but regretted her words at
David's suddenly solemn expression.

After a long pause, he said, "Absalom set them alight."

"Absalom? But why?"

"To get Joab's attention so he could ask him to petition me."

"He wants to see you?"

It had been two years since David permitted Absalom to return to Jerusalem, but he had not sent for his son in that time.

She thought David would say no more, but he shifted and looked back at the sky. "It's time to forgive him." Pain laced his voice. "I sense Adonai would want that." He looked down at her. "But how, Tabytha? How can I forgive him for killing my son?"

Compassion stirred inside her. She crept over to him, put her arms around his chest, and leaned her head on his shoulder.

"Adonai will give you the strength," she whispered. "Trust him."

Three days later, David sent for Absalom.

They were to meet alone in David's chambers, so even Gilia's man in the palace couldn't report precisely what took place. The Women's Quarters would have remained ignorant of the details of the reunion between the king and his son except that Maacah sent word to Tabytha. David was allowing Absalom to come to the Women's Courtyard after his meeting with the king. There, the prince would meet with his mother for the first time in five years.

As always among the king's women, the news of Absalom's impending visit spread faster than the fire in Joab's barley field.

Ahinoam and all who had sided with the queen over the years declared their outrage that Amnon's murderer would be permitted to set foot in the Women's Quarters again. Gilia threatened to disrupt the meeting, and Abital foretold that Adonai's curses would fall on their household that very day. Abigail and Pudu looked troubled, caught between honoring the king's wishes and loyalty towards their friend.

David had foreseen the trouble and forbade anybody except Maacah from going to the courtyard that afternoon. He even posted guards at all the entrances to ensure that Maacah and Absalom would be undisturbed.

Shortly before the meeting, Maacah's handmaiden knocked on Tabytha's door, breathlessly spilling out her message. Maacah was overwrought. She feared what the women would do to her when she left her room to meet with her son. Tabytha must come immediately to accompany her.

So like Maacah. Tabytha followed the servant down the passage. David had finally granted Maacah what she had pined for all these years, yet now she was too afraid to grasp it.

Maacah looked beautiful. Dressed in the finest of robes, with her hair piled into an elaborate style, she waited for Tabytha just inside her chamber. Tabytha considered it a welcome change from seeing Maacah lying in bed, disheveled and unkempt, but the impression shattered as Maacah's forehead creased with anger.

"Where have you been? I've been waiting alone all this time."

"I came as soon as your servant called me."

"Well, we are going to be late." Maacah touched a nervous hand to her pinned-up hair. "Absalom is an important man. He can't wait for us indefinitely."

"I'll walk you to the courtyard. I'm sure you want to be alone with him."

"No. Come with me."

"But David has forbidden ..."

"I can bring you if I want, can't I?"

And with that, Maacah lifted her head and regally swept out of her chambers, leaving Tabytha with little choice but to fall in behind her. The corridors were deserted, although several doors inched open furtively as they passed by, and a few children peered out at them from adjoining passages.

At the entrance to the courtyard, a guard blocked Tabytha's way, but Maacah turned on him.

"She's my friend, and I want her with me."

Tabytha felt strangely moved by that statement—*David's aloof wife considered her a friend*. Another insight struck her. Could it be that Maacah feared not the women but rather being alone with Absalom after all this time apart?

The young guard looked anxiously at the older one for affirmation before moving aside at his companion's nod.

Maacah and Tabytha stepped into the Women's Courtyard. It was strangely quiet, except for the men stationed around the perimeter. Tabytha saw Absalom instantly, not only because of his long hair and colorful robe but because, unlike the other men standing to attention, the prince leaned languidly against one of the far pillars. *As if he holds court in* his *palace.*

Maacah's sharp intake of breath told Tabytha she had seen her son too, but—ever the royal consort—Maacah did not run to him as Tabytha might have if Beninu had stood there. Instead, she walked down the steps with a dignified air and met him in the center of the courtyard, where they fell into a long, silent embrace.

On the steps, Tabytha wiped away her tears and watched as Maacah and Absalom eventually pulled apart. Absalom said something, and both mother and son laughed. It seemed like a good time for Tabytha to leave, but as she made her way back to the entrance, Maacah called for her.

"Tabytha. Come and embrace my son, lost to us all these years."

Tabytha had no desire to speak to the prince, but it touched her that Maacah wanted to share the moment with her. As she walked over to them, she admired Absalom's impeccable taste in clothing. The richness of his robe far exceeded anything she had ever seen David wear, and with his height and broad shoulders, the prince wore it well. He appeared to notice her perusal for he gave her his usual charming smile.

"Prince Absalom. I am glad you are here to see your mother again."

"Indeed." The prince's smile didn't waver. "But didn't my mother insist we embrace?"

She stiffened as he stepped towards her and pulled her against his chest. He still wore the same aloe and spice scent that she had always liked, yet this close the cloying smell reminded her of stepping into Maacah's over-perfumed rooms. When he released her, she took a step back, casting a glance at David's watching guards. Would they tell David his concubine had embraced his son?

"How very fine you look, my son." Maacah studied Absalom the way a starving woman might look at a food-laden table. "I thought it impossible for you to grow any finer, but I was wrong." She reached out and ran her hands through his thick hair. "It's as beautiful as I remember."

"Ima!" Absalom shook off her hand yet seemed both embarrassed and pleased by his mother's fawning. "Let's sit, and I will tell you of my meeting with my father."

Tabytha reluctantly followed them to the cushions on one of the steps. Absalom sat on the center cushion and indicated that she should sit beside him, but she ignored him and sat beside Maacah instead. At least the guards couldn't tell David she had embraced *and* sat beside his son.

"Tell me all." Maacah said. "How is it that Joab approached the king on your behalf?"

"I sent for Joab a while back, but he refused to come. The second time I sent for him, he wouldn't even receive my messenger. So, I thought, 'What is a sure way to get him here?' and devised the perfect plan."

"How did you do it, my son?"

"I set Joab's barley fields alight." Absalom laughed. "And before the sun had set, he stood on my doorstep."

"Was he angry?"

"Furious. But I told him his barns would be next if he didn't get me an audience with the king."

Tabytha didn't share Absalom and Maacah's laughter. "A bold and desperate man," the seer had said. What else was such a desperate man capable of?

"Yesterday, Joab sent word I should come and Abba would see me alone. And that I could come to see you afterward, which told me my life wasn't in danger."

"He wouldn't execute you after all this time." Maacah seemed shaken at the thought.

"It's impossible to know the mind of a king."

Tabytha thought how little he understood his father. David was, above all, a man of integrity and a man who loved his sons. If he had sought justice for Amnon's death, he would have done it long before.

"Joab met me today and led me to the king's chambers. As soon as I saw my father, I fell to the ground and bowed before him. And he said absolutely nothing, but when I finally looked up at him, I saw tears streaming down his face. Then he told me to rise, and he kissed me."

Oh David. Love for him swelled in Tabytha's chest. *Adonai truly did give you the strength to forgive your son.*

chapter 52

ABIGAIL

EXTRACT FROM SCROLL ד (hs GImEL)

Some days stay in my memory as if they happened last week rather than decades ago. Michal's arrival was one of those. I recall the soldiers' sideways glances as David led her to our house. Her crumpled gown and unruly hair, hints that she had been torn from her former life with no warning. The way David looked at her—youthful desire vying with uncharacteristic reticence. And the way she looked back at him as if she couldn't quite decide whether to throw herself or a knife at him.

Michal was a pretty woman who said little but watched everything warily. Her movements were restrained, but I sensed a deep well of shifting emotions inside her. Had her father, Saul, been like this? The thought that such brooding instability could reside in somebody wielding the power of a king unsettled me.

The house Ahinoam, Haggith, Pudu, and I shared with our children had always been full of talk and laughter, but Michal's arrival stifled some of that lightness. We no longer spoke as freely as before. The children were a little afraid of Michal, although, behind her back, they hissed and called her the serpent. I warned them to stop and show her respect, but the title she herself had spoken stuck, aided by the way she occasionally struck out at them like a slumbering snake disturbed.

The unease she brought into our house roiled inside me, too. Sometimes, I looked at her and saw the cowering girl she must have been in Saul's unstable household. I felt pity for that girl and for the woman who had suffered so many losses—her mother and sister, father and brothers. Yet Michal refused to talk about anyone in her past, especially the man who was her husband after David. I asked David about him once, and he told me, according to the soldiers who brought Michal to Hebron, this man Paltiel wept when they took Michal from him, and followed them all the way to Bahurim, where Abner threatened him into leaving.

"Do you think she cared for him as much as he did for her?" I had asked.

David's brow furrowed at the question, but eventually, he said, "Possibly. She asked me to send her back to him once."

I had wanted to ask him why he hadn't done it when Michal's unhappiness in Hebron was so evident, but I knew the answer for myself. As king, he could never show weakness, and what was weaker than letting another man take your wife as his own?

Still, I thought of that weeping man every time Michal lashed out at one of the children, every time she turned her back on me or the others when we tried to show her kindness, every time I sensed the anger simmering deep inside her. Sometimes, it was the only thing that kept me kind in the face of her disdain.

But Michal's arrival is not the only day engraved in my memory. Abner's visit is too. That day, David learned that even the closest of men can betray you.

But no. Even as I say it, I realize he already knew that some men could not be trusted, for why else would he send Joab and his brother to lead a raiding party on the day Abner came?

Abner was exactly as David had described him, tall and imposing. Something about him made me think of a long spear—the way he stood so straight, the sharpness of his gaze, even his cutting tone. No wonder men said Ish-Bosheth feared him or that he held such sway over the elders of Israel.

I watched from a distance as David greeted him and his men, and I saw that even David, the king of Hebron, deferred to him. I would have an opportunity to observe him up close, for David had instructed us to prepare a feast fit for a king, or in this case, a kingmaker. So it was I overheard some of his and David's conversation as I served the freshly roasted meat and bread.

"I've conferred with the elders of Israel and Benjamin. I promised you could deliver them from the Philistines and every other enemy they face. All that remains is for me to assemble the elders so they can make a covenant with you and declare you their king."

"What of Ish-Bosheth?" David asked.

Abner snorted in derision. "I'll deal with him."

"I don't want his blood on my hands."

"Well, be glad that other men do not share your aversion to spilling worthless blood." Abner didn't look at me as I refilled his wine cup. "Do you truly want this throne? Will you take what I offer you on a plate or not? It's easy enough to find another man to wear the crown, my lord."

The arrogance of his words shocked me so that my hand shook, spilling a few drops of red wine onto the sleeve of his robe. He turned his piercing gaze onto me for the first time that day. "You senseless woman. You will ..."

"This is my wife Abigail," David interrupted. "She can remove the stain if you give her the robe."

Abner's gaze stayed on me a moment longer and then returned to David. "Set the day, my lord, and I will assemble the elders. On that day, we will make you king of all Israel."

I moved away from them to serve Abner's men and heard no more of their talking, but throughout the day, my thoughts returned to the conversation I had overheard—*leave him to me to deal with ... what I offer you on a plate ... it's easy to find another man to wear the crown ... on that day, we will make you king.*

Why did the commander's words unsettle me so deeply? Still, I smiled at David's joy after he had bid Abner farewell.

"This is what we've been waiting for, Abi. Adonai's promise is about to be fulfilled."

"And spilling wine all over the man didn't make him want to find another man to wear the crown?"

David laughed. "Abner has always had a bent for the dramatic. But isn't he all I told you he was? Men don't call him the kingmaker for nothing."

Yet David's joy was short-lived. When the raiding party returned, Joab came to find him. David, in a particularly light mood, dueled with Amnon and Absalom outside the entrance of our house. .

"May I have a word, David?"

"Speak freely, Joab." David laughed as Absalom's wooden sword struck him on the knee. "Aim a little higher, son."

"Abner was here?"

"Yes." David lifted his hands in mock surrender to his sons. "You two are too strong for me. Run along while I talk to Joab."

"Why did you let him go? You know Abner son of Ner! He has come to deceive you and spy on you."

"Nonsense. He has spoken to the elders of Israel and Benjamin and has turned them to our side."

"Oh, the great Abner, the all-powerful kingmaker," Joab said bitingly.

"You fear he will take your place?"

"No, David. I fear your ambition blinds you to the truth. Abner is not our friend. He is our enemy." And with those parting words, Joab stalked away.

I had heard the conversation from inside, but now I came to stand in the doorway. David glanced at me, the lightness of the day faded from his eyes. "Abner's power threatens him."

"And he cannot forget that Abner's sword struck down his brother Asahel."

"It's good Abner is well on his way."

But Abner was not out of Joab's reach. Later, we learned Joab had sent messengers after Abner, and the commander had returned with the men to Hebron. While David slept, Joab took Abner into an inner chamber and stabbed him in the stomach, the same way Asahel had died.

The raised voices of Abner's men demanding to know where their commander was eventually woke up the household. David went out into the bristling tension of the night to find Abner's men and his own facing each other, knives drawn threateningly.

"Put away your weapons," he commanded before turning to Abner's men. "Why have you returned?"

"You sent for us," one man said belligerently.

"I did not." He looked around at the faces lit by the torches of the gate guards. "Where's Abner?"

"That's what we want to know, too."

David's gaze fell on Joab. He told me later a cold knowing gripped him at that moment. "Where's Abner, Joab?"

Joab flicked his head in the direction of one of the store chambers. "I have avenged the death of my brother," he said without a trace of shame.

At these words, Abner's men shouted with rage and reached for their knives, but David stepped forward and bellowed, "No! Enough blood has spilled tonight. You are outnumbered, and every one of you will die if you do not put your knives away now. Hear this, men of Israel, and return to tell your king Ish-Bosheth that I and my kingdom are forever innocent before the Lord concerning the blood of Abner, son of Ner. May his blood fall on the head of Joab and his whole family."

Then David took his robe and rent it, anger and grief combined, before pushing his way over to Joab. "Tear your clothes, Joab."

Joab stood defiantly before him.

"Now."

Only when David reached for his knife did Joab do what the king demanded.

"All of you," David shouted, "tear your clothes and put on sackcloth for Abner. A great man has been slain."

We buried Abner in the morning, and David walked behind the bier, weeping.

All Abner's arrogant promises died with him. If David were to become king of all Israel, it would not be by the hand of a man but rather by the hand of the only true kingmaker. Adonai.

interlude

michal

extract from scroll ב (hs beit)

David refused to send me back to Paltiel, but he did make one concession—he allowed me to send for my recently widowed sister-in-law, Hannah. On the day she arrived to serve me, I fell into her arms and wept. Mostly, I wept for the months I'd spent apart from Paltiel in a household in which I still felt like a stranger.

Before Hannah arrived, I had grown to realize that in order to belong here, I needed to let go of my love for Paltiel. No betrayal had ever felt greater, but I had to accept I was David's if I ever hoped to find some happiness and peace. So, I stopped refusing to go to him and tried to rediscover in him the man I had once loved.

Perhaps I would have succeeded over time, but Hannah's arrival churned up all my old feelings for Paltiel. She told me he still pined for me and had not taken another wife. He sent a small jar of perfume that he knew I loved. With Hannah sleeping beside me, going to David's bed felt more of a betrayal than ever before.

But I was glad to have her by my side when two men arrived with a special gift for King David. I've never had much to thank Adonai for, but for this one mercy, I am grateful—I was not there when the two brothers opened the sack and Ish-Bosheth's head rolled out of it. I'm thankful, too, that David did not rejoice at my brother's slaying but instead had his murderers executed immediately. Then he came to find me.

"Michal?" His expression was troubled.

"What's wrong?" I rose, and Hannah, beside me, rose too. The fact that he had come himself instead of sending a messenger concerned me even more than what I read on his face.

"Two men came with ... news." He stepped towards me, perhaps to draw me into his arms, but then stopped a pace away from me. "Ish-Bosheth is dead."

The shock struck the very air from me. "Are you sure?"

"Yes." Again, I thought he might take me into his arms, but he glanced at Hannah and then back at me. He nodded before turning to leave, and it was Hannah's arms I sank into.

Ish-Bosheth's death changed everything. Within two weeks, the elders of Israel came, bowing low before David and begging him to be their king. I watched it all silently from the shadows, simmering with resentment at how quickly and remorselessly they had changed their allegiance. Hannah and I still wore our sackcloth when everyone around us wore their finest robes. Nor did we partake of the rich feasting or dance with the other women on the day Israel's tribes promised to be loyal to their new king, David.

How could I not grieve that my father's dynasty crumbled to dust while David's was established? How could I not hate

Adonai for destroying my family while he blessed David's? I never felt more like an outsider than on the day the elders, who had once supported my father, declared David king of all Israel. I, Michal, daughter of a king, was destined to die in the house of my father's overthrower.

part 3

23 years since King David conquered Jebus,
to rule the twelve tribes of Israel
from within its mighty walls

chapter 53

Tabytha stood on Jerusalem's walls and watched the falcon drop from the sky, marveling at its speed. Next to her, Beninu raised his leather-clad arm and let out another long, piercing whistle. Tabytha kept her eyes on the bird and stood as still as her son had instructed as the falcon swooped onto his arm.

"Well done, Beninu." She remembered not to clap for fear of startling the bird.

"Yes, you did well, lad," the seer said from the other side of him. "He's responding well to your whistle."

Four years had passed since Beninu started meeting the seer to learn about handling falcons. The bird she and the seer had rescued died soon after Beninu had begun his lessons. Her son had been inconsolable even though the seer assured him the falcon had lived to a good age. It hadn't been long before somebody had brought the seer another injured young bird. Beninu named it Eshsha—flame—and spoke of little else between his visits to the seer. He even took to scouring the palace for lizards and mice for the young falcon.

Tabytha looked at her son with pride. Sometimes, she still couldn't believe he was ten years old. Only a head shorter than she was, Beninu had David's expressive eyes and her unruly curls. On the rare occasion he smiled, his face lit up with such joy that Tabytha felt she looked into the face of an angel.

Her gaze found the seer's, and he nodded at her. She sensed the warmth of his approval in that simple nod. He hadn't changed much in the years since they had met. His eyes were still filled with a fierce, sometimes frightening, fire, and only his graying beard hinted at the passing of time.

He stepped towards Beninu and stretched out his arm. "That's enough for one day." Beninu reluctantly let him take the bird. "See you next week, lad."

"Thank you, Nathan."

Tabytha had been surprised the first time she heard her son use the seer's name, but apparently, the man had insisted on it. Beninu had also told her sternly that Nathan was not a seer but a prophet of Adonai and every time she spoke of him as the seer, it showed her ignorant Jebusite roots. Yet, Tabytha continued to think of him as the seer.

Tabytha headed for the stairwell while Beninu lingered on the wall. She turned around and retraced her steps back to him.

"Are you coming, Son?"

"I always stay and watch the gate for a while."

She peered over the wall and followed his gaze towards the gate. "A more interesting view than we have from the Women's Quarters."

Guards and old men sat in a circle, and a lone trader led a donkey into the city.

"The best is when Absalom is here," Beninu said.

"He comes to the city gate?"

"Not often. He's usually a little way up the road with his chariot and men."

"Chariot?"

"Oh, Ima, you must see it." Her son's eyes lit with excitement. "And he's got horses to draw it and lots of men to run ahead of him. I tried to count them all once, but they were too far away and moving, so I think I counted some more than once.

"Do you think he would give me a ride in his chariot, Ima? Maybe I can ask Abba to command him to do it."

Tabytha thought of David's strained relationship with Absalom. The king may have forgiven his son four years earlier but still hardly saw him.

"Or you can ask Maacah to ask Absalom?" Beninu said hopefully.

"Absalom doesn't come to the palace often. But maybe the next time he does, you can ask him yourself."

Over the next few days, Tabytha often thought about Absalom, his chariot, and men. Why would the prince stand along the road leading to Jerusalem's gate? Did Maacah or David know of their son's unusual behavior? She thought of the last time she had seen Absalom, on the day of his reconciliation with David. How he had leaned against the pillar. His rich clothes. His confident air. She wondered whether the clothes and confidence merely masked what the seer saw in him—a bold and desperate man.

"Tabytha!"

The voice startled her. She spun around to find Miriam standing on the step above where she sat. The princess, smiling down at her, looked particularly lovely with her rosy cheeks and rounded belly.

"Miriam."

She rose and threw her arms around the girl, and Miriam laughed.

"I'm almost too big to embrace. That's what Hushai says."

Three years earlier, David had given Miriam in marriage to his closest confidant. Despite the age gap, Miriam seemed happy. Hushai treated his young wife with indulgent kindness, and often used her as a scribe. Thus, Miriam knew most of the politics of her father's court, something—Tabytha suspected—the princess enjoyed. Unlike Gilia, Miriam protected her husband's confidences and never spoke of them to the women.

"Your time grows close."

"The midwife thinks the babe will be born before the Feast of Atonement."

"That soon?"

Miriam nodded. "You won't believe what Hushai said to me the other day. He said he hopes it's a girl."

"No!" Tabytha had never heard a man say such a thing before.

"It's true." Miriam chuckled. "He says he has enough sons and now wants a daughter as beautiful and clever as her mother. And he insists that I teach her to read and write."

Hushai's first wife had given him four sons. Tabytha found it sad the woman had survived what killed so many others—childbirth—and then died from something as simple as a rotting tooth.

"Your husband's words are as smooth as honey. No wonder he has the ear of the king. But what about you? Surely you want a son?"

Miriam lay her hand on her belly and smiled. "I believe Adonai has shown me it's a girl." She had not altogether shaken her prophetic aspirations. "And we will cherish her."

Tabytha didn't doubt it. Miriam had grown into a particularly wise and gracious young woman. In that, she reminded Tabytha of Solomon.

"Did you see your mother today?"

"We were at the Shabbat market together. You weren't there?"

"I was with Michal. You know how she likes to meet in secret."

"Secret!" Miriam laughed. "Everyone knows you've been recording her story for years. Aren't you finished yet?"

"Nowadays, I don't scribe. Mostly, I listen to her and Hannah reminisce about Paltiel."

"The man she was with before Abba? What became of him?"

"He mourned Michal for nearly five years, and then his father found him a new wife. They have a few children by now."

Miriam shook her head and let out a long sigh. "That must be difficult for Michal."

"On good days, I think she's glad for him. She loved him."

"More than she ever loved Abba."

"She loved him too," Tabytha said. "In her own way. Michal didn't have an easy time of it."

"I never thought of it before. When I was growing up, she was just Abba's bad-tempered wife. The one he set aside."

"Sometimes I think your father may have loved her too. But too much happened. It pushed them apart."

"Abba's house was always destined for division," Miriam said sagely.

The words reminded Tabytha of something the seer had said on the day Absalom murdered Amnon. A wave of cold rippled over Tabytha as she recalled his words. *Warfare would come from inside David's own house.*

chapter 54

ABIGAIL

EXTRACT FROM SCROLL ⊓ (hs GIMEL)

I asked David once why he chose Jebus as his royal city—
the one from which he could rule all of Israel. He told me
all the answers I expected. That although Jebus lay in the
tribal land of Benjamin, it had never been conquered by
Israel before and would be accepted by all the tribes. That
it had fresh water. That it would be easy to defend. Then,
after a long pause, he said, "The truth is I didn't choose
it, Abi. Adonai did. It was never the City of David. It was
always the City of God."

We women stayed behind in Hebron when David and
his army, now drawn from all the men of Israel, set off to
conquer Jebus. Later, we would hear the stories. How the
Jebusites hurled rocks and insults at them from the walls.
How they declared their city invincible, claiming even the
blind and lame would be able to ward off the Israelites.
And for a while David thought they might be right. The
walls were well-built and strong. They towered up from the
steep, slippery cliffs of the long valleys below the city. If

David's army tried to invade, the slingers and archers on the walls would pick them off. And it was impossible to bring siege equipment into the valleys.

But Jebus had one weakness—its water supply. The city drew water from a spring, and if David and his men could find the source, perhaps they could use the water channel to enter the city.

After two weeks of exploring, a scout came to David and told him a cloth trader had told him the source of the spring lay within one of the well-guarded towers on the Eastern wall. This trader, Elik, now requested an audience with the king.

"Bring him to me," David ordered.

They brought a tall, dark-skinned man to David's tent. He bowed his head before considering David with a calculating gaze.

"Elik? My scout tells me you know a way into the city."

"I do."

"You are a Jebusite? Why would you help us?"

"My mother was a Jebusite. I was born after a Philistine ravaged her. I have always been an outsider. Never one of them." He looked resentfully towards the walls, visible from the slit in the tent.

"But you have a thriving cloth trade in the city?"

"I have been gone these last months to buy cloth, and now, they refuse me entry."

"Understandable considering their city is under siege."

"If I were a true Jebusite son, would they treat me that way? No. How much will you pay me to show you a way in?"

David had never met a man so disconcertingly direct.

"I am not a wealthy king."

"But you have your heart set on Jebus. I see it in your eyes. And you value the lives of your men. That, too, I see in your eyes. I know these valleys and these walls as well as I know the scars on my body. This bastard boy spent many hours alone and sometimes had to find a place to shelter for the night. Trust me when I say I can show you a way into the water channel that doesn't involve taking the tower. I ask again, my lord, how much is it worth to you?"

"Ten silver coins."

The trader laughed. "Make it a hundred. And I become the only cloth trader to the new king of Jebus. I hear you have many wives and daughters to clothe?"

"Forty coins. And yes, I will appoint you cloth trader to my household in the City of David."

"City of David. That has an enduring ring to it. Fine." Elik smiled. "Tonight. On the second last watch of the night while it is still dark, and the Jebusite guards are the most tired. Not more than ten men, or they will be seen. Tell them to meet me below the water tower. It's the one that's furthest east. There is a large overhanging rock that is a good shield against the city watch. I will meet them there."

He turned to leave but stopped at the tent entrance and looked back at David. "They might not care for me, but, my lord, will you spare the women, children, and even the old men of Jebus?"

"I will spare all who surrender to me and acknowledge me as king. And I will control my men. They will not rampage through your city. You have my word, trader."

David's men were the best of warriors. They could run long distances, survive in harsh, dry places, and fearlessly face down an enemy on a battlefield. They could kill with daggers and swords, bows, and arrows. Some had even mastered killing with slings and stones. But sheer silence met their king's explanation of how he planned to take the city. Ten men, David said, would creep in darkness through a narrow, slippery waterway and emerge amid the enemy. Every warrior among them knew this was a mission likely to fail, a mission that would end in death.

"Whoever leads the attack will become commander-in-chief of my army." David's gaze turned to Joab, who—he knew—already considered himself head of Israel's integrated army.

Years later, David told me with a hint of regret, there were two defining moments in his relationship with Joab. The first, when Joab slayed Abner, and the second, when David set the challenge to take Jebus. If David could never forgive Joab for killing Abner, Joab would never forgive David for manipulating him to remain his army commander.

The moment stretched out in silence. Finally, Joab spoke. "I will go, my king. You need only have asked, for my life is yours to command. And if I should return, I will continue to serve in my rightful place by your side."

Abishai immediately offered to accompany his brother. Next came Uriah, a Hittite by birth who could blend in as a Canaanite. Seven of Joab's closest men took up the challenge. David and the ten of them sat huddled around a fire that night, talking of what they would do if they made it through the waterway into Jebus. They agreed that at first light, David would move the army to the gate closest to the water tower as a decoy, for if the ten men managed to navigate the waterway, they would attempt to open the gate. At the same time, two units of archers would attack the tower from the valley below, drawing the Jebusites to the walls, away from the entry to the well.

David urged the men to sleep, but knowing the danger they faced, they all remained around the fire, silently sharpening their weapons in the shifting light of the flames. On the second last watch of the night, dressed in their darkest robes, they bade the king farewell.

"Adonai has chosen this city and will give you victory," David said. "Be strong and courageous."

Joab did not meet his gaze. At Joab's gruff command, the men slipped into the night.

Sleep eluded David, and he spent the rest of the night in prayer. At first light, he sent word for the army to prepare to move and called the commanders of the archers to instruct their men to take up places near the tower.

In the grainy morning light, David sensed rather than saw the flurry of activity on the enemy's walls as his army moved towards the gate. Calls carried from above them, clear in the crisp air, and David prayed silently they were to warn of the movement in the valley below rather than of imposters in their city.

The army reached its position, as close to the gate as David dared to go, while remaining out of reach of the Jebusite archers. He glanced to where his archers had positioned themselves, closer to the walls so their arrows could reach their mark. He knew too well that the enemy's arrows would do the same.

Help us, Lord, he whispered. The timing was everything in sending the signal to attack. He wanted to give Joab and his men enough time to climb the waterway, but if he waited too long, they might emerge from the well without the cover of distraction.

Eventually, though, the decision was forced on him as a bevy of arrows flew from the tower towards his archers. The shields men stopped most of the arrows, but not all.

"Attack!" David shouted.

David told me it felt like the longest hour of his life as he watched the futile battle around the water tower.

Occasionally, an Israelite arrow would find its mark, but most of the deadly arrows came from above. When he could stand the bloodshed no longer, he called the archers to retreat, hoping the deadly mock battle had given Joab and his men enough time to make it into the city.

Time stretched on, and just when his hope began to slip away, he heard a shout from the direction of the gate. He watched in amazement as the large wooden gate swung open, and a single figure emerged. *Joab.*

"Charge the gate!" David shouted, praying that the distance they had to cover wouldn't give the Jebusites time to cut down Joab and his men and then close the gate again.

But the gate stayed open, and as David reached it, he found Joab and his men in hand-to-hand combat with only a few defenders. The word had spread, however, and more and more Jebusites swarmed to the breach. Yet they were no match for Israel's warriors. Too long had they relied solely on their mighty walls to defend them.

When wave after wave of Jebusites had died to David's swords, David called out, "Men of Jebus! You have fought valiantly. Now lay down your swords in surrender, and I will spare your lives and the lives of all within these walls."

The sounds of the battle—clashing swords and bellows of anger and pain—muted slightly as his voice carried into the narrow streets. In a moment of uncertainty, both sides halted their attack, and then a voice responded.

"Lay down your swords, men." An older man with a wiry build and a long, bloodied sword stepped forward. "I am Ornan, the Araunah of Jebus." He limped towards David, dropped to his knee and lay his sword on the ground. Then he looked up at his conqueror. "My lord, I beg you to preserve the lives of my people."

"As Adonai is my witness, not another drop of blood will be shed."

At that moment Jebus became David's.

chapter 55

Tabytha hurriedly wiped away the tears, but Abigail had seen them. She reached for Tabytha and pulled her into an awkward embrace, careful not to touch the inky reed.

"I'm sorry. You've been here so long. You're one of us now, I almost forgot your past. I shouldn't have told you how David took Jebus. It must have been unbearable for you to record."

Tabytha shook her head. "David stayed true to his word and showed kindness to my people. Many more could have died if he was not a man of integrity."

"Your father was among those who died?"

A fresh wave of tears welled up in Tabytha's eyes. She didn't trust her voice and was grateful that Abigail didn't say anything more. They sat in silence for a while, before Tabytha straightened herself.

"Strangely, David reminds me of my father. From the first day I met him, I thought as much."

"In what way?"

"His strength. His kindness. Even his smile." She tried to swallow down the lump in her throat. "I remember the day of my betrothal so well."

"You were only a child."

"Yes." Tabytha laughed to dispel the heaviness in the room. "I remember my mother telling me to keep my mouth shut. Now, I understand she was telling me not to talk, but then I thought it was so the king and our elders couldn't see that my teeth were only half grown."

Abigail smiled. "Did I ever tell you David spoke of that day? He told me the Jebusite elders had made a covenant of peace with him and given him their daughters to prove we could become one people. He said they had insisted on it."

"David didn't want us?" Tabytha thought of the child she had been, of her distress and shame. Why had she endured it all for a man who didn't even want her?

"It wasn't like that, Tabytha." Abigail looked away. "The Jebusites saw his power and feared him."

"They thought having their daughters in his palace would keep them safe." Hadn't Tabytha's grandfather said as much?

"Something like that."

After another long silence, Tabytha said, "Michal once said the men in our families, who should have protected us, were the very ones to trade us away like cattle."

"Michal might know better than most. That's not my story with David."

"Ornan did that with me." Tabytha felt a surprising surge of resentment, followed by the insight *this* was how Michal had always felt. She didn't want to linger on the unpleasant feeling, however. She refused to become as bitter as Michal.

Abigail hesitated again as if weighing her words. "David spoke of you specifically. He told me one of those given to him was a child. *Only a little older than Tamar.* Those were his words. Your age, and the fact the men laughed at you, troubled him."

Shame washed through Tabytha at the memory of that moment, as sharp as if it had happened only the day before.

"Tabytha." Abigail squeezed her hand. "I'm glad you came. You have been a gift to us. It means more than I can say that you've given us a voice." She hesitated again. "I've been speaking to Bathsheba, urging her to tell her story too."

Bathsheba had always been an enigma to Tabytha. Even before the division in the Women's Quarters, the king's elegant wife had kept herself apart from the others. Gilia told with relish how Bathsheba had seduced David and deliberately fallen pregnant, forcing David to send her husband to the heat of the battle, where he died. According to Gilia, Bathsheba was the craftiest of women—with the sole ambition of seeing her son on the throne.

"It won't be easy to convince her," Abigail continued. "Bathsheba doesn't like to speak of those early days. She carries much shame."

Initially, Tabytha believed Gilia's narrative, but now she had her doubts. She remembered Bathsheba's genuine concern for Tamar. Would a "crafty, scheming" woman care so much or even feel shame as Abigail claimed? And Tabytha admired how much time Bathsheba spent with her sons. They had grown into well-mannered, thoughtful young men—perhaps the best of all the princes. No, there was more to Bathsheba than Gilia made them all believe.

"I'd like to hear the story from her lips," Tabytha said. "I've only ever heard it from Gilia's."

"Precisely." Abigail slapped the bench. "That's what I said to her. If you don't put the record straight, everyone will believe the stories of people like Gilia. You'll be remembered as the crown-seeker who led David astray. And you know what, Tabytha? She says she doesn't care."

"Truly? I would care. Wouldn't you?"

"I think so."

Tabytha carefully rolled away the parchment, corked the ink jar, and dabbed the last ink off the reed. She looked at Abigail, who stared out of the window in quiet reflection.

"Abigail? You say you're grateful I'm giving the women a voice. I wouldn't have been able to do so without the priest who taught me to read and write. You told me once you had heard of him."

"Wasn't he the one accompanying the ark of the covenant the first time David tried to bring it to Jerusalem?"

"I think so. He told me he had overseen the sacred relics."

"And nothing is more sacred than the ark of the covenant. What was his name?"

"Ahio." Tabytha smiled as she thought of the sweet, broken priest. "I want to write down his story, too."

chapter 56

tabytha

extract from scroll א (hs alef)

I asked David once if he knew what had become of Ahio. He said he would make inquiries, and, true to his word, he did. He asked the high priest, who apparently asked Ahio's father what had become of his son. Abinadab said that he had no son. One had been slain on the road to the City of David, and the other, useless to the core, was dead to him.

Surprisingly, my mother told me that Ahio had left Jerusalem to go to Gath, where he planned to seek out a Gittite called Obed-edom. Ahio visited my mother about three years after I went to the palace to let her know he planned to leave for good. She invited him in and gave him her freshly baked bread and goat's milk.

"Do you remember," he said, "you used to make me teach Tabytha in the courtyard?"

"I remember only that you kept Tawaassi from her real work."

My mother said she had smiled as she spoke the words, and he had smiled back through his tears.

"Tabytha kept me from falling for a while," Ahio said.

As my mother recounted those—his parting words to her—I understood. Teaching me had given him a purpose bigger than his sorrow and even bigger than the beer with which he had drowned it. He had stayed longer than I truly needed him because teaching me kept the grief from consuming him. After I left, nothing stood between him and what haunted him.

He didn't tell my mother why he chose Gath. Only when Abigail told me what she knew of the fateful day on which Ahio's brother died did I begin to piece it together.

She told me that during the reign of Saul, the ark of the covenant—the very throne of Adonai—stood untouched and almost forgotten in the house of a Levite called Abinadab. He had three sons. His eldest son, Eleazar, became the keeper of the ark while his two youngest sons, Uzzah and Ahio, grew up with it tucked away in a corner of their house, covered with a long length of linen cloth.

Abigail said everybody knew the stories of what had happened to the Philistines when they captured the ark. The statue of their god Dagon fell before the ark when they placed it in his temple. Every city to which they brought it was inflicted with tumors until the Philistines begged for it to be sent back to Israel. It came back—remarkably—on a cart pulled by two cows that had recently calved and had never been yoked before.

Yet even in Israel, the ark brought death. Seventy men of Beth Shemesh, who dared to open the lid of the ark and look into it, were struck dead. Like the Philistines, the villagers begged for the ark to be removed, so the men of Kiriath Jearim fetched it and brought it to Abinadab's house to be watched over by Eleazar.

Decades later, David conquered Jebus and remembered the ark. He decided to bring it to its final resting place in his city.

What a joyful celebration it had been.

David led the procession, singing and dancing with all his might, and the musicians and the people sang and danced with him. Ahio and his brother Uzzah guided the cart on which the ark rested. When one of the oxen stumbled, Uzzah put out his hand to steady the ark.

David was still singing when a wail pierced the air. Most of the musicians, not hearing the cry, continued to play. The dancers still danced to the beat of the music. But David stopped and looked back. Three men were dragging the oxen to a halt, and others were swarming towards the left side of the cart. For a moment, David feared the ark had fallen, but as the music stuttered to a halt and more and more voices began to wail, a cold fear gripped his heart.

He pushed through the crowd of worshipers and, bewildered, they quickly moved aside for their king. When he reached the oxen, he saw a young man sprawled on the ground. He recognized him as one of the priests chosen to lead the cart. The other man knelt over him, keening with such raw grief that David knew instantly the priest must be dead.

He pushed forward till he stood beside the grieving priest. The man had now wrapped his arms around the other's body and rocked back and forth. David could hear snatches of his anguished words. "Uzzah, my brother. No. No. No."

He knew he could not pierce the man's grief to demand answers, so he looked around at those closest to him and asked them what had happened.

When one man spoke and told him about the oxen stumbling and the priest reaching out to steady the ark, David's first reaction was rage. How could Adonai strike down a man for such a trifling thing? Didn't he hear and see the worship and joy of this procession? Wasn't he pleased that David brought the ark to rest in his chosen city?

But after his initial anger, something far heavier and deeper settled into David's heart: fear.

I realize now I had seen this same fear of Adonai in Ahio during all the years he taught me. But, whereas David let his love and worship of Adonai soften the edges of his fear, Ahio's fear mingled with grief and guilt until it was all-consuming. Until it almost destroyed him.

I think perhaps that was the reason Ahio went to seek out the man called Obed-edom, for after his brother's death, the ark stood in this Gentile's home for a short time, and brought his family blessings. Ahio went to escape his father's disappointment and his fellow priests' disapproval. Mostly, he went to speak to another who had lived in the shadow of the ark but had seen Adonai's grace instead of his wrath.

Ahio went to Gath to seek the other side of Adonai's face.

I wish I could ask him if he found it.

chapter 57

michal

extract from scroll ב (hs beit)

I found the City of David more tolerable than Hebron.
To begin with, I didn't have to share a room with David's
wives and their brood of children. The palace David
eventually built near the city's summit was as fine as any
I'd ever been in—much finer than my father's or brother's.
From the beginning, Hannah and I shared the quarters
that looked over the palace courtyard. It lay apart from the
other women's rooms, and mostly, we were left in peace.
Occasionally, David sent for me, and I would slip, self-
consciously, past the other rooms and through the Women's
Courtyard into the passage that led to the king's quarters.
To be honest, I liked getting out of my room and—although
I didn't tell Hannah—I was still attracted to David, and he
to me, I suppose. Why else would he send for me when he
had so many others to choose from?

But all that changed on the day he decided to bring that
cursed chest into the city. Over and over, his obsession with
Adonai drove a wedge between us.

How ridiculous it all was. The vast number of priests milling around the tent set up to house that old relic—couldn't they be put to better use? And the intolerable noise—cymbals, ram's horns, and the frightened lowing or bleating of animals, an endless stream of them brought for sacrifice. So extreme and wasteful.

Against my better judgment, I let Abigail talk me into watching the procession from her room. She had one of the best views in the palace, looking out onto the top gate of the city, the one they would bring the chest through. It had been three months since David tried to bring it to Jerusalem, and Adonai had slain one of the priests for merely reaching out his hand to steady it. I didn't say it to him, but I couldn't help thinking David served a particularly fickle god. Then again, all my supplications to Asherah had never opened my womb. Not for Paltiel, nor for David. I'd given up on gods and goddesses by then.

The whole city was in uproar that day. People thronged on the road leading to the gate and stood on the city walls. They lined the streets inside the city and hung out of windows or sat on roofs. The air thrummed with anticipation—a strange mix of festivity and solemnity. Like all the commoners, Abigail, Ahinoam, Eglah, and I stood by the window with a few of the smaller children, all straining to glimpse the old chest. I could read the excitement on their flushed, bright-eyed faces, but I couldn't share their emotion. Why had I even come?

"Look, there's Abba!" one of the children cried as the main procession reached the gate, and something surged inside me as I looked for David. *That* was why I had come, I admitted to myself—to see David in all his kingly splendor.

Then I saw him. Like all the priests carrying the chest, he wore a simple white robe up to his knees. He didn't look like a king. He wasn't even in the lead. Instead, he danced alongside the priests, singing and clapping and spurring on those he passed to sing and clap with him. I had never seen a more ridiculous, unbecoming posture for a king.

"Abba!" One of the children cried out of the window. Surprisingly, David heard that shrill voice over the clamor, looked up, and waved. The women and children all waved back, but I had seen enough. I turned and left the room.

David returned to the palace as sunset approached. From the window of my room, I saw him climb the steps of the palace courtyard. He still wore the priest's garb, and the sight of it filled me with a fresh surge of disdain. I reached for my fine robe and threw it around my shoulders. *This* was how royalty dressed. I didn't respond to Hannah when she asked me where I was going or to the guards who stood by the door of the Women's Quarters. Only one purpose burned through me—to tell David what a fool he had made of himself.

David stopped midstride as he saw me coming, and he smiled. When I think of that moment now, of David's last smile for me, something twists inside me. I thought then that the smile was a remnant of the foolishness of the day, but now I wonder if he wasn't simply glad to see me.

The words were on my lips before I could think about them. The words that changed everything.

"How the king of Israel has distinguished himself today, going around half-naked in full view of the slave girls of his servants—as any vulgar fellow would."

David's smile vanished. His gaze hardened, and his voice turned cold. "It was before the Lord, who chose me, rather than your father or anyone from his house, to rule over his people Israel, that I celebrated. I will become even more undignified than this and be humiliated in my own eyes. But by those slave girls you spoke of, I will be held in honor."

Then David turned and strode away, and I have never stood before him again.

chapter 58

Tabytha leaned over Haggith's shoulder and looked at the baby lying in the crook of her arm. She had dark grey eyes and a cap of thick black hair. Her forehead creased like an old man's with the effort of focusing on her grandmother's face, and her mouth moved as if already suckling.

"She's perfect, Miriam." Had Beninu ever been this small?

Miriam smiled serenely, her gaze not leaving her daughter's face.

"Was Hushai truly glad to have a girl?"

"Delighted." Miriam said. "I've seldom seen such an adoring father."

"Unbelievable." Haggith handed the baby back to her daughter as the infant began to fuss. "I've never known a man to take an interest in a babe. I remember David once said he only likes his sons when they're old enough to carry a knife."

"But surely he likes his daughters before that." Miriam laughed, opening her gown and lifting the baby to her breast. "Didn't Abba adore me as much as Hushai does Ruthie? Undoubtedly, I was as beautiful as she is."

"You had the same crop of dark hair," Haggith said. "But David's focus was on fighting the Philistines when you were a babe, and he hardly noticed he had another daughter."

"Perhaps. But Abital told me that the Prophet Nathan came to the palace on the day of my birth," Miriam said, furrowing her brow like her daughter had earlier. "Surely Abba would have considered that significant?"

"I don't recall that," Haggith said.

"How can you forget something so important, Ima?" This was precisely the kind of thing Miriam would consider portentous. "It was a few years after the first time Nathan came and told Abba that Adonai would make his name great and that his kingdom would be established forever."

"I remember the day of your birth, Miriam. I very much—"

"Not my *birth*. How can you forget Nathan coming to the palace to announce a *kingdom*?"

Tabytha smiled at Miriam's passionate outburst. The princess still had the same fiery streak as when she was a child.

"Well, your father already ruled all of Israel at the—"

"No. This was more than Abba being king. This was something far greater. A kingdom."

"Well, yes," Haggith still tried to defend herself, "and he had established that, too. All the tribes had sworn their loyalty to—"

"No, even greater than Abba's kingdom, Ima. Something yet to be fulfilled. Something ..." Miriam paused, grappling to find words to describe what she felt so deeply. "It's the very thing Adonai promised to Abraham." She took a deep breath and then, in a solemn voice, recited, "I will make nations from you, and kings will come from you. I will establish my covenant as an everlasting covenant between me and you and your descendants after you for the generations to come, to be your God and the God of your descendants after you."

Haggith seemed about to say something, but Miriam held up an authoritative hand before continuing her lesson.

"And then, when Adonai tested Abraham by seeing if he would sacrifice Isaac, he said that Abraham's offspring would bless all the nations on the earth. Do you see it?" Miriam's intense gaze found her mother's before turning on Tabytha. "Do *you* see it, Tabytha?"

"See what?" Tabytha hid her smile behind her hand. She well recalled these intense discussions with Miriam and Solomon when they were but children.

"Adonai promised Abba and Abraham the same thing. An *everlasting* kingdom. An offspring that would rule *forever* and would bless all people everywhere."

"Forever is a very long time," Haggith said.

"Precisely," Miriam said triumphantly as if these were the wisest words her mother had spoken all day. "And that's what I've been saying. This is not an earthly kingdom Adonai spoke of. It's a heavenly one."

As Tabytha reread a scroll on which she had copied several of David's songs, she heard a soft knock. She expected Abigail to enter, but surprisingly, Bathsheba stepped into her room with a soft rustle of robes and the whiff of scented roses.

"Bathsheba. Come. Sit." She hurriedly grabbed the stash of scrolls beside her on the bench and returned them to the clay jar. "Abigail usually sits here when I scribe for her."

"I'm not sure I want you to scribe for me." Bathsheba looked around uncertainly. "I thought I'd come and ..." The words trailed off. "I haven't been in this room since Eglah died. That must be well over ten years ago."

"More than that. I've been here thirteen years. She died the year before I came."

"So long." Bathsheba shook her head with an air of sadness. "Time passes strangely, doesn't it? Sometimes, we lose entire years of time, and sometimes, a day can feel like an eternity."

Tabytha studied her. Undoubtedly, Bathsheba was still the most beautiful of all David's women despite the fine lines of age around her eyes and mouth. She was tall and shapely, and her thick, loose hair shone with vitality. Bathsheba had an alluring air about her. Perhaps it was her hazel eyes that hinted at hidden secrets or her luscious lips or the way she moved with such soft, natural grace that one felt like a cumbersome ox beside her.

Tabytha felt a prickle of envy. No wonder many of the concubines, and even wives, disliked Bathsheba. She pushed her jealousy aside. "Abigail said you might want me to write your story."

A hint of a smile curved those lovely lips. "She's convincing. She worries about my reputation and wants me to set the record straight."

"Don't you want that too?"

"People will believe what they want to believe." Bathsheba picked unseen dust off the sleeve of her gown. "It suits them to think the worst of me."

Yes, it was simple jealousy. Tabytha remembered her own pang of it less than a minute earlier.

"Nothing I say will make them believe anything different. So why bother saying it?"

"Perhaps it's not for them. Perhaps it's for your sons and their children. Wouldn't you want your descendants to know the truth?"

Tabytha wondered why it suddenly felt so important to record Bathsheba's story. Was it simply curiosity on her part or a way to prove Gilia wrong? Or was it the same reason she recorded Michal and Abigail's stories—to hear the voices of women in a world that only valued those of men?

"The truth?" Bathsheba looked out over the darkening sky of Jerusalem. "Do we even know it ourselves sometimes? The truth is our hearts are divided and deceptive, even to ourselves. Truth is far more difficult to unravel than a scroll."

"But perhaps that's exactly what you can do now. Here." Tabytha patted the bench beside her. "Here, you can speak your heart freely. I think the time is right. Perhaps you are doing this for somebody else altogether."

"Who?"

"Yourself."

Bathsheba pondered this for a while.

"Will David read it?" she asked softly.

"He hasn't read any of the others."

Bathsheba finally nodded. "If I know he won't read it, I may be able to delve into my heart and discover at least some of the truth, even the hidden parts."

Tabytha quelled her excitement, not wanting Bathsheba to sense her curiosity to hear the most forbidden of all the palace stories. "Do you want to start now?" she suggested.

"It seems as good a time as ever." Bathsheba sat on the bench, silently watching as Tabytha reached for a fresh scroll, weighted down the corners, and then reached for a reed and jar of ink.

When Tabytha looked up and nodded to her, Bathsheba smoothed down her gown and nervously cleared her throat.

"I suppose it all began one warm spring evening as I purified myself in my courtyard." She watched Tabytha dip the reed in the ink, shake it gently, and turn to the blank parchment. "No," she said before Tabytha could write the first character. "No. That's not where it started at all. It started with Uriah hearing of the fearless king of Judah and his invincible god, Adonai. He traveled to Hebron to pledge himself to this Hebrew king and his powerful god. Later, when Uriah became my husband, he told me he had known from the beginning King David was a man like no other. A man worth dying for."

chapter 59

Bathsheba
Extract from Scroll ה (hs he)

I grew up in Giloh, a small settlement in the mountains south of Jebus. I am the granddaughter of Ahithophel, the daughter of Eliam, and my family's story has been woven into David's for as long as I can remember.

My grandfather was exceedingly proud to be of the tribe of Judah. "Our Father Jacob blessed us over all our brothers," he always said, insisting we children learn to recite the words of that blessing. I can do so to this day. "Your brothers will praise you. Your father's sons will bow down to you. The scepter will not depart from Judah nor the ruler's staff from between his feet."

Ahithophel's hatred for King Saul knew no bounds, and he ranted against him for wearing the crown that rightfully belonged to Judah. When there were whispers God had anointed another to be king, and he belonged to our tribe, my grandfather received the news with joyful, militant fervor, and we, his family, did the same. That's how it was, how it still is, with Ahithophel. When he turns his attention on you, you feel as if you are basking in sunlight, but it's as easy for him to turn away from you, and then what you wouldn't do to be in his favor again.

Like all of us, my father lived to please Ahithophel. When my grandfather heard of Saul's death, and that Adonai's anointed Judite was in Hebron, he went to seek out this promised king and swear allegiance to him. He took my father with him.

My father did not have his father's forceful charm or cleverness. He was a quiet man with few thoughts or opinions of his own. I used to think him weak, but now I understand that Ahithophel's long shadow had stunted his son like a plant growing under the overhang of a cliff. Uriah once told me my father changed on the battlefield. There, he said, Eliam became fearless to the point of recklessness, as if pure rage coursed through him.

Few would have believed this of my mild father, but I did. I too had been raised under Ahithophel's unyielding will and, over the years, felt something stirring in me I couldn't name until the day Uriah told me of my father's battlefield rage. Then I understood. What I felt moving, deep and hidden, was anger, and I wished that—like my father—I could vent it on an enemy.

Yet even those who doubted my father was capable of battlefield greatness couldn't deny he soon became one of David's most trusted warriors. Ahithophel forbade us from joining my father in Hebron, whose whole attention was to be on serving the king of Judah. We would be a distraction, my grandfather said. My father returned to Giloh only in the winter months with stories of the indomitable King David, of battles fought and victories won.

Ahithophel himself had also taken to spending months at a time in Hebron, becoming one of David's most trusted advisors. My grandmother resigned herself to this more easily than my mother. She knew opposing Ahithophel was like spitting into the wind.

I remember clearly the day my grandfather and father returned with the news that Saul's son was dead and that elders from all the tribes of Israel had come to anoint David as their king.

"We are as close as anyone can be to the most powerful man in all of Israel," my grandfather announced triumphantly. "And what a king he will be. Israel's crown is finally where it should have been all along—on Judah's blessed head."

In some ways, that day marks the end of my childhood, for I remember too how my grandfather's gaze fell on me that evening as I served the men their meal.

"Well, well," he said. "While we were off serving King David, our young Bathsheba grew up, Eliam."

I felt a flush warm my cheeks and quickly lowered my head as my father looked up at me. As always, there was something heady about Ahithophel's approving gaze.

"You are right," my father said. "Such a girl should be given to a husband soon. With her fairness, she will fetch a good bride price."

My father's words startled me. My sister, Eve, a year and a half older than me, had not yet been given in marriage. But I was starting to realize I had something my sister did not. Men noticed me. The village boys smiled at me. One of them, the rather handsome Reuben, had even begun to pick flowers and leave them under the tree where I sat to grind wheat. When my mother saw that, she insisted I wear a veil over my hair, like the married women did.

"Any man would want her," my grandfather said as he took a bite of the lamb my mother had prepared.

Anxious thoughts roiled inside me as I returned to the courtyard. I enjoyed the boys' attention. I liked seeing their hopeful looks when I smiled back at them. I liked the sense they were competing for me. For the first time, I had something I'd never had before, something akin to power over another. But now my father and grandfather were speaking of giving me as a wife to one man. What power would I have then?

When I reached the women, I couldn't hold back my tears. "They want to find me a husband!"

Far from seeing shock on their faces, I saw amusement. "Of course," my grandmother said. "What did you expect?"

"But I'm too young. Eve isn't married yet. Why should I be?"

"Nonsense. You have had your monthly bleeds for two years already," she said. "And we notice you dallying with the village boys. That must stop. The sooner you are given to a man, the better."

"If I have to marry, can it be Reuben?"

"Reuben!" They all laughed again, and my grandmother said, "Simon's son? His voice has hardly broken. How will he support a wife?"

"He likes me. And I like him," I added shyly.

"Liking has nothing to do with it." My grandmother gave me a stern look. "Ahithophel is an important man in Giloh, connected to the king himself. His fairest granddaughter will marry somebody of his standing, not a worthless, young goatherd."

After that evening, I lived with the gnawing fear that Ahithophel would arrive with a greying man of great standing and declare him to be my intended husband.

I was given a reprieve, however. The king summoned my grandfather and father back to Hebron within a month.

He had decided to take the mighty fortress of Jebus and needed Ahithophel's counsel and Eliam's sword.

Yet the attack on Jebus was not only a reprieve, but also the catalyst for what would come next. On my father's victorious return to Giloh, I first heard of the warrior whose bravery had given the Israelites the victory—a man named Uriah.

Uriah was not of the tribe of Judah. He was a Hittite. Yet, when he pledged his allegiance to David at the age of twenty, he changed his beliefs and name. No longer would he worship the Hittite's sun god. His new name boldly declared, *Yahweh is my light*. The Israelites didn't trust him at first, yet, over time, his unquestioning loyalty to their king won them over. He became one of David's mighty men, fighting alongside my father, Eliam.

Everybody knew Uriah to be fast on his feet and strong too. But it wasn't until the battle for Jebus that they saw his true courage. He was among the first to offer to climb the water channel with Joab, a mission that most believed would end in death. Once inside Jebus, Uriah saved the group of men from discovery by pretending to be a Jebusite commander, barking orders at inferiors. His Hittite accent, similar to the Jebusite's, ensured they passed through the city unnoticed and made it to the gate. After Joab himself, the men lauded Uriah for taking the city.

I pieced together the story of what happened next from snippets of conversation with Uriah and my father. Perhaps, over the years, the truth and how I imagined it took place have blurred. But I see it all in my imagination as if I was there.

In the celebration that followed the fall of Jebus, Uriah's fellow warriors thrust a cup of beer into his hands and lifted him onto their shoulders with loud cheers, chanting, "mighty Uriah, one of our own." They carried him to the fortress where David had just finished meeting with the Jebusite elders.

As the defeated Jebusites slunk away, David, Joab, and the king's advisors joined the warriors in their celebrations. Everyone spoke loudly and animatedly of all that had happened that eventful morning, leading to their conquering the nearly invincible city. Finally, David's voice rose above the men's.

"Today, I honor two men. Joab, who led the attack, I declare commander-in-chief of my army. As such, he is to be obeyed. When he speaks, he speaks for the king. And Uriah, without whose courage and quick thinking, we might not be standing here today." A cheer went up from the men. "I have no reward to offer you, Uriah," David said, "except my gratitude."

"I am yours, my king." Uriah bowed low. "I need nothing from your hand."

From the back of the crowd, somebody called, "Give him a wife, my lord!" The men broke into laughter, for all knew Uriah had flatly refused to marry, saying a wife would only come between him and serving his king.

David laughed too. "Do we have a fine enough woman to tempt such a hardened bachelor?"

"My daughter would, my lord," Eliam called. "There is no one fairer in all Israel."

"Well." David looked at Ahithophel standing next to him. "Let us talk more of this, then. She sounds like a woman worthy of such a great man."

"I doubt a warrior could afford my granddaughter's bride price, my king," Ahithophel said flatly. He had always sworn his offspring would marry within the tribe of Judah. A Hittite was not good enough for one of his own.

"In that case, I will pay for the bride myself," replied David.

Uriah objected, for what man could allow another to acquire him a wife?

Ahithophel stayed silent, knowing the futility of opposing the will of a powerful king.

chapter 60

bathsheba
extract from scroll ה (hs he)

I cried on the day of my wedding. I had seen Uriah briefly the day before when he and several of his fellow warriors arrived from the king's city for the wedding celebration. My father welcomed them, and my grandmother led me to meet him. I wore my second-finest robe, with a matching veil to cover my hair.

"This is my daughter, Bathsheba," my father said.

All the men turned to look at me, and I saw, with a jolt of pleasure, the familiar admiration in their eyes. But I saw none of it on the face of the man who stepped forward and inclined his head towards me.

"Shalom Bathsheba. I am Uriah." My name sounded harder on his lips than on the lips of my own people.

Uriah was tall and broad-shouldered, and at least he wasn't an old man. Still, disappointment coursed through me. Unlike handsome Reuben, there was nothing particularly remarkable about Uriah's eyes, unsmiling mouth, brown hair, and short beard.

I mumbled a greeting before fleeing to my quarters, where I begged my mother to ask my father to stop the wedding. She didn't. Our family would never live down the shame. The next day, wearing my finest robe and veil, I was led out by all the women and given to Uriah, the Hittite, in a short ceremony. The first, important part of our marriage—deciding on the bride price—had already been concluded by the men and witnessed by the king himself.

All that remained now was the blessing.

Uriah stood somberly under the wedding tent as I circled him seven times to show my submission and faithfulness. Then Ahithophel brought a goblet of wine and gave it to Uriah, who drank from it before passing it to me with the words of blessing to Adonai, the creator of the fruit of the vine. I wiped away my tears and drank from the goblet, too.

It was done. With the covenant ratified, I became Uriah's wife.

Our village feasted that day. I felt a twist of pain as I saw Reuben standing across the table from me. He looked up with a sad smile and lifted a goblet of wine in a quiet salute. I glanced hastily at Uriah. His gaze moved from Reuben to me in silent appraisal.

The feasting continued late into the night as Uriah and I made our way to the chamber prepared for us. We had hardly spoken to one another, and my heart thudded wildly in my chest as I looked at the sleeping pallet. I had heard what happened between a man and his wife, and the thought terrified me.

But Uriah turned to look at me and said, "All these years, I have slept alone. A few more nights won't matter. Let us get to know each other a little better." He must have seen the relief on my face, for he smiled. "You take the pallet. I'm a warrior, used to sleeping on the floor."

"Thank you."

He turned away as I removed my outer robe and hurriedly climbed under the blanket. I didn't watch him disrobe, blow out the oil lamps, and lay down on the floor.

Then, a terrible thought struck me. I lay on a cream cloth that was there for a single purpose. "They will want to see the cloth in the morning." I felt glad that he would not see the shame on my face.

"They will see the cloth. All blood is red, even a cut from my thumb."

I could not fall asleep. I was aware of him, his breathing, and his unfamiliar smell—not unpleasant but different. I doubted he slept either, and I was proved right when he eventually spoke.

"Who was the young man? The one who saluted you?"

"Reuben."

"He liked you."

"He used to pick flowers for me."

"Did you like him too?"

I held my breath, afraid, but he had asked it in a manner that appeared curious rather than jealous or angry.

"Yes. I liked him too."

"Is that why you cried when you drank the covenant wine?"

I could not explain that I cried because I felt too young to marry, because I feared leaving my family, because I was losing the admiration of the older boys and hadn't seen any of it in his eyes.

So, I simply said, "Yes."

We left for the king's city the following day. Even though the city lay within walking distance, Uriah insisted

I ride on a donkey. He walked beside me silently, his hand on the beast's rein. Two donkeys followed, carrying my possessions. The men who had accompanied him to Giloh were scattered ahead and behind us. I could hear their laughter and banter, but they did not direct it at me or Uriah. Occasionally, Uriah asked if I wanted to stop, but I always shook my head. Once, he decided for me, calling the others to a halt. He supported me as I slid from the animal's back and held out a water skin, so I could drink.

We arrived at the city gate at midday, and all the men, except the donkey boy, took their leave to return to their homes. I had been to Jebus as a child, but as Uriah led me up the narrow, winding roads, I looked around with interest. The houses were tightly packed together. There were people everywhere. The constant hum of sound—calling, laughing, hammering, clomping, and bleating—overwhelmed me after the wide-open quiet of Giloh.

At the top of the city stood an imposing fortress. Uriah saw me glance at it and said, "The king has taken the fortress for a palace. Our house is just below it.

We stopped outside a house that looked like all the others. "Here." He gave me his hand again as he told the boy to tie up the donkeys and unload the saddle bags. He led me up two steps and into a small courtyard. A storage area and an animal pen containing a goat made up one side of the courtyard. A covered kitchen with fire pit stood on the opposite side. Two narrow sets of stairs led to the upper sleeping quarters.

"We share the courtyard and kitchen with Ithmah and his wife, Orpah. He is also one of the king's men. Their room is the one on the right." He pointed upwards. "This is ours. Do you need help with the stairs?"

I shook my head, trying to hold back the tears. The house's layout was not that different from our own, but much smaller. Our kitchen and courtyard were always full of women—my grandmother, aunts, mother, and sister. We worked together, talking, laughing, and teasing each other. I belonged there, but here I was alone. There, I could look out over the mountains or walk to the river for water. Here, in the city, walls hemmed me in. It felt as if I could hardly breathe, as if this place would crush the life out of me.

"Bathsheba?" When I didn't respond, Uriah turned my face towards him. "Why are you crying? What do you need?"

"I want to go home."

I didn't know him well enough to identify the emotion that flickered briefly across his face before he said, "This is not easy, but you will adjust. Over time, *this* will become your home."

But even on that very first day, I knew that would not happen.

chapter 61

While sitting on the Women's Courtyard steps, Tabytha lifted her face to the sun and rubbed her aching right hand. She had been scribing for Bathsheba for three weeks already. The king's wife, who had initially been so reluctant to talk, now insisted on coming every night and spoke long past the time Tabytha usually went to sleep. Bathsheba had carried this story inside her for so long that now, uncorked, it came out in an almost unstoppable flow.

Tabytha opened and closed her hand a few times, trying to loosen it. She yawned and pressed on her tender temples. How could she be tired this long before midday?

"Bathsheba keeping you up?" Abigail sat down next to her.

"We're working hard."

"She said as much." Abigail gave Tabytha a searching look. "Apparently, you told her to tell her story for herself and no one else. Wise counsel."

"It always helps me to write down my thoughts."

Abigail glanced around and lowered her voice. "I'm not sure how he heard, but I thought I'd better tell you. David knows you're scribing for Bathsheba."

Tabytha felt a jolt of disappointment. She had promised Bathsheba David wouldn't see the scroll. They had agreed neither of them would tell him and had asked Abigail to do the same.

"Did he ask you about it?" Tabytha asked.

"He only asked if I knew. He might send for you."

That would be a pleasant change. Lately, it seemed he preferred the company of his advisors to that of his women.

"I've hardly seen David." She always hated admitting this to his more popular wives, but now it seemed to affect all of them. "How is he?"

Abigail frowned, but merely said, "As well as can be expected."

David's summons came later that day. Instead of taking Tabytha to the king's quarters, the royal guard took her to his counsel chamber. As she neared the room, she could hear a man speaking in urgent tones.

"... is winning the hearts of the people, my king. If we do not stop him, he will ..."

Another voice interrupted him. "Stop him, Hushai? Stop a prince from being kind to his own people? Surely the king wouldn't want that?"

She reached the door, and David looked up, smiling when he saw her. The three men with him—one of them Joab—followed his gaze. She recognized another as Miriam's husband, Hushai.

"We will speak on this later," David said. "Thank you, Ahithophel. Hushai."

Ahithophel. She studied the third man, Bathsheba's grandfather, with interest as he bowed and turned to leave the room. He had the same clear, hazel eyes as Bathsheba, but his gaze held a craftiness lacking in his granddaughter's. He was thin, his back as straight as a man half his age. Briefly, she met his gaze and sensed how easy it would be to be drawn into this man's power.

"Come in, Tabytha." David sounded tired, and as she approached, she could see the strain on his face.

She bowed. "My lord. I'm glad to see you are well."

"How are you? And Beninu? Still playing with birds?"

"I am well, as is your son. He is meeting the seer more than once a week now, for there is another injured young bird Beninu is helping him with."

David nodded, but his attention seemed to be elsewhere. "Sit." He indicated a small stool. "I hear you are scribing for Bathsheba."

She sat down and looked at her hands. "Who told you?"

"It's not difficult to deduce. I hear you spend every night together."

Gilia. Of course.

David turned his signet ring around and around. "Bathsheba's and my story is a delicate one. It could be used against me if it fell into the hands of an enemy."

"Surely it is safe in your own palace? In the room of one of your women?"

David's wry smile hinted at a man who had been betrayed too often. "I doubt it."

"She has hardly spoken of you. There is nothing for an enemy to use."

"But that will change."

"David." She dared to use the name she only spoke in their most intimate moments and waited for him to look directly at her. "I think Bathsheba needs to do this. It's why she is spending every night with me. The story pouring out of her is helping her. It's healing her."

He nodded at this. "I understand better than most how healing it can be to pour your thoughts onto parchment, but that scroll cannot fall into the wrong hands."

"Whose hands? The one you and your advisors were speaking of when I came in?"

"Not him." Then, more gently he said, "Hushai sees threats where there are none. I suppose that's why one retains counselors. Ahithophel agrees with me on this, and his counsel has never failed before."

"Who does Hushai think is a threat to you?"

"This does not concern you. What concerns you—and me—is Bathsheba's scroll."

"If you tell her to stop, she'll be disappointed."

David paced to the window and silently looked out over his city. It was, Tabytha knew, his way of thinking.

He turned. "Fine. Record it, but the scroll is mine as soon as you're finished."

"I told her you wouldn't read it. If she thinks you will, she won't be as honest."

"I am the king of Israel. I can read what I want." Coldness had crept into his voice. "Remember, Tabytha, who provides you with parchment and ink."

She lowered her head. "Forgive me, my lord."

"That's all. You may go."

She bowed and had reached the door when he spoke again.

"If you don't tell Bathsheba about this discussion, I won't read the scroll."

"What will you do with it?"

"Put it to the flame," David said slowly. "That way, we all get what we want. Bathsheba unburdens her heart while I am protected from an enemy's schemes."

On the way back to the Women's Quarters, Tabytha thought of David's words, "That way, we all get what we want." Perhaps David and Bathsheba would have what *they* wanted, but what did she, Tabytha, want? Was it enough to hear Bathsheba's story, to scribe night after night, knowing her hard work would go up in flames?

No. It wasn't enough. At that moment, Tabytha finally understood what she wanted the most.

The recording of time's events had always been done by men. *For* men. *About* men. Her scrolls were the stories of women, real women, and they were as valuable as every scroll David's recorder had ever penned. The king would never dream of throwing one of those into the fire, so why should he feel entitled to destroy one of hers?

Perhaps all that had happened to her—her father's death, Ornan giving her to David, Ahio teaching her to write—had been for a single purpose. Perhaps, as the seer had said, Adonai had had his hand on her all along and brought her to the palace for this one reason.

Tabytha's deepest desire was to protect and preserve the women's scrolls.

chapter 62

bathsheba
extract from scroll ה (hs he)

The months passed by, slow and intolerable. Uriah no longer slept on the floor, but I stiffened whenever he reached for me. I hated everything about the act of marriage. The roughness of his beard on my skin, his hands moving over me, the sharp pain, the lingering smell and feel of his seed clinging to my body. I would lie awake afterward and listen to his deep breathing, and despair would settle on me like a heavy cloak. How could this be my life? I had imagined it so very differently.

We shared the house with an older couple, Ithmah and Orpah, from Moab. Like Uriah, Ithmah was an outsider among David's men, and the two of them had formed a close bond. Orpah had cooked and cleaned for them for as long as Uriah had been in the king's army. She did not seem to like sharing the role with another woman. She watched everything I did closely and criticized my smallest mistakes. She was even harsher with her young maidservant, a girl called Simone, who slept in the courtyard's storage area.

Yet when the men were near, Orpah spoke kindly and laughed lightly. I disliked her for her falseness.

I became a different person in the king's city. At home, I had spoken my thoughts freely among the women. I had sung and danced with my sister and cousins. But here, I said little and did only what was expected of me. I detested the soulless woman I became as Uriah's wife.

I failed, too, in the most obvious of women's roles—I did not fall pregnant. Perhaps a child would have brought Uriah and me together, would have given me someone to love and pour myself into, would have softened Orpah's harshness. But it was not to be. Every month, I bled, glad only that for a few days, I would be unclean and wouldn't have to lie with Uriah. After my time of uncleanness, I would wait for the men to leave and perform the required ceremonial cleansing in the courtyard. I cried every time for the babe I did not carry and the nights of obligation ahead.

Sometimes, I would be at work in the kitchen and look up to find Uriah watching me. He did not have a particularly expressive face, but I thought I saw disappointment in his eyes. Surely, he had hoped for more from a wife. Yet, he never said it. Not once did he raise his voice at me. If he had, I could have shouted back and vented all my disappointment and pent-up rage. I could have pummeled his chest with my fists and screamed into the night. Then perhaps, spent, I would have fallen into his arms for comfort. I might even have found it, for Uriah was not an unkind man.

I also remember gentler moments from that year. Uriah sometimes invited me to sit by the fire as the men spoke about all the happenings in the kingdom. Since David became king, Israel's old enemies had joined against our united tribes. Listening to the stories of our enemies' schemes and the victorious battles the men had returned from, I would escape the confines of my small life for a short while.

As the fire cooled, Ithmah and Orpah would go to their room and leave Uriah and me alone. We would continue to speak softly, watching the last flames consuming the night's allotted wood. Together, we would sit and watch the final life trapped and moving in the dying coals until they were black and cold. We spoke of small matters. He told me how he had first heard of King David and left his people and religion to serve him. I told him how my sister, jealous from an early age, had sometimes pinched me to make me cry, hoping my grandmother would smack me. But my grandmother, no fool, began to smack us both, and the pinching stopped.

On one of these quiet nights by the fire, I asked him if he thought me beautiful.

He looked up at me with a small, rare smile and took my hand in both of his. "There is no one more beautiful than you, Bathsheba." For once, I saw in his eyes that he meant it. When I think of Uriah, that's the moment I like to remember.

Spring arrived. It was the time when kings went to war.

The men had left three weeks ago to besiege the city of Rabbah. Orpah had left that morning for Moab, having had word that her mother lay deathly ill. Only Simone and I remained.

Together, we had drawn enough water to fill the stone trough I used for my monthly ritual bath. It grew late, but I didn't mind. For once, I could bathe precisely when I wanted. Placing the oil lamp on the ground, I removed my clothes. I braced myself as I climbed into the icy cold bath, bending my knees so the water would cover my shoulders, and hugging myself to preserve my body heat. If I stayed in for a little while, it would begin to feel warmer. I closed my eyes and tried to loosen the tension in my body. On a hot summer night, few things compared to the pleasure of a cold bath, but the evenings were still too cool to make this enjoyable.

Long enough, I told myself and stepped out of the bath. I reached for the clean robe hanging over the goat's pen, and as I did so, I glanced up, startled to see a figure standing on the palace roof. They stood in darkness, but I was lit up by the oil lamp. I fumbled for the robe and quickly drew it around me. When I looked up again, the figure was gone.

I had all but forgotten about the person on the palace roof by the following evening. Simone and I were sharing the last of the bread we had baked that morning when a bold knocking on the door startled us both.

"Perhaps Isha needs yeast." Simone rose to open the door.

However, instead of our neighbor, a man dressed in the uniform of the palace guard stood in the doorway. He didn't even glance at Simone. His gaze rested on me. "Bathsheba?"

A sudden fear gripped me. "Is Uriah ...?"

"Your husband is well, as far as I know." A significant pause followed this statement. "I am Benaiah, King David's guard. The king sends for you. I am to accompany you to his palace."

"The king wants to see *me*?" What possible reason did he have to see me, a woman? Was there news from Uriah that this man knew nothing of? Had something happened to my grandfather or father? But no, surely the king would have sent a messenger.

"You may want to dress in something finer for an audience with the king," the man said. It was with that one word—audience—and his inflection as he said it that I began to understand.

Heat flooded into my chest, and my heart fluttered like a trapped bird. The king wanted *me*. The *king*! A tumble of unrelated thoughts assaulted my mind. *I was a married woman. He was the most powerful man in the land. I had nothing fine to wear. Would Simone tell Orpah? It had been the king on the roof of the palace. I would see the inside of the palace and meet the anointed of Judah. What would Ahithophel say if he found out? Would Ima cry if she heard? Should I say no? Could I say no?*

"I ... I will have to get ready," I said eventually, glancing at Simone. She stood, mouth slightly ajar, looking at the guard. I hoped she hadn't grasped what he was asking, but as she looked from him to me, I suspected that she had. "Simone, could you help me get ready?"

She nodded and followed me up the steps. By the time I reached my room, my body trembled as if I had just stepped from a cold bath. I went to the cupboard and found my finest robe. No, not my wedding robe, I thought with a flash of shame. My second finest, then. Perhaps not good enough for a king, but ...

"You're not going, are you?" Simone asked.

"What choice do I have? You don't say no to a king's summons."

"Tell him you are sick. Or unclean."

He already knows I'm not. "Simone, you need to promise you won't tell anybody. Not Orpah or Ithmah. Or Uriah." Something clenched in my chest as I said my husband's name. Better not to think of Uriah right now. "Promise me."

The girl looked a little surly. "Orpah is my mistress. I can't keep secrets from her."

"She's mean to you. I've been nothing but kind."

"Fine," Simone said eventually. "As long as you tell me what the palace looks like. And what the king was wearing and about all the serving girls and the guards, and the fine food and …"

"I'll tell you. So, do you promise not to tell anybody?"

"I promise." Simone suddenly seemed almost eager. "Let me brush your hair for you. I can pin it, too."

I shook my head. "Go down and offer the guard the bread. I will be down soon."

I sat a while until the trembling passed, considering what might lie ahead that night. A small voice told me I could still stop it from happening. But a thrill of wonder ran through me at the thought I was about to meet the handsome David, strong warrior, king of all Israel. Like Reuben and the other boys of my village, he had seen me and desired me. Here, no Ahithophel or Eliam dictated what I should do, no staunch grandmother wagged a finger at me. This time nobody stood between us. For once, I had the power to decide what I wanted to do. I had never done anything this reckless, but I reached for my finest robe and slipped it on, pushing aside the memory of the last time I had worn it. I brushed my hair and left it loose, covering it with a veil. I dabbed perfume on my neck, put on my sandals, and then slowly went down the stairs to the guard who would take me to the palace for a night with the king.

chapter 63

Tabytha and Miriam sat on the courtyard ground, their backs against the bottom step, where Haggith sat. Ruthie—beginning to sit by herself—sat between them, screeching and flapping her hands wildly. The women laughed and clapped, delighted at the little one's antics.

"This is what makes life in the Women's Quarters so beautiful," Tabytha said. "Watching the children grow up and their children after them. Laughing together." She looked at Haggith and her daughter and wiped away a stray tear. "Living life with friends."

Miriam laughed. "Why so serious suddenly?"

"I don't know." Tabytha shook her head ruefully. "One moment, I'm laughing, and the next, I'm crying."

"You're not pregnant, are you?" Haggith said.

"No." Sometimes, having only one child saddened her. Yet, considering Beninu's lack of relationship with his father, perhaps it was better that way.

"It must be all those late nights." Haggith smiled knowingly.

"What late nights?" Miriam asked.

"Tabytha is scribing for Bathsheba."

"Does the whole of the Women's Quarters know?" Tabytha sighed.

"Only those Gilia told."

All three of them laughed at that.

"I suppose that means Abba knows, too," Miriam said.

"He knows." Tabytha thought back to their meeting. "In fact, I saw Hushai when David sent for me to discuss the matter. He and Ahithophel were arguing as I arrived."

"Those two seldom agree on anything lately," Miriam said.

"Hushai sounded worried. He was counseling the king to be wary of somebody close to him. Do you know who they spoke of, Miriam?"

The princess shook her head and rose, reaching for Ruthie. "I do not betray my husband's trust. If he speaks to me on such matters, I keep them to myself."

"Sit, Miriam," her mother said. "Tabytha meant nothing by it."

"It's time for Ruthie to sleep." Miriam hefted the baby onto her hip and gave her mother a quick embrace before stepping up the first of the courtyard steps.

"I'm sorry, Miriam," Tabytha called after her, but the princess didn't turn back. "I chased her away." Tabytha gave Haggith an apologetic glance.

"I've done the same myself." Haggith shrugged. "She never divulges anything."

"It's been worrying me, though, that snippet of conversation. One of them mentioned a prince. David says Hushai is worrying for nothing, but then he wouldn't *want* to believe one of his sons is untrustworthy, would he?"

Haggith seemed unsettled at the thought. "David is a wise man. As is Ahithophel. If they're not worried, we don't need to be either. And since he forgave Absalom, David has a good relationship with all his sons."

"I'm sure you're right."

Haggith rose and stretched. "I grow too old for floors and cold steps."

"I'm going in too. Let me walk with you."

They parted in the passage. Back in her room, Tabytha pulled out Bathsheba's scroll and slowly let her eyes wander over the words. How much longer before David demanded this scroll? She couldn't shake the unease inside her. If Hushai was right and one of the princes posed a danger to the king, David might not let Bathsheba finish the story before putting this scroll to the flame.

Was Bathsheba's and her time running out?

Tabytha reached for a new piece of parchment and unrolled it beside the open one. She uncorked the ink, dipped the reed into it, and began to write.

I grew up in Giloh ...

chapter 64

BATHSHEBA

EXTRACT FROM SCROLL ה (hs he)

My heart pounded wildly as Benaiah and I walked the short distance between my house and the palace. Even though we walked in near darkness, I imagined everybody's eyes on me. I drew my veil forward and kept my head down.

At the palace gate, I hardly heard the interchange between Benaiah and the guards. I didn't look up as they opened the gate. I studied the packed earth and their sandals and heard only the strange pounding rush in my ears. *What was I doing? Was it too late to turn and run back to Simone?*

"This way," Benaiah said.

I looked up briefly to see the well-lit entrance of the palace, where another three guards stood watch. Thankfully, Benaiah led me across the courtyard to a dark side door. He knocked on it and spoke. A single guard opened the door. I followed Benaiah into a narrow passage lit by the occasional flickering torch.

"The floor is uneven here. Watch your step."

The passage felt cold and musty—not at all how I imagined a palace to be. Simone would be disappointed when I told her. We reached a curtained-off room through which some light shone.

"Wait here. I will announce you to the king." Benaiah slipped past the curtain. I could hear his voice. "She's here, my lord."

I had begun to shake again. *Fool! Fool! You shouldn't be here.*

Benaiah returned, holding the curtain aside and nodding for me to enter.

Hesitantly, I stepped into the room, not daring to look up, hardly daring to breathe, aware only of the curtain falling back behind me. *Too late. Too late.*

"Bathsheba." My name sounded soft on the king's lips.

Finally, I dared to look up at him.

The man standing a few steps from me was as handsome as I had heard, with a rugged face and dark eyes. He watched me with an intensity that I found both disconcerting and strangely flattering. Even without the fine robe and the royal signet ring on his finger, he would have carried an alluring air of authority and power about him.

I dropped to the ground in a deep bow. "My king."

He reached for me and drew me up.

So close. Too close. I caught a whiff of balsam and something deeper, richer.

"Your hands are cold," he said gently. "And you are shaking. Come, sit by the fire."

Only now did I look at my surroundings. The room was not large, but it was finely furnished—a room fit for a king. A fire crackled against one wall. Strangely, no smoke filled the room—a hidden vent must be drawing it away. Simone would like that when I told her. In front of the fire lay a carpet strewn with exotic-looking cushions. To the side stood a table laden with food, and two delicately carved chairs tucked under it. The torches burning in the wall sconces cast a warm and inviting light. There was no sleeping pallet, I realized with relief. This must be the king's private dining or meeting room.

I grew aware of the warmth and size of the king's hand on my own as he led me to the fire.

"Sit," he instructed. "Let me bring you some wine to warm you."

I sank down on the cushions, my fingers trailing over the silky fabric. The fire crackled warmly, a much larger one than we could ever afford to make. I pushed away the thought of our small courtyard fire. *Let me just enjoy this one.*

The king returned with a cup brimming with red wine. "Try this," he said. "A particularly fine wine from Tarshish."

I had never heard of Tarshish or tasted any wine other than the watered-down variety from our own valley. I took a sip of the red liquid. It coated my mouth, heavier than our Giloh wine, much stronger and, I suspected, headier.

"Good, isn't it?" The king took a sip too and settled down next to me.

The wine *was* good. I took another few nervous sips and felt its warmth traveling down my throat and into the rest of my body. The fire and the wine began to soothe away some of my tension.

The king was speaking, telling me of the delegation that had brought the barrel of wine and of other gifts he had received. Donkeys, gold, fine jewels, and even, once—he laughed—a caged monkey.

I laughed, too, as he told me how the monkey had escaped and jumped onto the shoulder of one of his advisors, grabbing the grapes from the man's hands.

"Not my grandfather, I hope?"

Momentarily, my question broke the light mood that the warmth and wine had spun around us, but the king recovered quickly. "Not even a monkey would dare insult your grandfather that way."

I took another long sip of the wine, trying to rid myself of the image of Ahithophel's stern face.

The king rose, fetched a platter from the table, and put it down between us. It was laden with freshly baked bread, cheese, olive oil, figs and almonds—enough to feed a family, I would tell Simone.

"Taste this, Bathsheba. The finest olive oil from the olive press across the valley." He tore a piece of the bread, dipped it in the oil, and held it out. My stomach churned at the thought of food, but I lifted my hand to take it from him. He smiled and shook his head, and I understood. Obediently, I opened my mouth and let him put the piece of bread in it. I hardly tasted the finest oil or the palace bread, conscious only it had been the act of one lover to another.

By the time I drained the last drops from the cup, the room spun a little, and everything about the evening felt soft and hazy. The king was surely the most handsome man I had ever seen, I would tell Simone. He told interesting and funny stories, and I found myself laughing freely.

He rose and filled my cup again.

"I fear you are trying to seduce me, my king," I giggled.

He leaned in closer and trailed a finger down my cheek towards my mouth. "Is it working?"

I saw the desire in his eyes and felt an echo of it stirring in my body.

"It may be working, my lord."

He smiled and took the cup from my hands, carefully putting it on the floor beside the carpet. Then he turned back to me and reached for the veil still covering my hair.

"I think it's time we removed this." As the veil fluttered to the floor, I remembered the moment Ima insisted I wear it. Uriah had been the only man who had seen my unbound hair since then. *Uriah.*

The king's one hand stroked my hair as the other pulled me towards him, drawing me into a long, deep kiss. When he drew back, his eyes were dark with longing.

"I've never seen a woman as beautiful as you, Bathsheba."

He leaned in for another kiss, this time pushing against me with his body, forcing us both to the floor. At that moment, something cold crept through the warm, wine-induced haze of my mind. *This is wrong. I am the wife of another.*

The king's mouth still claimed my own as I tried to speak, his hands fumbling with the catches on my robe.

"My lord, we shouldn't. I am ..."

"Hush. I sense you want this as much as I do."

"But my husband is ..."

"Far away. Come, let us enjoy the culmination of a beautiful evening together."

After that, his kisses stifled my objections. His cries of pleasure drowned my silent cry of regret.

chapter 65

Tabytha and Bathsheba sat side by side on the bench. For a long time, neither of them spoke. Finally, Tabytha reached for Bathsheba's hand that felt as cold as stone.

Bathsheba looked up and smiled wanly. "You won't tell anyone any of this, will you?"

Tabytha shook her head, but her mind spun with all Bathsheba had told her. Was what David had done to Bathsheba all that different from what Amnon had done to Tamar?

"Perhaps recording this is a mistake." Bathsheba looked at the scroll as if it was a particularly unpalatable piece of bread. "Let everyone continue to think I seduced David. That's better than them knowing the truth."

"That he forced himself on you?"

"But did he?" Bathsheba shook her head. "I should never have gone to him. One doesn't walk into the lair of a lion and expect to be unharmed. I brought this on myself."

"You were young and unhappy. And he was a king. What girl wouldn't go?"

Bathsheba shrugged and rose. "Speaking of that night has churned it all up as if it happened yesterday instead of years ago. It's time to bury it again. I hadn't planned to share so much, but ..." She took a deep breath. "Now that I have, I want you to promise not to show that scroll to anyone else."

"I won't." As Tabytha said the words, she thought guiltily of David's demand that she hand the scroll over to him. But he had promised not to read it, only to put it to the flame.

"Bathsheba?" Tabytha waited until the woman looked at her. "Will you come back tomorrow and finish the story?"

After a long pause, Bathsheba said, "There's as much pain in that telling. Even more, in fact."

"I would want to hear it from you," Tabytha said with all the feeling she could muster. Scribing Bathsheba's story had drawn the two of them together. It had felt like sharing secrets with Iuni years ago. "I need to know how you learned to love him after what he did. You *do* love him, don't you?"

Bathsheba nodded. "You've seen us together. Can't you tell?"

Yes, David obviously favored Bathsheba over every other one of his women, and Tabytha had always believed their love to be mutual. She thought back to those meals in the Women's Courtyard. Bathsheba had almost always sat beside David, her hand resting on his arm. She would lean in to whisper some small confidence to him, and his face would break into a smile. All the women had seen it and been envious.

"I've seen it. There's something special between you." She pointed to the scroll. "But that's what I want to understand. How did what you described—how did *that* turn into true love?"

"Not immediately. No. But there came a moment when we held each other and wept together, and I saw his heart, and he saw mine. That's when things began to change for me. For us."

"Will you tell me of that moment tomorrow? Please, Bathsheba."

The king's wife nodded slowly.

chapter 66

BATHSHEBA

EXTRACT FROM SCROLL ה (hs he)

In the days following my night at the palace, I felt strangely disconnected from my daily life. My thoughts were tangled loops of anxiety and regret. I lay awake at night berating myself for having gone and then could hardly rise in the morning. Simone quizzed me about the king's clothes, the room, and the food, and I answered her questions dutifully but refused to speak of the moments in his arms. If I thought of them, such a heavy feeling came over me I could hardly breathe.

I thought of Uriah often, of the way he might gaze at me if he knew the truth, of the words he might speak to me, and my throat would burn with tears. I wondered if he would expose and divorce me, and then, I wondered if my family would allow me to come back to them or if they would drive me away in shame. Where would I go? Would I wear the mark of the adulteress woman the way Cain had worn the mark of the murderous man?

But three weeks later, when Orpah returned from burying her mother, I was beginning to feel more settled.

Only Simone knew, and I had sworn her to secrecy. Uriah would never know. My family would never have to bear the shame or renounce me as their own. It had only been a single night, a solitary mistake, which now felt more like a dream than reality. I would carry on living in this small house in the king's city, would welcome Uriah home when he returned, would try to become the wife he longed for and deserved. I watched Simone carefully and made sure I stuck close to her whenever she was with Orpah. The girl appeared to be true to her word and didn't even hint at what had happened. Everything was going to be fine.

It was only when Orpah asked me if it wasn't time for my ritual bath that a fearful thought thudded into me. I hadn't bathed because I hadn't bled. Could it be ...? No! All these months with Uriah, my womb had remained closed. Surely one night with the king wouldn't open it? But another few fretful days passed, and still, the flow didn't come. Finally, I had to acknowledge to myself what I knew would be my undoing—I carried the king's child. Soon, my belly would swell with shame, and everybody would know of my unfaithfulness. Orpah would know. Uriah would know. My grandfather would know. *Everybody.*

In the early hours of another sleepless night, I made a decision. I had to tell the king. I didn't know what he could do, but as the most powerful man in the land, surely he could save me from my impending fate? Would he even care, though? I had to try. I could see no other way.

I waited for Orpah to go to the market and pulled Simone aside. "I need you to go to the palace gate and ask to see Benaiah."

"The guard who came for you?"

"Yes. Tell him that I have a message for the king." I swallowed down the wave of shame at having to acknowledge the truth. "I am with child."

Simone's eyes widened. "Are you sure?"

I nodded sharply. "Go. Speak only to Benaiah. Make sure nobody else hears."

Simone did as I asked and came home much later than I expected. Benaiah had apparently told her to wait while he spoke to the king and had returned with a message for me.

"The king says do not fear. He has a plan," the girl said.

"What plan?" I whispered sharply, for by then, Orpah had returned. Simone merely shrugged.

There was nothing I could do but wait. I spent the week pretending to Orpah I had my monthly flow and even had a bath at the end of it, looking up constantly at the palace roof as I did so. A day or two later, Orpah announced her friend's cousin thought he had seen Uriah enter the city at the trader's gate.

"Uriah?" My heart pounded wildly at the thought of seeing my husband again. The fleeting moment of anticipation was immediately swallowed by the weight of shame and fear of discovery. "Why would he be *here* instead of at the battle?"

"Perhaps he has a message for the king," Orpah said, and only then did understanding dawn. It was the other way around. The king had sent for *him*. This was part of the plan.

That night, two men arrived carrying a basket overflowing with food from the king's table, and a goblet of red wine. *Tarshish wine,* I thought with a guilty flush as Orpah held it up and sniffed it.

"The king sends these for Uriah and his wife to enjoy," one of the men said.

Orpah swiveled back and looked at me with a furrowed brow. "Why would the king send you fine food and wine?"

"I don't know. Perhaps a reward for Uriah's service." I recalled how that wine had made me feel, and I understood the king's plan a little better. He hoped Uriah and I would drink the wine and make love like he and I had. Then, it would appear that I carried my husband's child instead of his.

But Uriah did not come home that night or the next. The same friend's cousin told Orpah that Uriah had slept at the palace entrance with all the king's servants, and that he had left the city that very morning to return to the battlefield.

"Why didn't he come home?" I asked Orpah with a rising sense of panic. "Surely it's the least he could do to come home and greet his wife?"

"You know what these soldiers are like," Orpah said blandly. "Some strange sense of camaraderie won't allow them to enjoy themselves if their fellow warriors are in danger."

The king's plan had failed.

I can hardly remember the days after that but then came the moment that changed my life forever. I recall the smell of the bread baking, the tune that Simone was humming, the small fists of clouds against the bluest of skies. I can still hear that knock on my door, still feel the stirring of fear as I opened it to see Benaiah standing there, his gaze solemn, his mouth clenched into a tight line. And I remember his words and the way he looked past me as he said them and how I wished I had seen a trace of sadness on his face as he spoke.

"The king has received word that your husband Uriah fell and died in the heat of the battle."

I remember the strange moan that came—unbidden—from my lips and how I sank to the ground as the strength left my legs. I remember Orpah's voice behind me asking what was wrong, and the momentary confusion on Benaiah's face, as if he had not expected the news to affect me so. I remember the coldness of Simone's hands as she sank down next to me and reached for mine, the sharp wail of grief that came from Orpah's lips, and my sudden realization she had loved Uriah like a son, that she had loved him far better than I did.

After that, the days blur into a crush of people, endless wailing, hunger, and lack of sleep. Simone brought me figs in the middle of the night so that all those sleeping in the courtyard would not know that Uriah's widow was breaking the required seven-day fast. If grief was meant to steal one's hunger, I surely did not grieve enough, for hunger consumed me.

Then, the people were suddenly gone, and silence hung heavily over our house. Orpah still cried, but I hardly felt anything anymore. It felt insignificant that I carried a child, that all would know of my unfaithfulness, and that I would soon have no family or home. Uriah was dead, and my only remaining emotion was a flicker of surprise at the emptiness I felt at his absence, for I knew I had hardly appreciated him when he lived.

Then came another knock on my door. Three times, Benaiah stood there. The first had made me an adulteress, the second had made me a widow, and the third would make me the wife of a king.

The king had sent for me a second time, this time in broad daylight instead of the cover of night.

Twelve days after my husband's battlefield death, I became King David's wife.

chapter 67

Something stirred in the palace, a sense of unrest that
Tabytha could not quite define. She had first sensed it
on the day she heard the king's counselors—Ahithophel
and Hushai—arguing. She thought she saw hints of it on
Miriam's face as she rocked her baby and stared unseeingly
across the Women's Courtyard. Even here, at the Shabbat
market, she felt the unease. The guards spoke in low tones,
which halted abruptly as she passed by. There were fewer
traders, and those that remained kept glancing around
nervously.

"Where are the others?" she asked one of them.

"Most prefer to stay off the roads at such times."

"What times?" she asked, but he merely shook his head
and said no more.

She asked Abigail if she knew what was astir, and the
older woman said she didn't. Tabytha didn't quite believe
her. She quizzed Bathsheba, too, when she came to her
quarters in the evenings. Bathsheba said it had been a
while since she saw David, and all had seemed well with
him at the time.

Only Maacah gave her an unintended clue of what could
be afoot. On her weekly visit to the cloistered woman,

Maacah told her Absalom had been to see the king to ask if he might go to worship at Hebron.

"He told David he goes to fulfill a vow, but when he took his leave of me and kissed me on the head, he whispered, 'Wait and see, Ima. Soon, your son will step into his rightful inheritance.'"

Maacah smiled fondly as she spoke the words, but they left a lingering chill in Tabytha's mind.

She knew only one person would tell her the truth. So, she hovered outside the entrance to the Women's Quarters until she saw the slim figure of her son making his way to the gate.

"Beninu!" He turned and waited, somewhat impatiently, for her to join him. "I thought I'd come and watch you with the bird again." She fell into step next to him. "It has been a while since I saw him. How does he fly now?"

Beninu's slightly churlish expression lightened at her question. Her son didn't stop talking about the bird until they were on the city wall. The seer already stood there with the bird perched on his arm. He gave Tabytha one fleeting look before turning his attention to the boy. He passed Beninu a lengthy leather strip to wind around his arm and then carefully transferred the bird to him. For a while, Tabytha forgot the unrest of the palace as she watched the wonder and joy on her son's face.

"The warm air is good for flight today," the seer said. "You will see how high he goes. Release him and then call him back with this." The seer lay a featherless dead bird in her son's hand. "Your mother and I are going to walk a while. Do you feel you can manage him on your own?"

"Yes, Nathan." Beninu beamed proudly at this new responsibility.

Without another word, the seer turned. She followed him.

"You did not come to see the bird today," he said when they were some way from Beninu.

"I wanted to speak to you. Something stirs in the palace. In the land. What is it?"

He stopped walking and looked down to the valley. She heard sorrow in his voice as he said, "The fulfillment of the prophecy I gave the king when he sinned against the Lord."

"What prophecy? That warfare would come to his household?"

"That was a part of it."

"Is there another part?"

It seemed to her that his black eyes glistened with emotion. "Yes, Tabytha. That what he had done in secret would be done to him in the sight of all."

"What does that mean?"

The seer's gaze turned to the sky, and she followed it. Above them, the bird circled higher and higher. She looked towards her son's upturned face and smiled. When she looked back at the seer, he was watching her.

"Know that your son will be well. The falcon will ground him, and I will watch over him."

Perhaps he meant the words as a comfort, but they unsettled her. "You speak in riddles today, Nathan." She had never dared use his name before. "I know he is well. He stands right in front of me."

He inclined his head, a small gesture of respect. "Hold fast to all the words Adonai has spoken to you, both through me and the prayer songs of the king. They will strengthen you."

"You speak as if," she felt her voice rising with the threat of tears, "as if I will not see you or my son again. What do you mean? What is about to happen?"

"The sin of one continues to bring pain to many. As a single dropped stone brings a whole body of water to unrest."

"That doesn't seem fair. Why would Adonai do that?"

"Not Adonai. The king dropped the stone. Adonai does not stop the waves of pain. But he will not forsake those touched by it."

Then, the seer did a most remarkable thing. He stepped towards her and drew her into an embrace. Despite his age, his arms felt solid and strong. He smelled of dust and parchment. She rested her head against his chest and felt comfort and strength seeping into her.

He released her with a tender smile. "You are still that same strong girl who took on those boys with their rocks. The scrolls you have penned will endure. Because of you, the women's voices will be heard in generations to come. Shalom, Tabytha."

Without waiting for a reply, he turned and walked back to her son, leaving Tabytha standing alone, wondering why his words rung with the finality of a farewell.

chapter 68

bathsheba

extract from scroll ה (hs he)

My arrival at the palace caused a stir. From the first day, I was the subject of speculation and rumors. Some of them were far too close to the truth. My grandfather, who should have been delighted that his granddaughter had wed the king of Judah, wore a solemn expression whenever he looked at me. Few of the women were warm towards me. Abigail was civil, and Eglah as kind as she was to everyone, but the rest were wary, anxious about what my arrival meant for their own standing with the king.

Although I was flattered by David's attentiveness towards me, I sensed it only increased the women's antagonism. I spent much of those first months alone in my room—one of the finer ones in the palace. When it became known that I was with child, the rumors and resentment grew. By then, I had decided that the opinions of others mattered little. Here I was, a girl from a small village in Judah, married to the mighty King David and carrying his child. I had found favor with him, which would surely extend to our child. I had what every woman in Israel could only wish for. I did not need the friendship of others.

Our son was born perfect. He had ruddy curls and long lashes framing eyes that already seemed to be drinking in the world. His tiny fingers gripped firmly, and he fed lustily. For a few days, I couldn't believe it was possible to be so happy.

But then the prophet Nathan came with a message for the king. I would not have known of this except that David suddenly appeared in the doorway of my room that afternoon, his gaze on the child lying peacefully asleep in my arms.

"My lord." I began to rise from where I sat, but he held up his hand and stepped towards me. Only then did I notice that his eyes were red and his face mottled as if he had been crying. "What is it, my lord?"

"I came to check on the child. He is well?"

I nodded, smiling down at our sleeping son. When I lifted my gaze, David was looking at me, fresh tears brimming in his eyes.

"Something is wrong, my lord. What is it?"

"Nathan, the prophet of Adonai, came today." He took a deep breath. "He confronted me with what I had done. I sinned when I sent for you, Bathsheba. Not only against you and your husband ..." He looked away. "I sinned against Adonai, who gave me everything I have."

I looked down, ashamed. I hated thinking of that night, of what we had done. But this beautiful child lay in my arms because of that night. No, I would not regret it.

"It's in the past, my lord. Look at our son. Surely, he will bring us nothing but joy."

I briefly looked up to see David studying the child again, his expression as pained as when he had arrived.

David sensed me watching him. "Forgive me, Bathsheba. For what I did that night and for the pain I have brought into your life."

He cast one last look at our child and then turned to leave.

That night, my little son began to burn with an inner heat that would not be quenched. We tried everything we could—Abigail, Eglah, and I. We bathed him in cold water and dropped healing oils into his mouth. We rubbed his small, burning body with olive oil and frankincense, and kept trying to hold him to my breast. He would not drink, and every day, he grew weaker until his cries of pain were but a whimper. Abigail told me that David, refusing to eat and wearing only sackcloth, pleaded night and day for our son's life. I tried to add my prayers to his, but Adonai had always been a distant God to me, and I doubted he would hear my pleas.

Seven days from the time the prophet had come, from the time our son first fell ill, his whimpers finally silenced. His body stopped burning until it was cold as stone. Abigail wanted to wrap him in a shroud, but I refused to let him go. I cradled him in my arms, pressing him against me as if my own warmth could bring back his. As I ran my fingers through his curls, still wet from the fever, I wept for the son I would never know.

"Bathsheba."

I hadn't heard David, enter but he knelt by my side, looking at the child in my arms with the same anguish that I felt.

"I tried everything ..."

"I know, my love."

He pulled me against him, and we wept together. After a long time, he took the lifeless body of our son from my arms and lay him gently on the shroud that Abigail had brought earlier. As he wrapped the small body, he said, "It is time to let him go. We cannot bring back what Adonai has taken."

"You knew he was going to die. When you came that afternoon, you already knew."

He continued to wrap the body. "His death is a judgment on what I had done in showing such contempt for the Lord."

"If you knew, why did you even pray for him?"

"I thought Adonai might be gracious to me and let the child live."

"But he wasn't. He didn't."

The note of bitterness in my words made him look up. "This was the result of my sin. Adonai was justified in judging it."

"Our son was innocent, yet he paid the price for what we did."

"The price of grief is ours, not his. He is at peace now, Bathsheba. We will go to be with him one day."

Perhaps, I thought, but it didn't seem enough to me. Such a distant hope could not fill my empty arms or barren heart.

chapter 69

Finally, the unrest brooding in the palace for weeks broke like a sudden winter storm. David sent a messenger to Abigail, and in no time, the word had spread throughout the Women's Quarters. The women and children were to prepare to leave the palace by midday. Absalom and an army of men from every tribe marched towards the city to overthrow David. The hearts of the people of Israel were with Absalom.

The women wailed and wept, rushing around blindly, gathering their children, stuffing clothes and food into bags that could be slung over their shoulders.

Tabytha did not wail or weep or gather. She had known this moment approached. She stood in the center of her room and looked at her desk. The scrolls were her only true treasure. Would David spare a man to carry the clay pot that held them? She doubted it. Tabytha bent down and carefully pulled out one of the scrolls—Michal's. Could she wrap them all and carry them with her? She had to try.

"Tabytha." Abigail stood in her doorway. Behind her stood one of David's men.

"David has sent Benaiah for Bathsheba's scroll."

Tabytha glanced at the man Bathsheba had spoken of so often, the one David had trusted with his darkest secrets. He had an unyielding gaze.

"Let me look for it." She found Bathsheba's original scroll and carefully drew the parchment out of the clay pot, trying not to think it would soon be put to the flame.

She rose and walked to the door, holding out the scroll to Benaiah. "Could you send someone to carry the pot with the other scrolls? I know the king would want them saved."

"It's unnecessary," he said, "since you are to stay in the palace."

"Surely not?" Tabytha looked at Abigail and saw the truth on her face. "Why?"

"David has instructed the concubines to stay behind and see to the palace." Abigail's gaze slid away from Tabytha's.

"That's absurd. We are as much David's women as you are."

"The eldest Jebusite elder swayed the king's decision," Benaiah said. "He came this morning to say the Jebusite concubines belong not only to the king but to this city and its Jebusite people. He argued persuasively that they should remain here."

The eldest Jebusite elder? Ornan! She tried to understand her grandfather's reasoning. Perhaps, if he thought Absalom would defeat David, he believed he was protecting her and the others. But if David did not take them, they would be at the mercy of the invaders.

"Abigail! What will become of us if Absalom and his men take the palace?" She gripped her arm. "Please speak to the king. He will listen to you."

Abigail nodded. "I will try, but we have little time to spare. I need to prepare. Take care of yourself, Tabytha."

Tabytha would never know if Abigail spoke to David. If she did, it had been in vain, for his instruction remained unchanged. The nine Jebusite concubines and Puduhepa were to stay behind and see to the palace.

Tabytha watched from Abigail's window as the royal household fled Jerusalem. David led the way, surrounded by his guards. He stopped and glanced back at the palace for an instant, and the breath caught in her throat as she looked at him. Did he see her? Then he turned, lost to her in the press of guards and the flurry of white-robed priests around the golden ark. Tabytha thought of Ahio, who should have been there among them.

The administrators and palace staff came close on the priest's heels, followed by the women and children. She saw Maacah and wondered how she felt right now. Did she want her son to overthrow his father? Would she have preferred to stay cloistered in her room to welcome him? Tabytha looked anxiously for Beninu and finally found him walking with Bathsheba's sons. She willed him to look back as David had done, but her son walked head down, his shoulders slumped forward, probably wondering if he would ever see his bird again.

The seer's words came back to her. *Your son will be well. The falcon will ground him, and I will watch over him.* The words had angered her then, but now they comforted her. Beninu would return to the bird and the seer. Beninu, at least, would be well.

Near the back of the group, she caught sight of Michal and Hannah and felt a small kindling of rage that David even valued his estranged wife over her.

Behind the women came an army of men. She watched them fill the narrow street leading to the gate and wondered if there were enough of them to defeat Absalom's army of men from every tribe.

Tabytha stood at the window long after the streets grew quiet. As the king and his household had passed by, people appeared in doorways to call out, weep, and press food and water skins into fleeing hands. Now, the streets were ominously still. David's City waited warily for his son.

The palace was silent as a grave. That afternoon, the concubines drifted, one by one, into the Women's Courtyard. Tabytha sat on a step and watched them, thinking the women's reactions to this waiting time said much about them.

Puduhepa became motherly, bringing food from the kitchen and speaking loudly and cheerfully. Hurriya had her arm around the weeping Zurata. Suta's attention focused entirely on Bashemath, the only one of David's children who had remained in the palace. The girl, almost fully grown, usually did little more than lie and stare at the sky, her mouth open and her hands curled in on themselves. Suta had propped her up in a sitting position, and fed her small bites of Pudu's food.

The two cousins, Arinn and Aria, played senet, the Egyptian game they so loved. They had tried to teach Tabytha to play it, but she had little patience for it or for Aria's claims the game granted insight and influence over the gods and the afterlife. Yet today, she envied them. Their engrossment in the game allowed them to forget they might soon be the captives of a usurper. Namizi sat alone, carefully embroidering a flower on a garment. It would be for her daughter Anna, two years younger than Beninu.

Tabytha went to sit with her. "That's pretty, Mizi. Anna will like it."

Namizi looked up and gave a small, wavering smile. Her eyes brimmed with unshed tears, which she hastily wiped away with the back of her hand. "I'm a fool to cry. I can hardly see what I'm doing."

"You're not a fool. We're all afraid."

"Not Pudu or Gilia."

Tabytha looked at Gilia, who was berating Zurata for crying. "Perhaps they hide it better than we do."

"Gilia says it's time for a new, young king. She says David has become too set in his ways. And she says if she is to be someone's woman, she'd rather it was someone as handsome as Absalom."

"Gilia says a lot of absurd things. We are David's women, not Absalom's."

"Will our children be fine?" Namizi looked at her pleadingly. "They're too young to be without their mothers, don't you think?"

"The women and older children will take good care of them." Tabytha didn't tell her that Beninu hardly needed her or that he hadn't even come to say goodbye.

"But what if there's a battle? What if ...?"

"They'll keep the children far from the fighting." Tabytha reached out and squeezed Namizi's hand. "Anna will return to you, and you'll have that beautiful dress ready for her."

"You're not crying too, are you, Mizi?" Gilia's voice boomed across the courtyard. "What is it with all of you? You'd think we were being captured by some wild, ravaging Philistines."

"Let her be, Gilia," Tabytha said.

"Oh, Tabytha. The great defender of the women." Gilia turned on her. "Once so favored by the king. Now she languishes here—as discarded as the rest of us."

The words stung, as did the sudden realization, that with Abigail and the others gone, nobody would buffer her from Gilia's mean-spiritedness.

Tabytha rose and ascended the courtyard steps. Behind her, she could hear Gilia making another cutting remark and someone, maybe Sena, laughing. She did not turn back.

In the passage, she passed her own room and made her way to Abigail's. The sky reddened as evening approached. She stood again at the window from which she had watched David leave. In the distance, she thought she heard nickering horses. She looked towards the gate, but Absalom's army was not yet pouring through it. Dust hung in the air far beyond the gate. Was it merely dust blown up by the wind or the countless feet of Absalom's approaching men?

It wasn't too late. She could still escape and reach her mother's house before the invading army arrived.

chapter 70

Absalom and his army arrived after nightfall. From her room, Tabytha could hear the loud, triumphant shouting in the courtyard. Throughout the night, she heard singing, shouting, and occasionally a scream from the streets below. Were the men rampaging through the city like a Philistine army? Surely Absalom would rein in his men? He had worked too hard to win people's hearts—he wouldn't want to lose them now.

Ultimately, the scrolls kept Tabytha at the palace for she knew the remaining women would not protect them. Also, if Benaiah's words were true and Ornan had spoken to David that morning, her grandfather would send her right back. He had given her to David to win favor. No doubt he would give her to Absalom to do the same.

She must have finally fallen asleep that dark and restless night, for she startled awake to a rapping on her door and light streaming through her window. Her heart pounded wildly as she rose and threw on a gown.

She unlatched the door, amazed to find Miriam standing there, Ruthie on her hip.

"Miriam? What are you …?"

"Can I come in?" Miriam looked nervously down the passage. "I need to speak to you."

Tabytha opened the door wider, and the princess slipped inside.

"I thought you and Hushai left with the king. Why are you back?"

"Close the door. I don't think we've got long."

"Before what?"

Miriam looked at Tabytha—a long, searching gaze. "What I tell you could destroy my husband and me. And Ruthie. Swear you will not tell anybody else."

"I swear it."

"Abba sent Hushai back to know what Absalom is planning."

"As a spy?" Tabytha felt hope kindle inside her. David fought on. He had not given up.

"And to thwart Ahithophel's counsel."

"Ahithophel?"

"Yes. He joined Absalom in Hebron to plan this rebellion."

The thought frightened Tabytha. Bathsheba's grandfather was highly regarded for his wise counsel. If one man could give Absalom the crown, surely it was Ahithophel.

"But Bathsheba told me her grandfather revered David."

"So we all thought." Miriam reached for Tabytha's hand with her free one and squeezed it. "There's something else. I wasn't sure whether to tell you, but ..."

"Tell me." A sense of dread gripped Tabytha.

"Hushai told me this morning that Ahithophel's first counsel to Absalom on taking the city was to ..." She shook her head. "I'm sorry, Tabytha. Hushai tried to dissuade him, but ..."

"What is it?"

"Ahithophel told Absalom to sleep with the concubines." Miriam kept her steady gaze on Tabytha's face. "He said all Israel would hear of it and know that Absalom has set himself against David. It will make everybody more resolute for the fight ahead."

Tabytha put her hand over her mouth to stifle a cry. Surely, he wouldn't? They were still the king's women and under David's protection. But even as the thought arose, she knew they had lost his protection when he fled without them.

"I'm sorry, Tabytha. I thought it would be better if you had time to prepare yourself. I just ..."

"I'm glad you told me."

"They are busy setting up a tent on the palace's roof. Ahithophel wants it to be ... witnessed."

The city stirred with the news. Prince Absalom was to sleep with the king's ten concubines. Not only would he sleep with them, but he would do so in the sight of everyone on the roof of his father's palace.

"Have you heard?" Traders whispered it to their customers.

"Shameful." Women discussed it between themselves.

"A declaration of war. He can't come back from this." Men debated it at the city gates.

In one home in the city, a woman wept for her daughter, the youngest of the king's concubines.

However, her grandfather, the old Araunah, quietly commended himself for his role in bringing it about. With his granddaughter in the harem of the new king, he still held some sway in the palace.

On the mount of Olives, a bearded man with a falcon on his arm looked down on the city and thought of the courageous girl who had grown up to be so strong and gifted. *Be with her, Lord*, the man prayed, *do not let this break her*.

Absalom's soldiers took bets on how long it would take their leader to sleep with all ten women. They and the other young men of the city scouted out the best positions from which to see the tent, made of delicate enough fabric to see moving shadows inside. The men who said it would take four days won the coins. Absalom slept with two women on the first day, three on the second, three on the third, and two on the fourth.

Absalom first appeared on the roof at midday, right after the tent had been raised. He waved jovially at the gathered crowd before entering the tent. Soon, two men appeared, holding the arms of the first woman. The oldest of the king's concubines, she had arrived with him from Hebron. The closest watchers would tell later that the woman strained against the men as they thrust her into the tent, and that she had been inside for the shortest time of all the women. She emerged from the tent crying as Absalom stepped out and lifted his right hand in victory. The watching men cheered, for with this action Absalom had struck the first blow against the old king.

Some of the women had been docile, others had wept. But it was the last woman—the youngest of the concubines— who caused the greatest stir. On the streets of the city, they would speak of her in the days ahead.

This woman, it was told, had somehow shaken off the men's arms and walked with her head held high. She had turned momentarily to look across the roof at the walls and windows where the watching men sat or stood. Then, she had called across to them in a voice worthy of an army commander. "You are all traitors to King David, the anointed of Adonai! Absalom is an imposter, and his days are numbered!" The men walking next to her had grabbed her roughly, one of them silencing her with a large hand on her mouth.

Some said it was the woman's words that caused the watching men to turn and slink away. Others, that it was the roughness with which the larger shadow treated the smaller one in that tent. Still, they said the woman stepped out of the tent with the self-same dignity despite her torn robe, and that few men cheered when Absalom emerged and raised his hand.

Many of the common people on the street were secretly pleased the arrogant prince had been humiliated by a mere woman.

The mother of the concubine had smiled sadly when her son told her. "She always was a fighter, our Tawaassi."

The old Araunah had sunk his head into his hands. Far from bringing him the favor he longed for, the foolish girl had now made him a stench to this new Hebrew king.

And on the walls of the king's city, a lone man had watched his falcon rise and marveled at the strength hiding in ordinary, fragile things.

chapter 71

taʙythа

εxtract from scroll א (hs aleף)

As much as I try to forget that day on the roof, my body and mind betray me. Even now.

In the first few days, I was terrified to sleep, though I locked myself in my room and pushed the heavy desk against the door. Over and over, I imagined two men breaking through and dragging me back to that tent or Absalom himself breaking through and … no, no, no! I would try to pull my thoughts away from the scene in my mind, but they kept returning there.

When I drifted off, too exhausted for wakeful vigilance, his dark presence lurked in almost every dream. Sometimes I saw him. At other times, I dreamt his eyes looked at me, all the while burning with hatred for his father. Sometimes, I didn't see him, but I felt him ripping away my robe, exposing and shaming me. The worst dreams were of him clamping his hand down on my throat and snarling, "What did you say?" I would wake from those dark visions gasping for breath, my hands fluttering uselessly around my throat.

It always took a long time for the terror to subside. That had been the moment in the tent when I thought Absalom would kill me, the moment right after I said, "You are just like your brother, Amnon."

Miriam often came to my room to tend to the bruises and bring broth or bread. She coaxed me to eat small bites, even though I told her I wasn't hungry. She always brought Ruthie, whose happy chortling would bring me to tears. "What is it? Shall I take her away?" she would ask, and I would shake my head, unable to explain the overwhelming pang of love and fear I felt as I looked at the child, and how desperately I wished she had been born a boy. I finally understood the curse of being born a girl in this world of men who desired only pleasure and power.

Miriam didn't speak of what Absalom had done. She only once said, "I wish you hadn't made him angry. He wasn't like that to the others." She spoke mostly about the happenings in the palace, but I could not attend to the details. Still, having her there comforted me, and her voice soothed my troubled thoughts. One thing I do recall is her telling me Absalom had not slept with Puduhepa. He had apparently told her to get out of the tent when she reminded him she had been like a mother to him in Hebron.

I could not hide away forever. One afternoon, about a week after the day on the roof, I returned to the Women's Courtyard. A few of the others were there too. Hurriya and Zurata spoke brightly about the fabric they had bought, and Arinn and Aria played their game in focused silence. They hardly looked up as I arrived.

Suta sat by herself, arms wrapped around her knees, rocking backward and forwards.

"Where's Bashemath?" I sat down next to her.

"Asleep. Gilia is with her."

She looked at the women across from us. "Those four won't even speak about it. As if it didn't happen. They talk of gowns, games, and the weather as if nothing has changed."

"Perhaps it's easier for them that way."

She reached for my hand. "I heard about what you shouted on the roof. That was brave."

"And useless." I fingered the lingering bruise on my neck. "And foolish."

"Miriam told me he hurt you." She squeezed my hand. "It wasn't useless, Tab. They say the men turned away in shame after what you said."

I didn't want to think of that moment.

"How's Gilia?"

"She won't stop crying."

I thought of Gilia saying she would rather have Absalom than David. My gaze found the four women on the other side of the courtyard. We weren't all that different, Gilia, me, and the others. Each of us had our own way of pretending to be strong, of hiding what had been broken inside.

"Perhaps tears are what we need," I said. "At least they're honest."

Suta wiped one away. "I never told you, but after Bash's birth, I asked David not to send for me again. I couldn't bear the thought of giving birth again, of ..." Her tears were rolling freely now, but she still managed to say, "What if I'm carrying Absalom's child? What if ...?"

I let her cry into my shoulder, feeling anger building inside me. It grew until it pressed against the back of my throat, pulsing in my temples, beating through my bones. I raged at Absalom and Ahithophel, who had used ten innocent women in their battle for the crown. But I also felt resentment smoldering against David, who had left us unprotected.

If I'm honest, at that moment, a tiny flame of anger even kindled in my very depths against Adonai. He had allowed this to happen. Worse, he had ordained it to punish David in the same way he had taken Bathsheba's first child. The seer had known what was to become of us. Had David suspected it, too? Only *I* had not understood the seer's final words to me until it was too late.

What he has done in secret will be done to him in the sight of all.

What had started one night as David stood idly on the roof of his palace had ended inside a tent in the very same place.

chapter 72

Tabytha knew she would sleep easier with Absalom gone. She caught a glimpse of him from Abigail's window as he rode out of the city, surrounded by his warriors. Men from every tribe of Israel were gathered on the Mount of Olives, waiting for him to lead them into battle. What chance did David stand against a force that large, she thought with a hollow feeling inside. Absalom would return as king, and she would be his forever.

Miriam slipped into the room and came to stand next to her.

"I see Hushai rides on Absalom's right." Tabytha didn't take her eyes off the procession below them. "I thought Ahithophel would ride in the place of honor."

"Difficult for a corpse to do."

Tabytha turned to see if her friend mocked her, but Miriam's expression was serious.

"Hushai had word of Ahithophel's death this morning. Only he and a handful of people know. Absalom didn't want to tell the troops. They will consider it a bad omen."

"He's dead? But how?"

"When Absalom arrived in the city, Ahithophel told him to strike out against Abba immediately, but Hushai counseled him to wait and gather his troops from across the land, knowing that with a delay, he could get word to Abba." Miriam shifted Ruthie to her other hip. "When Absalom heeded Hushai's counsel, Ahithophel left for his hometown. Maybe he suspected what Hushai was doing and knew Absalom would be defeated. Whatever the case, he set his affairs in order and hung himself last week."

"Miriam! Is it true?"

"Two men from Giloh confirmed it this morning. They've been sworn to silence. You mustn't tell anyone."

"I can't believe it."

"I think Ahithophel didn't want to have to face Abba when he returned to the city."

"He'd be guilty of treason."

"Worse. Of betraying a friend."

Tabytha felt the first stirring of hope since David had left. If Ahithophel, the shrewdest of men, had believed David could defeat Absalom and return to be king, perhaps she could, too.

Perhaps David would still come back to her.

Tabytha spent the next two weeks reading the women's scrolls. It helped her forget what had happened and what *could* be happening, even right then, to the man she loved. For despite all that had passed, she knew she still loved him. Losing herself in the stories of Michal and Abigail helped settle the thoughts of her son and the fear that he might see his father die in battle. She did not unroll the copy she had made of Bathsheba's scroll. That story was too painful to read. It was the catalyst of all that came after.

In the third week, she left the palace, accompanied by Miriam, who insisted the guards let them pass. At first, the men were reluctant. The new king had told them that no one must leave or enter the Women's Quarters. Miriam stood her ground, and finally, they relented, one of them trailing behind the two women to Tabytha's old home.

Her mother, stoic as ever, stiffened when Tabytha embraced her and began to weep.

"What's done is done," she said. "Dry those tears, and let me call Atamu and Iuni."

Her brother, sister-in-law, and youngest niece were soon there. The girl stretched out her hands for Ruthie, who chortled with delight as Miriam handed her over.

"Where's Tuhi?" Tabytha looked at Iuni, who cast a troubled glance at her husband.

"Married to the tanner by the gate," Atamu said brusquely. "Fortunately, we received the bride price before the whole city went mad. Otherwise, he might have changed his mind."

"The tanner? The old man whose sons we used to play with?"

Atamu shrugged. "His wife died, and he needed someone to help with the hides. He gave me a good bride price for her."

The thought of her beautiful, vibrant niece now sold to an old man filled Tabytha with a familiar, heavy sadness.

Miriam sensed her mood. "I'm married to an older man, and we are both very happy."

Atamu gave Miriam an appraising glance before turning back to his sister. "What news of the battle?"

Again, it was Miriam who spoke. "Last we heard, Absalom's army marched towards the forests of Ephraim."

That had been more than a week ago. What had happened since then? Was David dead—perhaps already buried? Was Beninu safe? Was Absalom marching back right now to declare himself the rightful king to those who had called him a usurper, to laugh in the face of the concubine who had defied him?

"With so many men, Absalom will win a decisive battle," Atamu said. "David's body will be under a pile of rocks by now."

His words gave substance to Tabytha's worst fears. "You speak of my husband. And of Miriam's father."

Atamu addressed Miriam. "Isn't your husband Hushai? Didn't he turn on David?"

"You know nothing, Atamu," Tabytha said, wishing she had stayed in her room instead of letting Miriam persuade her to come.

"Hush now, both of you," her mother said as if they were still squabbling children. "Sit and have the last beer Iuni and I brewed last week."

The conversation turned to Atamu's latest venture to sell beer, which required their mother and Iuni to work fourteen hours a day brewing it. Her brother scowled as he spoke of the shortage of barley brought on by the uncertainty in the land. The women merely laughed and said they were glad of the shortage and the free time, and Tabytha found herself smiling for the first time in weeks, even more so as she saw Atamu's growing irritation.

"We heard what happened on the roof," he said suddenly, bringing the laughter to an abrupt end. "How you treated the new king in the sight of everyone. Ornan says you have made your entire family a stench to King Absalom."

There was a strange ringing in Tabytha's ears as she looked at her brother. Besides her Miriam stirred and Ruthie may have whimpered, but the rushing sound in her ears muffled everything else.

"He isn't king yet." Miriam's voice seemed to come from a great distance, even though she felt her friend's hand grasping her arm. "Come, Tabytha. It's time to go."

She allowed Miriam to pull her up. Iuni came and threw her arms around her and whispered, "He didn't mean anything by it."

Her mother was suddenly there too. "He doesn't speak for us all, Tawaassi. I am proud you stood up to that arrogant prince."

But all the way back, Atamu's words circled through her mind, and a new fear gnawed at her. What would happen to those she loved because of her brash words on that cursed palace roof?

chapter 73

tabytha
extract from scroll א (hs alef)

The palace rumors started the day after we visited my mother. There had been a great battle in Ephraim's forests and many men had died. One said hundreds of men, but another said many more than that. He had spoken to a Benjamite who had seen bodies littered across the land. One man said Absalom was dead, but another vowed he lived, for David himself had said the prince must not be harmed. The man who claimed Absalom was dead said he had hung himself in a tree, but the other said it was nonsense. He had heard it was the king's advisor, Ahithophel, who had hung himself.

That evening, a man rode into the palace, seeking Miriam. I went with her into the courtyard to meet him.

"My lady, I have word from your husband." He handed her a rolled-up scroll, and she quickly broke the seal, scanning the contents before passing it to me.

"Abba and Hushai live, but Absalom is dead," she said. "Hushai wrote this in Gilgal. The men of Judah have come there to bring Abba across the Jordan. More and more men from the other tribes are coming to bow to him in allegiance."

"He's coming back." Relief washed through me at the thought. "And Beninu. They're all coming back, Miriam."

We grasped hands and laughed with relief. David and his household returned. The rebellion had been quelled. The man who I feared, who still haunted my dreams, was dead and could hurt me no more. The Women's Quarters would once more reverberate with voices and laughter. Fleetingly, I thought of Maacah, who had lost the son she so cherished, but I pushed the thought away. David was coming back.

Another week passed before they arrived, and although the atmosphere in the city was festive, the king's party returned subdued. Miriam and I stood at Abigail's window, watching David lead the procession back to the palace, Hushai on his right. Hushai looked up and waved at Miriam, but David did not glance up. The new stoop to his shoulders told me the past weeks weighed heavily on him. I looked at the familiar faces behind him and saw the same heaviness. When the women and children finally trickled through the doors, it was obvious the time away had been an ordeal.

Beninu gave me a fleeting smile as I folded him into my arms. "Ima! I can't breathe."

I let him go. "Are you fine? Did you walk the whole way? You must be exhausted."

"I'm fine. Did you see Nathan while I was gone?"

I shook my head.

"The birds? Surely, he flew them."

"I didn't see them. But tell me what happened to you."

"It was boring. We walked and crossed the river and

hid in the desert for a while. Then we went to a town, and all the men, except Abba, went off to fight. And when they came back, Abba wept because Absalom was dead. Joab told him he must stop and go to the gates to thank the men for saving him. Then we came home."

There was so much my son's words didn't tell me, yet they revealed one important thing. The main cause of the somber feel in the king's party was Absalom's death. Abigail had told me once that David grieved deeply, and this was no exception. He had lost a son—a traitorous son who wanted him dead—but a father's love does not simply die with disloyalty. *Oh, David.* My heart welled up with pity at that moment.

That evening, I sought out Abigail. From her, I heard more. How a man named Shimei had cursed David as he fled from Jerusalem and begged for mercy on his return. How many men had been generous and brought them bedding, bowls, and food. How David had commanded the men not to harm Absalom and how he had been inconsolable when a messenger came with word of his death. She even told me of Joab's harsh words to David. "You love those who hate you and hate those who love you."

"But he lost his son, Tabytha," she said. "His own son."

I nodded and tried not to think of Absalom's angry gaze or hateful hands.

"How did Absalom die?"

"David suspects Joab's men killed him, but they all deny it. They claim they found the prince already dead, hanging by his hair in a tree."

"How's Maacah?"

Abigail shrugged. "I thought she would cry incessantly at the news, but she said almost nothing. She is like a sleepwalker."

Maacah had had too many blows over the years. Tamar, Absalom's revenge on Amnon, and now Absalom's death. How many blows until you felt nothing at all?

"I think you all had it easy," Abigail said. "Staying quietly at the palace."

I thought of the tent on the palace roof, of men watching and arms shoving, and hands on my neck, crushing the breath out of me. Abigail didn't know. Perhaps David didn't know either.

How long before someone told him?

The following morning, Miriam came to my room. Her expression reminded me of the day she had come to warn me of Absalom's intentions on the roof. Surprisingly, she came alone.

"Where's Ruthie?"

"With Ima."

"I'm not particularly fond of your early morning visits." I tried to sound jovial, but she didn't laugh. "It can't be as bad as last time, I suppose."

"I suppose."

It could only be one thing. "Your father knows what Absalom did to us?"

She nodded.

A wave of shame washed over me at the realization, but I fought the weight of the feeling. No! I was not complicit in Absalom's act. If anybody should feel shame, it was David for leaving us in the hands of his rebel son. "So, what now?" I asked.

Miriam looked down, fumbling with her gown. All her characteristic strength and confidence seemed to have left her.

"Does the king plan to punish us for what his son inflicted on us?"

She shook her head. "Not punish. No, he wouldn't do that. But ..." She took a deep breath. "Tabytha. I'm so sorry. You've been like a second mother to me." A tear ran down her cheek.

"You're scaring me." I pulled her into my arms. "What is to become of us?"

"You're leaving. Hushai says the king will provide well for you all."

"What are you saying?"

The princess took a few more steadying breaths and said, "Abba has told Hushai to find a house for you all. You are to leave the palace."

Suddenly, I understood. David would discard his disgraced concubines as easily as he had his disgraced daughter. He was unwilling to face us, as he had been unwilling to face her.

"Like Tamar," I whispered.

Something resigned had crept into Miriam's voice. "Like Tamar."

"When?"

"As soon as Hushai finds a suitable house. No later than the end of the week."

"I must speak to the king."

I would fall at David's feet and plead. I would remind him of the prophet's words that what the king had done in secret would be done to him in full daylight. I would tell him this was not our doing and would accuse him—why had he brought this on us? Why hadn't he taken us with him and protected us? Maybe, if I sensed him softening, I would tell him I loved him, that my son and all I held dear were here at his palace. That to be apart from him,

Beninu, and all the women who were sisters and daughters to me would break my heart. Perhaps I could still change his mind.

"I don't think he'll see you."

"Ask Hushai. Please, I beg you."

chapter 74

mIRIAm

letters found among the scrolls

Tabytha
I'm sorry I cannot come to speak to you. Hushai has kept me busy scribing an agreement. I begged him to talk to Abba on your behalf, and he promised to do so tomorrow.
M

Tabytha
Hushai says Abba said he won't see you. He also said the king is unwavering in his decision to send you all away and will not be swayed by any man or woman.
M

Tabytha
Hushai and I argued for the first time today. I asked him what he would do if a man did to me what Absalom did to you. Would he discard me as Abba is discarding you? He said I don't understand the shame this has brought on the king. I said he doesn't understand the pain of the women, inflicted once by Absalom's act and once by the king's abandonment. He only got truly angry when I said, 'What if a man did this to Ruthie?'
M

Tabytha

The house has been found. Tomorrow, you leave. I lay awake all night and could hardly breathe at the thought that tomorrow you will be gone. In the night, I thought of a way you might still be able to see Abba. We must try. Of all his concubines, he may still listen to you. I'll come for you this afternoon and try to bring you to this side of the palace. Be prepared.

M

chapter 75

In the end, it was surprisingly easy to get to the other side of the palace, where Hushai and Miriam stayed in quarters close to the king's.

Miriam arrived at Tabytha's door near sunset. Tabytha had prepared herself early in the afternoon. She washed and put on one of her finest gowns, although not the wonderful blue one of their first night together—that hadn't seemed right. She brushed her hair until it shone and left it loose, curls touching her shoulders, just as David liked it. She darkened her eyes and reddened her lips. She dabbed on the perfume he had bought for her once from a trader who claimed the royal women in the Phoenician courts adored the fragrance. She rehearsed everything she'd say to him and imagined over and over what he might say and how she would respond. Then she waited, praying that Miriam would come, that she would still see her husband and have a chance to convince him not to banish her from the palace.

It was a relief when she finally heard the knock.

"Quickly," Miriam said, and Tabytha fell in step beside her as she made her way to the Women's Courtyard.

"I told the guard Ruthie is sick, and I need your help to look after her."

"He didn't object?"

"I'm Hushai's wife," she said with a sideways smile.

Only a handful of older children were in the Women's Courtyard, and Beninu wasn't among them. Tabytha wondered fleetingly if the other concubines knew of David's plans for them. Had David told Abigail or Bathsheba? Surely one of them would have come to tell her after all she'd done to record their stories?

Miriam confidently knocked at the door leading to the main palace, and it opened immediately. The young guard inclined his head at them as they hurried past him.

Tabytha still feared he might change his mind and refuse her entrance.

The dank, winding passage reminded her of happier times when David had come to eat with them, when the women had sat mesmerized as he played his lyre and sang to Adonai. Of times when his gaze had fallen on her, and he had smiled. Her heart had always leaped with anticipation at the thought of spending a night in his arms.

"I must get back to Ruthie. I had to wait till she slept before I could leave. She will scream down the palace if she wakes to find me gone."

"Where's Hushai?"

"With Abba. I will call him so that you can be alone."

Near David's reception room, Miriam stopped and held up her hand. All was quiet.

"She's still asleep. Wait in this alcove until Hushai and I have passed by, and then go to Abba." She gripped Tabytha's hands tightly. "May Adonai grant you his favor."

"Thank you, Miriam." Tabytha swallowed, trying to ease the sudden knot in her throat. "No matter what happens, I'm grateful you gave me a chance to see him."

She tried to still the wild wingbeats in her chest as Miriam's footsteps retreated. She heard the princess's voice and then the deeper voice of Hushai. Moments later, they both rushed past her—Hushai asking anxiously after Ruthie—as Tabytha pressed deeper into the alcove.

Tabytha wanted to stand a little longer to calm her breathing, but she knew Miriam's lie would be exposed. Hushai would come back as soon as he realized what they had done. She forced herself to walk the last few paces to the king's reception chamber.

David stood with his back towards the door, looking out the window, as she had seen him stand so many times before when his mind troubled him. For a moment, Tabytha stood too, impressing his form on her mind—his stature and grey hair and the way his fine robe hung on his still-broad shoulders. David was the only man she had ever desired. A small, involuntary sob escaped at the thought, and, ever the alert warrior, David turned.

Afterward, she would think of that long, silent moment as he looked across the chamber at her. Was there an instant of softening in his expression? She thought there may have been, but she could never be sure. Perhaps the memory altered with her longing and the passing of time. However, she would remember clearly the first word David spoke was her name, and he did not speak it in anger but in resignation.

"Tabytha."

She came towards him, wanting nothing more than to step into his arms and lay her head on his chest, but as she reached him, he gripped her wrists and held her away from him.

"You shouldn't be here."

All her carefully prepared arguments crumbled, and she simply said, "Don't send me away."

He let go of her wrists and looked away, and in that moment, she knew she wouldn't be able to change his mind. The insight was strangely liberating. If nothing she said could make a difference, she could say anything she wanted.

"Did they tell you about the tent on the roof, David? Did they tell you what I shouted across to all the watching men? That they were all traitors to their anointed king? Did they tell you what your beloved Absalom did to the women you so carelessly left in his hands?"

His gaze held her own, and she could no longer read anything in those dark, impenetrable eyes.

"Do you know he tried to crush the life out of me? Perhaps it would have been better if he had, better than living out the rest of my days as your prisoner, paying for your and your son's sins."

"My lord." Hushai's breathless voice came from behind them. "Forgive me. Miriam deceived us. The babe is not unwell. She is ..."

"It's fine, Hushai. Tabytha was leaving."

"Shall I take her, my lord?"

David nodded, and Hushai stepped forward. He gripped Tabytha by the arm, and pulled her towards the door as David turned away.

"David!"

He looked back and held up his hand. Hushai stopped at the silent command.

"Send for Beninu," Tabytha said. "He longs for a father."

David nodded slowly. "You have my word."

"The scrolls. Can I take them with me?"

"Yes." He paused and said, "It will not be a prison. You will have everything you need for the rest of your days."

"Except you and our son."

A sad smile broke through his guarded expression. After a moment's hesitation, he strode towards her, and at some unseen signal, Hushai let go of her arm. David reached for her and pulled her against him, holding her head as she wept into his chest.

"Shalom, my gazelle."

Eventually, Hushai drew her away, and David let him.

So it ended, she would think afterward, like it had started—with a powerful king who saw her as little more than a helpless doe. And Michal's words would echo back to her at the realization.

We have been acquired and discarded at the whim of kings.

epilogue

tabytha

extract from scroll א (hs alef)

Abba is dead.

My jolt of grief as I read those words in Miriam's letter reveal my heart has not grown as cold towards him as I had come to believe.

David—my betrothed, my lord and lover, the father of my son—is gone. Since childhood, my life has been entwined with his. Even here, locked away from the world, wasn't I still his? *His* concubine to dispose of.

Who am I now that he is dead?

Even as I write that question, the answer rises in me, as clear as the water from Jebus's spring. I was born Tawaassi, but I became another from the day the Hebrew king laid eyes on me. The truth is I am Tabytha, David's widow.

It feels strange to dip a reed into ink and record my thoughts again. My days of doing this passed away when I had filled the last of the palace's parchment, mere months into my confinement. Ten years have passed since then, but with Miriam's letter came a surprising gift—a roll of precious parchment and a corked bottle of ink—with a line at the top of the letter saying David had instructed her to send it to me.

I cried when I read that, for David and I had always known that about each other—that the best way to understand the deep matters of our hearts was to pour them out into words, the way a spring pours out water from its depths. I cried, too, because even in his last days, David had not forgotten me.

Ten years. It feels like I have never lived anywhere but here, with walls around me and a guard at the gate. With only the distant, muffled sounds of the city to prove that there is a world beyond our own. Yet, at times, I feel like I left the palace only days ago. I'll awake from a vivid dream of Abigail or Beninu, and it will take me a moment to remember I am not in my room in the Women's Quarters but rather in a humble dwelling on the edge of the king's city.

The world stopped on the day David banished us. It shrank and intensified to the smallness and pettiness of ten scorned women and a broken, helpless child.

At first, I craved to hear news of the outside world. I begged the king's guards, who brought us food and water, to tell me something. *Anything*. Had they seen my son? What of the king? Had the Philistines attacked our borders again? But they were stoic and silent.

For a while, I convinced myself David would grow to miss us and would send for us. But when Suta died, Absalom's unborn baby still wedged in her body, and we didn't hear from him, I finally understood. We were as dead to him as the lifeless, shrouded form of Suta, carried away to the sound of Bashemath's wails.

The first letter from Miriam came a few months after Suta's death. She spoke of a revolt by a man called Sheba ben Bichri and how Joab had quenched it. More importantly, she told me my son was well and that his father—true to his promise—had sent for him often since I had left.

The next letter from Miriam came in our third year of confinement. She told me she and Hushai had another daughter. She also told me, to avert a spreading famine, David had appeased the anger of Adonai and the Gibeonites by handing over the last of Saul's heirs. Briefly, I thought of Michal when I read of their hilltop slaying, but it was the image of Saul's concubine Rizpah, keeping the vultures away from her sons' bones, that stayed with me. Rizpah, another king's forgotten concubine.

After that, Miriam's letters were few, and the affairs of David's court faded from my mind, replaced by the simpler, more tedious affairs of our household—rhythms of cooking, eating, washing, and sleeping.

Today's letter has jarred me back to my former life. David is dead, and surprisingly, Solomon sits on his throne. I remember that first moment in the Women's Quarters when two young boys hurtled past me, followed by the too beautiful Tamar. Little did I know her loveliness was the loose thread that would unravel not only the household I had just stepped into but also my future. Thinking back on those first moments, I recall the precocious prince's words. "An heir needs to know as much as he can to rule well." I see now what I could not see then. That even as a young boy, Sol had the confidence and cleverness to follow in his father's footsteps. Even now, I see evidence of his astuteness in the last line of Miriam's letter. It is an instruction from the young king that if I still have a copy of his mother's scroll, I am to burn it.

Ten years ago, this would have angered me, but time has led me to accept the will of kings. I move the olive lamp closer and reach for the clay pot that holds the scrolls. I draw out the copy of Bathsheba's scroll, completed the day before David sent Benaiah to fetch the original. I hold its edge to the flame and watch it catch alight, the sins of a king smoldering away into ash.

As the smoke curls up and catches in my throat, I think of the seer and the sadness I saw on his face the last time we spoke. Pudu and Gilia think Solomon will free us now that David is dead, but I know I will leave this house as Suta did, wrapped in a shroud. I know this because of what I saw in the seer's eyes that day—the sure knowledge I would not see Beninu again.

Now and then, I still stand in the courtyard, looking up at the small piece of sky above my head. Sometimes, I see a bird circling high above. I imagine it was my son's hand that flung it into the sky. I envision it dropping at his call and sweeping down onto his outstretched arm. I see my son's face then, and it is always that of a boy, alight with joy and freedom.

Thoughts of the seer make me think of Israel's God, who he and David both served so fervently. I sense him still—Adonai. Not in the way the seer or David did. They heard him speak and even spoke back to him. Not even in the way Abigail did, with the kind of faith that could turn the heart of a king. But on the very first day we met, the seer told me Adonai saw my heart and would be near me. I believe it, and so every night as I lay on my pallet, I speak to Adonai of my sadness, and I ask him to watch over us all—the wives and concubines, Beninu and my mother if she still lives, Tamar and Iuni and my nieces. And every night, something light settles on me, something that David might have called peace.

The first words I ever read of David's swirl through my

mind tonight. They comfort me. *Surely goodness and mercy shall follow me all the days of my life and I will dwell in the house of the Lord forever.*

May it be so, Adonai. May King David dwell in your house forever.

And one day may I do the same.

free harem scrolls companion resources

If you enjoyed *Harem Scrolls*, check out these two free companion resources:

ANCIENT BEAUTY TIPS:
BIBLICAL WOMEN SHARE THEIR SECRETS

A creative 7-day devotional on Biblical beauty, featuring Esther, Abigail and other women of the Scriptures.

"Your beauty should not come from outward adornment, such as elaborate hairstyles and the wearing of gold jewellery or fine clothes. Rather, it should be that of your inner self, the

unfading beauty of a gentle and quiet spirit, which is of great worth in God's sight." (1 Peter 3:3-4)

BREAKING NEWS: DISCOVERING THE HAREM SCROLLS

Newspaper clippings and social media posts that appeared in the first, unedited *Harem Scrolls* manuscript. These extracts from media reports reveal the complex archaeological and political implications linked to the discovery of an ancient cache of scrolls in Jerusalem. The fictional extracts reflect fascinating snippets of Joan's historical, geographical and archaeological research.

https://joancampbell.co.za/companion-resources/

about the author

Describing herself as a 'pilgrim and storyteller', Joan seeks to follow Jesus wholeheartedly, and shares her journey through blogging, devotional and fiction writing. She is the author of *The Poison Tree Path Chronicles*. The first book of this trilogy, *Chains of Gwyndorr*, won the 2017 Illumination award for YA Fiction. Her three other books, *Encounters: Life Changing Moments with Jesus*, *Journeys: On Ancient Paths of Faith* and *Soul Search: Questions Jesus Asked* are collections of short stories, reflections, prayers and art. *Encounters* was translated into French by Scripture Union France, and published as *Des rencontres qui ont tout changé*.

Joan Campbell

As a trustee for Media Associates International (MAI), Joan has trained Christian writers in South Africa, Ghana, Botswana, Hungary, Singapore and Mexico. Besides her training function with MAI, she also co-hosts their online poetry group, and builds community in her communication and social media role for the ministry.

The Harem Scrolls is Joan's first full length historical fiction novel.

Joan lives in Johannesburg, South Africa with her husband and two daughters.

Connect with Joan at https://joancampbell.co.za/

character list—alphabetic

Name	Description	1st Bible Reference
Abiathar	David's priest	1 Sam. 22:20
Abigail	David's wife	1 Sam. 25:14
Abishai	Joab's brother / David's cousin	2 Sam. 2:18
Abital	David's wife	2 Sam. 3:4
Abner	Israel's army commander / The king-maker	1 Sam. 14:50
Absalom	David's third eldest son (mother Maacah)	2 Sam. 3:3
Achish	King of Gath	1 Sam. 21:10
Ahinoam	David's wife	1 Sam. 25:43

Ahio	Hebrew priest / *Tabytha's tutor* *	2 Sam. 6:3
Ahithophel	King David's advisor / Bathsheba's grandfather	2 Sam. 15:12
Amnon	David's eldest son (mother Ahinoam)	2 Sam. 3:2
Arinn & Aria	David's concubines	2 Sam. 16:22
Asahel	Joab's brother / David's cousin	2 Sam. 2:18
Atamu	Tabytha's brother	---
Bashemath	Suta's daughter	---
Benaiah	David's personal guard	2 Sam. 8:18
Beninu	Tabytha's son	---
Daniel	David's second son (mother Abigail)	1 Chron. 3:1
David	King of Israel	1 Sam. 16:13
Elik	Cloth Merchant	---
Gilia	David's concubine	2 Sam. 16:22
Haggith	David's wife	2 Sam. 3:4
Hannah	Michal's companion / Paltiel's sister	---

hΛREM SCROLLS

Heber and Chava	Abigail's servants	---
Hurriya	David's concubine	2 Sam. 16:22
Hushai	King David's advisor / *Miriam's husband* *	2 Sam. 15:32
Ish-Bosheth	Saul's heir / Michal's brother	2 Sam. 2:8
Ithmah	David's Moabite warrior / *Uriah's friend* *	1 Chron. 11:46
Iuni	Tabytha's sister-in-law	---
Iyasala	Prince of Gath / Achish's brother & advisor	---
Jacoba	Abigail's handmaiden	---
Jeriel	Elder of Judah	---
Joab	David's army commander / David's cousin	2 Sam. 2:13
Jonadab	Amnon's advisor / David's nephew	2 Sam. 13:3
Jonathan	Michal's brother / David's friend	1 Sam. 13:2
Maacah	David's wife / daughter of King of Geshur	1 Chron. 3:2
Merab	Michal's sister / Saul's eldest daughter	1 Sam. 14:49
Mica	Mephibosheth's son (Jonathan's grandson)	2 Sam. 9:12

Michal	David's wife / Saul's daughter	1 Sam. 14:49
Miriam	David's daughter (mother Haggith)	2 Sam. 13:18
Nabal	Abigail's first husband	1 Sam. 25:3
Namizi	David's concubine	2 Sam. 16:22
Nathan	Prophet to King David	2 Sam. 7:2
Ornan	Lord of Jebus / *Tabytha's grandfather* *	1 Chron. 21:18
Orpah	Ithmah's wife	---
Paltiel	Michal's husband after David fled Saul	2 Sam. 3:15-16
Puduhepa (Pudu)	David's concubine	2 Sam. 16:22
Rizpah	King Saul's concubine	2 Sam. 3:7
Ruthie	Miriam and Hushai's daughter	---
Samuel	Prophet of Israel / anoints Saul and David	1 Sam. 1:20
Saul	King of Israel (David's predecessor)	1 Sam. 9:2
Sena	David's concubine	2 Sam. 16:22
Simone	Orpah's servant girl	---

Solomon	David's son and heir (mother Bathsheba)	2 Sam. 5:14
Sophereth	Solomon's future female scribe	Ezra 2:55
Suta	David's concubine	2 Sam. 16:22
Tabytha (Tawaassi)	David's concubine / scribe of the scrolls *	2 Sam. 16:22
Tamar	David's daughter (mother Maacah)	2 Sam. 13:1
Tuhi	Tabytha's niece	---
Uriah	Bathsheba's Hittite husband / David's warrior	2 Sam. 11:3
Uzzah	Ahio's brother	2 Sam. 6:3
Zurata	David's concubine	2 Sam. 16:22

FICTIONAL ROLE

On the next page, view the House of David.

HOUSE OF DAVID

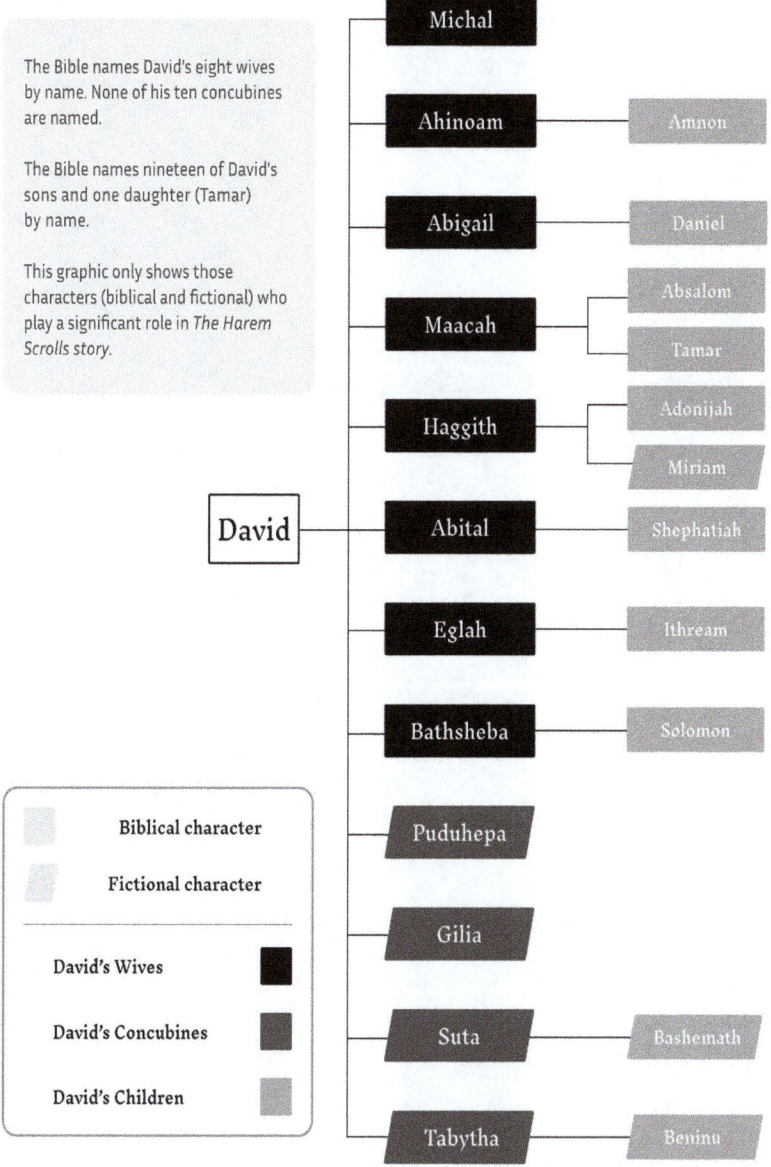

WIVES & CONCUBINES   CHILDREN

The Bible names David's eight wives by name. None of his ten concubines are named.

The Bible names nineteen of David's sons and one daughter (Tamar) by name.

This graphic only shows those characters (biblical and fictional) who play a significant role in *The Harem Scrolls* story.

David

Michal

Ahinoam — Amnon

Abigail — Daniel

Maacah — Absalom
       — Tamar

Haggith — Adonijah
        — Miriam

Abital — Shephatiah

Eglah — Ithream

Bathsheba — Solomon

Puduhepa

Gilia

Suta — Bashemath

Tabytha — Beninu

Biblical character

Fictional character

David's Wives

David's Concubines

David's Children

www.ingramcontent.com/pod-product-compliance
Lightning Source LLC
Chambersburg PA
CBHW070540030726
47505CB00001B/107